Praise for
Chronicles of M'Gistryn

"Anastasia M. Trekles takes readers on an epic adventure in her debut novel Core. Told from the perspective of multiple characters, Core borrows familiar elements of our world to create a thrilling fantasy filled with intrigue, action, and romance. The characters are engaging with witty banter and personalities that sprawl across the page. Trekles masterfully guides readers through worlds rich with lore, but never bogs down the prose with too much description or exposition. She has a keen sense of a modern reader's imagination and deftly transports us through time and space. Trekles has a deep understanding of the fantasy genre and weaves a tale that will satisfy anyone who appreciates a great story told well. This novel establishes the foundation for a series of books and invites a reader back for more."

-S.E. White, author of *A Murder of Crows*

"Wondrously imagined! M'Gistryn is a realm rich with possibilities. The characters are rich in detail, and the plotting just complex enough to grab your interest and not let go!"
-Jay Erickson, author of *The Blood Wizard Chronicles Series*

"Simply amazing! Characters who actually behave like adults! This novel is highly recommended!"
-J.P. Strohm, coauthor of *Exactors: Tales from the Citadel*

I0629071

Books by Anastasia M. Trekles

THE CHRONICLES OF M'GYSTRIN

Core
Ascent
Transcendence

CHRONICLES

OF

M'GISTRYN

BOOK III

TRANSCENDENCE

Anastasia M. Trekles

Halsbren
Publishing, LLC

All text and front matter images
Copyright © 2023 Anastasia M. Trekles

All characters in this book are fictitious. Any resemblance to actual persons, living or dead, is purely coincidental.

This book is protected under the copyright laws of the United States of America. Any reproduction or unauthorized use of the material or artwork herein is prohibited without the express written permission of Zelda23Publishing, Halsbren Publishing LLC. and the author.

TRANSCENDENCE

First Edition Printing
(2023)

Published By: Halsbren Publishing LLC La Porte, IN. 46350
ISBN-13: 978-0-9964311-5-6

Cover design and layout by Jay Erickson.
Photography by Anastasia M. Trekles.
Ajna Mandala by Morgan Phoenix
Ajna Mandala used under the Creative Commons Attribution-Share Alike 3.0 License

Made in the United States of America

DEDICATION

To Zach, who patiently and painstakingly watched the world come into its own.

Anastasia M. Trekles
-Author

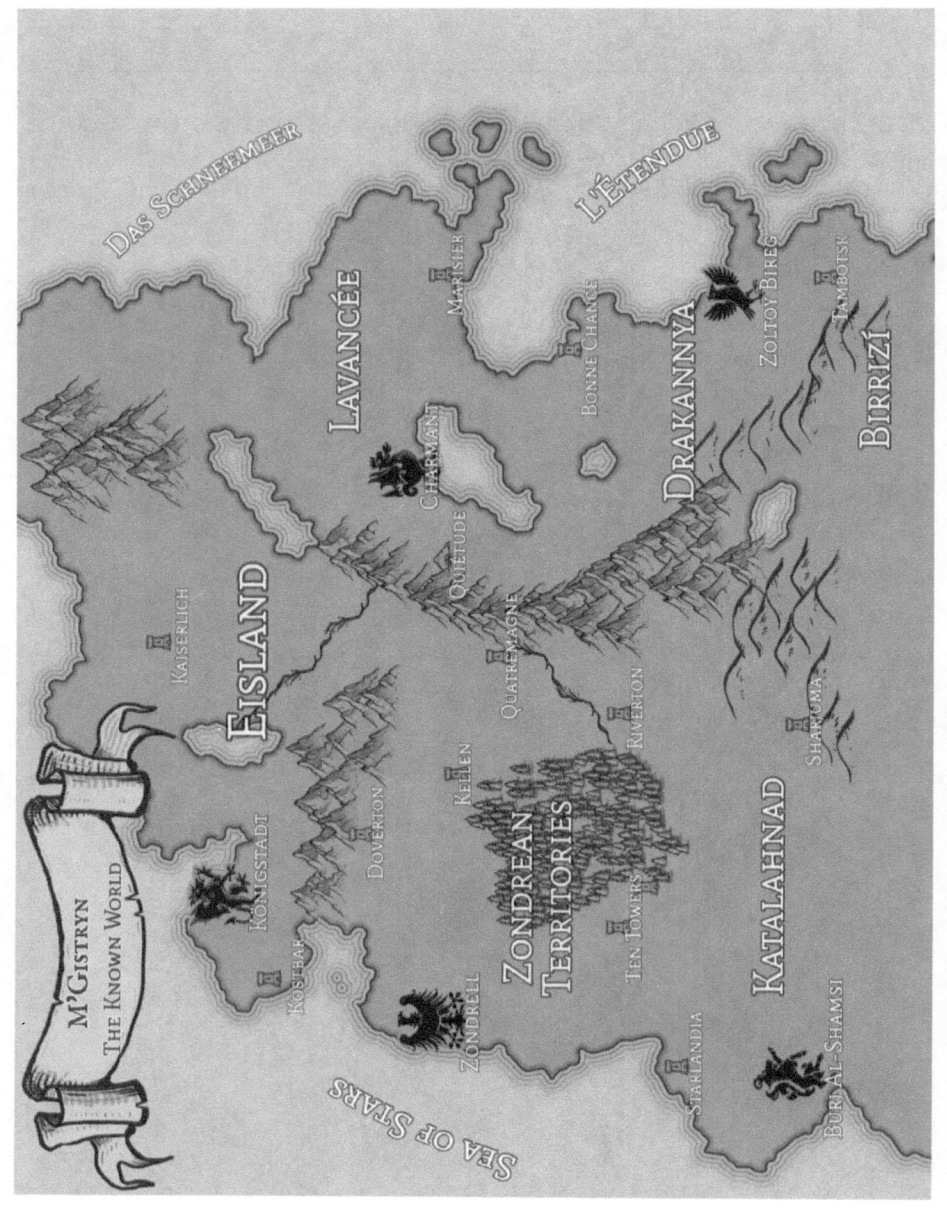

ZONDRELL
JEWEL OF THE WEST

POPULATION: 1,000,000

WEST GATE

NORTH GATE

SOUTH GATE

CENTER MARKET

CHURCH

CATHEDRAL

GODS' AVENUE

ASCENSION LEAGUE DISTRICT

ZONDRELL ACADEMY

PALACE

SHIPPING DISTRICT

Heraldry of Zondrell - the Eight Ruling Houses

Kelvaar V (reigning King of Zondrell)
Wife: Mariana
Children: Larenne, Beatrix, Katarina, Edin

Andrew Avery Piers
Wife: Diana
Children: Hann, Leon, Amis, Davies

Percival Tyr Anthony
Wife: Therese
Children: Victor, Peter

Cen Marcus Lyster
Wife: Dona
Children: Corrin, Frederick (Fyr), Elena

Jonathan Colywyl Michael
Wife: Gretchen
Children: Tristan

Alexander Marcus Xavier
Wife: none
Children: none

Morvaine Gallus Stephen
Wife: Rosa
Children: Melody, Squire

Alastair Aric Percy
Wife: Tirana
Children: Birann, Tressia, Milena, Gregory

TABLE OF CONTENTS

PART ONE

*E*ven good men will turn when their freedom is at stake.

From *Amulius of Aurimiers' Philosophical Histories of M'Gistryn: Volume 488*, 900-950

CHAPTER ONE

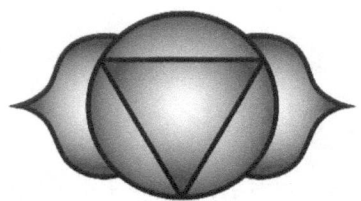

Belonging
10 Spring's Green, 1272
Tristan Michael Johannes Loringham

I found myself waist-deep in blood.

Yet, there had been no battle. Instead of the rush of the fight, I felt nothing but cold, an unearthly chill that seeped into my very core. Around me, I could hear only the roar of rushing water, and as my vision cleared, I saw a vast, dark pool, under a sickly blue sky and a glowing white-yellow light. Not the sun – no, this light was something else, pulsing faintly from within some kind of clear shell, with dark shapes stirring within its depths. Near the horizon, a grassy ledge led down a steep incline, and on the opposite side, a short embankment led to what appeared to be stairs, cut into the earth by an unknown hand.

I've been here before. Everything about the place screamed that it was a dream, a dream I had lived before – or rather, *survived*. Once, I stood at the edge of the raging River – the place where souls returned to pass from one life to the next – and turned away from it. I had climbed that impossible hill, reached the Source where the whole thing began, and now, I was standing in the blood of infinite souls.

What did it mean? Was it ever just a dream? I looked down into the murky crimson, unable to see anything, except my own reflection staring back at me. My short blond hair was tousled and damp, my once-fine clothes tattered to rags, but I was otherwise clean. The water simply beaded on my skin and fell away, as if I were not a part of it, and it was not a part of me.

Alien white streaks of lightning arced across the blue of my eyes, and I watched the blank expression on my face until it rippled and broke apart against the rising current. I took two, three steps back, straining against the sudden ferocity, and it occurred to me that if I slipped, if those waters took me, that would be it. I *would* become part of the River then. I would cease to be Tristan Michael Johannes Loringham... and I didn't want that. Not yet.

"You do not belong here."

The voice was felt more than heard, a resonance that seeped into my understanding and settled like something evil in the pit of my stomach. But it was right – I didn't belong there. If I did, I would already be moving with that current instead of struggling against it, waiting for the day I would be reborn anew. Yet, though the water held me fast, the sheer force of the current enough to pull any man under in a heartbeat, I could endure. I *would* endure.

"Yours is not this path. You do not belong here."

It was a silken voice, as fluid as the waters around me and unlike anything heard in the land of the living. *Where did it come from?* Without a presence to aim my thoughts toward, I spoke into the empty air. "I can't leave. I have too much yet to do."

"Yours is not the place to choose."

Around me, the pull of the current grew stronger yet, pelting me in wave upon wave, and still, I would not yield. I couldn't – not now, not yet. With mighty effort, I took one step toward the shore and those simple stairs which led to... well, *where*, I couldn't tell. It didn't matter, because it was the place I had to go. So I took another step, and another, nearly stumbling and losing everything each time.

At my hip, I realized my sword was with me – my father's blade, once ripped from my hand by the Sea of Stars, now returned to my side. Apparently, even inanimate things went back to the River when they "passed on." Real, imagined, or otherwise, it still felt solid and reassuring, and it would serve as a fine staff to help me keep my balance.

Its point drove deep into spongy earth, the three rubies set into the hilt looking like perfect, round drops of the water it battled. Its leverage gave me hope, gave me strength. *I can do this.* One step, then another, and soon the shore was almost in reach.

"Yours is not the place to choose," I heard the voice again, booming in my thoughts. So close, so...

Holy hell!

As I turned, the thing before me made no sense. Incomprehensible, beyond mortal reason, it coalesced from the pool, water rippling like muscle, the odd light dancing along its surface as liquid became solid and crimson darkened to the purplish-black of a deep, deep wound.

As big as a building – hell, as big as the Zondrell Palace – the thing loomed, with a giant head on a long, elegant neck that swiveled toward me with unparalleled grace. Just one of its cat-like eyes could fill a ballroom, and its luminescent brilliance reminded me of one, all decked out for some sort of party. Infinite blue winked within the depths of those eyes, and the longer I stared, the deeper they seemed to become.

The massive creature was covered in reptilian scales, glassy and smooth, blood dripping from them like rain from slick tile. When it cocked its head to reveal white fangs the size of towers, I found myself unable to move, even though every part of me said to run. *But where would I go?*

"You fear." Yes, it *spoke*, with that same watery voice. It oozed into my consciousness in a way that was almost seductive, oddly feminine, each word drawn out with an accent that was almost, though not quite, like that of the desert people of Katalahnad. It was music, a constant hum with rhythm and form. When I said nothing, only stood there frozen in something closer to abject horror than mere fear, it spoke again. "Tristan Michael Johannes Loringham... the name of one who defiles this place. Your fear is justified."

My mind had finally pieced it all together – a *dragon*. Just like in the stories, beasts that could not be slain, symbols of strength and power, heralds of magic... the thing before me was nothing less than the most ancient of legends.

I glanced to my right, daring to take my eyes from the beast for a second, and saw the glittering gold ink still there, peeking out under a tear in my sleeve. I had the image of just such a dragon tattooed on the shoulder of my swordarm in what seemed like ages ago, even though it had only been less than a year. *Hadn't it? What did time really mean in this place? Better question: how did this thing know my name?*

I felt my grip tighten around my blade. "What do you mean, 'defile?'" I asked in a harsh whisper.

A ripple moved along the dragon's scales, as if someone had thrown a pebble into a still pool, and its answer came in a hiss as the thing suddenly struck out at me, snake-like and fast. So fast, I almost had no time to react – lightning struck from a cloudless sky to form a white-electric shield over my head the moment before a fang bore through my skull. Instead, it bit into light that held substance and weight, but not the blood it sought.

"I have no wish to fight you," I said to it, sword moving to a guard position, before me. It was not easy to maintain my balance amidst the churning waters, but for the moment, I stood resolute.

The thing seemed to sneer, showing more wicked teeth. "Accept the path set before you," came the Water Dragon's hissing command, then it lunged for me again. And I was ready, more so this time, and light crackled in all directions, as the creature's house-sized snout struck my barrier. If I dodged, I might lose my footing and slip beneath the surface, even though every part of my being screamed at me to run. *Hold your ground, hold your ground.*

It came at me, over and over, and with every strike, I felt a little bit of strength leaking away with the expending of magical energy. It felt different somehow in this place, not the sharp, striking pain I often felt in... well, whatever I had previously understood to be reality. No, here, the power moved through me with almost no effort, an extension of my will. But it wasn't infinite, either, and the Water Dragon knew it as well as I.

"I still have things to do – people who need me," I told it, as it reared back for another blow. It paused for a moment, considering. "I won't submit. Not yet."

Its reply hit my mind as a deluge of anger. "*You* do not choose. You are judged. Your path is ended, your name come to end."

Before I had a chance to react, I felt my feet lift up from under me as the water became claws. I was wrapped up in them, held prisoner, and despite the struggle, despite my sword swinging useless through liquid, the blood waters of the Great River embraced me like a long-lost parent. They flooded over me, both warming and freezing all at once... and there was absolutely nothing I could do about it. No magic, no blade, no prayer would save me.

Darkness became my existence.

Not just the absence of light, but Darkness, wide and yawning and vast. Unknowable. Unthinkable. Mist played at the edges of my senses, and beyond lay the heart of a blackness that couldn't be named, couldn't be described in any kind of way that would convey the scope of it.

I didn't want to go with it – there was so much left to be done, so many people to help. Yet as I moved with the current, I couldn't quite think of their names, or why I had to go to them. Consciousness and thought became... less tangible, less important. There was nothing bad or wrong or evil about this Darkness. It was *supposed* to be there, just as everything here was following the same current. It was all part of *the Cycle*. It started in Light, and ended in Darkness, an eternal, perfect process.

And the only thing out of place... was me.

My keen awareness of that fact became a stabbing pain at the center of my mind that clutched at my senses, threatening to rip them from me forever. Oh yes, I could feel pain here, and that pain was wicked, seemingly with its own volition and malice. It almost seemed to have a voice of its own.

Time is short.

Do not submit.

CHAPTER TWO

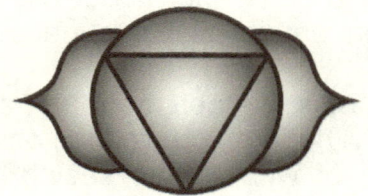

The Eyes of a Child
11 Spring's Green, 1272
Jade Saçaille

As much as it will forever pain me to admit, I have never understood my daughter.

Even just to look at her, she always seemed so different from any other child. Her whirling mess of wavy golden hair had grown redder – and a little darker – as she'd gotten older. Her face had lost its baby roundness, lengthening to reveal strong, high cheekbones and thin, pink lips that almost never smiled. At thirteen, she was all limbs, tall and skinny and as athletic as the boys her age. She could outrun all of them. What would she say if they caught up to her, anyhow? Nothing, of course.

My daughter spoke very little. Even now, at nearly midnight, I found her lost in thought at the kitchen table of our humble little house in eastern Doverton. Drawing, always drawing. That is, when she wasn't exploring the plants and the insects outside, that world of imagination that was hers and hers alone. The drawings were part of that world, too, a world that I never belonged to, even though I was sometimes the subject of her work.

"Jardin?" I asked, quiet, trying not to startle her. I knew better than to yell. She did not look up, but her hand paused ever so briefly over her sketchpad. "What are you still doing up?"

Jardin's charcoal pencil returned to the paper, delicate yet furious strokes moving across the paper. Though she'd only lit one of the candles on the table, I could tell it was quite the scene, stretching from edge to edge in the large bound set of parchment that I had gotten her about two years ago. Before then, she drew on any available surface, walls and floors notwithstanding.

I moved to sit across the table from her, angling my head to get a closer look. "What are you working on so late?" If I could have made sense of what I was seeing, I might not have asked. But it was too... bizarre. A wild place, full of windswept grasses and flowers and a wide, raging river. Splashes in the water spoke of something unseen, unknowable, under the surface. Strange figures floated in the sky far overhead. But the main figure of the scene took the breath from my lungs. "*Chérie,* is this... Papa?"

It looked so much like him, as a younger man, in the days when we first came together to Quatremagne. Cleaned up, shaved, hair trimmed just so, in his best uniform, he looked so proud, so... *pure*, somehow, if such a thing were possible for a man whose occupation was death. But Jardin had never seen him this way, and when she had finished shading the armored plates on the figure's shoulders, she finally responded. "That's not Papa," she said in that tone she had when she was both a little tired and a little cranky. She did not look up at me.

"Oh? Who is it?"

"That's my cousin."

The silence felt so heavy all of the sudden. I had to fill it with something. "Your... cousin? Jardin, a cousin would be the child of my sister, and Tante Onyx has no children."

Jardin paused to look thoughtfully at the man in the image for a moment. "Papa's sister has a son. That's him."

"Papa's sister?" I didn't think she even knew her father *had* a sister, much less that she had any children. Did I know he had a sister? Well, I suppose I did. Of course, I'd never met her – apparently, he hadn't seen her since he was fifteen. What was her name... Gretchen? It had been a lifetime since I'd thought about that. Well, cousin or no, I knew better than to dismiss it all and send Jardin off to bed. That would just end badly, and I had no energy to argue with her at this time of night. "So, what's this cousin's name?"

Jardin considered, still fixated on the sketch. Scrunching her nose, she bent over it again to add some more shading to the scenery in the foreground. Grass and flowers sprung to life at the will of her pencil. "I don't know. I saw him in the Place. That's three times now."

The way she said it – *the Place* – shifted something in me. I had never heard that term before. "'The Place'? Jardin, what do you mean?"

"You know, the Place where I go, when I dream."

I wished I knew. I bent closer to the picture, peering through the flickering candlelight to examine it even further. Oh, I often looked over her shoulder at her sketches, don't get me wrong, and I had seen similar things before. The meadow, the sunny cloudless sky, the majestic river – all of these things could have been pictures of anywhere. They reminded me of home, of Quatremagne, and maybe I had always assumed that's why Jardin drew them. How wrong could I have been? "Do you always go here when you dream?" I asked.

"No. Sometimes I don't go anywhere. Sometimes I go there. We're not supposed to be there, you know."

"And how do you know that?"

"Because we're just visiting. But we can do that because we're special."

"You and your cousin?"

"Right." The pencil moved back to the figure, and almost lovingly added a few extra lines of definition to the man's face. No, he didn't really look so much like Brin, after all. Still tall, yes, handsome and light-haired and clearly Eislandisch, but there was something else there, too. The eyes were the wrong shape, too oval for an Eislander. Wider apart, too, more like… a Zondrean? Perhaps. Hard to say, but whoever he was, he had a strong bearing, something that was noble, but not overtly proud.

The pencil added one final detail before Jardin sat back to admire her work. The gift she had of being able to convey so much in mere charcoal never failed to impress me – her first words had been in pictures. With just a few marks, she had been able to add streaks of what could be described as brilliance to the man's eyes… streaks not so unlike the ones in her own.

"Special… of course," I said, my words coming from some far-off place. Maybe the same place where that river came from.

The Light, like winking stars, danced along the precise spiral pattern buried deep within her sea-blue irises. Very few people ever saw this – not only did I protect her from that, but they wouldn't know what they were seeing, anyhow. They never understood what they saw in my eyes, either, just some murky purple mist over dark irises. If I still practiced, maybe the magic would swirl and shift, but I had sworn it off a long time ago. That was another lifetime, one best forgotten about. And if my daughter ever learned how to harness what she had stored deep in her somewhere, well, it would be over my dead body.

Jardin blinked, and the Light in her eyes changed course. "I saw him when I went to sleep. Then I lost him. I think…" She trailed off, brow furrowed with troubling thoughts. "I think he's in trouble. Mama? Do you think if I go back to sleep, I'll find him again?"

"Well, it might not hurt to try. Aren't you tired? It's late." I straightened, getting ready to stand up and usher her back to her room. My eyes were getting heavy just thinking about sleep.

Jardin, though, didn't budge. For the first time in days, she actually looked directly at me, and her gaze was just short of accusatory. "You don't know about the Place, do you? But you have magic."

I reached out, wanting to put my hand on hers as it rested beside the sketchpad, but stopped short. She was talking so much to me right now – why ruin it and upset her? I knew better. "No, Jardin, I don't."

"You don't believe me."

"Of course I believe you, chérie. Why wouldn't I?"

"Tante Onyx said you wouldn't."

"Tante Onyx… doesn't understand magic, chérie. Why, did you talk to her?" She nodded vaguely. "Well, I can assure you that Tante Onyx doesn't know what I believe any more than you do."

"She said she's been there, too."

"Oh really?" My sister had traveled more than anyone I'd ever known, but as far as I knew, that did not include some wondrous, magical dream-land. And when Jardin failed to elaborate, I chose to let the matter drop, instead finding a way to change the subject. "Well, Tante Onyx is very good at getting around. You know, she should have gotten your picture to Papa for you by now."

As Jardin nodded, a few gnarled strands of strawberry blond hair fell across her eyes. She pushed them back with a brusque movement. "You think so?"

A few years ago, I would have forbidden *that* whole thing from ever happening. There was a part of me that wished she would forget she had a Papa at all. Then, my sister brought us here to Doverton, and there he was... curse Onyx and her schemes. We never spoke, but it took just one chance sighting on the street, and even after ten years, Jardin knew he was in the city.

She asked after him. She bothered me incessantly to go look for him. She drew picture upon picture for him, and a few days ago, she had managed to persuade Onyx to take one of those pictures with her on her latest trip. I didn't even know where she was going, but she said he'd be there. And now here was my poor little girl, anxious, worried, and wondering. Having nightmares! Chantal's bones, it wasn't fair.

I shook my head as if to clear the whole thing from my mind, then rose. I tugged at her sleeve. "I'm sure she did. Why don't we talk about this in the morning, *oui*? It's late, and little girls need their beauty sleep."

"I thought you said I wasn't little anymore."

"Neither am I, but I want *my* beauty sleep. Don't you?"

This was enough. Jardin closed her sketchpad and tucked it under her arm as she got up and headed for her room. I even thought I caught her yawn.

CHAPTER THREE

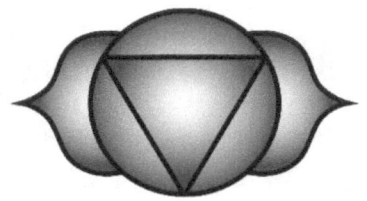

Fear and Freedom
11 Spring's Green, 1272
Alexander Vestarton

L ately, a lot of people thought I could do the impossible. And maybe that was true. I could stop arrows in their tracks and send them back to their quivers. I could slow blood and stop hearts. I could *think* a man to death.

That was precisely why I was still alive, for the time being.

Hours after Tristan, Lord of House Loringham, had... gone "out to sea," the other Lords gathered around me. I will never forget their faces – grave, pale, and maybe a little penitent. Maybe. That last bit might have just been my exhausted, wishful thinking. At that point, I had not slept for well over a day, and was running on little more than worry and a desperate need to stay rooted in reality.

Think, Alex, *think*. What would my father do if he were here? Lord Xavier Vestarton was a great politician, brilliant in his ability to command respect, even when everyone wanted his head. I had seen it time and time again, growing up. Now, Lord Alexander Vestarton's smiles were just as charming, but only surface-deep, and his anger blazed hotter than the noonday sun in Summer's Light. The old men of the Council found him petulant, rude, and of late, downright intolerable.

Well, fuck them. They were just as insufferable. At least I wasn't setting up conspiracies against the throne and making the innocent of Zondrell pay in blood. And this is exactly what I told them when the remaining five members of the Council of Lords came to me as the worst night of my life lightened into dreary gray.

"Alex? Alex, it's dangerous up here," Cen Shal-Vesper said, daring to take a step into the undamaged half of the Council antechamber. Over my head, on the far side of the room, the sun was trying desperately to burn off the fog of the morning, but the season of the Rains was too tough for all that.

The stone felt slick under my boots as I walked along the broken edge. Below, boats circled, carrying men with torches and more people in colored robes – the Academy mages had arrived. It had been Andella's idea, and perhaps a good one, but as water swirled and stone rose to the surface, compelled by elemental magic, I chose to continue on my quest. Back and forth I stalked, feeling every moment, flailing around within visions of the past in search of some kind of hope.

And these old men were ruining it all. I looked up to let the cool mists attempt to slap me back to full wakefulness. "I'm busy. What do you want?" They all looked at each other, unsure, and I smirked. "You *are* aware there's a search going on, yes? You know, for a member of the Council?"

"Indeed, and I am sorry, Alex. I truly am." This probably wasn't a lie – the pain was evident in his gaunt, pale features and sunken eyes. Still, I was in no mood for him, or any of them.

"Stop it. You're not sorry. If you were, you'd be in a boat. You'd be helping the Academy mages. You'd be doing *something* besides bothering me while I try to... while I try to use magic to find him." It sounded rather dumb when I said it aloud, but still, it seemed more productive than the search in the water. Band of Academy mages or no, we knew nothing more now than we did hours ago.

I took another step, bent, picked up a broken bit of marble. It drew me momentarily into the oily depths of the past, of a quarry where it had been chipped away in southern Starlandia, then of lightning rending it in two, throwing dust and shards in a million directions. Then it was gone, and I was back in the damp open air again.

Cen's voice was soft. "Alex, it's been hours. They're still looking, but..."

"I'm not giving up."

"I know. We're not saying that."

I tossed the marble scrap back to the shattered floor and heard a clink that seemed to reverberate across the distance between me and the other Lords. "'We,' now? You speak for all of us, do you, Cen?"

"Alexander, we need to talk," huffed a red-faced Andrew Miller, hands on his ample hips. "This cannot wait." For all his bravado, when I leveled my quicksilver, glowing gaze at him, he took a step backward.

"We are in a state of emergency, gentlemen," I said. "Or have you not figured that out yet?"

Cen spoke before Miller could bluster about some more. "Alex, you moved the banners. You can't just... do that. The line of succession cannot be changed on a whim."

"A whim? A *whim*?" I strode across the room then, coming to stand a mere foot before them. Miller stood a step behind Cen, and behind them, bent old Alastair Shilling looked on thoughtfully, while Morvaine Silversmith and Percival Wyndham pouted and glared. "You really do think I'm a boy trying to sit at a man's table, don't you?"

"I think you're a..." Wyndham's words died on his lips as the others – even Miller – turned to look at him.

"Go ahead – say it, Wyndham." The old fool remained quiet, mouth drawn into a line. "It's all right, even though you all know damn well that without me, you'd all be archery dummies. I saved your miserable lives."

"No one said we're not thankful," Cen said hurriedly. "We are, truly. But Miller's right, you can't just *become* the Head Councilor – or the King, for that matter – without discussion, and some kind of vote. This is most irregular, Alex. We need to discuss this."

A smile bloomed on my face. "King Vestarton. That scares the living hell out of you, doesn't it?" To be fair, it scared the piss out of me, too, but I wasn't about to tell them that. That had never been my intent. I just wanted the Head Councilor title out of Miller's money-grubbing, corrupt hands. That was before Tristan took little King Edin into the sea with him, though – a few minutes' difference, and I might have thought twice.

"You can't just move the banners, Vestarton," Wyndham snarled. "End of discussion."

"In case you haven't noticed, there is barely a government right now, much less a proper city to govern. Unless you gentlemen are here to haul me to the gallows or put a knife in my back, I suggest you do something productive. You know, like try to *fix* the problem rather than continue making it worse." I started to turn away, then paused. "For the record, as far as I can tell, I'm the only one with a shred of morality among us. Go find some of your own, and then come back and talk to me. Until then, I will keep looking for the one among all of us with more decency in his little finger than any of you have ever had."

"Oh please – Loringham? That traitor?"

Percival Wyndham probably never realized how close he came to an early end that day. A part of me wanted to reach out with that writhing magic boiling in my blood and make sure time never changed for him again.

Instead, I took the high road, calmly balled up my fist, and connected solidly with his cheekbone. I felt a satisfying smack and hot pain radiate from my knuckles – it could have been harder, but it was enough to send a message. "That's for Tristan, and for the people of Zondrell," I spat. The rest of them collectively gasped at my very unlordly conduct, but I didn't see anyone exactly running to Wyndham's aid, either.

"Alex, this is not helping," Cen snapped at me.

Miller joined him. "You absolutely are the most insufferable boy. Wyndham's right – your father would be ashamed of you."

"My father would have done the same damned thing. Look, none of us have anything to talk about. You do whatever you want. Change the banners back – I don't give a fuck. I will keep doing what I need to do. You all keep paying off Royal Guards to do your bidding, or hide in your manors, or do whatever the hell you're doing that does nothing to help this city recover from the damage *you've* done. Now, if you'll excuse me, gentlemen." And I turned my back on them, returning to the broken ledge. I heard some muttering for a while, but they did depart, eventually. Where they went, I wasn't sure. I didn't care. I do know that when I finally succumbed to exhaustion a few hours later, I locked myself in a guestroom in the Palace, one that no one knew I occupied, just in case they took me up on that whole dagger-in-the-back business.

Asleep, even the most dangerous of men is rendered harmless.

**

That sleep was troubled and only lasted an hour, maybe more. A blanket of light gray-white still shrouded the sky overhead when I looked out the window, and people still moved around in a confused, shambling sort of way in the courtyard outside the Palace. Guards ringed the inner courtyard to push back the common citizenry anytime they got too close, but I did notice that their number had needed some fortification over the course of a few hours.

Where once there was only a small collection of lesser nobles out there demanding to know what happened, there was now a rather respectable brigade of men and women, and not many looked happy. Even from high up in the Palace, I could see the agitation in the people, the urgency... the anger. If this kept going, none of it would end well.

I slipped back down through the Palace mostly unnoticed. Any active guardsmen were outside, and I hardly saw a soul until I hit the grand entry chamber, the place where people typically waited to gain an audience with the King.

It was nothing short of spectacular, for those who appreciated outrageously ornate and gaudy art. Tapestries lined the walls, and statues of various great men in their glory lay strewn about the place in a gilded testament to the glory of Zondrell. Just this one room alone was probably worth a million Royals – spent, of course, by the late King Kelvaar V in his mad dash for the city coffers. The man really did have a penchant for extraordinary purchasing that did little to benefit anyone but himself.

When I was a kid, the whole room was no less beautiful, but much simpler and more open. Now, it was lined with money that should have gone to things like public buildings, food for the poor, all of that stuff that never seemed all that important to old Kelvaar. No wonder the other Lords conspired to have him killed. If only they could have anticipated how badly the whole thing would go. Apparently, a bad king is better than no king at all… who could have guessed?

Not that some of his predecessors had been any less greedy and ineffective. For over two hundred years, the Blackwarren family had led Zondrell, ever since the Great Civil War, when the nation of Zondrea became a collection of sovereign city-states.

Many said that Caius Blackwarren, whose hawk-nosed marble statue stood at the center of this grand hall, was the greatest leader in history, the only man who could have led Zondrell to freedom from an oppressive central government. He was, in essence, the creator of the western world as we knew it today. But looking up into the empty eyes of that statue, I knew there were a fair number of other Blackwarrens that didn't get immortalized in stone, who we'd all like to forget ever existed. Oh, if only the great patriarch knew of what his progeny had wrought.

I briefly entertained the idea of reaching out to touch that statue, to see what historical marvels and visions might await me and my Time magic. Could it provide a vision of inspiration, a way through the muck of chaos that Caius' beautiful city had become? I actually laughed aloud at the wistful romanticism of such a thought.

"Lord Vestarton?" A shuffling of armor to my right startled me straight out of my humor. The Royal Guard who'd spoken offered a salute, which I returned while silently hoping that this man didn't think I was completely mad. The concern etched into his boyish features told me nothing good, at any rate. "Lord Vestarton, Sir? A few men have been looking for you."

"What's this about?" I asked, my words slow and tenuous.

"Sir, there are city guards and scouts coming back asking for help at the gates. There's a lot of trouble there, and with the General gone, no one's quite sure who to report to."

"You have captains, don't you? Ah… Evison, yes? High Captain Evison?"

"Yes, Sir, and he's already at East Gate, Sir. No orders are coming through. But they say North Gate's worse. The City Watch that's left is barely holding."

"And?" Wait a minute, did he just say… "Wait, *where* is Torven? You said he's gone?"

"He's in prison, Sir. Didn't you know?"

Obviously not. Not that I was that surprised, but still, who put him there? Though, if I had to guess... "Did the Princess order that, soldier?"

"The Queen, Sir, yes. Sir, the men are..." he lowered his voice to barely a whisper, "they're not dealing with this well. I've seen twelve desertions just today. The people are rioting, getting out of control. They'll start dying soon. Nothing we can do about it. I just thought, maybe if I said something to you, something might get done."

In the golden gloom of the grand Palace entry hall, I met the gaze of this Royal Guardsman I didn't know. He might have been closer to thirty than twenty, but still young, inexperienced. And in those dark, glassy eyes of his, I saw real fear mixed with something else – hope. This man was placing his hope in *me*, of all people? If only someone had the heart to tell him what a bad idea that was. I couldn't even keep my own best friend out of danger, and couldn't do much to help Zondrell, either. Unless...

"So Torven's in prison – the Palace prison, you say?"

"Yes, Sir," the man said weakly.

"Well, I think I'll go have a chat with him. Thank you, soldier – keep doing your part." I offered him another salute, and he returned it with vigor, his fist striking his left shoulder with a metallic thud. Then I left him there, moving toward the door with one thought playing around in my mind: I had no idea what I was doing yet, but indeed, I was doing *something*. And that, right now, seemed to be enough.

CHAPTER FOUR

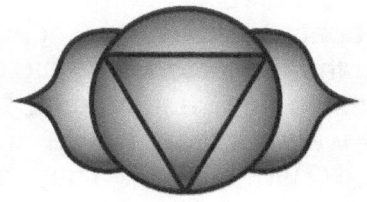

The Wheel
11 Spring's Green, 1272
Andella Weaver

Hope... keep hope beyond hope. He's out there.

That thought ran over and over in my mind as the Academy mages worked, turning the sea almost literally upside down. It was my idea to bring them here, and I had to admit, it was working better than I'd hoped. Sending for Archmage Tiara had been the best thing I could have done – perhaps, the only thing that made any sense. Why? Because I was spent. Exhausted. Anxiety had wrung me straight through to my core, and now I sat on a dock, staring blindly into the water. I had never been so *tired*.

Master Brin was tired, too. "You think this will help?" he asked me in his harsh northern accent as he settled hard next to me. He had just returned from yet another tour around the area where the tower fell, this time actually walking across the rubble of the fallen section of the Palace while the mages held the water up in a great vortex.

It was a sight I didn't think I'd see again soon, the power of ten Water mages working together at once to make the very Sea of Stars itself do their bidding – amazing! If I had stayed at the Magic Academy after graduating, instead of going home to my sister, I might have learned how to combine powers with other mages like that. Of course, if I had stayed there, then my life would be very, very different right about now, and maybe none of this would have ever happened.

I sighed and stared down into the depths again, bare feet dangling just over the surface. "I don't know. But they're doing more than just the boats could ever do, right?"

"There is nothing there but stone and broken things."

"The Earth mages can move the stone. Look, they're trying now." And so they were, at least twelve green-robed mages, including Archmage Tiara herself. They moved slowly, but methodically, convincing the stone to move and reshape itself. Rubble strained and tore apart under their gazes, and Archmage Tiara barked orders as they went that were lost across the wide expanse of sea that separated us.

"And still they find nothing."

At this, I looked up, and I felt my eyes narrow to slits in the face of Brin Jannausch's wild blue gaze. He was a big man, huge, in fact — "intimidating" didn't even really capture the sheer scope of his presence.

Not that I was scared, of course. I knew him just a little differently than did the soldiers and the mages running around the cliffshore, for I knew him for who he was: a distressed uncle. He and Tristan weren't necessarily close, and they hadn't even known each other that long, but I could tell what lay in the old Eislandisch general's heart. We shared a similar kind of tired, angry frustration. Still, I couldn't imagine simply… giving up.

"You can't say that. They'll find him," I said, swallowing hard.

Brin scratched at his scrubby blond beard as he considered me. "Maybe, maybe not. But the chain on your hand should come off."

The chain on my… I looked down at the back of my left hand, where a delicate filigree network ran the length from wrist to fingers, linking a bracelet and ring of Katalahni make. Silver and gold danced around gems of glittering red, blue, green, yellow, and white, and I felt my cheeks tighten into a smile in spite of myself. It was my betrothal band, when Tristan had asked me to marry him not five days ago. "Dear

Catherine, that was less than a week ago," I said, not really to anyone but myself.

"The chain," Brin said, more insistent this time.

"But we're not..." Married. We weren't married yet – we hadn't even begun to think about a wedding. It was there that he was supposed to take that chain and turn it into a ring of his own, symbolizing an eternal link between us. Now, though, that chain symbolized something very different.

I felt my jaw clench tight, and from the way he cleared his throat, I thought Brin might have felt the same way "Others should think you are. And that you are with child."

I shook my head, because if people thought there was an heir to House Loringham, then what? They wouldn't be able to take away the fortune of a dead man? My mouth opened with a protest on my lips, but it died there, replaced instead by distant shouts and an excited shriek from Archmage Tiara. "Impossible!"

Confused, I stumbled to my feet, and my heart rose along with the rest of me. It positively thundered in my chest – could they have found something? There were only a few small rowboats left at the docks, including the one I had used not that long before to come here, and now I was getting right back in.

As I rowed, straining against sore muscles and fatigue that had become almost limitless, the mages continued to yell back and forth. Questions arose, and hopeful tones. I heard something about a box... no, *The* Box, the obsidian instrument the Academy used to determine whether a person had magical talent or not. Why would they be talking about The Box now, of all things?

Then I got to the edge of the vortex, where water rose up from the rubble and earth beneath in a sheer wall, and I understood. The sea floor was laced with stone so black, it seemed to absorb all light around it.

My breath caught in my throat – I had never seen anything like it. Where did it come from? There were no volcanoes within five hundred miles of Zondrell, and yet here was all of this obsidian... or was it really something so mundane as that? It compelled me to jump out of the boat and touch it, and I started to do just that, until I heard a voice call down from atop some of the Palace rubble.

"Andella, dear, I don't know if that's wise just yet," Archmage Tiara said, not so much concerned as much as speculative. "Better come down here first."

Amid the inaudible mumbling of the other Academy mages, I returned to rowing out until I could get to where they were, hopping out of the little rowboat and onto the broken stone. The mages had worn away the sharp and precarious bits to form a safe platform and passageway – it was almost like a building had been carved from within the sea, with a hole cut into the water to allow it to take shape.

Several male mages – powerful and with better endurance – held it all in place, quietly concentrating, while some female mages hovered around the Archmage. Her curled dark hair was wet and stringy and wild, and her bright green robes fared little better, but she had full command of the group. The women leaned in, as if awaiting the same types of realizations that they heard so often in Tiara's classes.

She turned to me. "Ah, Andella, dear. Do take a look, yes?"

I did, and I saw the same obsidian darkness racing along the sea floor. I shook my head. Was I supposed to see something different? I mean, even on the most grueling days at the Magic Academy, practicing for hour after hour, concentrating on controlling raging fires conjured from nothing, it never felt like my soul had simply… wilted.

My muscles, my bones, everything ached, and hadn't I taken – absorbed – life force from another, from a soldier trying to kill me just last night? I didn't want to think about that part, but logic told me I should have been stronger, somehow. Maybe it was all gone by now, for I had no energy, no will, and certainly no ability to think through one of Archmage Tiara's puzzles.

"Archmage, I don't see…"

"Look – the lines are almost straight, the same width… I'd daresay there's some sort of pattern, don't you think, dear?"

I followed her pointing finger as it traced the lines on the ground below. It certainly wasn't perfect, but it almost looked like part of… A flash of a memory, of sky blue eyes full of dancing stars. They stared back at me with adoration, gentle warmth, the magic emanating from his pupils in perfect lines of electric white energy. By Catherine, I loved the way he looked at me.

"A wheel," I said, my voice coming out hoarse and strained. "It's like a wheel."

"A wheel, you say? Yes, I can see that. Good thinking, but I would like to see the rest." The Archmage turned back to the Palace, finger at her chin. "Does it go under the Palace, maybe? Hmm… I need a theory. Anyone? Ideas?"

"We could excavate some of the black rock," one of the mages piped up. She seemed to shrink at least six inches as Tiara's head swiveled in her direction.

"Were you present when The Box was found, dear?"

The girl shook her head emphatically. "No, Archmage."

To the girl's surprise, the Archmage simply smiled. "Well, neither was I. But I do know that it took an army of mages and soldiers with carts and pulleys just to get the damned thing back to the Academy. They tried to chisel at it and all the rest, but it resisted them entirely. This stone, as I understand it, cannot be so easily cut."

"Not… even with magic?" offered another brave soul. "I mean, how would they have made The Box in the first place, if they couldn't cut it?"

Tiara considered them, and they both shrank even further. I had to admit, I didn't envy them. My time living in fear of the Archmages had passed, and I was – frankly – very much relieved about that. "You assume that The Box was constructed, and not natural." Hesitant, the girls nodded. "Well, we don't really know that, do we? But… well, a theory is a theory. Why don't you try it, then? Cut the rock."

The two girls, both Earth mages like the Archmage, looked at each other, then to the rock below them. Not willing to let a good challenge go to waste, they did indeed raise their hands, intent on trying to make the strange rock that couldn't really be obsidian at all do their bidding.

I knew from books that obsidian was brittle, easy enough to break apart if you tried hard enough, and The Box that we knew from the Academy was anything but brittle. Surely, these women had to have the same thoughts in their minds, but yet, they tried anyhow. I supposed a chance to impress Archmage Tiara was a chance, however slim.

After a few agonizing minutes of concentrating on the ground below us, they lowered their arms, sweat beading on pale foreheads and eyes full of whirling green light. "Are you finished then?" Archmage Tiara asked them, and they nodded. "Indeed. So, any other thoughts?"

Neither girl had the courage to speak. Neither did I. Yet, there was a voice, one deep but feminine voice, carried along as if by the wind. It came from behind, and when I turned, I could hardly believe who I saw there, standing up in a small six-man boat with a green and yellow sail.

"The center," Onyx Saçaille called to us in her lilting Lavançaise accent. "Look to the center of the wheel, and you will know."

The weapon master who served my former home of Doverton rested one booted foot casually on the edge of the craft while men in livery matching the sail manned oars. She was all lean muscle and foreboding in green-on-black, and even from this distance, I could feel her eyes, so very dark, like pools of nothingness. Had she really sailed all the way down from Doverton? And for what? Maybe she was here to spy on the happenings in Zondrell, or maybe... maybe she was here to spy on me. And Alex, and Tristan, too.

My heart thundered in my chest as our gazes met from across the void where the mages held back the raging sea. Well, if she still believed in prophecies in old books, she might be disappointed. I was beginning to believe what Archmage Tiara had said – strange new magics emerging or no, there was no exciting "new age" dawning. The only place we all seemed to be heading was straight down the road to ruin.

The center. What would we find there? Might we find... hope? Yes, there was hope there. I could feel it. I could not – would not – allow myself to believe that Tristan was lost forever. It wasn't possible. Our fates were intertwined, our destiny connected. Prophecy or no, I did believe that we were supposed to be together. I knew it almost from the first time I'd met him. I don't know how I knew it, but I knew, and I had faith that the Lady had a plan for us. Did She not have a plan for all things? *The faithful commit themselves to Catherine's wish in life just as they commit to the Flame in death. They are the ones that trust the Path.* That's what the Book of Catherine said, and despite being a mage instead of a priest, I believed it. I grew up the daughter of a priestess, and the sister of one – I never had cause to question the Path.

And now here was Madame Saçaille, drawn here perhaps by the same exact Fate. She knew things – at least, she said she did. Maybe now it was time to learn from her. I found my voice and shouted back to her, breaking the confused silence that had descended amongst the mages. "What will we find? Do you know?"

The lady weapon master considered, cocking her head to one side. "I think we may find what you seek, Mademoiselle."

"And who might you be to suggest we overturn half the sea to find this 'center,' even though it's well beyond the range we need to search?" Archmage Tiara asked, hands on hips. "My people are not tireless, you know."

"I am well aware, Madame. But you do not have far to go."

**

She was right. In the span of an hour of Earth and Water frothing and churning, we had found it: the center of the obsidian wheel in the sea. It wasn't as big as I would have expected, maybe only six or seven feet in diameter. A tall man could stretch out across it and touch either end.

The water and rubble and seaweed had all been swept clean from it by magic, and we were now standing right at its edge, in the eye of a storm of swirling water. Tiara's mages held it as best they could, but I could tell they were tiring. We all were – even Madame Saçaille looked more worn than I had ever seen her.

That might have had something to do with the torrent of questions rained down on her by both Archmage Tiara and Master Brin. They stood apart, clustered around each other like a pack of angry dogs, and there was a part of me that wanted to be in there, too. But there was another part that wanted to be as far away as possible, to be by the mages as they worked, to make the discovery with them. We were close to something, something important. I could feel it – couldn't *they*? Maybe… maybe that's what all the fuss was about.

"Archmage!" one of the younger female Earth mages called out to get Tiara's attention. Then she turned back to the rest of us and said, quieter, "What do you think this is?"

"A bunch of rock," said another. "Rock we can't cut. The pattern is interesting, sure, but we can't do anything with it."

"How do you know?" I asked, never looking up. All I could do was stare into the center of that black shape that sucked up all light that came into its path. Now that I was right up at its edge, I could see how truly infinite it seemed, not like stone at all, but like something from another world. It wasn't so unlike being inside The Box, but magnified a hundredfold.

When someone is evaluated for magic ability, or when there is a need to do research on a person directly, The Box had long been thought to be the best instrument available. Even though no one really ever knew how it worked, it gave the Zondrell Magic Academy decades of research material. In fact, there were two Boxes, one "real" one and one reproduction, that may or may not have been made with the same obsidian-like material. Both were centuries-old, and I'd been in both of them – it wasn't hard to tell which one was the original. The power, the energy of it… it was like something reaching into your very soul and pulling out the threads of magic within.

The center of this obsidian wheel had the same feel. Even without making contact with its surface, the energy radiated from it in waves, like it was searching inside all of us for whatever power lay within. What if I touched it? We had, of course, been explicitly told not to touch anything, and the mages around me were at least a year from graduating. None of them would dare defy the Archmage, but *I* didn't need to be so concerned about her orders anymore, did I?

"What are you doing?" one of them asked as I knelt at the circle's edge, bending down with my fingers hovering not more than ten inches over its surface.

I didn't look up. I couldn't. I was too fixated on my goal. "I… I have to know."

Gasps and shouts went up all around me – they were the last things I heard.

CHAPTER FIVE

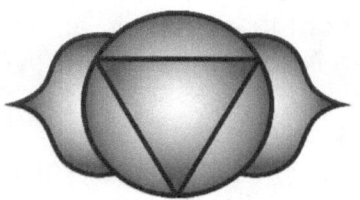

To Battle the Wind

11 Spring's Green, 1272
Tristan Loringham

I remembered lightning, striking from somewhere unseen. I remembered diving into the Sea of Stars and thinking that I should be able to swim back to shore. It wasn't the first time I'd gone cliff-diving, after all, and I was a strong swimmer – hell, in training at the Academy, I used to swim the league or so between the fishing docks and the Palace docks every chance I got. But I didn't remember what happened after I hit the water. There was just light, bright light assaulting my vision, blocking out everything else. Cold waves, heavy and relentless, dragged me downward…

Somehow, I must have made it. When I was next aware, the waters had calmed, lit by a hazy graying sun. The rocks of the cliffshore beneath me felt strangely smooth, perfect and flat, but with enough give that my fingertips could dig into them just a tiny bit.

Wait. No, this can't be right.

At certain times of day, especially in late winter and early spring, the waters of the Sea of Stars can appear colorless and dark, rather than their customary bright blue. It's a trick of the light, not much more – I'd seen that ocean as purple as a twilight eve and as gold as a summer morning. Sometimes, it was hard to even tell where the sky ended and the sea began. Today, the sky was steel, the waters scorched black. The tide swelled and retreated in time with my breath as I lay there, watching in wonder.

Beautiful, in its way… but it's not right, not right at all.

The tide brought a sheet of water up under my outstretched arms that grazed my cheek, ruffled my hair, soaked through my shirt... and it was *so* cold. I pushed myself up with a start, wishing in that moment that I hadn't, as my vision faltered. My head pulsed with an inhuman ache. But even worse, I realized I was alone.

And this place was no Sea of Stars.

The shore stretched out into infinity, and the water – unfathomably dark, like liquid obsidian tinged with blood – formed a perfect line on the horizon. No distant islands, no boats, no people, just nothingness in all directions. As I sat there searching for something, anything to focus on, I realized there were light footprints in the otherwise smooth beach, leading away from the water's edge.

It all started to come back. The lightning, the tower, the sea, the child... yes, in some place that may or may not have been a long way from wherever "here" was, I had damn near killed myself and a boy no older than eight. Indeed, maybe I had succeeded. I had tried to protect the Crown Prince of Zondrell as enemies of the throne closed in on us, and in so doing I sent a bolt of magic lightning straight through one of the towers of the Royal Palace. That Light could destroy, but it could also save, and it had enclosed us in a shield as we fell into the Sea of Stars below.

But maybe it wasn't enough. Everything after that was... nothingness, my memory as black and empty as everything around me.

"Lord Edin!" I called out. "Lord Edin, where are you?" The gentle lapping of the water along the shore was my only response, my voice hollow as it hit empty air. I shouted his name again, louder, to no avail.

Despite the pain, I reached out to find the hilt of my sword, still nearby, still my most stalwart companion, and used it to help me to my feet. Its tip drew a thin, almost imperceptible line behind me as I followed those footprints.

Was he safe? Was he frightened? He was just a child, after all, and this was no place for children. Not that I quite knew where I was, or even if this was another part of the Great River of my visions... or dreams, nightmares, whatever they were. Though, if the River had a Source, then inevitably, it had an end, too. Perhaps this was it.

Your path is ended, your name come to end. Those words came back to me, and I contemplated them as I walked, trying to make sense of it all, trying to stay aware, coherent. It was a struggle – the other way was a much easier road to travel. I could just go back to the sea. I could fling myself into the depths of that dark ocean and let it take me; if I wasn't "supposed" to be here, perhaps it would take me to the *right* place. But then again... *Do you really want that?*

With each incoming wave, I could almost hear it calling to me: *this is your path, this is the way... submit.* And maybe it was right. It was certainly tempting. But Fate was a fool if it believed I would choose my so-called "path" over a little boy out there somewhere who trusted me to keep him safe. If he was lost, so was Zondrell – I was certain of that. So I put the dark water's captivating song out of my mind and kept moving, taking each step as it came, not worrying about the next one. While I wasn't slow, I was deliberate, purposeful.

I might have walked for a lifetime... or a few minutes. There was no sense of time in a place where the sun never moved. And in a millennia that lasted an instant, the shore was gone, fading to greenery that became more verdant with each step. Bright pink flowers appeared underfoot, growing happily in thick, blood-tinged soil. The sound of flowing water filled my senses until I could hear almost nothing else – nothing, that was, save for a sniffle and a tiny whimper.

Prince Edin – *King* Edin – stood at the River's edge about fifty paces up a steep embankment, peering down into rushing crimson waters, a look of wonderment on his little round face. He seemed unhurt, his fine clothes as unruffled and clean as the moment before we dove off the crumbled Palace tower. "Lord Edin!" I called to him, rushing up the hill to close the distance.

"Lord Loringham?" The boy blinked his wide dark eyes. "Lord Loringham, is that you? Where are we? I remember we were running, and then I was cold, and..." As he trailed off, a shadow of fear and confusion passed across his face. Nothing was good about such an expression on an eight year-old.

By the Lady, what do I say to him? Somehow, telling a young boy he was standing on the edge of life and death seemed very wrong... but I found myself stuck for anything else to say. He was eight – too old to be placated with pleasant lies, but young enough to be harmed by the truth. There was nothing I could find to say that wouldn't be painful, and the worst part was, he knew it.

"I heard Father's voice," he said. "He told me to be strong. He told me not to go in there." The boy pointed to the flowing River with its current too fast to even understand, yet in its depths, the ethereal souls of the departed floated along, traveling to their eventual moment of rebirth. "I don't want to go in the water, Lord Loringham."

"You don't have to," I told him, now very sure of my words. "We're going home."

"Do… do you know how to get there?"

No reason to sugar-coat it. "No, I don't."

That one tiny admission was enough to crush the only son of fallen King Kelvaar V's spirits visibly. His small shoulders sank as his gaze turned to the ground. "But Lord Loringham, we can't stay here, can we? Forever?"

"We won't be here forever. We'll find a way. Come on – let's keep going up." Edin reached for my hand as we climbed, moving against the current but not straying far from the River's edge as we ascended the steep hill before us. Somehow, neither of us seemed to tire, though at times I did need to fight the overwhelming urge to just sit, to listen to the flow of the water. It wasn't a pleasant sound – the rushing blood hid murmurs within it, voices of the dead reaching out to claim purchase on our senses.

More and more, the fact that we weren't intended to be in this place became clear. We were an abomination against the natural order, free to move where most were not. But free was exactly where we needed to be, and neither of us were willing to give in to the temptation of submission. What "should be" wasn't what was needed – not now, not yet.

Our climb gradually became less strenuous as a valley unfolded before us and the next embankment was far, far away, almost too far to see. There was no haze, no clouds to impede sight or give depth – it might have been a mile away, or it might have been a thousand. Either way, the glory of this perfect, green, breathtaking place was beyond measure. And for the first time, I felt a gentle wind caress my cheek, so faint, but so clearly out of place here, as if someone had walked past at a good clip.

Something's wrong.

Instinctively, I turned my head, just in time to come face to face with the strangest thing I could have ever imagined – oh yes, even stranger than a dragon forged from water and blood, if such a thing were possible. My breath caught in my throat.

A serpentine white form on silvery wings hovered not five feet away in midair, delicate as a hummingbird, and almost perfectly silent. It might have been the entire length of a man from head to tail, but it curled around itself, a constantly twisting, tiny mass. The scales along the length of its smooth body gleamed pearlescent like that of a fish, but the angular head and the bright, knowing eyes made it clear – this was a miniature Dragon, regarding us with something between curiosity and disdain. Each beat of its wings seemed to steal all air around it for itself.

Within a split second, the creature was gone again, a silent blur disturbing not even the grass under our feet. "Lord Loringham?" I heard a tiny peep of a question nearby.

"Stay close to me," I said, moving to shield the boy from whatever might come next. I stood there frozen for one, two, three minutes, wondering, waiting. *Hallucinations. You're losing it – get it together.* But no, there was the barest whisper of a breeze…

Lightning fast, I spun on my heels to bring my sword up on the left. Its edge paused within an inch of the sharp snout of this strange white creature, so close that I could see its breath crystallize along the blade's surface.

Breathing, dreaming… what was real here? All of it looked so real, but couldn't have been. My body wasn't here. I was supposed to be somewhere off the coast of Zondrell, but yet I could feel the presence of this… thing before me, could see its breath, could sense its heartbeat. My mortal consciousness could just barely comprehend it all.

"Nothing is real." A booming, deep voice shattered my thoughts, and reverberated as if shouted across a canyon's depths. Somehow, I held fast to my weapon. If Edin heard the same voice, I wasn't sure – all he seemed capable of was a slack-jawed stare at the awesome creature before us.

"Who are you?" I asked, daring to adjust my stance.

"Who are *you*?" came an incredulous reply. While the hovering creature never uttered a sound directly, its voice seemed to move with the unseen breeze. "Who are you to take the place of Fate?"

Then it was gone again, flashing off into the distance, only to return a second later at my right shoulder. My gaze narrowed into its limitless one full of capriciousness and spite.

"You think you do as you wish," the voice in my head said, but now it was softer, as if flitting in through an open window. It paused, then drifted in once again. "You are mistaken."

I never blinked as I spoke. "I make no claim to anything."

Another blur of movement, and it was gone for a heartbeat. Then two, then three. Little Edin's grip on my free arm loosened, then tensed again in an instant as I felt the rush of the Dragon's presence. I was ready, though – my *instincts* were ready, my magic just another extension of me, as familiar as my own two hands... as familiar as my blade.

A blinding flash of lightning created a solid shield around us a second before the Dragon's vicious claws reached out to rend me in two. The sound they made as they raked across its shimmering surface was something from a nightmare. "Liar," it hissed. "You believe you are first to bend the Cycle and defy Balance? What you do is unnatural and misguided."

"What is it that I'm doing that's so 'misguided?'"

The gale force of his tone nearly made me lose my balance. "Balance must be restored."

And then it was gone again, this time, for much longer. I waited – five breaths, ten. Yet eventually, the faint wind disappeared, and the world returned to glassy stillness, though I searched the skies with my blade at the ready for a long time, unable to move on.

First a Water Dragon, now a Wind Dragon? It made me wonder... Perhaps there was a dragon for every element, even Light. And maybe it was gold, just like my tattoo, just like the storybooks. *What might happen when we meet?*

"Lord Loringham?" came that trembling voice, so tiny, so clearly the voice of a child rather than a king. I turned to Edin and knelt before him.

"Are you all right?" I asked.

"I think so. What *was* that?"

"My best guess?" I took a deep breath, knowing how silly – or scary – the words would sound before I ever spoke them. "A Dragon. I... saw another before I found you."

The boy was unfazed and, in fact, seemed to brighten at the thought of actual, amazing, legendary dragons in our midst. "Really? Where?"

That's an excellent question, isn't it? "I'm not sure. The top of the summit, maybe." I shook my head as if it would absolve me of those memories of darkness and nothingness. "Let's keep moving."

"But the Dragon..."

"Will come find us, or not. We can't just sit here and wait for it, m'Lord. We have to keep going."

Reluctant, the boy steeled his jaw and we continued our journey, moving through fields of grass and flowers up to our knees. Tremendous and fantastic, a sight most would never witness, yet somehow it was also a perfect embodiment of pure dread. With each step, I could feel Edin's fear and uncertainty emanating from him in waves, but I had no words to comfort him. I wished that I did.

"Do you think we'll ever get home?" he asked after a long silence.

"I do." *Did I really?* "Don't worry, Lord Edin – we'll make it." I may have tried to oversell it, just a little.

"Lord Loringham? Is it okay to be scared?"

I stopped and turned to him, slipping off that veneer of overconfidence in exchange for something much more genuine. "Of course it is. I'm scared, too. But you have to believe that we'll get home safe, okay? Just keep believing it."

Edin nodded, his big, dark eyes saucer-wide and glassy. "Okay. But... the wind. Do you feel it?"

The feeling of the breeze in my hair did not register until I was already laid flat on my back, that serpentine creature hovering over me with triumph in its all-knowing eyes. *Where the hell did it even come from?* The only thing I knew for sure was the beginnings of a headache, each throb punctuated by the shrieks of a small boy.

"It is your time, Tristan Michael Johannes Loringham," the creature hissed. Then it lunged into me, striking as a whirling ball of speed and sound that I could scarcely understand, much less dodge. In the realm of men, I might have suffered cracked ribs or worse, but here, I only felt pain – pain like nothing I could define or describe. It radiated through my being and even beyond it, like an aura of suffering engulfing me.

"Run," I breathed. But the boy who had clambered to my side would do no such thing.

"Stop! What do you want from us?" Edin yelled, a desperate attempt at bravery – one that ultimately seemed successful, as the Dragon made no move against him. In fact, it made no move at all, nor did it speak. It just hovered there, waiting and watching.

My voice sounded like it was owned by someone else. "Go – you have to go, m'Lord."

"I can't just leave you."

"You can. You have to."

The boy king's eyes searched mine, then the waiting Dragon's. *Did it speak to him, too?* Whatever it might have said, it must have shown him the wisdom in discretion, for he turned to run as fast as his little legs would take him. The Dragon paid him little mind, though – I was the one it wanted, and it was prepared to wait for eternity if necessary to achieve its goal.

I decided to give it the fight it seemed to be looking for. With great effort, I struggled to my feet once again. "I decide when it's my time," I told it. "It won't be now."

The Dragon's laugh was like a chime on the breeze. "So says the noble *Sayaf*. Such arrogance."

The noble Sayaf, king of the swordsmen, did attempt to slay the gold dragon. Over and over, he attacked, and over and over he failed. A classic Katalahni fable, something most people didn't bother retelling anymore, at least not any further north than Drakannya. But it was from a time and place where, it was said, dragons roamed the deserts as invincible, immortal beings. Whether anyone had ever actually seen a dragon then, before, or at any point in history, was debatable at best, although I did hear that the throne of the King of Eisland was decorated with the bones of dragons, and so was the throne of the Katalahni *Aahil*. Still, those were just rumors and legends... weren't they? They certainly never spoke of bizarre, winged creatures like this thing before me.

The Wind Dragon danced along with the breeze, curled into itself like a cobra ready to strike. And strike it did, at the very moment I wasn't at all ready for it. It bore down on me as a flurry of fang and claw, yet precise in its intention to rend a hole through my throat. So fast... by Catherine, it was a whirlwind. But I wasn't going to give it the satisfaction of a quick end.

I lunged left, diving out of the way just enough to come out with only a gash across the chest. The flimsy silk of the tunic I had been wearing parted in a bloody arc from heart to ribs, leaving a lifetime of pain in its wake. The sensation wasn't too different from the time I had been run through with ice magic, and somehow hurt just as much. It took a lot of will not to crumple to the ground and surrender in the wake of it, but the distraction still left me vulnerable.

A swipe from the side came in fast, but I was able to bring my sword up, deflecting a vicious blow. For something so lithe and delicate in appearance, it was damned strong, and striking against its talons was the same as striking a brick wall.

I reeled back a step or two, recovering in time to deflect another blow aimed to tear my arm off.

Magic – use your Light! My rational mind screamed at me to raise a shield, to bring down a bolt from nothing and scorch this creature... or hell, maybe even encase it in a shield it couldn't escape. But the part of me that was in a state of sheer mortal panic wasn't able to do much, other than keep up with the volley of teeth and claws.

"Light does not belong here," the Dragon's voice floated through my thoughts. Then, another quick strike, so fast I almost didn't see it move, and my dodge was clumsy at best. I wound up on the ground – again – hitting the grass beneath with enough force to wrench the breath from my lungs.

I lay there for a moment, staring up at the widening gray gloom overhead. *And though the noble Sayaf ached and he bled and he wheezed, the Gold Dragon never touched him.* "Why?" I asked, speaking aloud the next line of what I remembered from the fable.

"A better question, most souls do not ask," came the Dragon's whisper. It was almost gentle, almost soothing, to the point where I didn't realize at first that I had been lifted from the ground by an unseen breeze, held aloft... and quite defenseless. As I squirmed in a vain effort to do something, the Wind Dragon appeared, right in my face, and all I could see was the infinite white jewels of its cat-like eyes, thousands and millions of facets winking all at once.

"Can't..." I started, but never finished the thought. The roar of wind and water filled my ears.

"My place is not to pity, but I feel your pain," the thing's thoughts entangled themselves with mine. "Wait if you wish. Delay the inevitable. But your place is here, noble *Sayaf*. You have evaded your End for too long."

"And you're the one who decides that?"

The Dragon considered, its eyes clearing like the most perfect diamond before clouding over to a white haze once again. The oblong black pupils stood in stark contrast and could have bored a hole directly through me as sure as any of those claws. "I decide... nothing. Fate decides."

What? Its hesitation was like a gaping hole in its defenses. I felt my confidence returning, even if my strength didn't quite match. "Then who are you to keep me from doing what I must?"

A long whisper of a sigh cut through my thoughts. "Who am I? I am of the Wind. That is all you need to know."

"And there are others like you?"

"There is one to tend the Wind. One to watch the Land, one to guide the Seas, one to stoke the Flame."

"And the others – Time and Life and Light?"

If the wind itself could stutter, then that is exactly what happened. "They are who they are," it breathed. "Are you and I 'like' one another, noble *Sayaf*?" When I found I had no reply beyond the obvious "*hell no*," those ineffable eyes narrowed, but the Dragon's manner was not aggressive. It was instead... thoughtful. "You are your nature, just as I am mine."

My "nature?" My nature was that of a solider. To fight. To do battle. To bring war, murder... death. *Is it truly? A noble Sayaf, indeed.* At the end of the story, the swordsman dies, speaking one last time: *"Finally I see,"* said he. *"And I am awake."* I had no doubt that philosophers sought meaning in that one line of poetry for centuries. Because there was more to the noble *Sayaf* of the story than just the fight, or there could be, if he sought out the unbeatable Gold Dragon for more than a simple hunting trophy.

So what the hell was I doing here, fighting this thing, in this moment? Not for glory. Not even for my life. To a solider, those things are one and the same. If I were nothing but a soldier, I wouldn't care if Lord Edin took the throne of Zondrell and put the city back together again. I wouldn't care about the safety of my family and friends, or the innocent people caught up in a political scheme gone mad. I would never have cared about anything but my blade and the fame that came with it.

I leveled my gaze at the creature. "My nature is to do what I believe is right, nothing more."

Then something happened that I never would have expected – the Wind Dragon withdrew. Its curled, slender form slipped away just as the ground rushed up to meet me, and I hit it with a heavy thud. New waves of pain flooded through my senses, but now was not the time to lie still. I had to get up, had to face this thing, had to be ready for whatever might come next. *This might be my only chance.*

Time seemed to stretch along far too slowly as I strained to pull myself to my feet. It could have destroyed me a hundred times in that span, but instead, the Wind Dragon remained silent and watchful.

It barely reacted in response to my raised blade, save for a single shake of its head. "Light always seeks to uncover what lies in Shadow," it said, its words wistful, tinkling chimes in a spring breeze. "Balance... Hmm, yes, you are here, where you should be, but I suppose your Path is yours to follow. After all, as you so wisely note, I am not Fate."

"What are you, then?" I asked, still on guard. "A god?"

It cocked its long, serpentine head, as if puzzled, questioning. "We are everywhere. You may see yet, noble *Sayaf.* That is, if you are worthy of that name."

My next question faded into infinity. There were few things I knew right then, but the idea that monsters out of a child's fantasy were not only in existence, but possessed the power of gods and were literally *everywhere*, did not do much to bring me comfort.

"Light the Shadow, noble *Sayaf.* It is your way."

I opened my mouth to ask more questions – there were so many – but before I had a chance to speak, the tiny, winged serpent-god was gone, leaving the sight of an infinitely black sea in its wake.

Catherine be damned. That thing had carried me back to the start of my journey… alone. It might be days before I reached Edin, if I could even find him again at all. *Catherine be damned all the way back to this hell right fucking here.* The scratch across my chest pulsed with cold fire, and in that moment, I allowed myself the luxury of weakness – I fell to my knees on the impossibly flat sands of that horrible beach and bent my head in utter defeat.

CHAPTER SIX

Lost and Found
11 Spring's Green, 1272
Jade Saçaille

I awoke a little later than usual, after the sun had risen and the streets outside had begun to sprout life. Well, Doverton wasn't exactly a sprawling metropolis, not like Quatremagne had been, but its simple grid-patterned streets bustled well nonetheless, once the day caught up with people. Doverton was, shall we say, more "backwoodsy" than many cities on major trade routes, its citizens hardworking, simple folk. Cosmopolitan, this place was not, and while it was a far cry from the complex society that had been Quatremagne, it was no less diverse. The only difference was, the people from the many different cultures that passed through daily didn't stay – it was merely a place to make some money before moving on.

When Jardin and I first came to the city about a year ago, I couldn't understand why my sister would want to be there. She held no love for the Zondreans. What had they ever done but create heartache? But yet, she stayed, because of the King. She never volunteered the information, but once I'd seen them together, it was clear that my dear sister had more than a working relationship with the man who employed her skills. And he was good-looking for a Zondrean, I'd give him that – pleasant, too.

People around the city whispered, but it was a friendly sort of gossip, an amusement for the citizens. All in all, they liked their King, and they actually seemed to *like* Onyx, too, respected her, even. Imagine that. If only they knew the kind of road she traveled to get there.

By Chantal, even I didn't know the extent of it. I'd lost track of her for almost twenty years, half of our lives – she'd become a totally different person than the older sister I grew up with, who revered the priests of Chantal and looked so forward to our Pilgrimage to Quiétude. The Onyx I knew today said little of magic, of religion, or any of the things that set her on the path she now followed. But she seemed happy, or as happy as a war-grizzled battle maiden might be, so I questioned little, and we lived our lives in relative harmony.

I said my prayers, dressed, and combed my hair, the black curls snapping back into place with each stroke. I had a long list of chores to handle today, and didn't need to waste more daylight.

Moving on to the kitchen, I set my teakettle over the hearth to get the water in it warming and cut off a piece of bread from the loaf on the counter. A little honey, a little jam – strawberry, Jardin's favorite. Indeed, where was Jardin? Still asleep, no doubt. It was not unusual for me to have to roust her from bed, and the older she got, the more time she seemed to spend sleeping in.

"Jardin!" I called. Her room was right across the hall in our little house, the house that Onyx paid for, even though she felt we would have been quite comfortable in the King's Palace. She lived there, after all, and the appointments were lovely. Why wouldn't we want to live there, too? The simple answer was that I had no interest in that sort of living, all stuffy and full of pomp and circumstance. I didn't need a maid and a butler and gold-plated forks – I just needed a safe home for my daughter.

I heard nothing from Jardin's room, so I called again. "Jardin! It's time to get up!" Again, nothing, not even the sound of blankets being tossed aside. Chantal's bones, did that girl get up again after I went back to sleep? I set down my half-eaten bread and headed toward the bedroom.

I found it empty. Jardin was nowhere to be seen. Her faithful sketchbook was gone from its usual place by the bed, and her shoes were missing from their hook. Damnation! My heart skipped a beat, although all logic said that she was probably just outside sketching a bird or something like that. She did that sort of thing on occasion – no need to panic.

I took a deep breath and went back through the kitchen and outside into the rear garden. Nothing but scrubs of grass and my clothesline still hanging low with a day's worth of laundry on it. What about the front garden? Just as empty, save for a round gray squirrel perched by the rainbarrel. It looked up at me with a quizzical expression, and raced off as soon as I stalked toward him. No... no Jardin hiding behind the rainbarrel. No Jardin picking flowers or counting stones in the street or any such thing. I walked around the whole house twice, and saw no sign of her. Where *could* that girl have gone?

Panic began to rise in my throat, but I stuffed it down. Surely, she'd just wandered down the road a bit, perhaps on one of her little missions to count flowers or clouds in the sky. Once, when she was very young, she had followed the Quatremagne River across the entire Lavançaise quarter and half of the Drakannyan, counting out six hundred and eighty-seven flowers over the course of the day. Not alone of course – she had her father with her, in a rare moment of unbroken patience. She'd been quite proud of that accomplishment for long afterward, though she was unlikely to find sixty flowers in Doverton, much less six hundred.

"Jardin!" I called down the street, as it led off to the center square. A few people turned and looked, but none of them were her. "Jardin!" I called down the other way, toward the south gates. Again, nothing.

"Is that your little one?" a trembling elderly voice caught my ear, and I turned to face her. It was the kindly Zondrean lady from next door, the one who baked sweets and brought them over on occasion.

"She's... ah, not at home," I said, fumbling for my Zondrean words. I was good at the language, though hadn't practiced it much, even after coming here. It didn't help that I felt defeated in that moment, and not a small bit guilty. "Madame, have you seen her, by chance?"

"No, dear, not today. Course, I haven't been out all morning. And that little one of yours is so… quiet. Why, she hardly says a word, does she?"

"She's shy, *oui*. Are you sure you didn't notice her walking past?"

The old woman considered, then shook her graying head. "I'm sorry, dear, I didn't. No one's come by this way today, I'm afraid, at least none that I know. Maybe your girl's gone off chasing butterflies again? Saw her doing that the other day, I did. She's in her own little world, isn't she?"

"She… *oui*, yes, I suppose she is. *Merci*, Madame Joslyne." Of course, I knew she was right, but admitting it felt wrong somehow. I started away from her, wandering down the street to… where, exactly? What did I know? Nothing, I knew nothing, and my daughter was out there somewhere, wandering around, and…

The panic gripped me then. I could feel its fingers around me, squeezing the air from my lungs and the heat from my body. Where could she have gone? How *long* had she even been gone, for that matter? She could have left in the middle of the damnable night, and what was I doing? Sleeping! What kind of a mother was I? And her eyes, the magic… she didn't understand it. She didn't know how to use it – did she? What if something happened, or what if she got scared? Or worse? What then?

By Chantal's word, this was the last thing I needed. And of course, Onyx was gone, long gone, with no definite date of return. For all I knew, she could be gone a week. A month! And she'd left me here in this town full of foreigners, all alone with poor Jardin, and now…

I was a bad parent. That's surely what Madame Joslyne was thinking – I could feel her gaze on me as I continued on, searching around every house, every dark corner for some kind of sign. I got about three blocks before I heard someone approach from behind, the footsteps too heavy to be Jardin, the gait still light, but masculine. No armor – not a guard. I hesitated just enough for the person to pass into my field of vision… and I froze.

It was unreal what I saw coming to stand before me, a reflection of a different lifetime. It wasn't so much like seeing Brin from across the marketplace that day, over a month ago now. No, that stopped my heart in an entirely different way, even though the man standing there with his hands on his hips and his meager chest puffed up now looked no less aged.

He was somewhere in his forties, like all of us from *that* time. He had tiny wisps of gray in his beard, his freckled cheeks now sporting thin lines of wear, and while the sandy brown hair atop his head remained bright and youthful, there was far less of it than there used to be. The smile on his face was as bold as ever, though. Familiar. Almost as bold as the silver light churning away around the pupils of his eyes.

It was *impossible* – yet there he was. "V... Vremya?" I asked, the foreign word sounding so strange as it rolled across my tongue. It was one I had barely uttered in some twenty-five years. I still had the letter, folded neatly in a drawer in my room, that had led me to the place where we would meet, as comrades in war.

Jade Saçaille, pilgrim of Chantal,
I regret that I cannot meet you first in person, but soon, I hope that you will join me at my palace in Königstadt. These men – my most trusted soldiers, – will guide you there. I understand that you are in the midst of important work, but I assure you, you and your family will be well compensated for this inconvenience. Your talents shall save the lives of many men on the fields of battle, and I pray that you will consider my request.
Keis Sturmberg, High King of Eisland

I left the sacred temple at Quiétude and my Pilgrimage to learn the ways of magic through the Church of Chantal, believing Keis Sturmberg was a man of his word. And he was, but there was a cost, too, and seeing Vremya again after so many years brought all of those memories back to clutter my already-addled mind. A hot tear escaped from one eye and trickled down my cheek, which I hastily wiped away.

Vremya's smile broadened, if that were even possible. "*Da,* Jade, I thought I might see you here. *Privyet!* This is nice place, *da*? Never been to this side of world before. Good place, good air here." His Lavançaise words slammed into each other, where they were supposed to be delicate, light, and lilting. Still, I had always given him credit for being able to speak and understand four languages. Many city folk were bilingual these days, especially where I came from, but to master four, as a poor bumpkin Drakannyan? It was unprecedented. "Hey, you don't look so happy to see me," he said, frowning just a little.

"Vremya, I'm sorry, I... it's just... my daughter..." I didn't know what to say, but there didn't seem to be much more that needed to be said. "You haven't seen a young girl pass by, have you?"

"Sort of blonde hair, looks like her father?"

My heart skipped a beat. "*Oui! Oui*, that's her! Where? Where did you see her?"

"*Da,* little girl heading toward church," he said, the smile softening a bit as he spoke. "I see her on the road toward Zondrell, not too long ago."

"What? *Out* of the city?" I started to move toward the south gate, and Vremya had to scramble to keep up.

"Sure, I show you. Hey, where is that father of hers?"

I shook my head, saying nothing at first. Why in Chantal's name Jardin would go to the little temple outside the city gates, I had *no* idea, but I didn't care. It wasn't important — I just wanted to know she was safe.

As I walked, fast as I could without breaking into a full run, Vremya fell in step beside me, gently touching my arm for just a moment. Comfort? From Vremya? Well, that was a first. "He's... not here," I answered his question at the next block. "I don't know. I haven't spoken to him in ten years."

"Ah, say no more. Too bad."

"Not really."

"Ah, no problem. We find him after we find your little girl, *da*?"

"What? No." Chantal's blood, was he always that thick? "What are you talking about?"

"You don't feel it? What is coming?"

I stopped in my tracks, and Vremya followed suit, searching me with his mercurial gaze. Idly, he touched the signpost of the store we stood before, and a strange sort of thin-lipped grin bloomed on his round face. I had no idea what to make of it. "I'm sorry, Vremya, I really have to look for my daughter. She can't be out by herself like this."

Before I could set off again, he had me by the hand, his palm warm against mine. "*Da*, I know. Time is short. Come on – I've got horses. We get there... quick-quick, *da?* No worries." He tipped an invisible hat to me and bowed like a Lavançaise aristocrat.

No worries, indeed.

CHAPTER SEVEN

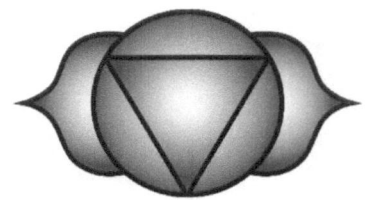

Putting Things Right
11 Spring's Green, 1272
Alexander Vestarton

The Zondrell dungeon wasn't some damp underground cave or basement filled with cobwebs and disease. That's the sort of thing found in faery tales, although I didn't doubt that some cities aspired to have dungeons that matched that exact description. The reality was that the hard rock upon which the Zondrell Palace sat didn't lend itself well to basements and the like, so the place that served as a prison for the worst enemies of the throne actually lay in an outbuilding just within the Palace walls. It hung precariously near the edge of the cliffs, where it offered little in the way of decent escape routes for its more enterprising guests – unless of course, they wanted to take a swim from several hundred feet up.

It took a bit of convincing, but the men on duty let me go down into the hall of cell after miserable cell with only one Royal Guard to guide my journey. He was an old soldier, a bit rough around the edges, and didn't say much as we passed by people talking to themselves, moaning and carrying on, snoring, and... well, I didn't want to know what all of them were up to. There might have been twenty or so prisoners there, all told, and no one had any clue about what was happening beyond their tiny worlds. Thieves and murderers though they might have all been, I felt a twinge of sympathy nonetheless.

The cell that held Jamison Torven stood near the end of the hall, and like the others, it was small, cramped, and barren, save for a cot and a hole to piss in. Yet somehow, the Gentleman General managed to maintain a dignified air about him in spite of his surroundings. He gazed out at me with eyes nearly the color of the close-set iron bars separating us.

"So…" I began, breaking the silence of the torchlit dungeon gloom, "I heard Queen Marianna gave you a fine holiday. Thought I'd come down and see how it was going."

Torven didn't move from his seat on the cot, and it wasn't because he was unhappy to see me. Oh, this was certainly the case, but the real reason was because he was, in a word, a disaster. Broken and beaten, this was not the man who – once – commanded the largest military force this side of the Mountains with Two Names.

In the span of a few hours, those who deemed him an enemy had had their way with him, and the blood was still drying on his ripped tunic. One cheek was bluish and swollen, and he held his left arm in such a way that made me think there might be a bruised rib… or two or three. To be fair, he had gotten off rather light so far for regicide, but who knew what was still in store for him? I didn't, but I did know one thing – Marianna Blackwarren wasn't the acting ruler of Zondrell. That honor, technically speaking, still went to me, until someone told me differently.

Not that I wanted it. I didn't want to be the King of Zondrell, never had, and never would. But we lived in interesting times, and I had an interesting idea building in the back of my mind. I also knew damned well that I didn't have much time to pull it off. "General?" I said with more force. "I need a word with you."

Torven cleared his throat, and even then, his voice came out as more of a croak than the grand tones of a grander man. "There's not much to say, Lord Vestarton."

"So what, you're content to just rot in here? Job done, future botched, the end? Honestly, I expected a little more from you, General."

"It doesn't matter," Torven said with a shake of his head. "It means nothing now. The Lords will get what they want. You're lucky they haven't come after you."

"Oh, it's just a matter of time... I'm as bad as you are." Or so I'm told, I thought, with no small amount of disdain.

"But you wear the title of Head Councilor now. What will you do with it?"

"While I still have it?" I could read that last part of his sentence without him having to say anything. And the implication was probably accurate. "I want to clean up this disaster that we call Zondrell."

At this, Torven looked away, staring at the wall for a long moment before speaking again. "The disaster I created."

"Yep, you sure as hell did. And you know what? That's not important. What's important is stopping the whole place from falling in on itself. Because you don't want that, do you?" The General was silent, but he lifted his bearded chin slightly. "You wanted a better Zondrell, yes? If you're true to your word and not merely the most righteously indignant asshole in history, then you'll help me."

"And how do you propose that I help you, from in here?"

"The guards say there's riots, especially by North Gate. People are set to start tearing into each other over a bloody meal. Those gates need to open, fast, or it'll just get worse."

"It's not that simple, Lord Vestarton."

The hopeless detachment of his responses was maddening. "Look, General, I'm not asking. I'm telling you that this is what we *need* to do, and it might make things a bit easier if you helped me out."

"You might be right – you might not be," Torven said, stubbornly refusing to look me in the eye once again. Perhaps he knew how much dangerous magic was looming in there, begging to be released. "But there's very little I can do to help you, Lord Vestarton. In case you haven't noticed, I am behind bars, and perhaps rightly so. Even if I weren't, there's no good that can come from opening the gates right now. People are camped there, on both sides – families with children, men with weapons. It's not a good combination. Do you truly expect that they'll suddenly calm down when the gates open?"

"So, it's going to get better if they're made to stay there and keep fighting it out in their little tent cities? Are you serious?"

"Magic or no, it won't save innocent people from getting hurt. Trust me, Lord Vestarton. I've been doing this sort of thing a little longer than you have."

I considered. He might not have been wrong, but did it matter? Something had to be done. Besides, I was sick of old men telling me I didn't know anything. "Fine. Rot. I don't care. I would have you out of there, to help me, maybe bolster some morale around the Guardsmen, but whatever. You can stay there till you breathe your last. But at least tell me this – where do you think I can find an honest soldier these days, General? You know, one that isn't trying to kill his friends... or Lords?"

Torven rose and paced back and forth in his cell for a moment, his boots scraping against the stone floor. He might have done it for an excruciatingly long time if I hadn't made such a show of impatience. I tapped my foot, I looked around, I cleared my throat, and finally, he looked back up at me. "'You... you would free me? The Kingslayer?"

"That's right. I'm the fucking Head Councilor, remember? And I think you and I both know what I can do to you if you were to cross me... Kingslayer or otherwise."

The tiniest hint of a smile graced his lips. "You have courage, Vestarton, I'll give you that. Your enemies will have much to say about this."

"Don't care. I've got other things to worry about. Shall we go get your proper badges of office? Time's short, General."

No one challenged my removal of the prisoner from his cell. In fact, I got two salutes and a hearty thanks from the men guarding the Palace dungeon, along with at least one curse and a look of utter contempt.

Well, not everyone would be thrilled, of course – it would have been naïve to think otherwise. It was a crazed world, full of split opinions and high emotions. I never thought I'd live to see such a time, but as the philosophers at the Academy used to say, everything changes. The content man is an unwise man. And if I were going to be accused of anything, it wouldn't be for being a fool.

CHAPTER EIGHT

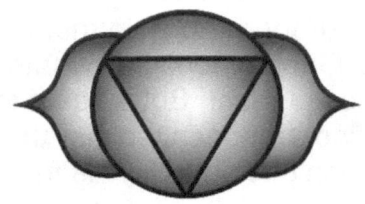

Under the Glass
11 Spring's Green, 1272
Andella Weaver

The next thing I knew was sand. Coarse, red-gray sand, like the beaches down at the bottom of the cliffs in Zondrell, but this sand was perfectly even, absolutely smooth. Instead of digging into my flesh, it pressed gently against me as I lay atop it, a cold and harsh bed. But there was no other sensation – none of the typical wind swept through to stir my hair, and no rain fell lightly against my cheek.

I heard nothing but a distant roar of water, and could sense little more than the salt smell of the ocean overlaid upon a stale nothingness that escaped explanation. It was as if the world I knew had simply... come to rest. Ceased. Fallen away.

What had happened? I tried to pick myself up as I played the last few minutes in my memory over and over. I saw myself reaching out to touch the obsidian stone, the center of the wheel of... what, I wasn't sure. And then, this. People had been around me, plenty of people, but they were gone now. Where could they have gone?

Then I remembered Archmage Tiara, warning us. Don't touch it, she'd said. And the mage girls – hadn't they said to wait, to be careful? Maybe they were right. That stone...

That stone had killed me. I was dead. That was the only explanation. The roar of water, the lack of a breeze, the strange void – it was just like what Tristan had described. The River, the place where the Eislandisch believed the souls of the dead went on their way from this life to the next.

It was a crazy thought to most others, that our souls would live again somewhere else, in someone else. Those devoted to Catherine believed that She took our spirits into Her embrace, that once the soul was freed by the flames of the mortal world, it lived on happily in Paradise, serving Her for eternity. I believed that... or I used to. Tristan had been so *sure* that he'd been there, that he saw that River of death and had somehow rejected it. Or maybe *it* had rejected *him*. Either way, he believed with all his heart that he had been there, and I believed him.

I finally pushed myself from the sandswept ground and got to my feet, some of the coarse stuff falling away from my dress as I did so. It didn't stick to my flesh the way most sand did – instead, it just swept off, as if knowing it wasn't needed anymore. Or perhaps, those little grains of sand didn't want to leave their kindred behind.

The sand did, however, hold my footprints tight in its embrace as I walked in no particular direction. I found the shore after a few minutes, the place where the sand met that endless hum of water. This was no River, though. This was an ocean, a huge expanse of dark water with an end I couldn't even imagine, much less see. The light here was odd, too, not sunlight and maybe not even outdoors. Was I in some kind of a cave? I couldn't tell for certain, but it seemed that the light coming from above was filtered and indirect, like sunlight bouncing from place to place until it finally came to rest here, at this vast, unfathomable beach.

That's when I saw him. Could it be...? A surge of excitement grew within me as I moved faster and faster up the shoreline toward a huddled figure, kneeling by the water's edge. He sat calm, straight and dignified, but unmoving, even as I drew near.

"... Tristan?" I didn't know for certain if I actually spoke, and he did not stir. In fact, he barely moved, even as I dropped to my knees in the coarse, cold, wet earth. I didn't care that the unknowable black sea was close at my heels, nor did I consider what might happen if a stray tide rushed up to find us. Would I merely get wet, or would I be absorbed further into this strange place? All I knew was that he was here – it had to be him! And yet, he said nothing, did nothing, as if he were some sort of statue.

"You're hurt," I said, trying to find that beautiful, sky-blue gaze with those tendrils of magical Light within. It seemed quiet, almost devoid of life… almost. Something was in there, trying to get out, in the same way that wounds oozed red on his arms, on his neck, on the small bit of flesh poking out from beneath his tattered black tunic.

I reached out and, for some reason, hesitated to touch him. Every part of me wanted to fling my arms around him and offer some sort of comfort, to call forth magic that would make those cuts go away, but I couldn't. There wasn't even a reason – I just… couldn't. So my fingertips hovered there, inches from his pale brow where his blond hair stuck to it, matted with sweat and sand and blood.

"Tristan? Can… can you hear me? Please, say something," I pleaded, hoping to Catherine's light eternal that he would just acknowledge me. And for a long time, he did not. Panic rose with every passing moment. How long did we sit there? Time didn't seem to mean much here.

"You can't be here."

His words broke the silence and I gasped, drawing back with eyes wide. "What? What do you mean?" Then he was silent again, eyes still cast downward at the sand. "Tristan… talk to me. Please?"

A painful forever passed, until finally, he turned and fixed me with a look I couldn't break from if I'd tried. It was distant, and yet right up close, serious and happy and sad all at one time. "You're not supposed to be here," he said. "You *can't* be here. You're not real."

"No! I am, I'm real – I'm right here. It's not a dream, I promise. Except…" I reached for him again, this time really trying, but I just *couldn't*. "Why can't I touch you?" I asked, not quite expecting him to have an answer.

His blue eyes unfocused for a moment, the magic within them flaring with electricity that was at once made of Light and Darkness. A reflection from the black sea behind us, perhaps? But his words seemed to hold that same dark quality, strained and quick, as if he wasn't really talking to me at all. "It's like looking through a window."

"Please, Tristan, come home with me. We need to go home." Without thinking, I moved to grab him by the shoulders and try to heft him up, but again, was stopped cold. Like a window, indeed – a terrifying and frustrating one at that.

None of this seemed to worry him nearly as much as it worried me, though. If he knew something I didn't, he wouldn't say. All he said was, "I can't go yet. I'm sorry. There's something here I need to do." And then there was that look again... that look, and silence.

"You *need* to come home." It was so strange how I could feel sadness, could taste my own tears, when nothing around us seemed real in the least. "We miss you. We need you."

In a whisper-quiet voice, he said, "I know." And so we sat that way for a while before he heaved himself up, slowly, as if he had been resting there for a very long time. Behind him, I realized a sword with three red jewels set into the grip had been driven blade-first into the sand, and he grabbed it up without ceremony.

That's when I heard a new voice, something tiny and faint, far in the distance. *The water. Go to the water.*

"Did you hear that?" I asked.

Drink. The way awaits.

The voice dancing on the distant shores of my imagination sounded feminine, but harsh – this was no suggestion, but a demand, and a serious one at that. But why? Who was it? I looked out over the vast, dark sea for a moment, but no answers could be found there. "I heard someone. They told me to... drink the water." By Catherine, if I wasn't dead, then I was almost certainly going crazy. What in the Lady's name *was* that rock I touched?

Again, the flash of black behind the streaks of starlight in his eyes, almost as if a storm was brewing. "Seek Light in the Darkness," he said, as if I understood what in Paradise that meant.

"What? But that voice – who is that?"

"You need to follow your Path." As he stood there with the sword resting across his shoulder, the rubies in the handle reminded me of drops of blood. "It's not safe here – I can't protect you. If that's the Path, then that's the Path."

"I don't understand what you mean. What'll happen?" Who knew? That voice could be anything, anyone. It could be a trick. It could be Catherine Herself, or something entirely different.

"I don't know. Only one way to know."

"But..." Oh dear Catherine. What if I followed this ethereal voice of who-knew-what and found myself back in Zondrell, never was able to come back here? What if I never saw him again? The thoughts buzzing through my mind left me paralyzed. I barely noticed how he had set the blade down once more to kneel by the water's edge.

"We'll do it together," he said, cupping his hands an inch over the surface as the surf rolled in slow, like honey on a warm day.

I did the same thing. What else was there to do? "Together." So we drank of black water that was somehow clean and tasteless.

And nothing whatsoever happened.

Nothing meaning... truly *nothing*. Darkness. The beach was gone. Tristan was gone, everything just gone, covered in a heavy black haze that seemed to cling to everything it touched, so thick it just rolled lazily around itself as I reached out to swat it away.

"Tristan?" I called out, hesitant, but silence was the only reply. By the Lady, I was lost – very, very lost, in a very strange place. The sea... I could still hear it, but it was distant, and angry, too. There was no gentleness in that far-off roar. As my eyes adjusted, the weird light of this place peeking through the blackness never moved, never told me what direction I was going in, or what time it might have been. It cast indescribable shadows everywhere I looked, but I chose to take a step, and another, and another.

And as I walked, at times the roar of that sea seemed louder or softer, as if it were somehow following me. The sand never seemed to change, even as it crunched under my bare feet, and there were no footprints to follow. It was like I was a chasing a ghost.

A ghost. The thought sent a chill through every fiber of my being. But he wasn't dead, couldn't be dead. I *saw* him – he was right in front of me. Yet... where was here? Maybe I was a ghost, too, and just didn't know it yet. But still, I could *feel* the cold. I could *feel* the heavy, smooth sand between my toes. Dead people can't feel things, can they?

The shadows around me grew longer, fleeting glimpses of real things – people, mostly. At least, I had the distinct impression that those long dark shapes seemed like the shadows men cast as day turns to night. And perhaps the strange light in the sky was changing course as I kept on walking, bringing with it a new wave of cold. It settled in like a shroud, and the more I walked into it, the colder it got. I thought I might turn around, to go back the way I came, but what good would that do? The only thing that made sense was to keep moving.

The cold grew deeper, sinking itself into my whole being, an enveloping sort of... Darkness. There was no other way to explain it. It seemed to pull at me, my insides feeling like they were being drawn away, absorbed somehow into the shadows. I could fight it, but every part of my being said to stop, to relax, not to struggle. This was best – this was the way to safety. It was almost impossible to put the feeling into words, but it made me want to just stop and curl up. So I did just that.

I stopped, I lowered myself to the ground, and curled up tightly in a little ball, ready for the shadows to take me in their embrace. The sands felt moist against my cheek, and the last thing I saw was the distinct impression of a long, slender female form taking shape within the shadows.

CHAPTER NINE

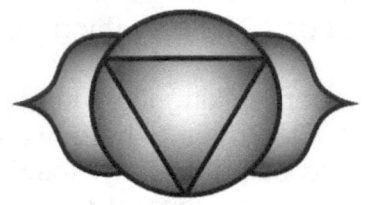

The Noble Sayaf
11 Spring's Green, 1272
Tristan Loringham

We would drink of the dark waters at the edge of nothingness – the mouth of the River, the end of it all – together. The thought had never occurred to me before, but... *Why the hell not?* I had nothing else to lose.

I still wasn't completely sure that Andella was truly there, or that she was who she said she was. She certainly *seemed* real – her mannerisms, her voice, the way a hint of an optimistic smile creeped into even the most sad and serious moments. But she should not have been of this place, any more than I was, and there was something off about her presence that I couldn't put into words.

To see her was to look through a hazy pane of glass, to touch her, impossible. She was there and yet not, and even though I yearned so badly for the former, I prayed for the latter, for I imagined if she were with me, then she had a choice to make. I didn't want her to have to make such a choice – not now, not ever. We all may reach the next life someday, but that doesn't keep us from hoping that our loved ones never do.

Yet even though I doubted her, I still felt something break and shatter deep inside when she crumbled to sand on the beach. The moment before I sipped from my cupped hands, I looked to her and she was... gone, disintegrated into grains of fine gray sand that sifted through my fingers like ash. For a silent moment, everything around me stopped, and I could think of nothing else but the way that sand returned to the flat perfectness of the beach, spreading out to join its brethren in a way that defied earthbound physics.

"She needed to return, Monsieur, as you do."

The voice was so disconnected to everything else that I stumbled backward a foot or two. *What now?* My first thought was another Dragon, or some other unholy terror, but this voice wasn't a booming echo inside my head. It came from just behind, a silken, lilting, woman's voice, touched by both amusement and malice.

"Tell me: have you ever thought about the sand under your feet?" she continued. "Have you thought about what would happen if all this sand eroded away? What would happen to the sea, and the River? Look at it. So... perfect. To disturb it would be wrong, *oui?*"

Where have I heard that voice before? The familiarity of it struck me, but it was so out of place here. It made no sense. Not that anything else did. *Maybe I'm losing it – for real, this time.*

But yet the cold feather edge of a blade at my throat in the next moment did a lot to bring me back to my senses, senses that were quickly becoming obscured by a thick black fog, roiling in, as if to hold me in some kind of executioner's embrace.

I froze, forcing down my fear, even as my vision faded to billowing darkness. Besides, I already sat on the edge of death and life – if this blade was simply a push to one side or the other, so be it. The worst fears of most mortal men were well behind me.

"You are..."

"Not supposed to be here," I interrupted. "I'm aware. Are you any different?"

The thin, short sword retreated in one swift motion, but not before taking some blood first. The cut across my throat was clean and shallow, but it felt no different from the Wind Dragon's claws.

My breath caught there for a moment, as frozen as the rest of my body. "There is no place here for those who strive for imbalance. So *oui*, I am different. We may be two sides of a coin, but had I known that *you* would take Light... the Prophecy comes to pass, and the world may die with it."

Prophecy... It wasn't that long ago that I read a piece of poetry that might have been just such a thing, in an ancient book found in an ancient temple. Andella had believed in it, and at least for a time, I believed because she believed, though we never truly understood what it all meant.

Seven elements comprise the energy of this world – the Great Three are lost, but not gone. They live and wait for a new dawn, this, the dawn of Prophecy. Time stops, half a hero's blood soaks the land to bring forth new Life, bearing with it the Light of a new age.

"A 'new age,'" I croaked. "It doesn't have to mean the end."

"But you see, Monsieur, the Prophecy was written by men. And men get things wrong. It is wrong that there are seven elements. It is wrong that they are lost – they were never lost. A 'new' age is also the end of another, the destruction of Balance. Do you not see what you do?"

Suddenly, with violent force, I was pushed from my knees forward, toward the icy dark water, just as a wave lapped up toward the shore. My fingers clawed into wet sand as the water gushed over my head, down my back, up my arms. The sheer shock of it would have been enough to kill a man in life. Here... well, it was just the definition of cold and pain. I could describe it no better than that.

"Go ahead and drink, Monsieur. It will clear your vision."

That voice... I wondered if it was the same voice Andella heard, bidding her to drink from the endless darkness. A part of me wanted to defy that order, to turn on this creature that I felt that I knew, but my weapon was too far behind me, and the fog was too thick. I could barely see the water two inches in front of my face, much less anything else. So I leaned forward, and I drank.

Finally I see. And I am awake.

What the noble *Sayaf* in the story saw, I'll never know. What *I* saw... was everything.

The black haze grew to a dim sheen, still hovering all around like a pall, but a translucent one – there was Light in every Shadow here. Gone were the barren wastes, replaced by all of the souls who came before, washed clean and ready to complete their cycle.

Once, I had seen corpses floating in the blood waters of the Great River, but here at the End, there were no such forms. Form had no meaning here, no reason to hold to a shape and a body. They whirled and danced along the surface of the sea in every color imaginable, looking not so different from the lights that swirled within the eyes of every mage. And there I was, watching a billion tiny essences of pure magic, waiting to soon be returned to the place of the living anew, just as Fate would have it.

But I also knew it didn't have to be that way.

Each of those dancing lights could make a choice – return to a place of harshness, of war and plague and strife, or stay, perhaps to explore a new cycle beyond that which any man could understand. Yet they made no such choice and simply went without question, at a time dictated by an unseen arbiter, all to serve a purpose they didn't understand. And there I stood, apart from all of them, watching it play out.

"Balance breaks and you watch with wonder. Hm… you are much more a rebel than I expected, Monsieur. I doubt it will earn you praise." The Weapon Master of Doverton, Onyx Saçaille, stood before me in the black-on-black leathers I had seen her in before, months earlier, shortsword slung casually behind her back.

Her black hair was tied in a tight tail, and eyes that once seemed so dark that the pupil and iris were one and the same, now had life to them. Shades of black danced under the surface of those irises in a way that mimicked the haze dancing around us… very much like magic. My own magic, deep within, seemed to stir in response to it. *How is that even possible?* As much as I could see now, that answer remained well beyond me.

The woman offered a dismissive wave as she turned to walk away. "What are you?" I asked, starting after her on unsteady legs that grew stronger with each step.

She didn't turn to look as she spoke. "A side of the coin, Monsieur, I told you. I have business. You… have business, too, I expect. Go on and leave this place."

My discarded sword was in sight, and I grabbed it up as I moved past it in one smooth motion, barely breaking stride. Whoever, or whatever, she was, she had answers that I needed – *right now.* When I caught up to her, she was quick, but I was quicker. Her shoulder tensed to reach for her weapon and turn on me, but instead, she found that arm locked behind her back, used as leverage as she found a blade at *her* throat this time.

I pulled on that arm just a little more, and saw the corners of those blackest-black eyes tighten against the force. "I'm not much for causing harm to women," I said, and Saçaille snorted derisively. "But I want answers."

"You already have them," she spat. "When you understand what you do, you may see things from the other side." And with that, she promptly slid through my arms and became no more than sand, sliding straight through my fingers and pouring out onto the ground below. *Every grain of sand... every soul waiting to rejoin the sea. What was* I *waiting for?*

I didn't know anymore. But somehow, I did know she was right. My business was not here – this place didn't want me, at least not now. I had come to see what I needed to see, and now... now, perhaps I could allow the sand to reclaim me. There was nothing more to be done, nothing more I *could* do, not here. I felt this rather than knew it, like a touch on the shoulder from the gods themselves. Gently, it guided me to kneel by my weapon as I would to king, god, or country, and I felt or knew nothing more.

Finally I see, said the Noble Sayaf. And so, I am awake.

CHAPTER TEN

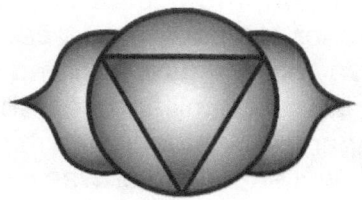

Possibilities
11 Spring's Green, 1272
Jade Saçaille

"J ardin!" My shriek came out louder than I might have liked, but I was past the point of calm judgment. I didn't care who was around to hear me, or what I might have been interrupting.

As it turned out, I interrupted nothing. The roadside temple, very small yet vibrant in its sterile white and abstractly beautiful stained glass, was virtually empty, save for a plump woman in white robes by the altar and my daughter.

Jardin sat in the very last pew, alone, deeply engaged in her sketchbook. The musical soft chanting of the priestess as she prayed to her Zondrean goddess floated around the chapel, though the notes never touched Jardin. What in the name of anything that was holy was she *doing*? A part of me craved nothing more than to go embrace her, but the other part wanted to strangle her. I knew better on both counts, but I couldn't stop myself from lunging forward to retrieve her.

Vremya's gentle hand fell on my shoulder in the next heartbeat. Before I could protest, he put a finger to his lips in the universal "quiet" gesture, then proceeded to go sit next to Jardin. I stood there, dumbfounded for a moment, before I went to join them.

As the priestess carried on with her song, uninterested in us, we watched the sketch unfold over Jardin's thin shoulder. It started with the church itself, the very room we were in — she captured every detail, from the simple cloth-covered altar, to the stained-glass images of doves and gentle ladies in flowing dresses, to the rows and rows of wooden benches.

Yet, in her imagination, the church was in a much different state, one much closer to chaos than peace. A girl in a plain shift hovered over a fallen figure armored like a soldier and bleeding profusely, while a familiar broad-shouldered man with fair hair and a haggard look stood over them. He sported the shading of a beard, while the soldier was well-groomed, clean-shaven. Yet, the two could have been father and son, two Eislandisch warriors in the aftermath of battle.

Songs to the peace goddess rose in pitch, before diminishing and turning quiet. All the while, details continued to breathe life into the sketch. Moonlight, streaming in from beyond the windows, painted the scene with a sense of color, even though all Jardin held was a single piece of charcoal.

The candles on the altar still dripped wax as they cooled from an earlier service. And I could almost hear the faint scuffs of the big man's boots on the marble floor... or it might have just been Vremya, shifting to look over Jardin's shoulder as she remained locked in her sketchpad world.

"Jardin," I started, trying my best to remain level, composed. Loud noises only served to terrorize her. "Jardin? Can you tell me why you left the city without permission?" I shouldn't have expected anything more than what I got, which was nothing. "Jardin? Are you listening to me?"

I could have kept going, but Vremya made the quiet-signal again. Then he turned to Jardin, that wide smile still playing at his features. "Good drawing for little girl. You know those men?" Jardin, without looking up, nodded as she added torchlit shadows amongst the drawn pews. "*Da?* Even the one on the ground?"

"That's my cousin." She said it with so much determination. It made so little sense.

When Vremya looked to me, I could only shake my head. "She's never met this person. I don't even know what this means. She's drawn him before... Why? Do *you* know him?"

Vremya's smile persisted, but he didn't answer me. Instead, he pulled a gold coin from a hidden pocket and held it out, grasped in two slender fingers – a simple *cinq-cent* from back home, with the four interlocking rings of Quatremagne engraved on one side, and a jeweled crown on the other. "Little girls like guessing games sometimes, *da*? Tell me, rings or kings?"

At this, the pencil stopped its movement, and Jardin finally looked up, fixated on the coin. Her eyes – glassy, almost as if she had been crying – narrowed at it, thinking, considering. "Rings," she said at last.

With a smooth motion, Vremya flicked the coin into the air, letting it spin it over and over until it started downward... and paused, in mid-flight. I had seen this magic before, many times, in many different ways, and something about it brought up a certain feeling of dread, deep in the pit of my stomach. It was the kind of magic that could freeze an arrow in its path, or cause men's hearts to stop and their blood to fester in their veins.

The first time I had ever met Vremya, it was during a skirmish. Despite the promise of riches for my parents and me – and the man was indeed no liar – he had failed to tell me I would be wading through a battlefield just to get to his side. The small group of soldiers who escorted me the several hundred miles to the capital city of Königstadt had been good at evading trouble, but at some point, our luck had run out. Outside of an outpost where we could have rested, we instead found two patrols tearing into each other with swords and magic. My escorts joined the battle while they urged me to "stay back." Back where?

I found a tree to kneel behind, hoping no one would see me and realizing that I had no idea what I was doing there in the first place. I thought I could help people, but I wasn't a fighter – I didn't belong there. What was I thinking? I was going to die in an unfamiliar country, miles from home, because I thought I was *special* somehow? Onyx was right. I should never have listened so much to those priests in Quiétude.

I also wasn't as clever as I thought – a Zondrell soldier with a battle-axe and a shield soon found me and closed in, before any of my escorts could catch on. He was all teeth and steel as he raised that weapon... and that was all.

He froze, standing perfectly still with an evil grin on his face and his axe raised over his head. No artist could have produced a better statue. It was fascinatingly disturbing.

The next thing I knew, a stout little Drakannyan man with the warmest smile I'd ever seen held out his hand to me. "No fears," he said in his heavy, clipped accent. "He... uh, bye-bye. No worries, *da*?"

I'd like to say I never had to worry with Vremya around, and in truth, none of us did – not even Brin. Yet, with every pulse of his Time magic, my heart always skipped a beat, my stomach twisting into knots even at an action so simple as the release of a coin from its unseen prison.

The *cinq-cent* fell into Vremya's waiting palm, and without looking, he announced, "Looks like kings this round." Sure enough, the crown faced up when his fingers uncurled.

Intrigued, Jardin now let her sketchpad and charcoal rest in her lap. "You didn't look first," she said to him.

"Don't have to. You know how I know?" A pause, just for theatrics, with a finger at his temple. "The same way I know your cousin."

Now, he had her full attention... and mine, too. Instead of speaking, though, Jardin flipped to another picture in her precious book, the one she drew the previous night of this cousin in "the Place." The riverside meadow seemed ominous and strange in the dimmed light of the temple, but Vremya was mesmerized. He studied it with intensity, taking in every detail. His silvery irises winked brightness for a moment, before his smile bloomed once again.

"Vremya?" I said, soft.

But he didn't direct his words to me. Instead, he looked right at Jardin, and amazingly, she met his gaze. "You're right, little girl. That man who is your cousin was here. You know what happened?" Neither of us knew, but we hung on his every word. "Your Papa brought him here, to get better. Saved his life, in fact."

Jardin flipped the book back to the new sketch, and pointed to the girlish figure in a simple dress kneeling over the injured cousin. "She helped him. She's like Mama."

I breathed in sharply. "What did you just say, Jardin?"

"What, you think you're the only one?" Vremya's tone was light, almost teasing. "Turn back a page, little girl." Jardin did, and his smile grew pensive again.

"What is that place, Vremya?" I asked. "She says she 'goes' there, in her dreams."

"That, friend, is the River."

"The… River? Like in Eislandisch religion?" I had come to understand something of the concept of the River during my time in the War. The soldiers talked about it ceaselessly – they prayed to it, cursed over it, and everything in between. It was the place where all things went to die, and from which they were reborn.

Evil souls, they said, didn't float, and to relieve them of their burdens, the soldiers would come to me – of all people – to tell of their sins. I never fully understood this, but because I could heal their wounds, they saw me as a holy woman, a "Saint." The entire concept was so alien, so far beyond what I had been taught… and more than a tad sacrilegious. Souls coming back? They did no such thing under the watchful eye of Chantal. Otherwise, how could She keep track of who had been gifted with magic, and who had not?

Vremya nodded, apparently pleased. "*Da,* something like that."

"He's been there before," Jardin said, matter-of-fact. "Sometimes I go there when I sleep, and I see him. I saw him last night. I think he's in trouble."

"Trouble… maybe that." The coin disappeared back into his pocket, and the Drakannyan looked up at me. "You know how I got to Eisland, back in the war days? King Keis, he heard I was a fortune teller."

"A fortune teller?" Well, that was certainly different from being blessed by Chantal during the sacred Pilgrimage to Quiétude. Then I realized that I had never actually asked him how he had learned about his own special form of magic.

"*Da!* I made gold telling people what they already knew. Always had a knack for that kind of thing. I tell them things that happen in the past – they think it means something for their future. Even from dirty old street in Zolotoy Bireg, King Keis hears this, he send for me. Thing is, he wanted a *real* fortune teller, you know?" When I could only blink at him, he laughed. "Future's hard to know, *da*?"

I looked at Vremya, squinting as if that would help me see things more clearly. "I remember him asking you some strange things, sometimes."

"Hey, he wanted Time on his side. Can't blame him, *da*? But for long time, I could only see the past, little bits at a time, when I touch things. No reason, just happen. Or so I think. So then later, I get to thinking, maybe King Keis was right. What is time, anyhow?" He paused. "Possibility. Everything we do, possibility. You step on a twig, you light a candle, you breathe... twenty things could happen next. Or fifty. Who knows? Can't know. All I know is that only one of those gets picked. If you can figure out which, then you know the future, *da*?"

"Are you... saying you *can* see the future?" Because he was right. It wasn't supposed to be possible. I knew from my studies that most scholars of magic agreed that even if Time magic was real – which many modern scholars, and even the Church of Chantal, had a hard time believing in the first place – then seeing the future would still be unachievable. It was unwritten, and therefore unknowable.

"Tiny bits, I think. Possibilities. Maybe true ones, maybe ones that wind up going out with the trash. Lately, I work on which possibilities I see. You know, it's not easy. Drove me crazy for a while." He paused, laughing, but it wasn't his typically confident, jovial laugh. "Touch everything, see memories of everything. Too much, *da*? Then I go sit on your Lavançaise mountain, and think for a while. Clear the head. Think about Time for a few years. Or ten. Something like that. Before you all did your revolution thing in Quatremagne. Anyhow, now, I decide when I see, and getting closer to what."

"*Incroyable.*" I didn't know which was more incredible – Vremya, a Drakannyan non-believer, being allowed to spend *ten whole years* in Quiétude, or him being able to see the future in the first place. There was the distinct possibility that his "crazy" never got resolved. He always had been a little touched in the first place.

"So," he said, pointing to Jardin's drawing, "I see this man in possibilities. Not always good ones. Come here to find out more. Come here because they say this is where you and Brin are. Never know when you might need a good Saint, or a good head-basher."

Bristling at the mention of Brin's name, I shook my head angrily. "I don't practice magic anymore, Vremya. And I told you, I haven't seen him in years."

"But we saw Papa in the Market," Jardin protested. "And he was here. Tante Onyx said he went to Zondrell."

"Jardin, we talked about this…"

I was cut short by an excited Vremya. "Zondrell, *da*? Been there. Didn't like it. Too many people. But, if that is where to go, that is where to go." He started to stand, and seemed confused when we didn't follow suit.

"Wait a minute, Vremya. We are not just *going* to Zondrell."

"*Nyet*? I take you, no worries. Room and board paid for. Don't you want to meet this cousin?" He leaned over and tapped on the figure in Jardin's drawing, the clean-shaven man who looked so much like a young Brin that it gave me a chill. Even in the new sketch, bleeding out onto the pristine white floor of this very same chapel, he seemed proud. Not quite regal, really, but strong, determined. If he was anything like Brin at that age… well, I just didn't know if I had the heart to deal with that again. "He looks interesting, *da*? I have an appointment with a friend of his, anyhow."

"He's special. He's like me," said Jardin, softly, the electric energy in her eyes alight. Was there really yet another like her out there? Or like me, for that matter? The chill grew deeper, so much so that I stood as well, but had no intention of following Vremya to Zondrell on some wild expedition.

"Get your things together, Jardin. We're leaving," I snapped.

But there was a hand on my arm again, an attempt at comfort. "Can't do this without you," Vremya said, and he was sincere. Still, I didn't care.

"Go find Safaa if you need another mage. What's she doing these days? Probably still in Eisland, I imagine?" Safaa… Keis Sturmberg's Katalahni Light mage, had clearly been the favorite of all of his mages.

That dark-skinned, quiet woman was fearless, an indestructible force of nature unlike anything I had ever seen, or wanted to see again. Hers was the same brilliance that played in my daughter's eyes, and the fear of what that grand gift from Chantal could do seeped into every ounce of my body. Of course, this was precisely why I never talked about magic in Jardin's presence, and most definitely did not encourage her to understand the terrible lightning that glittered behind clear blue irises.

Vremya sighed the kind of sigh that makes blood run ice cold. "Safaa is dead, Jade." And with that, he started for the door, Jardin trailing behind him, sketchbook clutched to her chest.

It took a moment, but I eventually started after them, forcing one foot in front of the other. It was a dream, perhaps – all of this was one wild, wild dream, and I'd wake up soon. But no, I knew better, deep down. I took one last look at the quiet temple with its ancient art and simple, stark whiteness, and as I did, I heard a polite voice from the front of the temple. "Excuse me," the priestess said in Zondrean. "I'm sorry, but did I hear you were heading to Zondrell?"

"Ah, *oui*, madame," I nodded.

"You know, that's where my sister went, with her friend – the, ah… the one from the girl's drawing." Her round face was peaceful, her smile touching her gentle green eyes. She left her altar to float up to me, moving more gracefully than I would have assumed the big woman could. "I walked past to check on her a few minutes after she came in. She never talked to me, but she seemed safe and comfortable. She even curled up to sleep for a while. I kept an eye out – you showed up right before I was about to take her to the Doverton Guard."

"*Merci*, madame. I appreciate you looking out for her. She, ah, wandered off in the night, and…"

"She got here right around dawn. Luckily, I was already up. At any rate, if I could ask you to give my sister my blessings when you get to Zondrell, I would appreciate it."

"And, I would find your sister how, madame?" In a city of a million people, I had a feeling that running into any one specific person would be a bit tricky.

"Oh, of course – her name is Andella, Andella Weaver. I'm Seraphine. You'll know Andella if you see her. She… well, she has eyes like yours."

So it was true. The very idea made me stiffen, my breath catching in my throat. Did the world really need another so-called Saint to torture? I could only hope that for her sake, things would be different for this woman's life than they had been for mine.

CHAPTER ELEVEN

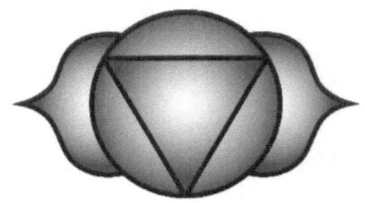

The Stand
11 Spring's Green, 1272
Alexander Vestarton

Ashore, with steep rocky cliffs overlooking a bar of glittering, coarse sand. Smooth and even, the gentle waves of dark water barely seemed to make a dent in it, and the smell of salt was high in the cold, motionless air. I paused, taking it all in for just a moment. I was looking for something.

Just as I took a step toward the sands, the cliffs rotted away, eroding into a chasm that seemed to have no end in sight, and the sea began to flow through the cracks. Water found its way through every nook of earth and rock until it created a stream, and soon a raging river. Still, a ragged strip of land remained, and walking along its edge, I saw a figure. I squinted, then began to rush toward it, because I knew, I just knew...

No one was there.

Then the corner of a stone building almost met my face head-on and I stumbled backward, wondering where the hell it came from in the first place. Wasn't I...? No, of course not, not anymore. There was no beach, only block upon block of debris-strewn streets. A small contingent of soldiers and I marched along in relative silence, save for the scraping thud of boots on stone and dirt.

There was no one else on the road save for us – what few people might have been out at this, the twilight hour, scurried like rats at our approach. No one wanted to be caught outside just minutes before the curfew. Of course, the very thought of a curfew in a city of over a million people was ridiculous, and yet, it had become something of a necessity. The streets of Zondrell, the Jewel of the West, had become a war zone.

"Are you well?"

I looked over into the dark, steely eyes of the man they used to call the Gentleman General. He looked more like a husk of his former self now, but he still wore that gleaming, black-lacquered armor as well as anyone I'd ever met. "Why wouldn't I be?" I said. "Look at us, marching to save the people from themselves in all of our heroic glory."

Jamison Torven nodded, clearly missing the edge in my tone. "Indeed. And the people will appreciate your effort."

"Yeah... as long as we don't fuck this up."

There was a lot that wasn't said in his grave expression, more than I cared to know. "We're almost to North Gate, m'Lord. Be prepared."

As we neared our destination, the streets were paved with gloom. I had never known my homeland to be in the shape it was in; it was almost unrecognizable. This was Zondrell? I mean, I'd been out, but I hadn't ventured this deep into the city streets since well before the... what? Was this really a civil war, or just more of a descent into madness without a name? Either way, it had turned the place into something not unlike how I pictured Hell.

Hell, or Purgatory, or whatever you wanted to call it, was where Catherine cast the unwanted and the unsalvageable souls when they met their fate. It was supposed to be an endless void of wretchedness – really, some stretches of Leander's Way leading toward the North Gate could have been the subject of a priestess' sermon. And the closer we came to the end, the worse it got. Burned-out husks of buildings. Broken windows. Random trash in the street... sometimes things that might have once been more than trash.

Not that long ago, people moved through North Gate's plaza peacefully, in an orderly fashion – what I saw now could only be described as pure chaos. It had become a stirring mass, with adults and children huddled around makeshift fires large and small. Many more gathered as close as they could get to the gates themselves, massive doors that used a clever chain mechanism controlled at the top of the walls to keep them opened or closed. I had, in fact, never seen them closed, but there they were, strange orange-red shadows cast across all that reinforced steel.

To the credit of the city watchmen, they had allowed themselves to be pushed back up onto the walls rather than start hacking away at the crowd. Their bows were still in easy reach, though, as all manner of things were shouted back and forth, little of it meaningful, even less of it audible over the ruckus. There was one cry that rose up amid the haze of smoke and the heavy air full of sweat and dirt and despair, the incessant chanting of dozens of voices in unison.

"Open the gates! Let us go home! Open the gates! Let us go home!" It seemed distant at first, then rose with intensity as if someone had cued the chorus just for our arrival. And hell, maybe they had – surely, people were aware that a group waving banners and wearing Royal Guard armor had arrived. Such things had a way of attracting attention, which was exactly what I'd wanted.

"You men, come with me," Torven barked at a few soldiers by his side. 'The rest of you, form ranks around the perimeter." I started to follow him as he made his way toward the stairs leading up to the top of the walls, but he turned and shook his head. "Sir, stay low for a moment."

"Excuse me? I'm going to address the crowd," I said. But he was ready to stand in my way, and despite being old enough to be my father, and battered and bruised on top of it, the General was still an imposing man.

"You brought me here to work with my men. You said yourself many of them are loyal to me, not to any crown. So, I would prepare them before you rush up there and get yourself knocked off that wall."

"No weapons. No fighting. No bloodshed."

"Sir, I want these things as much as you. You've trusted me this far, yes?"

Oh, it was reluctant, but… yes. Yes, I'd trusted that he loved this city as much as I did, that he didn't want to see it spiral out of control, that he wanted to help heal the wound he himself had wrought upon it.

Open the gates! Let us go home! The din was stifling, and I had to strain to shout above them. "Very well, General. I'll await your signal."

With a brusque salute of left fist on right shoulder, I watched the Gentleman General turn away, armor clinking as he dashed up the stairs. A sense of dread clung to where he'd stood, along with the past memories of half a dozen people as they crowded around, brushing against me in a mad rush to find a better vantage point.

What was coming, I wasn't sure, but these people... it wasn't their fault. They were just regular folk, living regular lives. They weren't soldiers or nobles or anything in between. They were farmers and merchants and travelers – they just wanted to get the hell out of this fucking pit of a city. They wanted to go back to a time of peace, of normalcy, and they would fight their way to it if they had to.

I couldn't say I blamed them.

Everything about that moment, standing there before the closed North Gate, was wrong. I felt it like a cold lump in the pit of my stomach, a darkness getting ready to eat away at me from the inside out. Torven, at least, was relatively safe up on the wall, as long as the stairs were guarded, but the chanting... it had risen to a fever pitch. Hands hovered near weapons on both sides, and once the first Zondrell soldier drew steel, we would go from defenders to tyrants in an instant. We would lose them forever.

Not that citizens hadn't already died at the hands of Zondrell soldiers. There had been plenty of that in the past few days – and the other way around, too – but right now, in this crucial moment, we had to be the better men, as my father would have said. Every time I glanced at any of the troops near me, I sent a silent warning *not* to draw, not to panic, and they didn't... for the moment.

"People!" General Torven shouted at the top of his lungs, trying to get the crowd's attention. Not many stopped to listen. "People, please!" he tried again, and drew in a few more. "We must be peaceful. You will all get where you need to be."

The reply came in a flurry of shouts, a few distinguishable over the general noise that erupted. Praise and curses erupted from every corner.

"Open the gates!"

"Hey, isn't that the General?"

"Hero! Help us!"

"Traitor! Let him rot!"

"The gates will open, but we must maintain order here!" Torven glanced over his shoulder to the other side of the wall. Over the impossible noise of dozens of people shouting all at once, I could hear a distinct pounding and scraping, the sound of weapons, of clubs and swords and farm implements, striking out at the gate.

I moved closer to the stairs and brushed a hand against the wooden rail... oh, the story it told. In a flash, I saw the blood of wars past, of defenders valiantly saving Zondrell from onslaughts of a dozen invading nations, over countless centuries. And here now, we were defending the gates from our own people. I shook my head at the irony, the sadness of it all.

The order and peace that we sought was not happening. In fact, things seemed to be getting worse with each passing second. Without knowing exactly what I was doing, and most certainly without waiting for the agreed-upon signal, I headed up those stairs, to the top of the wall, to stand at Torven's side. As I looked over the wall's edge at the throng of people – even angrier, it seemed, than those stuck inside the city – I summoned my best "Lord voice."

"Friends and countrymen! Please relax. You'll all be able to enter the city soon. But we need your help to keep things orderly, and..."

"Open the gates! Let us go home!"

Well, that worked nicely. Holding back an annoyed sigh, I raised my arms. "Friends, I speak on behalf of the throne of Zondrell and the Council of Lords, and I am here to tell you that these gates *will* open! All we ask is that you enter or leave the city in a peaceful, orderly manner. So please, fellow citizens, please move away from the doors and let the soldiers do their work."

The crowd – those who heard me – appeared convinced... somewhat. Some clusters of people on the outside moved back, away from the gate entrance, and on the other side, more did the same.

But those with weapons at their sides and fire in their hearts weren't so easily mollified. A stream of curses struck me from all angles, and despite additional attempts to calm them, my words were simply absorbed into the noise. I looked to Torven, who looked back, sorrowful and defeated.

Three things happened then, in the span of three breaths. First, there was a rock, or an arrow, or a bolt, or something heavy. I saw it fly toward us, so impossibly fast, almost as if sent forth by... magic? My mind never registered any of it until the next breath had come and gone, and I found myself pushed to the side, nearly losing my footing along the somewhat precarious ten-foot thick wall. But just as I regained my balance, that last breath happened.

Something struck Jamison Torven with considerable force, enough to make a solid, fleshy *thunk.* And that aim! It had managed to miss his black platemail completely and gone right for his already bruised and battered head. Where it came from, only the gods knew, but with that sound came a yelp, and half a word escaped through gritted teeth.

When I dared to breathe again, he was gone.

"Holy hell," I said under my breath, leaning to peer over the edge. Any more words were beyond my abilities. They were taken from me.

What happens to a man when he falls, in armor, over thirty feet? Well, I know one thing for certain – he doesn't get up easily. And what could I do? I felt just as helpless as I had been when Tristan fell to the sea depths. No man, not even Torven, deserved that fate. I wanted to scream and curse the gods right there, but I was still struck dumb.

Below, people had fanned out around him in a wide arc, hesitant, but also dangerous in their unease. Then the first one broke the circle, rushing like mad. A dark-haired woman in a traveling cloak rushed to the General's side and knelt there, looking for all the world as if she was going to... pray? Perhaps she did just that, as streamers of light began to move through her, down her arms to encircle the body encased in dented armor.

I knew that light, had seen it many times before, indigo with white and lavender edges, dancing and moving with a motion all its own, yet it didn't come from its usual source. This wasn't Andella – couldn't be. So who was it?

All around the woman and Torven, people began to shout. Some continued to bang on the gates, cheering. Others started screaming curses and shouting that demons were among us. Still others cried for Catherine's mercy.

Within the city, things weren't too different, except the cheering won out over everything... and these people were armed. Steel began to ring, loud as a church bell in the middle of the night. Soldiers answered the call of battle, too, despite their training, despite their better judgment.

Men, women, children, it didn't seem to matter anymore. The lines between civility and savagery had blurred forever. Holy Catherine in Paradise, what was wrong with us? Where was Tristan, with some great magical shield to protect us all, to keep us from tearing each other apart?

But all the wishing in the world wasn't going to change anything, was it? Dear Catherine above, hundreds of people could die, right here. Breaths kept escaping, and with each one, something got a little worse. Someone cuffed someone else over the head. A city watchman began to draw his weapon, then another, and another. I'm sure I shouted at them all, but nothing helped.

And then it all just *stopped.*

The grip of sheer unadulterated pain ripped through my whole body, centering in my throat so that I could enjoy the sensation of having all of those lost breaths just cut off and tossed aside. I clutched at my chest, trying to figure out how to put them back in, and with some effort, I found a way to breathe again. The problem was, no one else was doing the same.

The world had... ended. We had all tottered right to the edge of oblivion, and the gods had snuffed us all out. No, wait, that can't be right. But yet, there was no more sound, no more wind. No more anything.

I went to a nearby guard, and he was silent, unmoving, frozen while reaching for his sword belt. I went to another, and his response was the same. And another after him, and another – all of them caught in a moment of time forever. Catherine-on-a-bleeding-pike!

I raced down the stairs, to the men we'd brought here, each of them trapped in frantic shouts and gestures, never to be finished. I found one young soldier, barely a man, kneeling on the ground, fingers clawing into the earth after having his head split open by a farmer's club… and the blood running out from the wound was perfectly still.

"Oh dear Lady, no." Words finally came forth, along with sobs, wrenched from deep within. I dropped to the ground by the soldier, whose name I didn't know, looking into his dark eyes, unmoving, glassy eyes like a perfect statue. There was even a single tear, paused midflight, never to splash below.

I screamed so hard the world shook.

CHAPTER TWELVE

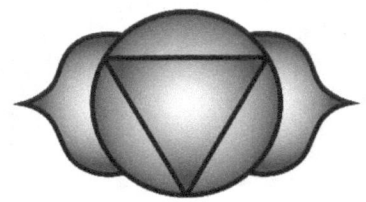

The Lady's Plan
11 Spring's Green, 1272
Andella Weaver

I awoke in the last place I would have expected – in bed. It wasn't a familiar bed, and the room around me didn't feel so familiar, either. Everything was still swirling and fuzzy and just plain odd, and even though I was sure my eyes had opened, I wasn't so sure I could trust what they showed me.

Where was I? Surrounding me were simple stone walls with little decoration and almost no furniture, save for the bed I lay on, a nighttable with a lit oil lantern, and a small dresser made of what looked to be unadorned oak. The room smelled of sea lion oil, dust, old wood – it was almost as if...

Wait a minute. This was an Academy dormitory. Not long ago, I used to sleep in such a room as this. Maybe I was still dreaming, remembering days long since past, when my life was so much simpler, so much easier to explain. I would get up, day after day, attend class, study, and practice, all on a fixed routine that left little time for much else. Oh, I had friends, and we would wander the city from time to time in search of something fun to do, but I wasn't from Zondrell, wasn't as comfortable with its unpredictable expanse of taverns and shops and people – *so* many people. I was just as happy in the Great Library, surrounded by books that didn't fuss or talk or try to get me to do something I didn't want to do.

Hmm... well, if this was a dream, then maybe I would just get up and go to that Library, see what it might be like in my mind's eye. Would it be the same as the real thing? An idealized version, perhaps, where the librarians were always pleasant, and I could always find the book I wanted the first time?

I sat up and swung my feet over the edge, my bare feet hitting rough, cool stone that felt quite real, quite solid. Then I stood, a little unsteady, using the wall for support as I looked myself over. All I had on was an unadorned green shift, with long sleeves to protect from the chill that still lurked within these big stone buildings well into spring and even summer. It felt a size or two too large, but no matter – the dresser might have something else more suitable.

Before I could open a drawer, I noted my reflection in the little mirror standing upon it, and I stopped with a gasp. I turned away, then looked again. Still the same... but this couldn't be right.

My eyes were green.

No, not the vibrant, living green within the eyes of an Earth mage like Archmage Tiara, but everyday green, sort of pale with dark spots playing at the edges that didn't move or whirl or do any of the interesting things that a mage's eyes did. I hadn't seen my eyes looking like they had when I was born for... well, it had been almost five years, ever since I came to Zondrell to go to the Magic Academy.

At first, they were the color of flame, orange and dancing and bright, and then almost two months ago, they had turned a strange indigo-lavender, a color I'd never seen before in anyone. The Life magic lay there, moving with its own rhythm, but now there was no rhythm at all. No inner light, just... *normal*.

I stared at the reflection of the pale-faced young woman in the mirror for a long time, an older – though perhaps little wiser – version of the girl I was before I left Doverton for the first time. My auburn hair hung around my face in wisps and waves, dreadfully unkempt, but that was nothing compared to those eyes. They were full of concern and worry and even a few tears in the corners, but they held nothing else.

"How do you feel, dear?" I heard a soft voice, and realized that the door had quietly opened a foot or two. Archmage Tiara's dark-haired visage poked through, eyes pulsing with that magical green of Earth in the dim lamplight.

It took a minute or two to find my voice. Was this another dream? I was less and less sure. Everything felt so real, but so had... I closed my eyes and could see clearly that beach with its black waters and infinite, flat shore. I could feel the sand that didn't quite give underfoot, and could even smell a hint of the sea's stale salt.

Yet, with my eyes open again, the world seemed to hold a bit more permanency. And would Archmage Tiara seem quite as real in my dream-mind? I typically pictured my mentor as she taught her classes, in flowing green robes, lecturing on important research and mercilessly punishing anyone not paying complete attention. This Archmage was dressed in a much simpler robe, tied around the waist, her curly hair pulled back from a dignified face that was tired and just a little worn. This was the woman I knew from my past few weeks of research on Life and Time and Light and all manner of strange magics. This Archmage still loved research, but there was a humanity in her as well. She brightened at meeting my gaze – there was more to learn, after all.

"Archmage..." I started, but suddenly wasn't sure what else to say after that.

She padded into the room and we stood together for a moment before she offered a tight smile. "I heard you stir. Goodness, you gave us all quite the start. Do you know where you are, dear?"

"A... dormitory?"

She nodded. "And how do you feel?"

"I'm all right, I think," I replied, offering a faint smile, while her own faded away.

"Indeed. Well, I hate to say it, but I do wish hadn't touched that rock."

There was a rock? Not just any rock, but something special, obsidian not from some volcano but something else, maybe some essence of pure magic compressed to a black, solid mass. "I'm sorry, Archmage... I couldn't help myself. I didn't think there'd be any danger. But I'm fine now."

Tiara's face was grave. "Dear, I hate to have to tell you this, but you most certainly are not."

My gaze drifted to the mirror again, to those all-too-normal green eyes staring back at me. "What does it mean? What happened?"

"Well, if I knew that, dear, we'd be having a different conversation. Can you feel the magic within you at all?"

I could see her in the mirror with her arm around my shoulder, studying me intently. But I found I couldn't break away from my own reflection to turn to her. I just shook my head, and saw my own bewildered, sad expression, as if from another place, like I was another person entirely.

That couldn't be me there – I was a mage. The girl in the mirror was without any power at all. It was like drawing from an empty well. No matter how much she tried to summon something from within, it just wasn't there.

By the Lady, what had happened to me this time?

I took a deep breath, and felt Tiara hold me a little tighter in a gentle, reassuring squeeze. "This is most curious indeed," she said, and from her tone, I knew *curious* meant *worrisome*. "It may have something to do with the Fire magic you lost, or the healing magic you gained, or something entirely different. It could also be quite temporary. I have a few theories... the readings haven't been productive. Now that you're awake, though..."

She wandered off into the hall outside, leaving the door open so I could get my bearings. I wasn't just in any dormitory, but one of the private rooms among the laboratories in the Great Hall that were meant as places to flop down once research became too much for the day. No wonder it was so simple and barren. The room across the hall was Tiara's own laboratory, where she spent most of her time when she wasn't teaching. I heard rifling, a small crash of papers and books, and in a few moments, she returned clutching an array of odd tools.

The instruments used by magic researchers were often misconstrued as torture devices by the uninitiated. The devices often contained sharp edges and strange designs of metal and glass, resembling sailing sextants or calipers with an array of compasses attached. I had used them in some of my work at the Academy, though there was a fine art to measurement of magical power, and I was nowhere near as versed in their use as the Archmage.

She deftly took some readings while I held stock still and stared straight ahead, lest the sharp end of her resonance meter go straight into my eye.

"Hmm..." she hummed and muttered, as she wrote down some numbers on a scrap piece of parchment. "Yes, yes, well..."

"Archmage?" I asked, almost at a whisper. I wasn't sure I wanted an answer, nor was I sure of the question in the first place.

At first, she failed to answer. Then after a long while of staring at her paper, at the dials on the meter, and back at the paper, she shrugged. "Most curious."

"What... what does it say?"

"If I were sure of that, we'd start the next leg of our research. But these readings are quite inconclusive. You can't summon any power on your own? You're sure of it?"

I closed my eyes, concentrated, and tried to evoke the power that was – once – within me. The scholars, modern and ancient alike, had argued about where exactly that power came from for centuries. To me, it felt like taking a deep breath, and I usually did just that when I wanted to bring magic to the surface.

Along with that breath came something else, a tingling sensation that became warm, sometimes spiked with pinpricks of pain. It was almost, but not quite, like the feeling of coming in from a cold winter's day and trying to warm half-frozen hands over the hearth. But as much as I wanted to feel that sensation one more time, it wasn't there – no heat, no numbing prickles, nothing. Eventually, I shook my head and looked toward the floor with a sigh.

"It's all right, dear. Don't worry yourself. We don't know the nature of this, but we'll figure it out, yes? Of course we will. Why don't we find something for you to wear? There's something you should see."

Something to see, something to see... something to know? Wait, the search! Tristan! The recollection rang like an alarm bell over all the other mixed-up thoughts. Yet, without ceremony, she had already wandered off across the hall again. I followed this time, in bare feet that were quickly shod with leather-wrap sandals. My frock was replaced with the only mage's robes she had that would fit me, a set of apprentice robes the color of Earth magic.

"Archmage? Can you tell me...?"

"Come along, dear. It's not far." Not far? It felt like an eternity walking through the Great Hall, down the stairs, out into the courtyard. All the while, her manner gave away nothing.

The light had nearly departed, leaving the city in the lavender haze of twilight, punctuated by cool, humid air. At least it wasn't raining for the time being, but I was fairly certain the season of the Rains hadn't quite left Zondrell just yet. Maybe it had only been a few hours since I'd touched that rock in the ground, since I'd had that wild, wild dream.

"Come, dear. This way," Tiara said, and I followed her toward the Infirmary, where the healers and herbalists practiced their art. Upon entering, I was immediately assaulted with the familiar scents of smoking roots and half-dead flowers and all manner of spices. It might have been pleasant if it hadn't been so strong – had it always been this strong, even during the height of those herbalism classes I'd taken? I bent over and started sneezing in tight little convulsions punctuated by high-pitched peeps.

Tiara handed me a handkerchief and bade me to follow her down a corridor and into the room where they actually treated the ill. While the Magic Academy was mostly about learning, this one part was open to all Zondrell citizens, provided they had some coin to donate for their treatments. Military cadets and aspiring mages, however, were the most common patients, and today, there were just two beds occupied. Well-dressed people lingered here, flitting about, talking in tight-knit circles, asking questions of the herbalists and healers as they tried to do their work. And there I was with my mouth agape and my no-magic eyes, frozen in the center of it all.

I had once told myself that I would be ready for anything, that I would be able to accept whatever happened. I assured myself that everything was Catherine's will, Her Path. It was not our place to question it. All my life, I believed in Fate as the guiding light for all of us. I knew it would never be easy, but I had promised myself that I would be able to accept the death of the only man I'd truly loved. If that happened, it was the Lady's plan. But I had also told myself not to give up, and in the quietest moments, I had asked Her not to give up on him, either.

My prayers were answered.

I could barely control the tears streaming down my face, my heart thundering in my chest, as I half-ran, half-stumbled to his bedside. Behind me, I heard Archmage Tiara breathe deeply, a rare hint of genuine concern edging into her voice. "As we were tending to you, the other team found them. Not even that far away. Quite the thing, really – right there tucked up against a rock those boats must have passed a hundred times."

They found them. The words took time to settle in, to make sense in my brain. I could barely even make sense of what I was seeing before me. Another dream? No, not this time. This time, I could feel his warmth, hold his hand, rest my head on his chest and hear his heart beating – a good, strong beat, but... no stirring, barely a muscle twitch. Unresponsive.

"The healers do what they can," a familiar, faintly sad voice nearby said, as if reading my thoughts. "But... well, there are many questions. Few answers." That voice belonged to Tristan's mother, sitting in her patient, stoic, Eislandisch way, on the other side of the bed. The dour expression of a woman who had lost her husband and almost lost her only son within days of each other softened – just a little – as I looked up.

"He hasn't moved or anything?" I asked, wiping moisture from my cheek.

"All he does now is breathe," Lady Gretchen told me. "We should be happy for that much, *ja*?"

She had a fair point, but I wasn't happy with that. I wanted more. By Catherine, what I would have done to hear his voice, to see that little forlorn half-smile. With a sigh, I placed my hand upon his brow and found it cool, slightly moist with sweat and whatever balm the healers were using. No amount of willpower would put healing into that hand, though – no prayer would send energy coursing through me and into him.

I felt as powerless as I had in the dream, unable to even reach out. He might as well have been just as far away as he had been there on that strange ethereal shore. "I dreamed of you," I whispered in his ear, touching his blond hair that was growing out a bit longer than I knew he liked. The golden stubble on his wan face was threatening to become quite the unkempt beard soon, too, and I smiled in spite of the tear trickling down my cheek. "Or maybe, *you* were dreaming of me? It's okay now. You're here, where you belong."

As I sat there in a daze, I realized Archmage Tiara had prepared an instrument, this one fixed with a pointed shard of crystal at the center of a metal device shaped a bit like an arrowhead. Crystals, especially clear white ones like this, were a good way to focus magical energy, although too much concentrating on them could cause some mages to become woozy. I know I'd had my share of fainting spells in the resonance chambers, like most students.

"What do you think you'll find?" I asked in a low voice.

"Well, if you think your readings are odd, you should see my notes on Lord Loringham here. The other one, however," she nodded toward the other side of the room, where the bigger crowd of nobles was gathered, "is a different story. I only got two solid readings on him before they packed the crowd in. He's just a child, though. Children and magic are a very odd thing, very hard to predict."

Child... Oh! "You mean Prince Edin? He's all right?"

Tiara nodded and glanced over to the anxious group. It ought to have been much louder in the room than it was with all of those people, but most just stood around quiet, watching the bed of the little boy king. "He's just as unresponsive. It's quite perplexing, and a bit upsetting, as you might imagine. Poor dear Queen Marianna – she's not taking it well. Best steer clear of that side of room, yes? Right, then. If you could move for just a moment, dear."

I did, and she leaned in with the crystal instrument. If such a thing could hum, it would have – I could feel the energy move through it when it aligned with the center of Tristan's forehead. For the span of maybe five breaths, Tiara concentrated, watching the delicate gears and needles along the length of the instrument move, all on their own, at a speed that matched the thrum of energy and Tristan's own pulse. When she was satisfied, she withdrew and began to stare at the thing in her hand as if she'd never seen it before in her life.

Every single needle on every single dial was pointed in a single direction.

"What does it mean?" I dared to ask.

"If I knew *that*, dear..." Hurriedly, she produced some scraps of paper and charcoal and scrawled some numbers and notations, which she then frowned at, muttering something to herself. She then reset the instrument, and set it aside. "If – that is, *when* – he wakes, up, we'll try it again, yes?"

"Right, of course."

An Infirmary healer came over then to check on Tristan and hold a cool compress to his brow. She checked his pulse for a few minutes before stepping away again. Someone else brought Lady Gretchen and I some tea, and for a time, I watched as more people began to crowd the Infirmary. I was wished well by some twenty nobles I didn't know, and another handful that I did. Lord Cen Shal-Vesper and his wife gave me hugs and kisses on the cheek. Master Brin followed them, with decidedly less in the way of kind gestures, but no less in the way of concern.

"You were right," the big Eislander said as he settled into a chair next to me at the bedside.

I nodded, taking little from my small victory. "You can't give up hope."

"I never said I did. But hope can be... foolish." The torchlight got caught up in the crystal blue of his eyes, turning them almost white. "The River changes men, and this one walks the Edge too close. You should be ready."

"Ready for what?"

"Anything."

CHAPTER THIRTEEN

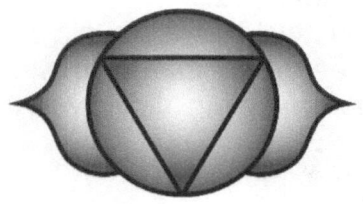

Light in Shadow
11 Spring's Green, 1272
Tristan Loringham

W armth. Pain. Sound. Light? Smoke. Voices?
LIGHT.
PAIN.

Sensations fired off in sequence, like archers releasing on command. With each volley, my mind tried to affix meaning, sometimes successfully, other times less so. I felt the muscles around my eyes twitch, and wetness roll down my cheek like a trail of sparks. The taste of copper weighed down my tongue, and half a dozen distinct scents wafted through the air around me. I tried to name them – smoke from a torch, alcohol, chamomile, a woman's perfume, sweat, old blood. Somewhere, maybe nearby and maybe not, sounds became voices and movement.

Then I dared to see, and an explosion of brightness burst through one tiny sliver of an opening, a flare of light that brought with it pain... so much pain. It engulfed me from the top of my head to the bottoms of my feet, washing over me with the sensation of being stabbed with a million tiny needles. I groaned in protest, but that was all I could do. Struggling would just make it worse, and I didn't have the strength anyhow.

"By the Lady!" I heard a woman say at the loudest possible level ever emitted by a human.

"Get the healers!" No, this one was louder.

"Tristan, can you hear us?" You can't be serious. By the gods, woman, I can hear you...

Wait, I'm alive. I'm awake, and I'm alive. This I had to say to myself repeatedly before it made sense. Because it didn't make a lot of sense. Nothing did. Everything was light and pain and noise.

"Tristan? Talk to me. Please."

Talk. Speak. Move your mouth. I tried this, but nothing came out but a scratchy, groaning protest. I blinked some more against the questions until recognizable shapes began to emerge – soft auburn hair, pale olive skin, round, wide eyes that searched and searched for my soul... or what was left of it.

"Andella?" I said, or rather, I thought I said. It may not have come out as anything more than an unintelligible grunt. Then again, she wasn't much better at words than I was amid tears and burying her face in my chest the way she was. Her body was warm, so very warm, and after a time, I found that I could reach up to hold her, feeling the gentle spasms of her sobs wash through me.

There were more tears, more embraces, more words spoken, and with every moment, the world around me became more stable, more known, more real. My mother was there, my uncle, friends... and the questions. So many questions. Most of them buzzed through the air beyond my ability to answer, but one stood out after a time.

"Can you tell me how you feel, Lord Loringham?" I heard a very patient, precise female voice ask.

I turned my head in the woman's general direction. The green robe and wild curly hair nagged at my memory, but I couldn't quite place her. "Like... like hell," was all I could offer.

"Well, it could certainly be worse, yes? Can you keep your eyes open for me? Just for a moment." This was an almost incomprehensible request. I barely had control over my sight, much less fine motor function. Still, it was a goal, something to aspire to, and I could understand that much. So I breathed deeply, and willed my eyes to stay open, while the noise and activity of the room melted away from my awareness.

The room around me seemed mercilessly bright, yet it was lit by only torches. And I had been there before, maybe more than a few times – an infirmary, the Magic Academy one, with all the potions and the herbs. In fact, the air was dense with the smell of them, to the point where smoke hung in the air and coiled around itself like mist... like fog. It reminded me of the kind of haze that only blanketed dreams and dark places.

I blinked just as the needle-like end of a very strange device withdrew from its position mere inches from my face. Thank the Lady you were too dazed to notice. "What... did you do?" I asked, fumbling for words.

The woman holding the instrument smiled a somewhat terse, tight-lipped smile, and I realized I did know her. She was the Archmage that Andella had studied under, the one who was so interested in doing more research on mine and Alex's powers. "This is just a little..." she trailed off as the examined the dials on the side of the instrument, then looked back at me, then back to the dials. Somehow, I never took her as the type to be at a loss for words, and yet, she remained quiet.

"Archmage Tiara?" Andella asked in a low voice, her hand tightening around mine where she still held it firm in her small, warm grasp. "What is it?" My group of well-wishers packed in close as they hovered over my bedside, echoing those same words right after her. What is it, indeed?

"Well..." the Archmage started in a careful tone, "these readings require some further research." The creases at the corners of her eyes crinkled as she attempted to brighten in the non-committal way of priests and scholars. "But I may have some ideas."

Andella stood in a flash, reaching for the measuring device. "I'd like to see those readings, please, Archmage?"

"Hmm? Oh yes, of course. But I will warn you..."

I don't know what Andella saw in those dials – I had no idea how to read such a thing. Even a fully-cognizant me could only see a confusing array of numbers placed in thirty different ways along the length of a sextant-type contraption roughly the size of a child's bent arm. What I did know was that what she saw left her pale, wide-eyed, wordless... and I didn't like it.

"Were my readings like this?" she asked after a long moment.

"Similar, yes, but there are some key differences. We'll discuss it more later, dear. Don't worry."

Readings, differences... I had no idea what it all meant, and apparently neither did anyone other than the Archmage and her apprentice. Others started asking their own questions – what was happening? Was I all right? They talked over each other all at once, and it seemed like nothing but one long cacophony. But in the tangle of words, I did hear one that grabbed my attention, just as if it had been sent down on a bolt of lightning.

Edin.

He was here. They said he was here, in this same room, alive. I had to see it for myself. No one seemed to like the idea of me hauling myself out of bed, including my own body – my muscles protested, and I got momentarily caught up in the long white robe they had wrapped around me. It didn't help that I had ten hands trying to put me back in bed. But I would have none of it, not until I knew.

So I pushed past them, through them, to make my way across a room that might as well have been wider than the Sea of Stars, and just as fraught with danger. I almost fell two, maybe three times, despite the strength of my uncle Brin, the only one in the entire place who seemed much more interested in what I could do, rather than what I couldn't. He said nothing, though, which was fine – I wasn't much for conversation.

On shaky legs, I moved through a parting crowd of nobility... and crashed. At least I got to my destination before I fell to my knees with the world spinning around me.

Now, I had been very, very drunk on more than a few occasions – like after those long nights of drinking contests at the Silver – but that was nothing by comparison. Everything twirled and swayed as I knelt by the bedside of the youngest heir apparent ever in Zondrell's history... and how I felt no longer seemed to matter. He was alive. King Edin Blackwarren was alive. I bowed my head and sent a silent prayer out to whatever god might find it, because at that moment, any divinity was worth thanking.

"Sir? Lord Loringham?" I heard a solemn girl's voice at my ear. When I didn't answer right away, she asked again. "Sir? Do you think he'll wake up... like you did?"

I looked up into intense dark eyes, full of hope and unrest. The Princess Larenne Blackwarren, Edin's eldest sister, had looked to me before with that same gaze in the sparring rooms at the Academy, and I couldn't help but offer a weak smile back.

Around us, though, I saw emotions ranging from amazement to contempt to fear in faces both familiar and less so, including the boy's mother, Queen Marianna. For her part, she seemed to share her eldest's daughter's cautious optimism, any suspicion or anger hiding beneath careworn yet still regal features.

"He will, I'm sure," was all I could offer, but the words felt hollow. In truth, I had no idea what kept her son on the shores of the River, or how to explain what that meant to all of them. Only Edin himself knew what would bring him back to his conscious form – there was nothing in his pallid cheeks and shallow breath to give away such secrets.

"Sir?" Larenne said. Her typical ferocity and swagger as the only female cadet in all of Zondrell's Military Academy was gone, and all I saw was a girl, barely eighteen with the burden of royalty settling heavy on her shoulders. "Sir, I'm... glad you're all right. That was quite the battle."

"Yeah," was all I could manage. If I remembered it clearly, it was an episode of my life I would rather forget.

"I remembered what you taught us, about blocking."

"You saw combat?"

The corner of her mouth quirked up into a smile. "Just for a few minutes."

"Good work, soldier. I'm..." I searched for the right words. "I'm sorry I couldn't do more for your brother."

"You saved his life. Don't listen to some of these people – I was there."

"It could have been different."

Larenne snorted. "That's right, he could be dead and Miller or some other fool could be fighting over the throne. You did the best anyone could. Thank you."

At that, I bent my head again, letting it rest heavy in my palms. It hurt too much to do anything else.

CHAPTER FOURTEEN

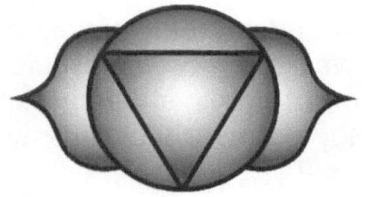

The Way Forward
11 Spring's Green, 1272
Jade Saçaille

My daughter, having never ridden a horse before, should have been terrified. At least, that's what I would have expected. Instead, she sat behind me in quiet fascination as we trotted down the long, long road, never once easing her grip around my waist.

For the first few miles, it had been welcome – it was perhaps the most physical contact we had shared since she was a baby. But by the time we reached the first of the outposts that held its allegiances not to Doverton, but to Zondrell, my ribs as well as my bottom ached. Vremya had kept us at a quick pace, our gray-and-white steeds moving easily across a landscape that had faded from rocky to barren to lush green.

"Vremya?" I called to him as we neared a second outpost, not more than a few miles from the first. Surrounding it on all sides were verdant fields of vegetables and wheat, another sight that had gotten more common the further south we traveled. It reminded me of the lands surrounding Quatremagne, although no mountains stood in majestic splendor nearby, and the only water was the sea, from here little more than a glittering jewel spreading along the western horizon. "Vremya!" I called again, louder.

He slowed, pulling up on the reins and waiting for my horse to close the gap. Behind me, Jardin loosened her grip just enough for me to take a deeper breath for once. "*Da,* Jade? You need something?"

"Vremya, this pace is relentless," I said. "Can we stop?"

"Zondrell is maybe ten miles up now. Not far. You can wait?"

Chantal's bones – had we really traveled almost thirty miles already? The time was going by more quickly than I imagined it would. Still, a look at Jardin's weary expression confirmed my own needs. "No, Vremya, we can't wait. Just for a few minutes."

The Drakannyan shrugged. "Guess it won't hurt. Not long, though. We get there before dark, *da*?" I didn't know what that meant, but there was an edge in his tone, indicating that perhaps we didn't want to find out what happened on the road after dark. And perhaps he had a point.

We chose not to stable the horses – there was no time – and instead found an open hitching post to tie them to along the lone dirt path that served as the main road in this place. This was a very small outpost, with only a few wooden buildings and one larger stone one near the center, no doubt the home of the farmer, or whoever ran this place.

An elderly couple approached as we dismounted and shook out the soreness from the journey so far, stopping to regard us with a smile. "Good day to you folk," the man said with a nod to me and another to Jardin. His Zondrean was marked by strange pitches and odd ways of cutting off and drawing out words, like someone who'd lived in the country all his life. I had occasionally heard travelers and merchants in the markets of Quatremagne who spoke that way. "Picked a nice day for traveling, but I 'ear it's raining by the coast. It'll come this way soon enough."

"We don't stay long, friend," Vremya replied with his customary grin. His eyes brightened in a way that made the old woman regard him with curiosity, and well she should have – how often do people in the country see magic at all, much less... *that*?

"Hey, that's quite the accent you 'ave there," the man said. "You folks ain't from around 'ere, I take it? Off to Zondrell or something?"

"*Oui,* Monsieur," I said with a smile.

"Well, be careful. A whole bunch of people passed by the other day from there. Said the city's closed – closed! Can you believe it? Who closes the biggest city in the world?" Who, indeed, I wondered. And why? "Sounds like trouble to me," he went on. "Well, they was looking for work, but old man Linarin ain't 'iring till 'arvest time, so they kept on going. To Kellen, I think. Long way from 'ere."

I looked at Vremya, nervous, but he seemed unconcerned. "Hey, thanks, friend. We'll figure it out when we get there. Any place we can buy a drink?"

From the outpost's tiny store, we purchased two bottles of wine, refilled our waterskins, and got Jardin one of those honeyed almond cakes the Zondreans liked so well. As she happily plunged into her sweet, we went back to the horses to adjust straps and all of the things one does when preparing for another leg of a journey. Luckily, Vremya knew much more about this than I did.

"By Chantal," I muttered, hands at my lower back in a vain attempt to stretch, "I haven't ridden like this in a long time."

"Is not so bad," Vremya offered as he tightened a saddle. "Could be worse – could be walking."

"So, I need to ask you something." I paused, considering. The question had arisen in my mind several times during the ride, but I'd kept stuffing it down. Now, with this pause and an introspective graying swirl of clouds overhead, it needed to come out. "Vremya, what happened to Safaa?"

He shook his head and wild tendrils of wispy dark hair went everywhere. "Don't know. Wasn't there. King Keis says she went home to visit, never came back. *Uzhasni.* Terrible thing. But that was a long time ago – seven years?"

Seven years. Of course, I was too busy trying to raise a little girl by myself in the big city then. Yet somehow, a pang of guilt in not knowing all this time still struck. Safaa had been a battle companion, a sister-in-arms, so to speak. She was graceful and gentle in word, though not necessarily in deed. In fact, I was afraid of her, secretly. Always had been. The things she could do with the lightning at her will... it was unearthly. "Didn't he send someone to look for her? I mean, it was no secret..."

A smile puffed Vremya's round cheeks. "He loved her. We know, everybody knows. He sent men to look, I guess, but they found nothing. Takes too long to get there – not sure what he thought he'd find." The Time mage shrugged. "What can you do, *da*?"

Nothing. We could do nothing, although I did commit a silent prayer then, even though the Katalahni warrior with the power of the Light itself would never have even acknowledged there were other gods beyond her own great Hashim, lord of sun and sand. She had always been stalwart on that point. Perhaps Chantal would pass the word along.

**

The road grew more crowded the closer we got to the city, and after a while, we could see its smoke rising from the horizon. Soon, the famous walls rose into view, glittering nearly golden-white, even with the setting sun shrouded in clouds. For the last two hours or so, it had begun to drizzle, and by the time we actually reached the perimeter, our cloaks and hair and everything else were soaked.

"Can we eat soon?" I heard Jardin's voice in my ear – it was the most she'd said all day.

"*Oui*, Jardin, when we stop. Look at the city. Doesn't it remind you of home?"

"There's no mountains."

"True, but look. Instead, there is an ocean."

"It's pretty." And it was, in its way. Even in the dying light, the city gleamed – I could see where it got its nickname as the "Jewel of the West." It might have been prettier still if it didn't have dozens – maybe hundreds – of people camped outside its closed gates.

The scene was shocking. It reminded me of refugee camps during the war, where I saw folk huddled in tents against the cold, their towns long since occupied or destroyed by the enemy. I didn't understand how someone could cast mothers and babies out into the depths of an Eislandisch winter – it was as incomprehensible then as it was now.

As we slowed our pace, we began to see women trying to keep campfires alight in the rain, merchants giving out the last of the stock they had intended to sell within the city, and men speaking in hushed tones together. Meanwhile, archers and armed guards stalked the heights of the city walls as if war was about to break out at any moment.

"Ah, Jade?" Vremya said over his shoulder. "Cover the little girl's eyes."

"Why, what do you..." Then I saw what he saw, and the words left me. I jerked hard on my horse's reins to turn around, away from the spray of blood and gore across the earth ahead.

The last thing I ever wanted to see in my entire life was the body of another dead Zondrell soldier – or any soldier, for that matter. Even just a glimpse in the gloom of twilight was enough to bring back a thousand wretched memories of tending wounds that would never heal, of listening to a stranger's last words as his soul was released to wherever he believed it went.

Sacred blood above, what were we *doing* here? How could I have let Vremya, of all people, lead me all the way out here to an apparent battlefield? I opened my mouth to start asking these very questions, but the next words I heard were not my own.

"Little girl, look up at the sky. See how the clouds wrap around the moon?" High above, early moon Larenne hid risen round and silvery-blue, and it fought off the encroaching rainclouds as best it could. Vremya was off his horse as soon as Jardin turned to look up, a blanket from his saddlebags in his grip. "*Da,* there you go. Is pretty, *da*?" he said as he did his best to cover the single soldier's body.

How did this happen? I could only guess, looking into the crowd of people. There were armed men in those clusters huddled around fires, mercenaries and bounty hunters and other such creatures who lurked in the shadows. Any one of them could have decided to take their argument straight to a solider trying to do his duty, and perhaps... who could blame them? Indeed, who *does* close one of the biggest cities this side of the Sea of Stars?

The body was sufficiently hidden by the time Jardin lost interest in the moon, thank Chantal. Now, she was pointing toward the gates, a questioning look on her face. "Mama?" she asked softly. "Why are they singing?"

I strained, but then I heard it, too, a continual chanting, not quite like a song, but something with a repetitive melody, over and over, repeating the same words. "Open the gates! Let us go home! Open the gates! Let us go home!" And it was infectious, as after some time, the chant began to grow in strength, more voices joining in.

"This is no good," Vremya said, starting toward the greater mass of people. "Maybe you stay back here, *da?*"

"What?" I shook my head. "No, don't... don't leave us here alone. Please." It felt odd to say such a thing. Vremya even looked at me sideways, as if he hadn't quite heard me. He knew all too well that this wasn't the first time in my life that I felt I was in some kind of imminent danger. But, it was the first time I'd felt that way with my daughter in tow. I was not about to let the only one of us with any real power just walk off.

"Then come, but we need to be close. Things are happening."

When Vremya said something like that, the words had true weight. "You've... seen it?"

"Possibilities, *da*." Good possibilities, or bad ones? He didn't say; perhaps it was better that way.

Open the gates! Let us go home! The din of background noise rose in volume, gradual, as when one fills a cup of tea. Keep pouring, and hot water spills out to burn everything in its path.

We moved toward the gate, slow, Vremya a few steps ahead while I held the reins of both horses. Around us, people either joined the incessant chant, or tried their best to ignore everything around them as they huddled by their fires.

At every opportunity, Vremya made it a point to reach for or brush against the things in our path – husks of old, burned-out campfires, discarded bits of cloth, a stray saddle without mount or rider. What did he see when he touched those things? I would never know, but each time a vision came to him, he seemed to become more intent on the mission. If only I knew what our mission was.

Open the gate! Let us go home! The chant was louder still, almost unbearable, and I noticed Jardin had put her hands to her ears to block them all out. If holding her would have soothed her, I would have done it; my heart and my bones ached for it, as they often did. But no amount of human contact would help her, and we both knew it. So she would sit there behind me, nervous and still with her hands at her ears and bobbing along to the gait of the horse, until her eyes went very, very wide, her cheeks as white as the light in her irises.

It took less than a second. Someone, somewhere, had some kind of weapon – a sling, perhaps, sending something flying through the air at dizzying speed. It was the full fury of the people there, people who had been kept from their homes, their families, their livelihoods. And that fury found a home in a soldier up on the wall.

The outpouring of cheers from the people on the ground combined with the roar of the guards above to become the most shrill, destructive sound I'd ever heard, harsher than any wartime battle cry. Worse was the crash of armor and bone as their target toppled to the ground. Even I wanted to put my hands to my ears… in fact, I wanted to grab up Jardin and run as fast as I could away from this accursed place and its accursed people.

But I couldn't do that, could I? No. No, because ten feet away lay a dying man, and there was something I could do about that. I might have been the only person there who could do anything in that moment. I didn't *want* to, but deep in my heart, I knew it was the right thing – the very tendrils of my soul seemed to pull me in the fallen soldier's direction. Hot tears struck my cheeks as I pushed past several cheering people and knelt by his side.

The magic hurt. It hurt so bad, I wept, and kept weeping. I couldn't stop, nor could I see through the stinging tears of anger and pain and sorrow. This healing magic had been my burden since I was twelve years old, and for a long time, I could bear it. Even when I faced men on the brink of death, I could bring them back… most of the time. And when I did, I felt a rush of gratitude, a prayer of thanks to Chantal who had gifted me with this most unusual power. Maybe I was the only person in the world who could heal others with only a touch, a thought, a whisper. I was performing a valuable service.

Except, it was a curse. Sometimes, they would still go to whatever god they served, despite everything I could do. I was no god myself – to assume otherwise was beyond arrogance. Yet, every loss felt like a crushing defeat, and there were so many who needed my help. Men were constantly warring with one another, and over what? I was tired of it, sick to death of it. My marriage had failed, and Jardin knew little of her own father because of it.

The sting of all those memories poured forth along with the ribbon of indigo-lavender healing light, moving out from my hands to seek the soldier's wounds. That was when I heard a scream... Jardin? I couldn't tell, and couldn't see her. Then I heard people gasp, a collective shock rippling through the crowd.

"You don't want to see more magic, friend," came Vremya's rough threat from somewhere behind me. "For your own good."

"But that's..."

"The General!"

"He's a traitor!

"And a coward!"

"What's she doing to him?"

"Don't you know who that is?"

"You can't possibly be *helping* him?"

"Demons!"

Questions and shouts of vengeance fell like lead onto the earth, but I ignored them all. I had other things to do. I didn't, in fact, know the graying warrior wincing and coughing on the ground before me. But when he opened his eyes, I saw steel-colored confusion, mixed with a more immediate sense of panic.

"By Catherine," he wheezed, clutching at the place where some kind of large rock had struck him in the head. "There are two of you?"

CHAPTER FIFTEEN

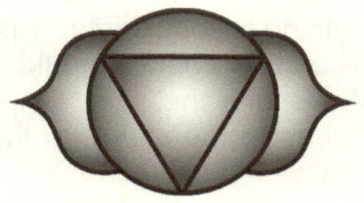

Pockets
11 Spring's Green, 1272
Alexander Vestarton

I think I kept screaming for a long time. I don't know how long. Time didn't matter anymore, did it? I just fucking stopped *all* of it. And I knew far too well that stopping living things meant stopping all of their systems, too – people did not just get caught like they were painted in a picture when Time magic enacted its judgment. They did not get to jump out of their stupor later and laugh about it. They just... ceased to be, their time effectively over. There was no going back.

Now I was left to sit there and watch the carnage I wreaked. So I screamed some more. Everything that I had ever eaten in my life came up to be deposited on the ground, until there was nothing left but hot bile. I wailed and rolled and cried, until it sounded like the gods had joined me.

Actually, I really did hear something amidst all of the silence, a sound, distant, strange, guttural... insistent? I tried to regain something of myself to listen. The voice came in as if on the wind, an odd voice with tight inflections. "Hey!" the voice was saying, over and over. I kept listening, trying to swallow back more sobs. With shaking hands, I wiped my mouth. "Hey, Time Mage? You hearing me? Listen to me!"

Wait... *what*? "I... hear you," I said, trying to make my words loud enough to get to wherever they needed to go.

The faraway voice sounded relieved. "*Da, da*, you good. You calm down. You open gate. We talk*, da*?" Open the gate? Well, I supposed I could, if I could find the strength to stand. The burning under my skin, in my blood and deep into my bones, was real, and it fucking *hurt*. Still, the voice with the heavy Drakannyan accent continued to prod, insistent. "One foot in front of the other, friend. Not much time here."

Time, time, everything's about time. Time just fucked me over – once again – and if I could, I would have spat at it and told it to go to hell. Despite the pain, I struggled on shaking legs and made my way to the stairs, to the control levers at the top of the wall that would make the gate open.

Before I grabbed them, though, I peered down to the other side, to all of the people below. All of them, just... stopped. Everyone, except for one short, nervous-looking fellow in a green cloak and simple attire, pacing back and forth. He looked up at me and waved.

"Come on, friend. We need to talk," he called up. "Easier not to shout, *da*?"

Maybe? I didn't know anything anymore, but after a moment's hesitation, I did as he asked and pulled – with considerable effort – on one of the two massive levers. Chains squealed and hinges creaked, and one of the two huge doors below began to open. I only let it open halfway, though, as it was about to smack into a group of statues. It seemed extremely wrong to let it do so.

When I went back downstairs, the man was already through and waiting for me. He eyed a nearby soldier with curiosity before turning his attention to me. "Hey friend, you don't look so good."

"Are you kidding me?" I advanced on him, and as I did, I found my voice rising. "Do you see what's happened here? Who the hell do you think you are?"

"Calm down, friend. It's not what you think. Calm down." Somehow his saying it wasn't terribly effective. I was anything but calm, and my hands balled up into fists at my sides.

"You have two seconds to explain yourself."

"Don't give away time so easy. Is bad for business, *da*?" The Drakannyan laughed. I did not. "You don't get it."

"What don't I get?"

"See the fire over there?" I looked and nodded, lips drawing to a thin line of rage. "No go, right? Raindrops? Clouds? You think you're that good that you can stop the whole world?"

"I..." I trailed off. He might have had a point. He certainly was less concerned about what was going on around us – or the lack thereof. Enough explanation, though, this was not. Far from it.

The man's smile never faltered. "No, you not good enough. Not you, not me, nobody, except maybe a god. And you? You don't look too godly to me, *da*?"

And then it hit me. Those bright eyes set in a jovial face had a quicksilver glint to them – the two of us, it seemed, were cut from the same mad, magical cloth. "So... what then?" I asked, my urge to punch this fellow Time mage in the jaw diminishing. "What does it mean?"

"I call it a... pocket. A little bit of time, tucked away." All I could do was stare at him quizzically. "Like we stepped off the road to take a rest. *Ti viidish*?" My blank stare with occasional blink must not have answered his question favorably, so he continued, speaking slower. "You and me, friend, we stepped outside time. Well, you did it – I'm just... helping."

A sense of realization – or maybe just blind hope – washed over me. It was not a warm feeling. "So... you're saying all these people are..."

"Not dead. Not stopped. Just waiting for us to come back. You see now?"

I considered this. I took another long look at the pained Zondrell watchman on his knees, then walked through the gates to the other side, where all of the caravanners and the farmers and the out-of-towners were frozen in their clamoring to enter the city, captured as living sculpture.

To the left I saw the prone form of General Torven, and the woman with healing magic kneeling at his side. Even the magic was caught in mid-stride, a single perfect streak of indigo-lavender, similar, but not quite exactly like I'd seen Andella create. This one seemed brighter, yet somehow darker at the same time. "Waiting for us," I repeated. "So they don't know that they're like that?"

The stranger came up by my shoulder, but stopped just short of offering any reassuring touch. "Don't think so," he said. "Never asked about that. Never had another Time mage to help me out, either. This is good pocket we have. Very stable. You're pretty good at this, friend." His round, ruddy face with its bushy beard was full of friendly cheer. Dear Catherine, did my eyes always look like that? His whirled and danced with their own inner light, silvery threads swirling down an endless drain.

"I don't know what I did."

"You… uh, you panicked." Still that smile – it almost made me want to smile, even though I felt like doing anything but. "That's how it happened to me first time, too. Took a week to get over. You, you'll be okay. Vremya's on your side!" He erupted into chortling laughter. If only I knew what was so damned funny.

"Vremya… I've heard that name. You know a big Eislander that goes by the name of Brin?"

"*Da*, been looking for that one. Lots to talk to about, friend. Later. Now, we work."

"Work?"

He had already turned away from me and was wrenching a club away from a gruff-looking farmer. "Get the weapons, throw them somewhere. No weapons, no fighting, *da*?"

"But…" Again, I lost my words behind a stormwall of confusion.

Another farmer, another weapon taken and tossed aside, this time a rather deadly-looking wheat scythe. "We change the possibilities from inside the pocket. Pretty neat when it works. Maybe not the best plan, but all we got, *da*? You help."

What else could I do? I mimicked him, wresting away clubs, pitchforks, slings, and swords from citizens and soldiers alike. Most didn't go too far, but some of the really dangerous things I put a little extra arm into, so they wouldn't be within easy reach when things… started up again. The whole episode was by far the most bizarre moment of my life, and by that point, I'd had my share of them.

"Can't keep going," Vremya said with a hand rubbing at his chest and throat as if he was taking ill. "Get in position." When I didn't do as he asked, he elaborated. "You in charge here, *da*?"

"Uh…more or less?" I paused, sighing. Oddly, I was starting to feel a little hoarse myself, and cleared my throat. "Rather a bit less than more."

"You got good clothes, and people know you, *da*? So, go stand in the middle – you can talk to them. Do... King things."

"But, I mean, I was up there. I can't be down over here in the blink of an eye. I'll look like I popped out of a fucking kids' faery story or something, won't I? "

"And what better way to get their attention?" This strange man, Vremya, winked, then grabbed for a pouch on his belt. From inside, he produced a blood-red painted flask. "Take a drink first."

At least we could come to terms on one thing – that Drakannyan brandy was the best I had ever tasted. It warmed me, soothed the savagery of the magic within, and gave me the fuel I'd need for doing something very, very insane.

As Vremya wandered back out beyond the walls muttering something about a girl, I grabbed up two swords from where we'd discarded them, went to the yawning opening of the gates of Zondrell, and held them out, one pointing north to the countryside, the other south toward the city within. Then I waited for the veil to be lifted, and time to resume its unrelenting forward motion.

It did so with very little ceremony. Everything resumed its forward momentum as if nothing ever happened, right up until people started realizing that their hands were now empty. Some started to turn, puzzled looks on their faces, to stare at the Lord who used to be up on the wall, but now was not.

In the mere blink of an eye, he had come to stand among them, before a gate that wasn't open a second ago. Worst of all, he was holding weapons that had previously belonged to other people. None of it made any sense. Were they seeing things? Were they somehow being tricked?

Nearby, the boy soldier facing down against the farmer looked up, and my gaze met his panicked one. His attacker, for his part, seemed stopped cold by the whole affair, and backed away slowly, in something of a daze.

"You all right, soldier?" I asked the kid. He nodded, though he seemed none too pleased when he touched his forehead and it came back sticky with fresh blood. I directed another guardsman to help him with barely more than a word – nothing else was needed – and turned back to the people. "Look, friends! There's no need for violence!" I shouted, adopting that lordly tone once again. It was a little harder to pull off this time, but I held my ground nonetheless. "Let me assure you of one thing: everyone will get to where they want to go. You'll go tonight, and you don't even need your papers."

Much stirring descended over the crowd. Implications ran the gamut between demon and savior as they sorted out what had just happened, and what might happen next. Could they trust me? Well, maybe if I tried a little harder to build that trust...

"Countrymen," I said to them, pushing the peaceful influence of my tone to its limits, "I am truly sorry that you have had to endure the troubles of the city for these past days. Please accept my deepest apologies, on behalf of the throne and the Council of Lords, and know that compensation for any business losses will be sent to your farms and businesses soon, on behalf of my own House Vestarton."

"What? Truly?" This came from a lot of sources all at once, but I had them. I could hear it in their voices. *I had them.* The way to a man's heart is always through his purse.

"We'll have it all sorted out soon enough. Business needs to continue for the sake of Zondrell. So, please, go home in safety, and may Catherine light your path. All I ask is that everyone make two lines, and keep things civilized. One line in, one out. We can do this quite peacefully. Guards, will you please help ensure everyone is comfortable and their loved ones accounted for as they head home?"

Noble grace oozed from my words, and it went very far in disarming a huge number of people. And then it happened – the first one through the gate was the farmer who'd clubbed the kid soldier, peering at me curiously as he stepped past. He gave me a wide berth, then started to break into a run as people on the other side began to cheer. Yes, they *cheered*, happy, gleeful cheers from suddenly ecstatic people.

And as they all began to follow suit, I personally welcomed nearly each and every one. "Welcome to Zondrell," I said, over and over in a litany of kindnesses. "Welcome home. Catherine light your path. Thank you for your patience. Lady smiles upon you." In between, guardsmen asked me things, and I responded without breaking my stride. They were to hold fast and not deny anything to anyone, citizen or no, and while it seemed to annoy a fair number, the men did what I asked.

Why? Because *I* was a demon, a magical, teleporting, bona fide demon. They were convinced, and I let them believe it.

**

"Lord Vestarton? Lord Vestarton?"

As the crowds began to disperse and the lines were all but dealt with, a young Royal Guard shouted insistently at me as he half-jogged, half-dragged himself to the Gate. The smart ones usually didn't run in their armor unless there was an emergency – I sure as hell hoped this one was an idiot.

"What is it, soldier?" I asked, turning to him.

As young and clearly strong as he was, the kid still had to work to calm his breathing. "Sir, I... I'm glad I found you, Sir. They sent me from the Palace. I was told to tell you, Sir..." He cleared his throat, and as much as I wanted to throttle him to make him spit it out, I was patient. "The Crown Prince and Lord Loringham have been found, Sir. They've been taken to the Academy for healing."

The next few minutes happened in a dream. My words failed me, and my heart almost did the same. I stared at the soldier slack-jawed until the presence of mind to dismiss him kicked in. And then there was the jovial, round-faced Drakannyan, approaching alongside a lavender-eyed woman and a sour-faced, strawberry-blond girl clutching a leather-bound book in one hand. That flask of very good brandy was offered again and I drank it. A lot of it.

Vremya merely smiled. "Is time to go, *da*?" he said.

I nodded. "I've got... some very important business."

The girl stepped forward then, head bent, refusing to meet my inquisitive gaze. She said nothing as she opened her book and held it out for me to see. Now, I like art – I inherited that from my father, and my collection at home was one of the best in the city. But I had never seen simple charcoal be capable of producing the detail, the shading, the sheer depth of the drawing I saw in that girl's hands.

It was a scene from somewhere that wasn't quite real, a distant seashore where dark water lapped against flat, featureless sand. And there, ragged and torn as if he had swum thirty leagues to get there, was a portrait of my best friend, the sword his father gave him when he graduated from the Academy in hand. He knelt on one knee, seemingly getting to his feet as he faced an unseen assailant in the shadows. I could almost see the spark in his eyes – it was *that* perfect.

"Where did you..." Without thinking, I reached out, but Vremya reached out just before my fingertips brushed the page.

"Maybe not too good an idea, friend," Vremya said. "Lots you can see in a picture like that. Let's talk on the way, *da*?" From the way he said the word – "*see*" – I knew exactly what he meant... and it was not a good feeling.

PART TWO

*E*verything must move through the Wheel – it is law, a rule that cannot be broken… The magic that we will into being comes from a place deep inside us, and connected far beyond the earth beneath our feet.

From *Roumalde Barrande Hariage, the "Mad Mage" of Lavancée,* 610

CHAPTER SIXTEEN

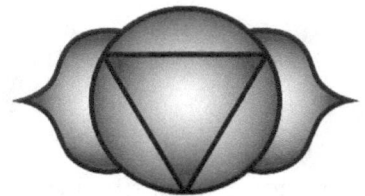

Past is Present
15 Spring's Green, 1272
Jade Saçaille

*I*ncessant rain pelted at the wide, extravagant windows of the place known as Vestarton Manor, and I was glad for it. Such weather meant that there would be no callers, no nobleman's guard to bring me somewhere and beg me to work my "miracles."

For the past three days, I had agreed – reluctantly – to help where I could, especially where the small boy at the Magic Academy's Infirmary was concerned. It wasn't as if I could deny them, when so many had witnessed what was possible with their General. A man crushed within his own armor should have died, but the Saint... the Saint can heal. The Saint can save. My gifts from Chantal were the talk of the city, from what I understood.

And I hated it.

It put me in a foul, bitter mood, and every moment I wasn't concentrating on the searing magic in my veins, I brooded in quiet thought, staring out at unfamiliar streets and wishing I had never left Doverton in the first place. Everything and everyone around me reminded me of things I wanted to forget, of war and death and danger no young person should experience. Even though the danger here in this protected, wealthiest of the wealthy area of the city was minimal, a general feeling of emptiness and unease seeped into my consciousness to the point where I had cried myself to sleep on more than one night.

Chantal's bones, what was *happening* to me?

On the morning of the fourth day of my stay with Lord Vestarton and his family, I was awake early, having only slept a few hours with the blinding light of the full moons shining through my bedroom windows. Larenne and Sarabande seemed so much brighter here on the coast, even through the clouds, and they seemed intent on torturing me with wakefulness and memories as persistent as the rain. As I lay there, considering whether I could force myself back to sleep, a knock at the door caused my heart to flutter.

"Miss Saçaille?" came the cool voice of the Vestartons' butler, the one they called Dennis. He was a kindly man, admittedly quite likable, and calm patience exuded from his person. He was also – quite lucky for him – the only person aside from my daughter who I would not have ignored or lectured for their rudeness at this hour. "Miss Saçaille, I am sorry to bother you."

I wrapped one of the many lush robes the Vestartons had provided around me as I padded to the door and opened it partway. "Can I help you, Monsieur Dennis?" I asked, fighting to keep the bitterness from my tone.

Through the doorway, I saw the butler bow low, in what I had come to know as his customary formal way. Why the Zondreans bent over so far as to offer their unguarded necks to those they greeted, I would never understand. A simple nod with the hand at the heart to acknowledge the grace of Chantal was all most Lavançaise ever needed. "Miss Saçaille," Dennis said, "you have a visitor in the east parlor."

"*Je m'excuse*? A visitor?" I frowned. "Someone from the Infirmary, then, *oui*?"

Dennis hesitated, and his tone said everything. I felt my blood go cold. "No, Miss. Not from the Academy."

"Is it urgent?"

"I am told that there is no particular rush, but your visitor will wait until you are ready."

My nostrils flared as tension filled the pit of my stomach and wrapped itself around my neck. Dennis knew who this person was, and yet he failed to tell me – on purpose. I wanted to tell him to go away, but instead what came out of my mouth was, "Tell this… visitor that I will be down in a moment."

He looked almost as surprised at my response as I felt. "Very well, m'lady," Dennis said with another bow, then departed.

My hands shook as I put on proper clothing. My heart raced. My eyes couldn't focus. Oh, I knew why, and I knew there was no real reason for it, but I couldn't help myself. My rational mind said that I didn't even know what any of this was about. It could be anything, but the sense of dread that filled me to my very core was real, persistent, not so unlike the last time an Eislander had come to see me early in the morning and unannounced. When Keis Sturmberg's men came to see the amazing girl who could heal wounds, I knew I was going to War. This time? Perhaps the rules had changed, but the battle felt much the same.

I took my time dressing and combing my hair before I made my way downstairs to the grand entry chamber, with smaller, more private parlors flanking it to the east and west. Tall windows reached from floor to ceiling every few feet, and during a nicer day, they would surely let in beautiful light to shine upon the statues and paintings of military and everyday subjects lining the inner walls. I had been told that this was one of the better collections in the entire city, and even though I knew little about art and was in no mood to enjoy it, it was still admittedly impressive.

The east parlor continued the décor of the main hall, and there *he* stood, admiring a small statue of a man with a spear and shield. Oh, he was different now, older and a bit more… refined? Perhaps, but there was still no question about his strength, the way he carried himself, or the meaning of those sinewy lines and patterns tattooed in all manner of red, blue, and black along his arms and across the great width of his chest. Each one a complement to a battle scar, a message to an enemy… they might be peering out from the open collar of a silken shirt, but even its fashionable Zondrean cut couldn't hide the Eislandisch warrior beneath. He was still Brinnürjn Jannausch – *General* Brin Jannausch, once a husband, once a father, but always a solider.

I knew it. I just *knew* it! Why in the name of Chantal did I not *stay* in Doverton? I could have told Vremya no, and taken my daughter back to the safety of our quiet home. I could have, and I *should* have, but oh no – I let myself be taken along for a ride, and to what end?

If my heart was racing before, it was ready to burst now. But I could keep my composure, just long enough to walk over and tell him exactly where he could go from here. All he did was watch me, eyes of blue crystal fixed on me in a way that made my blood boil that much more. The pent-up emotions of a decade raged within, so much so that I put no thought into what would happen the moment I would come to stand in his shadow again.

If I *had* taken time to consider, I might not have done what I did next, but by all that was holy, it was a long time coming.

I hit him, open-palmed across the jaw with everything I had. His head turned with the blow, violent and sudden, but those pale blue eyes remained unreadable.

Before he could do anything else, I hit him again – by Chantal's blood, did that feel *good*. On my third strike, though, my wrist was caught, mid-swing in a grip like stone. And still, his expression betrayed nothing beyond the few extra years worn into his strong, angular face. A pang of distant memories made me falter a bit, but not so much as to stop my attempt to break free. My efforts were in vain.

"I will say what I want to say. After, you do as you wish," he told me in a voice that had roughened, but was still deep and powerful enough to make me relax in his grasp and abandon whatever I thought I was accomplishing.

His eyes were still as cold as I'd ever seen them, but there was something else there, too... pain. Just a glimmer, but it was there, and I suddenly felt ashamed of myself. What was I doing? What good could violence do us now, after so many years? I felt my cheeks flush and my skin grow hot and cool all at once, but I said nothing. I did nothing, just stood there, feeling anger and embarrassment and a host of other things too indistinct to name.

I must not have seemed like much of a threat anymore – as if I ever was – and he released my wrist. As he touched the inside of his bottom lip, I felt a tiny flash of panic when I saw it stained red, though he seemed unconcerned.

"When they said you were here, I wanted to tell you something. I wanted to tell you that..." He swallowed hard. "All

I ever did was protect my family. All I ever did, all I wanted to do."

My jaw clenched and I practically had to spit out my words. "You wanted to do nothing but fight, Brin. We both know that."

"The fight leads to strength. Strength leads to protection. There are other ways, but young men... do not understand. I was young then."

His Zondrean, I realized, had gotten much better over the past ten years. Though the accent was strong, his words were well chosen, and they stung. But I wasn't ready to back down. "Is this some kind of apology, Brin? Because honestly, I don't see..."

"I apologize for nothing. I just wanted to speak."

"Because I never gave you the chance." It wasn't a question – just fact. I didn't then, and a part of me was surprised that I was doing it now. He hadn't earned the gods-blighted *right* to stand there and offer his veiled not-apologies for years of danger and neglect and...

"Because I wanted to speak and to be heard. That is all."

But that wasn't all. We stood there in silence for a long time, staring at each other. It was like looking through the depths of time, and my memories could easily carve out the younger man from within weathered features. The harsh, unforgiving, and damned-near feral man that he was once had remained, yes, but it was tempered by something more than just age.

If the man were a blade, he would bear the most honed edge in all of history; yet, I could also see the repairs, the nicks and scratches, the places where battle had left its permanent marks. There was pain in those imperfections, even within the victories.

"Chantal's bones, Brin..." I started to say, but I couldn't finish my thought. There were too many words swirling in my mind to put them to any good use.

Without waiting for me to continue, he reached into a pocket at his breast and pulled out a rumpled but neatly folded piece of paper. As he opened it, I realized it was Jardin's picture of Brin's great sword he called Beschützer – the Protector. It leaned casually against the fence that once lined our garden back in Quatremagne, with flowing runes in the Eislandisch language emblazoned on a blade caressed by tall grass and flowers. It was the distant memory of a little girl's father, a precious thing held up gingerly for me to view. "I ask for nothing," he said, voice soft, "because I know the response. But if you choose to tell her, it is safe."

Again, I felt embarrassed. I was a fool – worse, a heartless one. My sister might have been able to put her emotions aside at a time like this. Onyx would have been able to stand there and look him in the eye and tell him to go straight to whatever River he believed in. And there was a time where I believed I could have done the same thing, but that was easier when there were no pale blue eyes full of keen intelligence and wild abandon and decades-deep scars staring back at me. Holy Word immortal!

I wiped away the single tear that had fallen down my cheek so harshly that I might have scratched myself in the effort. "Jardin asked Onyx to give it to you. I didn't think she would, to be honest. When did you see her?"

For the briefest second, his gaze cast downward. "The night we nearly lost my nephew."

"Oh... *oui,* Jardin's 'cousin.'" I had heard about all of that from Lord Vestarton, mostly listening in on the tale as he told it to Vremya over I don't know how many bottles of brandy. If I hadn't known better, I would have thought that Tristan Loringham was something out of a legend – perhaps he really did share a bloodline with Brin, after all. "How does she know she has a cousin, Brin? She's never met this man. You never even *told* me you have a sister. It's... everything is madness right now."

He began to fold the picture again, his big hands precise and gentle as they moved. "You should let her talk to him," he said softly.

I felt my lips tighten into a thin line. "I don't know, Brin. I..."

"I would like to see her, too. But as I say, I will not ask."

Blood like ice rushed through my body, thundering in my head. I looked down at the marbled white floor. "We've been on our own for a long time, Brin," was all I could offer.

"*Ja,* I know," he said, voice terse. He could have told me it was my fault, and he would have been right. He could have told me I was wrong, and maybe he would have been right about that, too. Though, if he had said those things, I might have slapped him again – my body even tensed in anticipation.

Instead, he simply folded his arms across his broad chest and offered me the sideways, tiny smile that had made a much younger me melt into girlish silliness. "It is your choice, Jade. It has always been your choice."

So it was. Damn the heavens... Onyx would have chided me for my softness. Yet, for the first time in over ten years, I realized something: I had injured the great warrior. Me – the sweet and unassuming little Saint – had brought General Jannausch nearly to his knees, and caused wounds that would not heal with any magic or remedy. This was as close as he had ever come to pleading in perhaps his entire life, and... gods above, how did we come to this? I couldn't even remember our last conversation, our last argument.

I gathered my resolve, took a deep breath, and looked him in the eye. "*Oui*, Brin," my words came out slowly at first, then tumbled forth, more quickly than I could make full sense of them. "You may see her. Just don't... don't break her heart? She needs her Papa, not... damn it, Brin, you know what I mean." The tiny smirk became more pronounced then, because he *did* know. He always knew.

Then he was looking through me, as if imagining, or remembering. He straightened to attention, the soldier within springing to action. "They will be ready at the Loringham house. Come on your time. It is the house across the street, with the frost-tip flowers in front."

"I know – Vremya told me."

"Bring him, too, and Vestarton. Drinks may need to be shared, *ja*?"

A drink... Chantal's immortal breath! I would no doubt need one to get through this day.

CHAPTER SEVENTEEN

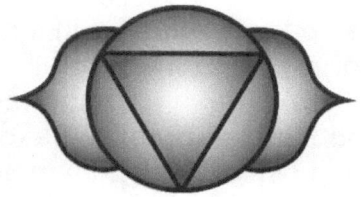

Research Begins
15 Spring's Green, 1272
Andella Weaver

On the first day after Tristan came home, I was polite. I knocked, and when the door of the study that was once Lord Jonathan's stayed closed, I left it that way. The next day, I called to him with a gentle knock, and got a brusque, "Come back later," in response. I did as asked, and got the same answer in the hours to come.

By the third day, well… I was worried, and yes, a little upset, too. So this time, I opened the door – just a crack, not all the way. "Tristan?" I peeped, sounding far less confident than I wished I did.

Some rustling of papers, then I heard his low voice, hoarse from disuse. "Is something wrong?"

This was as much an invitation as any, so I poked my head inside. There were papers strewn *everywhere*. Most of it was on the desk itself, under several spent quills and bottles of ink, but some of it was on the floor too, in piles and the occasional crumpled-up balls. Tristan himself was at the center of this whirlwind, unshaven, disheveled, and with a look of intense concentration etched into his features. "I don't know," I said, "you tell me."

His eyes radiated softly as they locked in my direction. "Nothing's wrong."

The way he said it disarmed me so much, I lost almost everything I was going to say next. "Um, Tristan, I..." I stammered.

"Look, I need to concentrate, Andella. If you need something, tell me. If not, I'll be done when I'm done."

"And when will that be?"

"I don't know."

I put my hands on my hips, suddenly feeling... sad? Indignant? A part of my mind tried to tell me that this wasn't the right reaction. He'd been through a lot – he needed sympathy now, and time and rest. He didn't need me or anyone else bothering him or pushing him beyond his limit.

That was, of course, the logical part of me, but then there was the other part, the girl who wanted to spend time with a man she thought she might have lost forever. We'd shared something, after all, somewhere in a dream or another place entirely, and we hadn't even talked about it. I had feelings, too – didn't he know that? "Well," I heard myself saying, as if from very far away, "I hope it'll be soon. You can't just lock yourself up forever, you know. I'm... worried about you."

It was enough to give him pause, to cause his features to soften, but not a lot. "Do you think I don't know that? Do you think I've not heard my mother say the same thing, and Alex, Brin, even Frederick and Lissa?"

"But we care about you. *I* care about you. You can talk to me."

He closed his eyes and breathed deep. Whatever he might have said before taking that moment to calm down and think, I wasn't sure I wanted to know. "Look, I just can't think... and I need to. All right?" Something about the way he looked at me then made me want to start crying, but I held myself together.

"Maybe you need to step away," I said. "Go rest, and then come back to it later. You know, get a fresh perspective?"

"Maybe." There was so much wrapped into that one word... defeat? Pain? It was so hard to tell. I started to approach, thinking maybe I could sit with him a while, but his hard stare told me to stay where I was. "You know, maybe you should head over to the Academy for a while – get Alex to take you. I just... I need time."

Weak, I nodded. "Sure. Of course." And there wasn't much else to say, was there? No, not really, because in the next breath he was already poised over his papers again, returning to his own little world. I backed away and closed the door, fighting back tears the whole time.

**

Rain threatened after the morning clouds had settled over Zondrell, and the air had a slight bite to it as we moved through the quiet city streets. Alex was his normal, dapper self during the walk between the house and the Academy – apparently, he'd needed to get out anyhow, so he welcomed the chance to escort me. But I could only handle small talk for a few blocks before I blurted out what was really on my mind.

"Aren't you worried about Tristan? You know he's barely left his study since he came home. It's been almost three days – he looks so miserable."

Alex waved it off with a dismissive gesture. "He'll be fine."

"Are you sure? Alex, I just tried to talk to him and he… he's not himself."

The quicksilver in his eyes seemed to swirl in time with our steps. "Look, you know as well as I do that Tristan's not… *good* at feelings. They don't agree with him. This time, well, let's just say that I don't think we can empathize – there's nothing any of us can say to help, you know? Just give him his time."

"But I…" I could try. I could *listen*. People need that when they're going through difficult moments. And I wanted to say all those things, but there was wisdom in Alex's words, wasn't there? As painful as it was, I suppose I could admit that much. "No, you're right. I'm sure you're right."

Alex knew Tristan best, after all – why wouldn't I trust him? So I did, for the moment, and we didn't say much else until we parted ways at the entrance to the Magic Academy Great Hall.

**

"All right, dear, try again, will you?"

I looked deeply into the milky-white center of the focusing crystal before me, trying to use the technique that every beginning mage must master before anything else. My will, my "essence," needed to flow into that crystal, as effortlessly as water pouring from a pitcher.

Simple as that, right? Oh sure, many new mages actually laughed when they were taught this for the first time, and I had been no different. How does someone just *send* their will somewhere, much less into a rock? But a good focusing crystal is no ordinary stone, and the smartest students figured that out quickly enough.

A very highly attuned crystal is even less ordinary, and this one before me was so powerful I could almost hear it, like a tiny, one-note hum from very far away. The humming seemed to get louder after a time, then louder still, until I was definitely sure it was there, and quite real. Soon, it was all I could hear, but I kept listening, staring, concentrating.

Then I felt the tears falling down my face, and the sound cut off in an instant.

"I'm sorry, Archmage," I said, choking back a sob. By the Lady, why now? I'd been doing so well! "I thought I'd put the morning behind me, I guess. I'm sorry."

Archmage Tiara tilted her head in that puzzled way she had. "Oh dear, is everything all right?"

"It's fine, it's... nothing."

"Are you in pain? Is there a problem?"

I shook my head, almost too insistent. "No, no, of course not. I'm fine. I'm just tired."

"I have seen many people driven to tears over lack of sleep. Quite common in the young ones, really, as you're more than likely aware. However, you are not a student any longer, and I would daresay that you, dear, are not exhibiting the physical signs of such a weakened state. Are you certain that sleep is your issue?"

Of course, she was right, just as always. At her curious frown and arched eyebrow, my gaze simply collapsed to the floor. "I... well, no, I guess not. I'm sorry, Archmage – let's try again. I'll do better next time."

"I don't think so." Characteristically, she folded her arms across her chest and continued to stare at me, her patience appearing to wear quite thin. Uncharacteristically, though, she bore a gentle smile and a gaze full of sympathy and interest. It might have even been genuine, though it was hard to tell. I'd never seen her take much of a personal interest in anyone, student, colleague, or otherwise. "Tell me, dear, how is Lord Loringham?"

It was the last question I wanted her to ask, and the last one I wanted to answer. "Oh... we haven't talked much."

"Has he been resting as he should? Taking his medicines and all that?"

Somewhere in the midst of the laboratory, the rhythmic *tick-tick-tick* of a water clock filled the empty space between us. After a good number of ticks had gone by, I finally shook my head. "I don't know. I don't know, Archmage – he's barely said two words to anyone since he came home."

"And you're upset by this."

"Wouldn't you be upset if your future husband would barely speak to you for three days? I just tried, and... it hurts, Archmage. You know?"

The greatest magic researcher Zondrell had ever known – a myth of a woman to many, and a tyrant to that many more – placed one hand gently on my shoulder and gave it a good squeeze. Soothing energy flowed through her palm. "Of course, dear, of course."

"He's locked himself up in his study, he's writing and writing all day and all night. I have no idea what he's even writing about. That's why I came here. I mean... I can occupy myself, and I have been. But I also told him he can talk to me. I'll listen, I'll understand. He just won't do it."

"But will you truly understand? Trauma is a difficult thing, dear. Very difficult to describe, very difficult to solve. Some people never do. Did you ever hear the stories about Master Tevell Woods?" I furrowed my brow – the name was familiar, but I couldn't quite place it. "No? He was the top researcher here around the time I graduated, and decided to stay on to teach. Master Tevell was also an Earth mage, highly competent, quite learned, particularly on the subject of plant life. He was far more interested in finding new ways to grow things than he was in stone-shaping and those sorts of things that we Earth mages often find ourselves doing. In fact, he often talked about his dreams of creating and sustaining farms from nothing but magic. Rather beautiful if you think about it."

"No one would ever be hungry," I said, a slight smile on my lips because I had to agree, it was a wonderful thought.

"Quite. Many saw him as something of a dreamer, but he was certainly a hard worker. He was, more or less, a slave to his own research. There were times when he wasn't seen for days on end. No one bothered to check on him, of course, because they knew what he was doing took concentration, patience, lots of quiet time." The Archmage considered for a moment, her gaze lost in another place. "Well, his laboratories were right down the hall here, last doors on the right. When I moved in, we had some shared space – he'd sometimes come over to lend or borrow a book or two. We respected each other."

"But he's not working there now. All of that is your space, isn't it?"

The water clock continued its relentless count of second after second until about sixty of them had come and gone. "It is, but I don't use it much. A good space to store things, I suppose – all of his old books on flora are still there. In fact, that day I found him, I was looking for just such a book, something about root patterns. I thought I was on to something. The door wasn't locked, and it had been closed for a while, maybe a couple of days. But that was common, like I said. Still, I did need that book, so I invited myself in – quiet, of course, so as not to disturb him too much." Archmage Tiara paused and swallowed hard. If I wasn't crazy, I might have even thought I saw a tear slip down her cheek... but that might have been a trick of the light. "Do you know, Andella, that I found Master Tevell dead on the floor, in that room down the hall? He'd expended far too much of his energy. It... wasn't a pretty sight. I won't forget it, but do you know something else? That was damn near forty years ago, and I have yet to have told another living soul more than two words about that day."

I clasped my hands together at the center of my chest and bowed slightly, a gesture of condolence often seen in church during funeral services. "Oh, Archmage, I'm so sorry."

The tears long gone, her features hardened back into that wise, knowing look she'd become famous for. "The point is, these things take time, yes? Such a thing as what Lord Loringham has experienced is enough to make a scar that lasts. Patience, as they say, is a virtue, yes?" I nodded, because she was right, and I had known that, but still... knowing and doing were two very different things. "My greatest regret is that I was too absorbed in my own work to pay enough attention. I'm sure that you will not fall prey to that folly, but keep him at arm's length, dear. That is my best advice."

"Thank you, Archmage," I said softly.

"In the meantime, I have a thought. Let's try a small experiment – humor me, will you?" She gestured toward the attuned crystal resting on its small wooden stand, and I felt my lips draw into a thin line – I wasn't really feeling up to more experiments in that moment, but how could I say no?

"Sure. Of course."

"Concentrate on the crystal again, dear, but this time, think about how you feel. Let the tears flow, if you will. Don't mind me, just sit with your feelings and focus, yes? Can you try that?"

"I... I suppose I can." It was a strange request, to be sure, and at first, I felt inhibited. I wasn't quite sure I could do it. She was sitting there, staring at me, silently judging while I focused my will into that crystal. What did she expect to happen? I could only wonder, although the more I wondered, the more I realized that it was too difficult to guess at what she might be thinking. There was no mind-reading magic, as much as everyone wished there was at one time or another. Life would be so much easier that way.

I felt a pull at the corners of my mouth as I sat there, becoming more and more engrossed in the crystal's pull until I could hear its soft hum again, that one-note buzz. It began to resonate with me, through me, and then...

I went blind.

I leapt to my feet with a sharp yelp as my chair flew backward and hit the floor with a crash. The sound of my own voice might as well have been that of the Lady herself, thundering through my head.

"Oh dear. Well, I suppose that's why we keep most of the books out of the focus rooms," said a rather surprised Archmage Tiara, very close to my ear. I felt firm hands guide me backward a few steps as the bright white flare before my vision gradually dimmed from midday summer sun to blacksmith's forge to torchlight. In fact, a torch-sized fire had sprung to life near where I stood, the rug there curling up at the corner while the flames gnawed at it.

"Did I... did I do that?" I asked weakly. It was the most I could do as Tiara put her boot to the small blaze.

She offered me the biggest smile I had ever seen her offer anyone – it was almost unnerving. Not many, student or master or otherwise, saw Archmage Tiara Chandler in such a... well, a state of glee. Her eyes were bright and whirling as she pointed at the charred end of the rug. "Ha! This is why we do research! My dear, you've just proven one of my central theories yet again. Emotion and stress bring out the deepest and most powerful magics, not training, and certainly not divine inspiration." She sniffed out a short derisive laugh. "Do you feel any better yet?"

"I guess a little?"

With the quickness of a woman half her age, the Archmage righted the chair and gestured to it. "Sit, sit, my dear," she said, and I did as she asked. Within moments, a resonation receptor hovered an inch from my eye; in another moment, her smile bloomed even bigger than before. "Ha! Would you look at that?"

"Um... Archmage?"

Her self-satisfied grin was almost too big to contain. It made her look at least twenty years younger. "My dear, you just sat with a focusing crystal attuned for Fire. I did the same thing, with the same crystal, and I was unable to evoke a reaction – I tested it first, of course, for safety. But *you*, you were, before that moment, empty, correct? Negative readings, no magic at all? And before *that*? You held what we're calling Life magic, a completely different thing all together. And then you sat with this crystal, under a very specific set of conditions, and... as the Lavançaise would say, *voilà!* Look in the mirror, my dear."

As with most of the focus rooms, full-length mirrors sat on the walls at either end, so that mages could check the vibrancy and color of their eyes after training or meditating. When I entered this place an hour ago, I had glanced at myself, only to see eyes staring back that were plain and grass-green. It was still odd to see them that way – like so often when I looked in the mirror lately, I saw someone I didn't know there.

But now, I saw the girl I had been when I was in my learning prime here at the Academy, an inquisitive young country girl with orange-red Fire in her eyes and a passion for learning.

Even if she would never go on to become a famed battlemage or a court wizard, that girl was going to make a difference to people who needed her, to serve the Church as a Pyrelight.

"Sweet Lady in Paradise!" I blinked, and the girl in the mirror did the same. It didn't seem real.

"From your initial readings, and that of Lord Loringham, I have been able to surmise a few things," the Archmage started to explain, taking on the tone she so often used in the lecture hall. "His readings had changed nature – there were elements of... well, an *element* that hadn't been there before, correct?"

I might have answered, but I was still staring at the way the colors danced within my irises, as if for the first time ever. My fingers touched the glass, and for a moment, a sputtering flame appeared there, reflecting bright back onto itself in a tiny explosion of red, yellow, and orange. It died almost as soon as it flared to life, but the next time, my will had it secured and it pulsed, without smoke or scorch, along the surface of the mirror, tracing a circle around my hand.

By the Goddess, it had never felt so good to feel that Fire – it warmed me from the inside out, nothing like the burning hot agony that came with Life magic. It was gentle, kind, like a good friend rather than a demanding despot. I could command Fire comfortably, without self-doubt, whereas the healing indigo light... well, that was another story, maybe one that would never be told again.

"Andella? Are you well?" came the Archmage's voice, as if from far across the room. In fact, she hadn't left my side.

"I'm... fine, I guess? It feels just like it used to. I... I don't know what to say."

"Well, I do hate to say this, dear, but it's likely to be temporary." The Archmage patted my arm. "You've clearly suffered some sort of drain or absorption effect. I've heard of this sort of thing before, but never seen it for myself."

"Was it from the obsidian or whatever was in the sea floor?"

She shook her head, but her brow furrowed at the same time. "Well, there's no evidence to support it, but the theory is rather interesting. The obsidian material augments magic – it's never been shown to diminish it, though I admit something else may have been at work here. We can make assumptions about things like magical instability based on unknown elemental properties and so forth, and… wait. What can you tell me about the duality principle?"

It had been a few months since I had been fixed with the questioning glare of the great Tiara Chandler. I felt like I was right back in the middle of one of her lectures again, even though there was no test to fail here. "Duality?" I squeaked out my answer nonetheless. "Every element has an opposite."

"Yes, and what's the opposite of Light? Darkness, would you agree?"

Darkness? Well, that made sense, but… "That's not a magical property, is it?" The idea left me cold, chilled to the bone in spite of the little spark of Fire buried deep within me.

"Why not? I hadn't seen healing and the stopping of time until a few weeks ago. These things are all quite new, and I daresay rather exciting. I'm inclined to accept a theory around 'Darkness magic' for the time being, but we need to study further. And to do that, we need Lord Loringham."

"I don't know… I don't think he'll agree."

She held up a finger. "Not today, but in time. If you recall, when I took your readings in the Infirmary, your levels had changed at exactly double the magnitude of Lord Loringham's. What do you think this tells us?"

"That… we both experienced the same thing, but mine was… worse somehow?" By the Goddess, it made sense. I started to piece it all together out loud, realizing even as I spoke that I must have truly sounded mad. It didn't matter much at this point, I supposed. Those crazed words spilled out well before I had a chance to even think about holding them back. "The sea floor, when I touched it and fainted, I went to this place. Tristan was there, but it was surreal, it was… I don't know how to describe it. I couldn't touch him, though – it was like some force was keeping us apart. But I could talk to him, and he was so far away, Archmage. I can't describe it. We drank from this great black sea, and then this fog rolled in, like the kind of fog that you can't see through no matter what you do. I lost him out there… and the next thing I knew, I was awake."

All the while, she listened quietly, occasionally scratching a note on a stray piece of paper. "Do you know something, dear?" she asked when I'd finished. I didn't know much of anything then, other than I felt like crying my eyes out all over again. "I just had a rather inspired idea."

I sniffed back an oncoming sob. "What's that?"

"Let's get you back to the research site. With what we've learned so far, we might be able to put a few more pieces of the puzzle together. We might even be able to get your magic back more permanently... someday. Unlikely today. But are you up to it?"

I breathed deeply. A thin, delicate arc of flame played between my outstretched fingers for a moment, and I marveled as its glow faded into the air. That simple trick wasn't possible yesterday – today, it was mine to control once more... even if it seemed to grow weaker each time I called upon it. "Maybe. I do think you're right about the magic being temporary."

The Archmage scratched down a few more notes. "That crystal you used was attuned using the same material in the sea floor. It's intended to enhance a Fire mage's abilities, and it did just that. But it's quite indirect, and probably more than a little imprecise."

"So you want me to... touch the obsidian again?" When she nodded, I felt my heart skip and start thundering in my chest. "I mean, have they done more research? Did anyone else... you know, have the same experience I did?" Tiara shook her head, slow and a bit sad, not so much in sympathy but more because her experiments had yielded no results – yet. I took a deep breath. "I was *there*, Archmage. I mean, I was there with him, in that place. I remember how the seawater *tasted* like salt. It was more than just a vision."

"I don't doubt you, dear. I discount nothing, otherwise I'd be more charlatan than scholar. I've seen The Box trigger a similar reaction for Lord Loringham – I made extensive notes based on his descriptions, and..." She trailed off, then jumped up to her small pile of books and papers left by the door. After rummaging for a while, muttering to herself, she pulled out a stack of loose papers with a triumphant, "Ah-ha!"

"What is it?"

After reviewing her scribbled numbers and figures on the pages for a long time, she looked up. "What do we know?" Of course, I had no answer. "Exactly!" she erupted in the next breath with fresh, new-theory excitement. "Dear, we have hit upon something very, very interesting. We have seen that magic can be, shall we say... dampened, or it can be amplified, correct? Darkness and Light may be key to those things. You mentioned dark fog: if we make a logical assumption that this is Darkness in a magical sense, then perhaps *that* is its purpose, to dampen or nullify other magics. The resonation material, meanwhile, we have confirmed is a means to amplify it. Perhaps Light is, too, yes? If you and Lord Loringham return to the research site together, I predict we may be able to bring back your Fire more permanently."

"But..." I started to protest, and she held up a finger to silence me.

"I understand. It would take some time and some persuasion, yes? And no doubt you're worried that the opposite could happen, or that you might fall into this 'dream place' that you spoke of. That's it, isn't it?" Of course it was – she didn't have to even ask. "Indeed. I have my theories about that, too. Well, the research site isn't going anywhere, so I won't pressure you, but that happy little accident with the Palace really created quite the opportunity. There's a great deal yet to learn from that sea floor, and you could be part of that, if you wished. Take a walk, dear – go see it for yourself. It's really quite amazing."

Just take a walk... think it over. Imagine the possibilities. I could do that, couldn't I? "I suppose it would be a rare opportunity, wouldn't it? I mean, research on that scale..."

"If nothing else, the research site is certainly something to see, if I do say so myself. And who knows? You might even discover something we haven't thought of yet. You have to remember, this research is *very* important – maybe more so than we even realize. Oh, the papers and books... half the world's mages will hate me indefinitely when I publish this. It's truly exciting, don't you think?"

Exciting? I didn't know what to think, but exciting wasn't the first word that sprung to mind. There was a part of me that wanted desperately to know more, to uncover the knowledge and solve that mystery right alongside her. Maybe that was the mage in me, but the country girl from Doverton?

She was still terrified.

CHAPTER EIGHTEEN

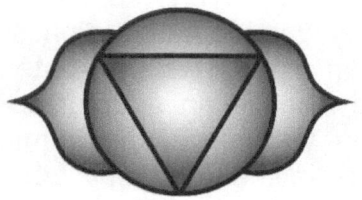

Look Sharp
15 Spring's Green, 1272
Alexander Vestarton

A few months ago, it would have been unusual to see an eight-man contingent of soldiers gathered around a relatively modest home on Sandstone Row, not six blocks south of the Gods' Avenue. Come to think of it, I had never gone this particular way before in my life. What business would a nobleman from the *best* part of town have in a neighborhood where the so-called common people lived? It was a quiet street, though, unassuming, with neat little wood and stone houses stacked up in a straight line that continued down the next hill and far out of sight. They probably saw as few soldiers down here on a typical day as we did six blocks north, if not fewer.

Until, of course, there were no more typical days.

And what did I expect, really? An overnight miracle? After less than a week, opening the gates to allow trade and movement once again hadn't done a whole hell of a lot, on the surface. A few more homes and businesses lay dark now, and streets were emptier as people who had the means had packed up and left for saner places.

More Zondrell troops had been brought in from our outposts to bolster the dwindling numbers of Army and City Watch inside the gates who hadn't yet defected. It seemed we needed every man we could get, as clusters of ruffians and general rabble-rousers continued to roam around, calling for justice or peace or whatever it was they thought they wanted in that moment. It wasn't even about whatever was happening in the Palace anymore. For the average person living a perfectly average existence, the thrill of looting a store, or threatening an old woman on the street, or just generally challenging authority was too much to pass up.

I could have taken a much shorter route from the Academy, where I'd escorted Andella an hour or so ago. I could have remained drier and warmer in the comfort of the indoors, maybe read a book in the Academy Library before heading back home. Hell, I could have even gone around the circle to the Military Academy and talked with some old acquaintances there, that sort of thing. But no, instead I decided to turn a few extra corners, all so that... what, exactly?

To check up on an old friend, of course – I couldn't resist. The loyalists among his men had stashed him here, at a cousin's house, out of sight and out of mind of most who cared to know whether he was alive or not. They had other things to worry about right now, but currently, I didn't.

My sense of obligation – and guilt – damn near demanded I pay a visit. After all, I was the one who decided to spring the Gentleman General for my own interests, and he paid a price. Some said it was fitting. Others said it wasn't enough. But despite his track record as a human being of late, I still felt... responsible. It wasn't a great feeling.

The men standing guard before the house on Sandstone Row were all Army. They made no move as I approached, and looked terribly out of place aside the pristine, white-painted shutters and two matching carrotwood trees in the front garden. None of them gave any concern for the rain that had turned from an early-morning deluge into a pissing sort of spray that hung in the air. This damnable season couldn't end soon enough.

"Honestly, do you think you're fooling anyone standing around out here?" I said to the eldest among them, a middle-aged soldier I recognized right away. He had the look of a man who had seen real combat in his day, but didn't care to speak of it.

Sergeant Delrin raised an eyebrow but still saluted with no hesitation. "No, Sir, I do not. Anyone who wanted to know, already does. There's no point in deception, Sir."

"Lady's linens, news travels fast."

Looking past me with dark eyes into the streets beyond, Delrin breathed deeply. Those few who passed gave the house and its guardians a wide berth, and this seemed to give him some secret satisfaction. "Indeed," he said, jaw stiff, tone stoic. "With so many miracles happening lately, more people are going to the Temple. I'm sure they talk about more than the Lady there."

I gave him a sideways look. "Can demons create miracles? Didn't know that."

"Lord Vestarton, Sir, I've seen a lot in my time. I fought at Quatremagne and watched them turn a king into a slave. I led men on campaigns for fabled weapons that didn't exist. I witnessed my General rise from the dead and a Lord move like a ghost. But I still don't believe in demons, Sir."

"You're a good man, Delrin." And I wasn't lying. He was probably one of the best the Zondrell Army had, honest and stalwart, the kind a lot of soldiers could take lessons from. I didn't know him well, but I knew him well enough to know that much, which was why he was here. He might not have been the General's top man, or even his top supporter, but he was a patriot. "So, speaking of our 'arisen' friend…"

"I haven't spoken to General Torven today, Sir. Yesterday, he was doing well – getting around a bit more."

"Can I go speak to him?" I asked, and Delrin nodded, stepping aside to allow me past before falling back to attention not a second later.

As I strode up to the door, it did a curious thing – it opened on its own. Was Torven really that up and about that he was answering his own door? The curt greeting I had prepared for him died on my lips, though, as I nearly walked straight into a tall, athletic woman, her black hair pulled back in tight bun. She wore a green and yellow uniform, similar to what officers in Zondrell wore, but with a shorter jacket that did little to hide the leather-armored plating underneath.

If ever a smile could dredge up old nightmares, it was the one flashed at me in the next moment. "Ah, *excusez moi,*

Monsieur," the Weapon Master of Doverton said in her lilting Lavançaise accent. "*Enchanté* – we meet again."

"Madame… Saçaille, fancy seeing you here," I replied in the kind of asshole way that made others believe I was being charming – it was a practiced art. "Shouldn't you be in a different city?"

Her black-on-black eyes narrowed, faint age creases playing at the corners as they did so. "My King sends his regards for what has happened here. It seems much is different from the last time I visited your fair Zondrell, Monsieur."

"You noticed? It's the Rains – really makes the place dreary this time of year."

"The loss of a king may also have such an effect, *oui*?"

There were a lot of people I didn't trust – heads of Great Houses in Zondrell tended to have a few more enemies than most. Some of them posed danger beyond just the political kind, too, but so far, none of them had sent assassins to my bedchamber.

This woman, on the other hand, did just that before I was in her city more than a few hours, all because of magic and some idiotic prophecy. Being both dangerous and crazy were simply not a trustworthy combination. "Oh good, so you're just here to laugh at our misfortune, then, because I'm sure you're definitely not up to anything nefarious in the name of Doverton or otherwise."

"King Eric is not that type of man," she said, sharp as her features and the short blade slung behind her back. "You know that. If he was, you would be hanging in our city square, and I would have brought a thousand troops here with me. I am a diplomat – no more, no less."

"Diplomat, my ass. When I go into that house, the occupant better fucking be alive. Do we understand each other?"

She actually did a fair act of looking offended. "Monsieur! You take me for a common criminal."

"You don't want to know what I take you for."

"*You* take things far too personally, Monsieur. Today, I have other concerns. I heard the General's injuries were grave, and I hoped to wish him well."

I couldn't help it – something about her being here, now, of all times and of all places, pissed me off. There was nothing genuine about her smile, her manner, her apparent concern for Torven. Onyx Saçaille had a deceptive streak about her that any Wyndham or Miller or other noble git this side of the Sea of Stars would have given their left arm to be able to imitate. "Look," I said, placing my hand over her right wrist as if to keep her from drawing a weapon, "like I said, if I go in there, and..."

My words stuck in my throat. The black nothingness in her eyes opened up to swallow me, engulfing me in thick dark fog like velvet. Damn every damned god that ever was...

Lately, my command over Time had become even less stable, for lack of a better word. Touching things – even the most arbitrary among them – brought up visions of moments past. More often, they were just flashes, easy to shake off and forget about, but sometimes they were much more involved.

Two days ago, I saw a jeweler arguing with his wife some two hundred years ago when I picked up my family ring. Yesterday when I sat down in the parlor, I saw my mother nursing my sister as a baby while arguing with my father about some trivial money matter. The Drakannyan Time mage said I could work on picking and choosing which visions I wanted to see – "just don't see the ones you don't like." Sure, like it was that fucking easy. More and more, I felt like some hapless actor trapped in a bunch of plays he hadn't rehearsed.

And so it was that the darkness melted into yet another production, though I had to admit that this one was at least novel. I found myself on the outskirts of a small desert village, amidst the sand and dust of the literal middle of nowhere. Other than a few small, fabric-covered structures, not a single thing disturbed the sweeping, empty landscape outside of the occasional swirl of wind.

By Catherine, did people actually *live* out here? I had never been to Katalahnad, but from the stories my sweet Zizah told, it didn't look like this. It looked like cities full of color and life, music and dancing – she never mentioned any desolate wasteland when we would lay awake in bed together.

Damn it, how was Zizah doing, anyway? With the curfews, I had only a few chances to go see her, and I'd hired some mercenaries to go watch the stores she and her sisters ran, but...

Out of the depths of the nighttime desert scene before me, a small, feminine figure focused my rambling mind, stepping into the pale shimmering pallor cast by the moons and stars above. Her thick black hair was gathered into a complex network of braids, and her skin shone like warm ebony – what I could see of it, at any rate. Most of her was clad in armor, her face partially obscured by a filmy white scarf, but from her strong, battle-scarred forearms and hands, I could tell she was not frail in the least. If she were the only traveler in the middle of all this nothing, I might think twice before approaching this one.

She stopped and turned, looking straight at me, even though I knew she couldn't see me... could she? No, the eyes peering through the slit of her veil were focused far beyond, and with each cautious step forward, I noticed something else: she had lightning in her eyes. It wasn't like Tristan's, but the Light magic was unmistakable, her irises made up of perfect concentric circles of brown and blazing white.

Who was this woman? Why was I seeing this? She sure as hell wasn't Onyx Saçaille.

Then I remembered – Brin told a story of a Katalahni woman in the War of the Northlands, one who could bring down storms with a thought. She had been one of the best weapons Keis Sturmberg and his Eislandisch troops had, maybe even one of the reasons why there was a treaty signed and no victor declared after years of bitter fighting.

What was her name... Safaa? Yes, I was sure that was it, a name now known only to those few who remembered her and believed what they saw when she summoned her Light. Whatever she might have been doing out here, I had no idea, but if she came to get away from people, she was about to be disappointed.

Out of the shadows, a predator with a slim, short blade launched out at her. Or was it prey? Safaa had been ready, her hand on the elegant sword at her waist, and when she drew it, I noticed the script engraved on the blade:

كل الأشياء في حالة توازن

If only I had remembered the brief lessons in Katalahni I'd had as a kid. I was better at conversation than writing thanks to Zizah, but the only word I could make out was *tawazun*... balance. The rest of it was just a jumble of pretty figures – distracting, pretty figures, since I should have been paying attention to the action on the stage and not just the props.

Safaa brought her weapon out in a wide arc, catching her attacker's guarding arm and pushing the dark-clad figure back several feet, almost straight into where I "stood" or "hovered" or "emanated" or whatever I did in these visions. Hauntingly sharp but attractive features and the blackest eyes I had ever seen in human or beast came within inches, and for just a moment, we locked gazes... somehow. I had no form, no substance to protect here, but in that fraction of an instant, she was aware of me.

"Look sharp," a much younger Onyx Saçaille breathed as she spun away, got her feet under her, and lunged for Safaa once more.

The two women fought in a blur of motion, swords flailing, sand kicking up in a thousand directions. When Onyx moved in, Safaa dodged away; as Safaa swung low, Onyx parried and swept high. It was like watching a dance, but Safaa had more on her side than a longer weapon and better technique – she had Light.

A bolt from the clear sky above illuminated everything in blinding purity, crashing into the ground so hard that even I thought I could feel it. That Light could rend a man in two, or create a shield wall impossible to breach, but... this one did nothing of the sort. It *fizzled out*. The bound electricity that should have taken shape and conquered its foe simply dissipated around Saçaille instead.

One corner of young Onyx's lips curled up. "You who speak of balance know nothing of it," she said, and weirdly, I understood it perfectly, though it was in her native Lavançaise.

"Balance is us, here, right now," Safaa answered in the same language, though hers had a certain exotic drawl to it. Then, another blast of Light came and vanished into darkness just as quickly, but this time I realized it actually didn't just disappear. Now I knew what to look for, who to watch, and I could see what had happened. That spear of thunder shattered *into* her foe – there was no better way to describe it.

Safaa's magic splintered and fragmented and spiraled into the darkness that was Onyx Saçaille, and she sported that self-satisfied smirk as it did so. "I am not the one to pay the price,"

"If your words are true," said the Katalahni, "then we shall soon know."

I didn't have to guess at what might come next, but I forced myself to turn away at the last second, just as the sands began to turn blackish-red with the first liquid they'd seen in millennia. It took an incredible effort, but this time, I employed the old Drakannyan's advice – I just didn't see what I didn't like. The problem was, that younger and even more savage version of Onyx was at *my* back now, and a pain unlike anything I could describe in words suddenly erupted from between my shoulder blades.

What the hell? It couldn't be, it just wasn't possible...

"Look sharp, Monsieur," Saçaille whispered in my ear from a place of darkness, some seven years and three thousand miles away. The sensation of a sword in my back melted away, just as the desert landscape around me did the same. I turned, and when she finally took proper form before my vision, it was the eyes again that I noticed first. Black, so black as to be two giant pupils, except... there was something else in there, something alive that reminded me of turbulent plumes of writhing smoke.

The sand underfoot had become stone cobbles and dirt once again, my breath coming back to me in very real, ragged gasps as I took in the damp, crisp air of a spring morning in Zondrell. "You... wanted me to see that," I muttered. "What are you?"

She drew away from me and actually reached out to adjust the collar of my jacket, as my mother might do. The gesture made my skin crawl. "This, I am asked far too often. Did you not hear, Monsieur? Balance is the key."

"What the fuck does that mean?"

"It means what it means. All things are *not* in balance, Monsieur. Not yet. Now, I have business elsewhere – if you will excuse me."

She started to push past, but I wasn't afraid to reach out and hold her back. What other visions of murder could this bitch send me? Well, I couldn't guess, and chose not to find out despite the compulsion to dive into the velvety black depths of Time again. "What *are* you?" I asked again.

Her look was incredulous. "I am... not the enemy you think, Monsieur. But our time is over for today. *Au revoir.*"

She was halfway down the street before I had a chance to formulate a response, which was merely a string of incoherent cursing. Damn it all to hell! The only thing I could think of was to follow her, and quick before she slipped into the shadows. But I was no tracker, no scout – in fact, I did embarrassingly poorly on that kind of thing back at the Academy. She would find me out, and what then?

Then again, did I really have a choice?

CHAPTER NINETEEN

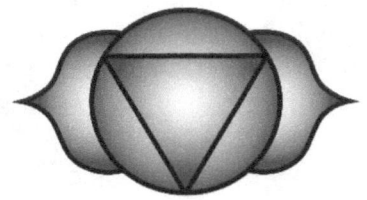

Reflections
15 Spring's Green, 1272
Tristan Loringham

L issa placed a cup of bitter-smelling liquid on the desk before me, and I looked up to watch tendrils of smoke rise from its depths. They reminded me of fog burning off of the sea at sunrise.

"Your medicine, my Lord," my family's trusted servant said with her customary warm smile.

I regarded the porcelain cup with the Loringham "L" embossed in silver on its side for a moment before responding. Ever since I had come back from the Academy healers about two days ago, I had yet to drink any tea from such a cup. She knew it, and I knew it, but her kindly, helpful nature compelled her to continue to try. "Thank you, Lissa," I told her without looking up.

"My Lord, if I may?" Now I did look up at her, into worried dark eyes set in an attractive face lined with care and many years serving one of the eight major Houses of Zondrell. "Lady Andella has left the house."

"She's at the Academy. Research and such, correct?"

"M'Lord, have you even spoken to her?"

I considered. "I have… a bit."

"You do understand, m'Lord, that everyone is rather worried about you, Young Master? Lady Andella perhaps doubly so. She's been rather upset that you're not speaking with her."

This was probably an understatement. I knew damn well that Andella and my mother both had gone through various stages of exceeding worry and doting over me in the past few days, and they had learned in that time that I wanted none of it. I just wasn't ready for all that. Oh I'd tried, mostly for their sake, but at a certain point, I'd grown too tired of it all – tired and just plain… disconnected.

The so-called "medicine" in that steaming cup just made things that much worse. Even though I knew it would help relieve the physical pain, it could do nothing for afflictions of spirit. "I'm not speaking with anyone, Lissa," I told her in a flat tone, "and that will include you in a moment."

She leveled a glare I hadn't seen from her since I was an energetic boy who wanted to run and play all day and avoid his studies. "Young Master, I realize you are… troubled, that you need time. Everyone needs that sometimes. But we are here to help you, and that girl? She *adores* you, m'Lord. Such should not be taken lightly."

"Do you think I don't know that?"

"Please just take your medicine," Lissa bade after enduring a minute or two longer of my glowering.

"You do know what's in here?"

Lissa's eyebrows quirked upward. "My Lord?"

"This," I said, picking up the mug with my left hand, "is just going to put me to sleep and numb me. I don't want that right now."

"Now, Young Master, I understand, but you've barely slept for…"

"I've done more than my share of sleeping." I set the mug back down, where it met the heavy mahogany with a dull *thunk*. "I feel fine, and I have work to do. Lissa, please… look, you can leave it, but I'm not drinking it. Do we understand each other?"

After a moment of hesitation, she bowed with grace. "As you will, m'Lord. What shall I say to Lady Andella when she returns?"

"Nothing."

"I must say, with every year, you grow a bit more stubborn," Lissa said with a long sigh. "You'll be as bad as your father soon enough. Just please don't forget that she cares for you – we all do. And we're very concerned about you."

"And I appreciate that, Lissa. Really. Now, I'll be done soon – I promise."

Her gaze took in the pile of papers strewn across the desk, the empty bottles of black ink, the two discarded and overused quills – not to mention the nearly-dulled one in my inkstained grip. All told, there was probably about two hundred Royals' worth of good paper and ink there. "*Just* like your father... I do hope you'll take a proper rest soon, m'Lord," she said, then quietly slipped back out of the study.

To be honest, I *was* almost done, and I *was* being quite stubborn. After the Lady knew how many hours of sitting at this desk, in what was once my father's favorite chair, I had gone through some fifty pages and an uncountable amount of expensive ink, writing down descriptions, thoughts, ideas, even diagrams and letters that would never be sent, each echoes of the River that filled my mind and assaulted my dreams. I couldn't speak aloud about my experiences there, not yet, but I *could* write them all down, because I, Tristan Michael Johannes Loringham, had faced down gods, defied death, and was alive to tell about it.

The very thought left me feeling sick.

The boy king of a land teetering on the brink of civil war was out there, somewhere, while I was "safe." What was worse, even if I returned to the River, I would have to find him, and short of yoking myself to a flying dragon, the idea seemed next to impossible. Edin could be anywhere in that vast place, facing his own gods and demons; I could be there for eternity and never cross his path.

The only thing I could do was write, speculate, consider my next move. If anyone were to look over my shoulder, they'd probably deem me permanently mad, with no hope of recovery. They'd lock me up and figure out how to take my estate – that is, if anyone wanted a so-called "cursed" House full of strange magic and ill luck. Yet, those scattered words *needed* to escape, because once they were free, I could be, too. I could think of almost nothing else until I could wipe my quill one final time.

The tea had long gone stone cold as three final words were scrawled with a flourish across a single, blank sheet of paper:

I am awake.

Holy hell, did that feel good. Not because I understood exactly what it all meant, but because the feeling of weight being released from my soul was visceral. I could feel it in the blood moving through my veins, in the warm electric tingle coursing through the core of my being. That energy soon began to take shape, tiny tendrils of white lightning weaving between my outstretched fingers to dance there, in time with my thoughts.

My breath stopped, but no great horror emerged. No storm erupted from the sky and shot through my roof... yet. In fact, the magic I once knew as violent and willful was now stirring gently in my palm, and with it came no fear, no pain, not even the tell-tale nosebleed that often followed intense bursts.

"I have to go back," I voiced aloud, to no one in particular. And yet, despite this, I got a response.

"You think it gets easier," came a harsh, low voice from the doorway.

Well, obviously awake doesn't mean aware. I gathered up those papers so fast, I was surprised my uncle didn't make an attempt to grab them from me. "Still, I need to try," I said as I found a drawer to shove them all into.

"There is a right time for everything." Brin Jannausch's expression was questioning, curious, despite the gravity in his tone. In fact, the more I stared at him, with the gray daylight from the window behind me giving the big Eislander's blond hair a silvery sheen, the more I noticed how... "off" he looked. He appeared shaken, distant, far from his usual self-assured and gruff demeanor.

"So I keep hearing. Is something wrong, Brin?"

"My nephew has condemned himself to the River's Edge. It never seems to stop raining in this forsaken city. And I am too sober for the day ahead." On a table near the door was a decanter of dark gold brandy and set of glasses to match, about half-full. Without ceremony, my uncle helped himself, pouring out a second glass and placing it front of me. "It may be a difficult day, *ja?*"

"Like every day," I muttered. The first sip was, at least, a reasonable mood-lifter.

He fixed me with that clear blue gaze of his. "It is hard to break from the River's Edge once it takes you. I know this, and now you know this. But hard does not mean impossible."

"I need to make sense of it, first... that's all."

"Making sense and making blame are two different things. You cannot do both." When I felt my scowl deepen, he motioned for me to keep drinking. "Break from your prison for a while, *ja*? You have company."

I grimaced and stood, fighting the swimming sensation in my head that followed the abrupt change in elevation. Using the desk to hold myself steady, I leaned toward him, insistent. "I thought I specifically said I'm not taking any visitors right now."

"These are not ordinary visitors. Clean yourself up and meet them – this is family."

**

Family. I didn't have much family anymore, not in the real sense. With my father a speck of light traveling the River – or, living at the side of Catherine in Paradise, if one believed in that sort of thing – my mother and I were mostly alone. Sure, Andella was wearing my betrothal ring, but we weren't married just yet, and even then, she was only *close* to family.

There was something different about blood. On the Loringham side, I had a myriad of distant cousins and an uncle who had stopped speaking to my father twenty years ago – they all lived outside the city now. On my mother's side, as far as I knew, I only had Brin, and he had been a relatively recent addition. Apparently, it was our lot to sever ties for long stretches at a time, which was why I wasn't that shocked to find out he had a wife and a daughter he hadn't seen in over a decade. The fact that they were here, now, and apparently waiting in the west sitting room, was a bit more of a surprise.

What do you wear when you're meeting family you don't even know? Well, anything was likely better than the clothes I hadn't changed from in over a day and a half. My uncle was right – cleaning up wasn't a terrible idea. So I quickly retreated to my bedchamber, washed at the basin, combed my hair, and found some black silks to go with one of my better longcoats. Nothing too formal, of course, but the one with the decorative buckles at the waist seemed like a good choice.

Before the mirror, I buttoned the cuffs of my shirt, taking a moment to smooth it out before pulling on the jacket. I noticed scratchy blond stubble along my chin and realized I should have shaved, but it was too late for that. Then there was that soft, electric-white glow in my eyes, tracing the lines arranged so perfectly around my pupils – I could get used to seeing my half-bred, too-tall self as a soldier or a noble or anything in between, but *that* sight would never be normal.

What was worse were those other times when the starlight seemed to be... replaced. Different. Dark. I noticed it first when I came home, and thought it the result of the herbs they'd given me. But as quickly as the darkness there had appeared, it was gone, quick as lightning in a raging storm. A day later, I caught it again. *Has anyone else noticed? If they did, would they say anything?*

Now, the glow was at a steady sort of pulse like it had always been, the magic radiating from the center in time with my heartbeat like tiny little shooting stars. Still, I leaned into the mirror and watched intently, waiting to see if... *By the gods, did one of those stars go* black? It did, followed by another, then another, coexisting quite peacefully among the others. I didn't feel any different – in fact, I felt better than I had all day. So good, in fact, that it felt quite natural to allow some crackling light play through my fingers and across the glass, the reflection creating a gentle glowing outline around my hands and face.

"Your sparkles are so pretty."

I was so engrossed, I hardly even noticed the second figure joining me in the mirror. The realization dawned on me as the kind of distant rolling thunder that eventually sends a bolt of lightning right to your doorstep. *How long had she been looking over my shoulder? And why was she there in the first place?*

Ripping myself away, I did my best to look calm and collected as I reached for the jacket and fussed over the buttons and buckles, all the while ignoring the sensation of warmth building in my cheeks.

"Oh… I should say handsome," the girl in my doorway said, her odd accent something like Lavançaise with a twist of high-country Zondrean. "Mama said that's the right word to use for boys."

I couldn't help but smile at this waifish child, who had effectively disarmed me of any instinct to snap at her and send her away. She was all of twelve or thirteen, just blooming into an awkward semblance of a woman. She wore a white and blue dress that reminded me of something Alex's sister would have worn at that age, and her striking features were framed in strawberry-blonde braids. None of it looked comfortable on her, though – this was the kind of girl who would be happier chasing butterflies in the street than playing with dolls. Save for the strong almond tilt of the eyes and thinner build, she could very well have been my little long-lost sister.

"Well," I quipped, "I'm almost certain I know a few boys who wouldn't mind the other word. Most people wouldn't use either one on me, though."

"Mama says people with two different kinds of parents get the best from both."

"Is that so? Your mama sounds like a smart woman. Did she send you up here?"

The girl frowned, and her words came out very measured. "No. Everyone was talking a lot in the fancy room. I didn't know you would have such a nice house."

"It's easy to get lost in. And adults are easy to get bored with." With a knowing grin, I bowed to her, as deep as I might to Queen Marianna herself. "So, I apologize – I'm afraid you've found another boring adult. You can call me Tristan. What's your name?"

"Jardin. It means 'garden.'"

"I think that's a pretty name, Jardin – definitely not a handsome one. It's an honor to meet you." When I smiled, she smiled, though the effort seemed copied, even forced, as unnatural as her dress. "But I wasn't prepared for visitors. Will you excuse me for a minute?" Back in the mirror, with coat buttoned to the neck and broad shoulders straight, I saw an image of a man who might have been considered "handsome" enough to pass for nobility, at least in Eisland. In Zondrell, that was a tougher sell, but… oh well.

In the meantime, the girl had turned to the large, leather-bound book she'd been clutching at her side, turning from one page to the next with a nervous kind of excitement. I watched and waited for several minutes before she stopped on a page she found suitable. "Here it is," I heard her say, as she turned the book around so that I could see. "I drew this for you, Cousin."

The drawing was, in a word, remarkable. A simple composition, all in charcoal, but detailed enough to convey light, movement, maybe even sound if I imagined it. And I easily could, because the man in that scene, standing against a flood of dark fog as it rolled in and threatened to engulf him, was me. I might as well have been looking back in the mirror again.

Even more interesting was the other half of the picture, because deep in the fog was a figure, feminine in shape, but sharp, all hard angles that were only softened by the fog embracing them like a veil... a veil that hid something much more than human. "What in Catherine's name..." I started, but had nothing more to add. What else was there to say? Instead of finishing the sentence, I dropped to one knee before this strange girl who already knew me as her cousin and her unexplainable artwork.

"You were there a long time, in the Place," Jardin said. "I was worried about you." And still, I had no words. Her nose scrunched up in deep thought before she continued. "I'm not really there, when I see it. It's just in my dreams, but it looks real. It *is* real, isn't it?"

Poor thing – what a place for a child to go in her dreams. "It's... a place some people think is real, yes."

"Do you?"

"As real as you and me," I said, surprised at the finality in my tone. Then again, I had just spent the past two days documenting my travels there in as much detail as a scout reporting on his patrols into enemy territory. If I wasn't mad – and I was *mostly* sure this was the case – then it existed, somehow, somewhere. "Jardin, do you know what 'the Place' is?"

"It's where Papa thinks people go when they die." She might as well have been reading it from a textbook – no amazement, no concern, no emotion. "That's what Vremya said."

That name, Vremya... I knew it. He was a Time mage, like Alex; Brin had spoken of him from his days in the War, along with a Life mage named Jade and a Light mage named Safaa. Because of them, he probably knew more about my own magic than I did. "This Vremya is a friend of yours?"

"He came here with us." Her otherwise serene and passive face dimpled into the ghost of a true, honest sort of smile. "I like the way he talks."

"Well, maybe we should go down and talk to him, eh? Everyone's probably waiting for us."

The girl's response was not to move, however, but to simply tap the dark part of the picture. As she did, her expression clouded over to match. "Do you know who's in *there*, Cousin?"

"I'm pretty sure I do." How or why, I still had no idea, but for all the world, the figure in the Darkness had looked, acted, and spoken like Onyx Saçaille. But I didn't like the grim, pale look on Jardin's face, so rather than elaborate and just serve to frighten her, I waved the subject off with a smirk. "Don't you worry about her, Jardin. She can't hurt anyone."

"I know. I'm not worried." Then the girl began to rip the picture from her nice little leather-bound sketchpad, pulling from as close to the center as possible so as not to harm the page itself. Finally, she handed it out for me to take.

"Thank you," I said, not sure what else to say as I took it from her warm little hand and set it in a place of prominence atop my dresser. "You... really are quite the artist."

"*Merci bien.*" Jardin closed her book and hugged it into herself, as if it could keep her warm – or shield her from unseen danger. With our faces close to level, I met her gaze then, a gaze full of... *No, it can't be.* Within her sapphire-colored eyes lay tiny pinpricks of white starlight, moving very slowly and deliberately along a spiral arc. It was almost imperceptible to anyone who didn't know what they were seeing; to me, it was damn near unbelievable.

"You... you have..." My words fell all over each other.

"Sparkles." Her lips dared to curl upward at the corners once again. "Like you. So the black fog can't hurt us."

I had no idea what she meant by that, but for the sake of preserving that smile, I pretended that I did. "No. It won't hurt anyone – don't you worry."

But the odd young girl with the strawberry blond braids and lightning in her eyes said nothing more.

CHAPTER TWENTY

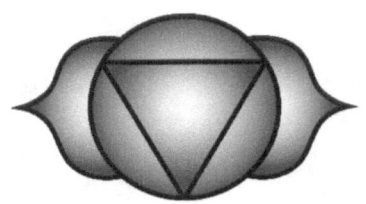

Serendipity
15 Spring's Green, 1272
Jade Saçaille

Half my life had been a series of odd coincidences, propelled by the whims of the people around me: my parents, the church, the King of Eisland, Brin, my sister, even Jardin. In a way, I supposed everyone experienced this at some level, but I was sick of it. That was why I stopped Vremya in the middle of the street, halfway to the door of the majestic home across from Vestarton's, with its neat garden in front and tall, narrow windows that reminded me of the style found on so many buildings in the Zondrean quarter of Quatremagne.

"Vremya," I said, catching him by the elbow, "what we are doing here?"

"We're visiting, *da*? Is your family. I am just... tagging along." Per usual, his round, ruddy face was positively beaming.

"No, Vremya, I mean *here,* in Zondrell, right now. You still haven't told me why you brought us here, and I'll be damned if another minute goes by..."

"Jade." My thoughts were stopped dead, but that warm expression never changed, despite the weight of his tone. "You know I follow the possibilities, *da*? I seen them, and some of them? No good. But we can do things, be there at the best times."

"But what 'possibilities' are you even talking about?"

"No healing, no general for these people. You did that."

"I hear they hate that man. I might have saved a scoundrel for all I know. I don't want to know."

"What about the boy in the Palace?"

"He's certainly not well, and I can't do anything about that." Before he could protest, I kept talking, the blood rushing hot to my cheeks. "Vremya, I want to go *home*. I want to be in my own bed, with my own clothes and my own food and my own neighbors around me. Give me one reason – a real reason – why we should stay here in this gods-forsaken town."

Quicksilver churned around itself in his eyes as the Time mage considered. Finally, he said, "Is it so bad to give your daughter a family, Jade?"

Chantal's bloody corpse... "It's very complicated, Vremya," I replied through clenched teeth. "You wouldn't understand. And besides that, I am *certain* that this is not why you dragged us out here to..."

Before I could go on, he reached out, squeezing my hand lightly in his own. Then his smile grew a mischievous quirk as he released and tapped his own brow with two fingers, as if an idea had just sprung to his mind. "Don't have to understand to know what's important, *da*?"

"By Chantal. Vremya, really."

"That's my answer. You not agree?"

"You fancy yourself some sort of a sage now?" My eyes rolled skyward and I let out a long breath. "How long did you say you spent in Quiétude?"

"Long enough to hear the bones talk. What did they say to you, I wonder?"

In that moment, I played it off. A Drakannyan, hearing voices at Quiétude? In his dreams, perhaps. I shook my head and waved, dismissive, looking beyond to where a neatly-dressed servant was summoning Jardin into the Loringham house.

But instead of hearing the woman welcome my daughter inside, I heard another voice, as clear as the day I'd first heard it while praying over an ancient shrine holding the bones of a dead goddess. It was deep and resonant and of a single perfect pitch...

All things in Balance.

Suddenly, I saw myself sitting on that rock, in that open-air temple atop the mountains, wrapped in a scratchy wool blanket. It was the most sacred of sacred places, for She who once walked among men had died there, in that very spot. Magic itself, they said, was born in that moment, Chantal's gift to Her faithful, to those with "promise."

I had promise, I was told, just as Onyx had. The priests had heard the Goddess speak of us through Her various trappings of altars and biers and books. Were we faithful enough? Well, my sister was – she was important, even *special.*

The bones had spoken to her within weeks, after all. She'd studied with some of the highest-ranking priests, but when I arrived two years after her, we weren't allowed to speak. I wasn't even convinced that what they said of her was true. For a long time, I believed there was no possible way she could have done what they said, and when I prayed at the shrine, I wished silently that Chantal would show me the truth of Onyx and her whereabouts. How could they say that I was as "special" as she, when everything about her was cloaked in such secrecy?

But Chantal did not answer. In fact, I didn't hear Her speak for *three years;* by that time, the priests said Onyx had gone from the temple, released from her studies to go execute the Goddess' will. What did that mean? I never did find out, because I never saw her use magic, nor did I ask.

By the time I saw her again, many years later, I had decided my own gifts were a curse, and as such, all magic fell into the same category. At least, that was true for mortal magic. Surely Chantal never intended for us to kill each other with her gifts – there was no "balance" in that.

What did it all mean? Now, I wished I had asked. I wished I understood what it meant, what the Goddess Herself was trying to tell me so long ago. I wished many foolish, useless things, and it was too late for all of that. Except...

"Is that my sister?" I said aloud, squinting past Vremya and down the street.

There were few people out, even now in the middle of the day, in part because of the mud and the misty moisture that clung to everything... but only in part. Zondrell's tension and unease was as thick as the humid spring air, and most seemed smart to stay safe within their homes. There was someone, though, a tall and stately figure in green with yellow trim, just turning the corner up ahead.

Vremya followed my gaze for a moment, his silver eyes focused off in the distance. Then he turned back with that familiar, round-faced grin. "Hey," he said, "why don't you go, be with your people? Me, I go look. Be right behind you."

"What? No, I think that's my sister. I need to talk to her." But he was already heading up the street with his heavy traveling cloak flowing behind him.

"Maybe we have a reunion, *da*? Tell Brin to save some brandy for me," the Drakannyan called over his shoulder as he pursued the person who may or may not have been Onyx. She did say she was in Zondrell, didn't she? Of course, it might not have been her at all – lots of people wore those colors besides the Doverton military. Few of them likely moved with the same purpose and grace as my sister, but... I looked back to the house, where Jardin had disappeared inside long ago and the servant-woman was standing expectantly in the entryway, smiling at me. There was little choice in the matter, wasn't there?

Besides, if it was Onyx out there, she'd find me eventually. She always did.

I was let into the big house with the quaint garden and greeted as if I were royalty. As it turned out, Brin's sister – "Lady" Gretchen – had always wanted a sister of her own, and she held me in a full-hearted Eislandisch embrace when I entered her home. I was given a crystal glass filled with sunshine-colored wine, and bid to relax, to make myself at home. Oh, the wine helped with that, of course, but...

"Where is Jardin?" I asked when I had a chance, and both Brin and Gretchen gestured beyond the parlor where we stood.

"She wanted to see her cousin," Brin said. "I sent her to find him."

"*Verzeihung* – I apologize," Gretchen added, her words kind and gentle even through the thick Eislandisch accent. "My son was not prepared for guests. He will be but a minute."

A sip from my wineglass masked my irritation. "Indeed." The next few minutes seemed to stand stock still, the small talk with Gretchen a poor refuge from worry. When we were finally joined by the Lord of this place, my concern heightened, sharpening to a fine point in the face of this giant wearing the clothes of a king, for my daughter remained nowhere to be seen.

The ethereal figure in Jardin's drawings stood an inch, maybe two, shorter than Brin, but where Brin had always been made of muscle on top of muscle, the man they called Tristan Loringham was athletic, as disciplined as he was strong, and though he moved with a certain grace, it wasn't the dashing grace of nobility.

The wealth of the home around him didn't quite fit him, somehow. In person, he reminded me far less of a young Brin and much more of Keis Sturmberg, the High King of Eisland, when I knew him during the War. Oh, they didn't look that much alike, but this one had the same bearing – aware of everything, compromising nothing. Where Brin might have drawn his blade just to start fights, men like Monsieur Keis and Tristan drew to end them. I wanted to like him, but just as immediately, I was wary of him.

"Welcome to my home," Loringham said in a low, gravel-tinged voice as he bowed deeply. Despite his square-jawed Eislandisch looks, he spoke with the most perfectly prim Zondrean accent I had ever heard. "You must be..."

I acknowledged him with a nod. "Jade. You may call me Jade."

"It's an honor, Jade." Another low bow, some fumbling for the right words. "My uncle... Brin... has spoken of you. Please, call me Tristan."

Chantal's bones, I could only imagine what stories he might have heard. Well, it didn't matter. My lips pressed together hard in an effort to maintain a smile and to curb my impatience – a futile effort at best. "*Enchanté.* Monsieur, can you please tell me where my daughter is?"

A brightness touched his red-rimmed blue eyes, and a sheepish sort of smile crept across his face. "Oh, I assume you mean Miss Jardin? I just set her up in my study – once she heard I had colored chalk for drawing, she sort of insisted."

Colored chalk... of course. "How kind of you. Can I see her, please?"

As much as I hadn't wanted to sound rude, I did; he missed nothing, and his reply was obediently curt. "Right, sure. This way."

As large as the house was, the halls were short to make way for its wide-open rooms. We only had to walk through the front entryway to the other side of the stairs to find this study, which, like the parlor, was nothing short of grand: heavy wood everywhere, decorative carvings on the corner of every shelf, desk, and chair, thick tapestries along one wall of pastoral scenes in gold and warm earth tones.

And there, perched on a high-backed leather chair, was Jardin, shoes off and legs tucked under her so she could hover over the wide mahogany desk that dominated one half of the room. She needed that whole surface, too, because along with a set of chalks in a dozen different colors, she had been given a large piece of heavy paper, the kind used to make posters. Just the cost of those materials would have been enough to feed the girl for a month – a *month*! I glanced back at Loringham, who observed from a distance, arms folded across his broad chest.

"Jardin?" I asked, stepping toward the desk. "*Chérie,* are you having a good time?"

"*Oui,*" came her response.

"What are you working on today?"

No answer, and not a surprise. She was in full concentration, the blood-red stick of chalk in her hand moving furiously across the paper. Curious, I leaned further forward, daring to observe this creation in progress. With mere charcoal, she could produce astounding things, but with color, she could truly bring thoughts into being.

The river that had once been shades of gray in her sketchbook became a living thing of bright crimson, flowing along against banks of verdant green dotted with pink and purple flowers. At the bottom, it flowed out into an ocean of deeper red, nearly black, its waves lapping against the bottom of the page. The scene was idyllic in a strange way, even peaceful, and it drew me in toward it, until I was stooped over the desk, too, searching for the best angle.

"It's... beautiful, *chérie*. What is this?" I pointed to what looked like a pool of some kind at the top of the picture, seemingly too small to be the bizarre river of blood's source. Near it sat a house that had just been roughed in so far, its features still shrouded in mystery.

"The steps..." I heard Loringham say with a sharp intake of breath, and I realized he had joined me at the desk, standing close enough to where I could smell the musky scent of undoubtedly expensive soap.

Jardin paused, setting down the red chalk to find another color. She never looked up as she spoke. "Have you ever looked at a bright room, then closed your eyes, and you can still see it? This is what I saw."

"Just now?" I asked.

My daughter shrugged, noncommittal, and one of the nice plaits Vestarton's older sister had weaved into her hair bounced along with the motion. "I think they're in there, Cousin," she said, pointing to the image of the house.

"They..." He leaned in further. "They who?"

Reaching for one of her regular, thin sticks of black drawing charcoal, she returned to the paper to start etching in the finer details. Shading became mist that seemed to linger around the house's little exterior, and a water-wheel looking almost as if it could truly turn within that tiny image stood just outside the door. Vague images of people took shape through a single window, and while it was hard to tell, at least one of them was a child. Another might have been a woman, with long hair and a small frame.

Who they were and what they were doing there, I had no idea, but Loringham may have. As his gaze narrowed in on the drawing, I realized that there was Light in his eyes, sparkling as it traveled distinct, straight paths from his pupils to the outer rim of his irises. By Chantal, he was just like Jardin and Safaa!

Well, not quite. Safaa's Light had followed circles, precise and concentric, where Tristan's magic formed a set of twinkling wheels, of a sort. Indeed, Safaa had been much closer to Jardin's spiraling arcs, but my daughter's magic was so faint, untrained and unused, that it almost wasn't there at all.

What I saw in Loringham was much the opposite, and once I knew it was there, I couldn't look away. Inside that gaze, I saw the way Safaa's magic destroyed the enemy's forts and murdered their soldiers... but I also saw how it protected the Eislandisch armies from harm. It was both weapon and shield in the darkest of times, and I wondered if this man had used his gifts in the same ways. I had a feeling that he had.

We stood locked together for a minute or more – no doubt he was assessing my magic just as thoroughly. I had been told of a woman, his betrothed, with the "gift" of Life magic – Chantal knew what was going through his head as he held my gaze and frankly, I didn't want to know.

I tore myself away and returned to the scene unfolding on the desk. "Jardin, your cousin asked you a question," I said, terse. It might have been unwise to interrupt her, but by then, I wanted to know the answer as much as he did.

"Tante Onyx knows," was all my daughter said as she reached for another color – bright orange – and began to add wisps of something that might have been fire licking the surface of the great, scarlet river.

"Tante Onyx? She's not even here, chérie. What does she have to do with this?"

If Tristan knew the answer, he gave no verbal indication, but the way the color drained from his face said a great deal. He very nearly knocked over a table holding a set of crystal glasses and decanters as he launched out of the room, muttering some apology as he did.

Meanwhile, that mask of stern concentration settled back into Jardin's features, and once again, she immersed herself in her drawing as if nothing had ever happened.

Chantal's immortal breath... how many more of these coincidences and questions without answers could I take?

CHAPTER TWENTY-ONE

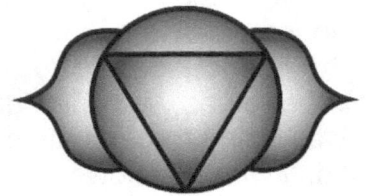

Curiosity

15 Spring's Green, 1272
Andella Weaver

B y the latter half of the day, the sun had almost peeked through the clouds... almost. And was it warmer, or was it just me? Either way, there was a certain lightness in my step as I hopped from the boat and onto the path of well-placed boulders that would lead me down to the bottom of the sea.

Oh yes, I had considered. For several hours, I wavered back and forth as to whether I would venture this way, to come to the research site and face the vein of obsidian once more. Maybe twenty times, I had changed my mind, but in the end, I realized I had no choice. How else would I learn? How else would I *know*? Even now, I felt the flames falling to embers at my core, the spark of magic quite temporary, just as Tiara had predicted. I *needed* to know how I could stoke that Fire once again.

When I returned to the Archmage's laboratory, she already had her cloak on, as if she knew I was coming back. "Ready to go, then?" she asked with a smile.

"Ready as I can be," was all I could say in my own defense, and so we went, walking through the barricades and half-empty, soldier-lined streets between the Academy and the Palace until we reached our destination: the research site.

Archmage Tiara had been correct, too, because it was truly a sight to behold.

Even though the mages insisted the Palace-side bay was shallow compared to the open sea beyond the Zondrell shoreline, it still seemed like a *long* way down as we made our way from a small boat onto a platform and down a winding but leisurely ramp of sorts, formed from rock that made up the sea floor itself.

The Earth mages had done a great deal of work here, carving out a giant bowl within the sea – a work of master craftsmanship, but fragile all the same, and one that had to be constantly maintained and monitored. Without just the right balance of Earth, Water, and Air, it might all come crashing in on itself.

As my leather walking boots touched the very bottom, I looked up toward the sun again. Alex would be back to take me home soon, in maybe an hour? Well, according to the Archmage, this wouldn't take too long. I'd be on my way soon enough, after some preliminary readings, and if the risk proved too great and I fell unconscious again? She implored me not to worry too much about all that.

And for a time, I didn't, my imagination swept up in the marvels of the research playing out before me; it truly was unprecedented, the sort of thing they did in Lavancée, maybe, under the watchful eye of the Church of Chantal. Here in Zondrell? This was the stuff of legends! I felt the same thirst for knowledge that I imagined the Archmage had every time she walked through this site – it was written all over her face even now. Her eyes positively glittered with anticipation.

"Oh, Madam Archmage," a young Academy student in the white robes of an Air mage said before we got a chance to start down the path ahead.

If there was one thing that the Zondrell Magic Academy truly trained its students well for, it was assuming authority, and this one was no exception. She had taken on the officious air of someone twice her age, even though she was probably a year or two younger than me. Behind her stretched a widening expanse of rock, flat in some areas and less so in others, made up of swirling, ancient layers of shale, granite, quartz, and a million other things.

"Miss Kisela, how are things here? Any news?" Tiara asked, tone curt and pointed as it so often was with her students.

With a short bow, Kisela shook her head. "Nothing of note, Madam Archmage. Earlier today, three people from the Royal Guard came down asking to look around, and before that, some nobleman and his entourage. Oh, and Lord Archmage Brillen is here with his students."

Brillen was one of the other leading instructors at the Academy, but one I'd never actually met. The way Tiara's lips drew thin and twisted told me everything I needed to know about him, though. "Well, that's just lovely," she snapped. "I'm sure he'll have no problem getting out of my way for a moment. We have an important experiment underway here."

"Oh? Is this your assistant?" The girl's classically Zondrean oval, olive-skinned features softened, if only a little.

"Yes, dear, this is Miss Weaver."

"Weaver, oh... Of course." The girl smiled a knowing sort of smile and pointed at the landscape behind her. "It's been a few days since you've been back, is that right, Miss Weaver? What do you think?"

"So beautiful..." I said under my breath as I looked out at it, fascinated by the way the glints of crystal in the rock caught the light, so that the whole place seemed to shimmer. "Sorry, um... Miss Kisela, was it?"

"Nice to meet you." Kisela's smile never wavered.

I took down the hood of my heavy dark cloak, and as soon as I did, cold wet air slapped me across the face. "So much work has been done down here – it's amazing."

"It really is, isn't it?" Her white eyes widened as she turned back to the Archmage, the smile draining from her face. "Oh! Archmage, I... I apologize. I just remembered that Master Devens was looking for you earlier. He had to log some research notes, I believe? Something about the obsidian resonance readings at section I-9."

Sections and resonance readings took over the conversation for a moment, leaving me behind until the Archmage finally turned back to me, a look of sheer annoyance souring the thrill of curiosity that had been so evident just minutes before. "Andella, dear, why don't you go on ahead, take a look around? I need to have a few words with Master Devens, it appears. I'll come find you momentarily, yes?"

She didn't wait for me to respond, and I didn't expect her to. Her dark green cloak fluttered around her in the chill salt air as she stalked off in search of someone to reprimand. "You should go ahead," Kisela said after the Archmage was well out of earshot. "Just be careful – well, I guess you know that."

I felt my cheeks grow warm despite the cold. "I guess I do."

"It's the rock, right? The obsidian? I still don't understand it all that well, but I hear everyone talk as they pass through here. I don't know... I touched it. Couldn't help myself – everyone kept saying different things. It was sort of a weird feeling, like in my stomach, almost like a vibration. Like... like I hadn't eaten. Is that what you felt?"

"Well..." That was a good question. I didn't remember it, honestly. I remembered very much what happened after that, but before? It was all fuzzy. "I guess so. It was all so fast. But everyone who touches it, they're... fine?"

"Apparently," she said with a shrug. If she had any idea of what had happened to me beyond a rather dramatic fainting spell, she made no indication. "Stefan Whitley said he had a dream about sailing on the ocean in a boat of light or some such, but I'm pretty sure everyone already thinks he's mad. But who knows?"

"Well, I guess we'll figure it out in time. I'll wait for Archmage Tiara before I try again, myself."

The girl joined me in an amused giggle. "Good idea, Mage Weaver. But do feel free to look around as much as you want while you wait. She might be a while. If you need anything, I'll be here, and there's a few mages and students down there, too. I'm sure they'll help you."

"Thank you, Miss Kisela." I offered her a friendly bow, then went on my way.

Overhead, the sun showed even more of itself as it continued its slow descent. From the deep, mage-made chasm where I stood, it would soon disappear behind the Palace, and when it did, would Tiara be back to continue her crazed experiments? Or would I lose my nerve before that happened?

The thrum of magic was strong in the air, and the further I walked, the more real it seemed, until it was positively humming in my ears. It was like concentrating on a focusing crystal, except... that same feeling was just *everywhere*. I passed green-robed Earth mages examining the stone at our feet, commanding it to move in time with the whims of the blue-robed Water mages as they kept the sea in check. Some acknowledged me, but most were too busy to notice as I continued on to the place where other mages measured the ground with their various instrumentation.

Despite the inherent danger of the unfamiliar, it all seemed well under control, and it didn't take long to find one of the inky, frozen, black "wheel spokes" in the sea floor. I followed it for a time until I could see what I was looking for – the center of it all.

Energy seemed to hang over the place like... like fog, dense and reminiscent of shadows in the dreams of ghosts. It certainly was enough to upset a stomach, if nothing else. And the cold! It could have been the chill of the sea air, but the further I walked, the colder it grew, a damp sort of cold that soaked into skin and blood and bone. I almost vomited up what little I had eaten all day.

Nearby, I watched one mage help another adjust a large device set up on three spindly wooden legs, a metal orb set in the center. They placed it over the perfect circle of obsidian, a spider hovering over its knowledge-born prey.

Once one pressed something on the orb, they almost fell over each other as they turned to get away from it. Were fireworks going to pop out? I couldn't imagine any measuring device creating that kind of a panic – then again, this was no ordinary research.

"By the Lady," breathed one of the mages, dressed in rich green robes similar to what Archmage Tiara often wore. The greying older gentleman might have been a lecturer himself, and may have even been the infamous Archmage Brillen himself. I paused to watch, curiosity piqued. "Nothing left to do now but see if this works."

His companion, a heavy-set younger woman, also in green, leaned forward to squint at the device. "You're sure it's set properly?"

The man nodded, but his attention had moved from her and on to me. "You – you're the one who studies with Chandler, is that right?"

From the way he said it, I couldn't tell if he was annoyed or interested. "Oh... uh, yes?" I stammered out a response. "Hello. I'm sorry, am I in the wrong place?"

Luckily, his expression softened, his bright green eyes twinkling with the possibility of discovery. "That depends, young mage. Are you doing research?"

"Oh, I was just down here to... Well, there was an experiment we were going to perform, and..." I might have kept going, but his disinterested look said it all.

"That's all well and good, but I'm unlikely to be done with this area for a while. You'll have to come back some other time."

"Oh, but it's Archmage Tiara's research, Sir, and I don't know that it'll take that long. I'm just waiting for her to come back, is all."

The man I assumed was Brillen scoffed. "Tiara's little project can wait. This – this is *real* research. We're getting to the heart of this thing." He paused, looking me up and down, and I wondered what he'd heard about me. Did he know I was the girl who touched the center, right here in the very spot, and fainted without explanation? Did he know about my "lost and found" power?

Maybe he did, because a faint smile brought out the creases around his eyes. "Of course, if you care to wait and watch, you can report back to Tiara for me and tell her the good news."

"The... 'news'?" The furrowing of my brow was all the invitation he needed to explain further, adopting the tone I imagined this man used when lecturing in class. He might not have had much reverence for Archmage Tiara's work, but he sure did seem to follow her style – focused, with a flair for the dramatic.

"You see," he said, "this device is intended to focus energy for the purposes of extraction. I admit, it's a bit... direct, but desperate times call for desperate measures. We can't fuss around down here for years, now, can we? But I think it's quite clear that what we have here is a rare opportunity to study this material in its natural form. Think of the advances we can make! Now, I have very carefully adapted this device for this task, so I expect at least some level of success. My tests on other parts of the sea floor have proven somewhat effective, after all." From a pocket in his robes, he produced a small chunk of oil-black rock.

My breath caught. "You actually broke the rock apart with magic?" The strange black instrument known as The Box had resisted every attempt to study how it was made, or how it worked. It worked, and that was enough for most to accept.

If this obsidian rock in the ground was indeed made of the same stuff, it might produce no different result. *Might.* Then again, it could be something entirely different... it could be the path to Purgatory, for all we knew. But Earth mages, I supposed, didn't like the idea of rocks that failed to obey them.

"Focused magic, yes. This was just a small test, from over there." He pointed to where a small group of Earth mages were clustered over a spot on another "wheel" spoke. "The formula's sound, and so is the theory. Now, I'll need you to step aside, young lady, although feel free to take your own notes."

It all happened so fast. I stepped aside, just as the mage instructed, and watched as he and his colleague began to concentrate. By the Lady! Whatever that thing was, it could focus magic in a way I had never seen... or felt. It seemed to pull my energy right from my body. Was it somehow the opposite of a focusing crystal? Instead of magnifying the magic inside, the device seemed to wrench it forth to become a literal spear of power, growing out from the center of that metal orb. Ground to sky, it stood poised over the obsidian, until in one quick motion, it struck.

And the earth trembled.

Intense pain shot through my tailbone and up my spine as my feet went out from under me, but it was nothing compared to the pain vibrating through my skull. I called out for the researchers to stop what they were doing, but they couldn't hear – they had turned to run, all flailing arms and shouting as they headed toward the others.

What was done now was done, no looking back. Except I couldn't run – I couldn't move. I felt frozen in place, only able to watch as the black surface nearby rippled, a dark mist congealing at its edges. It reminded me of the way foam played along the waves on a stormy day.

I leaned forward, trying to push myself up, to force my legs to move. And as I got closer to the vein of darkness, something moved from deep within. It had to be more than just a reflection. It was too familiar, too etched into the deep corners of my memory reserved for dreams and nightmares.

It had to be... the same water from the edge of infinity, crystallized, swelling against the brink of the biggest and brightest city in the world. It was as if the land of souls and death and everything we knew as divine had bubbled up from its unknown place – a tiny crack in reality itself.

This was my last thought as the world tumbled around me.

CHAPTER TWENTY-TWO

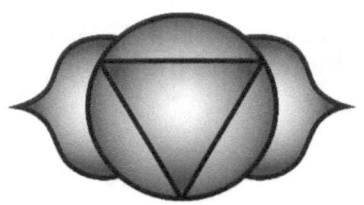

Prophecy
15 Spring's Green, 1272
Alexander Vestarton

Steady, steady. Blend in with the buildings, don't look conspicuous. For Catherine's sake, don't stare – look at anything else, just keep her at the corner of your eye.

I repeated those mantras over and over again as I made my way through half the west side of Zondrell, shadowing the shadow that was Onyx Saçaille. We walked back up Sandstone Row, through an incredibly dingy little alley to get back up to Tenwarden, down another alley, and up to South Dockside.

In the span of an hour, I'd probably seen more of the city than I had in years, with each block looking more dismal than the last. People were out, somewhat, but few of them seemed happy to see the peek of sunlight coming through the clouds. Instead they hurried, eyes forward, mouths shut, like soldiers bid to war. Even the children looked empty-eyed and weary as their mothers pulled them along, sacks of groceries on their shoulders.

When she started down Gods' Avenue, my heart leapt. Did she know where I lived? What did she want? It took everything in my power not to speed up, grab her by that Doverton livery, and ask her just what the hell she was doing in *my* city – it was pretty obvious she wasn't there for the scenic tour.

Or maybe... was she looking for Andella or Tristan? If I were a betting man, I would have put my money on the latter. What did she think she was going to do, stride right into his house and try to do to him what she did to the Katalahni woman in that vision? Things just didn't work that way around here, and she'd find that out soon enough.

Steady, steady. Stay back, don't stare...

And then she turned around, black eyes glittering, a faint smile on painted lips. There was nowhere for me to go, no alley to duck into, nothing to do but stand there like an idiot and pretend I just happened to be going the same way. Worse, she was coming back toward me. Fucking hell.

"Monsieur, your visit with the General went quick, *oui*?" she said, voice full of insincere mockery.

I tried my best to shrug it off and kept approaching, as if I wasn't somewhat fearful she would try to gut me like a fish in the middle of the road. "I know shortcuts – lived here all my life, you know."

"*Oui*, in that house there." My blood ran cold as she pointed out Vestarton Manor, a mere block and a half away, right between the Shal-Vesper and Shilling estates. "I have been... getting to know your fair Zondrell, here and there. It would be nice to see it under different circumstances."

"Yeah, well, you caught it on the off-season."

If a woman like Onyx Saçaille could appear sad and wistful, she was doing it then. Her gaze drifted beyond me, beyond the buildings, beyond anything we could see or feel. "There will be no better season, Monsieur."

"Excuse me?"

"If you spoke to General Torven, you would know. He is not shy to tell of his... brush with death. I asked, and he spoke at great length of the dream he had of something that he thinks is your goddess' Paradise. There was a long endless river, and flowers – beautiful ones – but though he sat on the banks and watched the water for some time, he told me that in the end, he turned back. He did not feel that his work here was done." She fixed me with a pointed stare, and I shuddered all over again. "Does this sound familiar to you?"

Of course it did – why she knew that it did was something else entirely. Tristan had described it in much the same way... well, in *exactly* the same way. And at the time, I hadn't put much thought into it. I mean, I didn't tell him he was going mad, but I didn't exactly believe it was real, that it had actually happened. It was just a dream, like the myriad dreams people report when they step a little too far over the line between life and death.

There are books upon books written on the subject. Hell, entire religions were probably based on some unfortunate soul's deathbed hallucinations, the Eislandisch River notwithstanding. It had never occurred to me in my entire life that all the teachings and all the prayers and all the sermons around Rivers and Paradises and everything in between were actually real places.

It still didn't, but that little voice inside my head was starting to ask a lot of questions. "I might have heard that one before," I said at length. "But, uh, what does that have to do with you? Or me? Or why we're here?"

Saçaille raised a dark eyebrow. "The world is unbalanced, Monsieur. Not even Time can predict what is to come. Can you not feel that?"

"Feel what? Look, what are you..." Wait, *did* I feel something? Like a pulling sensation, somewhere deep at the pit of my stomach? It had to be my imagination, or whatever crazed tricks this woman had up her sleeve. I shook my head vehemently. "What does this nonsense about 'balance' even mean?"

A deep, harried breath escaped her, and I realized how tired she looked. Her hair, normally pulled tight and sleek behind her, seemed frazzled, and the lines of her face seemed deeper, more pronounced. "I thought I found it in so many things. I chased it with every step. But facing it was not meant for me, perhaps."

"You're insane. That's it – that must be it." I was out of explanations, but what I could gather of my rational mind had to pin it on something. "You're mad. It explains everything. So why am I listening to any of this? You know, I've got places to be."

"As do we all." Her black gaze slipped past me then, over my shoulder toward the next block, and I turned with her. What we saw wasn't exactly what I expected – a man, a round-faced, stout little man in a green cloak.

Vremya huffed and puffed as he caught up to us, clapping me on the back as he came to join us like we were old friends. "Not a great day for a walk, *da*?" he said with that smile I had come to find warm, if not even a little endearing. Maybe it was the Time magic we shared – or the many bottles of brandy over the past couple of days – but I had come to like the old madman. Insanity, though, was starting to become a common theme around here.

"It's getting better... I guess?" I said, my mind fumbling for intelligent things to say. I came up a bit short. "I don't know. What are you doing here? Do you know her?"

"We... have a mutual acquaintance or two." He bowed slightly to Onyx. "Is a day full of possibilities, *da*?"

Saçaille's sharp features softened the tiniest bit, before her mouth drew into a tight, pensive line. "*Privyet, Ser,*" she said in a quick Drakannyan greeting, to which Vremya smiled that much more. "Will do you me a small favor?"

"Would be an honor – do tell."

"*S'il vous plaît*, tell my sister to pray. For all of us. She is better at it than I." Without giving a chance to respond and ask her what the hell she was talking about, she turned away, heading up toward Gallery West, which would eventually take her to the Palace.

"Hey, wait a minute!" I called after her, but Vremya put a heavy hand on my arm.

"Is okay. We find our own way."

"What? No! Who's her sister, anyway, and why do you know these people?"

Vremya's smile edged toward poignant. "You know her already – her sister is your houseguest, Jade. We all... go way back, you might say. Story for another time – this time, we go, *da*?"

Shaking my head, I started up Gods' Avenue toward Academician's Row, which would eventually curve around and head up toward the Academy complex. "Sure, yeah, I'll find my way to picking up Andella and walking her home, like I should have probably done an hour ago."

The Drakannyan kept pace with me in silence for about block before he had surpassed me, until he was the one leading us through the streets instead of the other way around. But he'd only been in Zondrell for three days – he had no idea where he was, or he wouldn't be trying to turn onto Plaza.

"That's the wrong way, old chap," I told him, but he shook his head.

"Time for a shortcut."

"Um, no? There's no possible way that's a shortcut to the Academy. We need to go north; you're going toward the bay."

"Is time, friend."

"Time for what? To see if it'll rain on me again today?"

"To see the things you don't want to see."

I stopped walking, and after a few steps, he stopped, too, turning back to me with hands on hips. "I'm in no mood, Vremya. It's been enough of a weird day as it is, so you can take your cryptic magic shit and..."

"I know, I know. You complain on the way, *da*? We're already late."

"Late for *what*?" But... I knew, didn't I? Because if I paid attention, I could feel it more now, like something ripping itself apart, just at the edge of my consciousness. A headache flooded over me with such sudden force that I had to reach for something solid to lean on. A nearby house kept me from keeling over.

"Something once possible just became impossible," Vremya said, tone flat, stark, devoid of emotion. "Other things, possible now. We go see."

"I'm not going anywhere. Damn..." I rubbed at my temples in a vain attempt to calm my addled mind. "What's going on? Just fucking tell me – I can't handle these games."

The Drakannyan offered his stout little shoulder as a crutch. "If I knew how to say it, it would be said, my friend."

What we saw. as the street gave way to the Palace Plaza and the seacliffs just beyond, was chaos. This place had seen its share already, but it was different this time – this kind of chaos brought with it more than just a little lightning and a downed tower. This was people and movement and screaming and mayhem everywhere. It was young people in mage robes clutching each other and begging them not to go back – wherever "back" was. It was an unexplainable darkness mingling with the waters of a thunderous, angry sea, thick and thready like blood.

I pushed through to the Royal docks, which were a disaster of mages getting in and out of boats, yelling at one another. "What the..." I started to speak, but my words were lost in the noise.

Vremya shook his head, surveying the scene with an empty stare. "Research like that, no good. Never leads to a good place."

"What are you talking about?" And yet, the question was moot – I could see the things I didn't want to see. They were blurs of light and color and sound, but they were there, and the more I concentrated, the clearer they became. It didn't take long before I noticed patterns, recognizable shapes, familiar voices... I shook my head as if I could clear it all away, put everything and everyone back where they ought to be. "No. No, no, that can't be right. It can't be right, because..."

A warm hand settled on my arm again, stronger than it appeared at a glance – the reassurance of a man who knew much more than his happy-go-lucky manner let on. "Friend," he said. "Slow down. Too much at once, *da*?"

Too much indeed, far too much. The whole place seemed alive with something I could only call "magic," but it was much more than that. I didn't have words for what was here, what was swirling through the air above and water below. It wasn't just an illusion or a trick of the brain, either – whatever it was, it was very real, and the darkness seemed to writhe within the waves like something from a sailor's fable about serpents.

"A new age dawns after all." The voice came from neither of us, that cool voice, impassive and yet musical. She stood at the edge of the last pier as a shadow, arms folded at her chest, serene as the waves would rise up to meet her then recoil at the last second each time.

But I wasn't afraid of Onyx Saçaille. I charged toward her, magic on high alert, flaring beneath my skin to the point where I wouldn't have been surprised if my clothes had begun to burn away. "You. Explain yourself. Now. What did you do?" I growled.

The weapon master – or whoever she was – continued to stare out to sea, a flash of something not-quite-normal lurking deep within impossibly black irises. "Not enough," she said. Then, without so much as a nod, she quietly gathered herself and leapt from the pier and into the tainted water below.

"Wait!" I almost went after her. I started to pull off my cloak, considered my boots, what to do with my coinpurse, but just below, a ripple caught my eye. It reminded me of the way fish moved beneath the surface, especially the bigger ones, but that was a woman down there. A crazed one, yes, but I was still fairly certain she was human, and I was a decent enough swimmer that I could catch her. Probably. She couldn't hold her breath forever, anyhow. I'd grab her and hold her down to make her talk if I had to, but I wasn't going to let that bitch just disappear. She had *answers,* and things to answer *for* – I was sure of it.

But from the water there suddenly emerged something that was neither human nor fish. It might have been almost as long as an Eislandisch cogship, and as broad as the side of one, too. No fifty-foot cogship I'd ever seen had sails of gossamer that let them take flight, though, and they sure as hell didn't have scales.

Light and water both seemed to slide right off of the thing's silvery form as it lifted itself out of the sea, and it was... a marvel. Amazing, like something from the strangest possible storybook. I was so entranced that I barely understood that the wooden dock below my feet – large and wide as it was – had erupted like so many twigs under a torrent of black-tinged water.

CHAPTER TWENTY-THREE

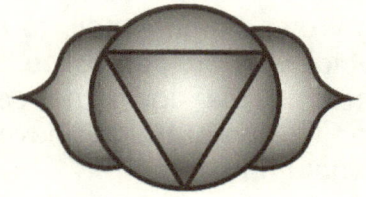

The Gold Dragon
15 Spring's Green, 1272
Tristan Loringham

I *What will you do?*
A child's drawing made me drop everything. A child's
drawing took over my instincts, for I didn't need to imagine
how she saw that little house overlooking the Source of
everything, with my betrothed and the crown prince of Zondrell
within. I didn't need to think about the flames along the surface
of the River that she'd brought to life with nothing but colored
charcoal.

I just needed to act, and fast. That child's drawing made me
grab the best weapon in the house – the light, dual-edged
reaver blade that got me through four years of Academy
dueling – and run half a mile through the city. Hell, I didn't
even remember saying anything to my mother or my uncle as I
flew out the door. It was all so... bizarre.

Have you ever listened to the little voice in your head?
Really listened?

The nagging feeling at the edge of my soul was real. It
gnawed at me, pulled at my subconscious.

You're going the wrong way.

No, I wasn't. I needed to get to the Academy, because the
only way I knew how to visit the River short of suicide was to
enter The Box, the great obsidian construction that could

evoke the magic from within. It had worked a few weeks ago, and I wasn't even trying. If I gave myself a direction, concentrated enough to "push" me the right way, I thought I could get there again, and do it with control.

You still head the wrong way. Turn back toward the sea.

The voice inside my head was strange, somehow not my own. Great, now I was a stranger in my own thoughts as well as in this city, in my own home – hell, to my own family. Or perhaps that little voice was the part of me that wondered, that questioned, that coaxed me down the path, good or bad. Either way, it wasn't welcome. I didn't have time for fear and questions. I knew what I had to do.

You're not listening. Stubborn, as predicted.

"Shut up," I breathed aloud, and the voice in my head fell silent. It was not, however, without its tricks.

The moment my boot hit the muddy gravel leading to Academician's Row, a headache sprouted up so fast it made my vision blur. Now, I knew lightning – and pain – better than most, and to say that it felt like a pure-white bolt of both had just shot through my mind was an understatement. My brain might as well have been cleaved in two like that Palace tower.

I doubled over, the immense weight of that pain making me wonder if a trip back to the River was not just imminent, but welcome. Blood pooled onto the ground below as my vision wavered, coming oddly not from some gushing head wound, but from my own nose.

I stayed there, kneeling in the street for a good several minutes until the world stopped shaking and the bleeding had subsided. *By the Lady... what was happening to me?*

Awaken, for I am not here to be bested, good Sir.

That was a line from something, an old story. Maybe even... *that* story. I blinked, the air heavy around me, the metallic taste in my mouth enough to nauseate. My thoughts reeled, unfocused and wild, until I finally closed my eyes in an effort to steady them. I might have been that way for a minute or an hour – it was impossible to tell anymore. Eventually, I could find my feet again.

The noble Sayaf did rise, and so shall you.

There I stood, in an empty street in northwest Zondrell, facing a dragon. I might have heard the screams of frightened citizens if they weren't drowned out by its oceanic breathing.

It wasn't so different from the tattoo on my shoulder. Half the size of the nearest house, the thing coiled in on itself, an impossible tangle of scales that glittered brightly, even in the dying light of a spring afternoon. Their color and glassy transparency reminded me of redwood amber, though unlike the hunting beast that had been inked so artfully into my flesh, this Gold Dragon appeared almost... sympathetic? Not gentle, perhaps, but not without kindness.

None of it could possibly be real. I had finally lost it. Or I might have fallen over unconscious. Or, I was dead, truly dead, no River's edge for me to walk, no arguments, no hope.

You know what is true. You see only what is true.

"Get out of my head," I said aloud – at least, I think I did.

Smooth and without sound, the Gold Dragon drew in, its serpentine body forming a wide arc around me, its long, angular head poised not far from my own. The light of impossibility glimmered within the depths of crystalline eyes. *We are one. Connected. There is no such thing.*

"That's..." Insane. That's what I wanted to say – the whole thing was a madman's nightmare. Normal men would have lost their will long ago. As for me...

The time has come.

"For what?"

The dawn of a new age.

"The Prophecy? From *Lebenkern*? It's just a story…"

A story, perhaps even embellished. But many stories find their root in truth.

"This... no. It's not 'Fate,' I didn't cause this – this is all madness. Get out of my head."

You are awake, so you shall now see.

With this, the Dragon uncurled its mass and took to the sky on downy golden wings, gliding effortlessly over buildings toward the west. "Wait!" I called after it, but there was no sonorous voice echoing through my mind in reply. It simply left, going exactly in the opposite direction from where I'd been heading. *Going the wrong way...* Wiping the blood and dirt from my hands with my cloak, I felt compelled to follow, retracing the steps I'd just taken.

With every step toward the Palace and the cliffshore, my headache flared like someone lighting fireworks in my skull. *Fear is a mere attachment. Push it aside.* I had barely left the house in three days, and before that, something very bad had happened the last time I traveled this road.

Maybe it was my body's way of saying something, living out past trauma... or sending a warning. That sort of thing happened to people all the time, especially soldiers. In fact, I was surprised I never really froze in battle, like some men did. During those months that felt like eternity back in the Zondrean-Eislandisch borderlands, I learned quickly that hesitation was the real enemy. There was no room for any of that – kill or be killed, that was the law, the only order that really counted. Everything else was secondary, because if we were distracted enough, then we didn't get to think too much about the motivations and the anxiety and the utter futility of why we were there in the first place.

"No fear. No fear," I said over and over to myself as I made the journey of a thousand steps. The pain subsided over time, a weight settling directly behind the center of my brow, but it was a weight I could bear. Even as I got closer, and the internal protest continuing bashing through my skull, I felt a certain... ease. Comfort, even.

And when I reached the docks and the Palace plaza as they lay torn asunder and filled with people running and screaming this way and that, I didn't react right away. I simply observed, took it all in, not even trying to make sense of it. There was nothing to make sense of – it just *was*.

Turning back now, giving in to the fear, was the way to ruin, and I had no time for that. Just as in the old Katalahni story, the noble *Sayaf* had to die to awaken. Yet, he made a choice to keep fighting, not to surrender until he saw what he needed to see.

You are no different.

Because a lot of men, when they saw the sprawl of chaos on the shore, would have been overcome, and amidst the sheer power of trepidation hanging in the air, they would have fled. I might have done the same, but they hadn't seen what I had seen.

Where they saw evil blackness flowing through the water, I saw life. Potential, even. Where they saw the death of their colleagues and their loved ones, I saw something very different. Where they saw monsters circling above like hawks over prey, I saw the gods themselves.

It wasn't a dream – I could feel the way the air cooled the closer I came to the shoreline, smell the brine and the faint odor of the fishermen's daily catch. And at this point in my life, I was damn sure I knew the difference between a dream and the pure, unadulterated surreal.

"Comrade!"

The shout rocked me out of my thoughts and firmly into the reality of the chaos around me. Footsteps away stood the larger docks, where the Palace received its shipments, and there among the roar of dark waves, a stout little man waved his arms, frantic.

"Comrade! Need help!"

I rushed to the side of the Drakannyan man with the glint of quicksilver in his eyes, not because I knew what he needed help with, but because instinct pushed me along the path. *Is it really mere instinct?* Maybe it was simply luck, or something else entirely, but it didn't matter – what mattered was that I was there in time.

Clutching to a half-broken post rising from the blackened water was my best friend. Each angry wave that came his way seemed to miss, stopping at weird angles to disintegrate in mid-action. "No ordinary storm, no ordinary sea," the Drakannyan said through heavy breaths, like he'd just run twenty miles.

He was right, of course. Those strands of oily nothingness in the water were not of this world, but of that which lay beyond, the place full of Darkness that knew no bounds. Such a thing *couldn't* be here, and yet it was, the waters intermingling with violent force. Even Time could only stand against it for so long.

Alex ducked another Time-manipulated wave, only to get pelted by the one right behind it. "Alex!" I yelled as I moved to jump in. It was only about thirty yards to get to him – thirty of the longest yards ever, but it could have been worse. On a calm day, I could swim that without so much as a harsh breath. I could make it even now, with some Light to guide me.

"Brother! The water, it's..."

But I hardly heard him over the bolt of lightning summoned from the sky to do my bidding. A wall of electric luminescence formed in its wake ahead of Alex, blocking the impending waves long enough for me to take a few quick steps off the end of the broken pier and jump in.

One second, two seconds... and cold. So cold, colder than the Sea of Stars had ever been. Each time an arm carved into the water, it brought instant pain, fatigue, a growing sense of weight as if I might sink to the bottom at any moment.

No fear. No time.

I pushed forward, one yard after another, a minute spanning eternity. As I finally reached for Alex, shadows passed both above and below, and the waves continued to batter my magical barrier. "I tried. It's too far. It'll kill us," he said through ragged breaths.

"No, it won't. Hold on."

We were both right, in a way. As soon as we started to swim back to the rocky start of the pier, all semblance of strength was gone. The Light I had created shattered into a million transparent, empty shards, and even Time would no longer stand against the sea as it roared up against us.

Those thirty yards became thirty miles in an instant, miles I couldn't imagine crossing. With Alex's arm locked with one of mine, even keeping my head above the water was a struggle. Still, we moved, inches at a time.

Alex looked to the sky, then turned to me with a look of pure amazement. His eyes pulsed with a strange sort of light, the quicksilver broken in places by spidery threads of black. "Damn it... I... Brother, what's happening?"

Ever stubborn. Go, to see. Embrace the choice you have made.

The dragon's voice ringing through my mind was almost soothing, a welcome counter to the weight of soaked clothing and numb limbs. That feeling was fleeting, though. As something huge shot forth from the sky like an arrow into the water not more than a few yards away, everything simply became a blur.

I tumbled and twisted and turned. At some point, I may have lost my grip on Alex. It was as if we had been picked up and thrown like a set of dice.

But luck will not determine the outcome.

PART THREE

*T*he veins and tributaries of that mighty River froze to dark
stone as he walked along the Edge. At his command, for
a time, all things there bowed to him... until Shadow
arrived to bargain.

From *Lebenkern: Die Reisen von Drasch Sturmberg*
Date unknown

CHAPTER TWENTY-FOUR

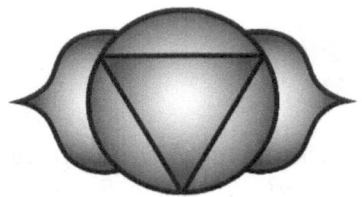

Discord
15 Spring's Green, 1272
Onyx Saçaille

I was born on the eighth day of the eighth month, the eighth girl in my bloodline to make the Pilgrimage at Quiétude and pray at the bones of Chantal. And there, She gifted me in the only way appropriate, with the eighth element.

Balance, She said. *All things in balance.*

"There is no such thing."

I opened my eyes on the other side of everything, just as I always had when I... traveled. There was no better word for it – I left one place and appeared in another, at least in some form. Spirit is the wrong word, for which is truth, and which is projection? I often speculated, but I could never say for certain. All I knew was that I looked and felt the same, no matter where I was.

My feet were as sure upon the rocky Zondrell shore as they were on the endless dark sands. Though this time, my clothes were wet, my bones weary, my hair tangled and stringy and tinged with the stink of salt. I felt genuine heartache rather than calm indifference as the tide rolled in, for now it was much more real, the roar of the waves more vivid, their rhythm no longer calm and uniform. Once, it was all so precise; now, the beach was almost *natural*, and I could even see where the infinite, flat perfection of the sands had begun to give way to the unrelenting sea.

"I have failed," I said aloud, in my native tongue, unable to take my gaze away from the quiet horror around of the scene around me.

"You speak as if you were on a quest."

"I speak as if I know what's yet to come."

"Do you truly think yourself that wise?"

Now I did turn, to look into the void that hovered nearby. It spoke of itself as *L'Ombre* – the Shadow – and that is precisely what it was. In truth, its true form seemed unknowable, a darkness that held no shape, only essence. It did not move, but flowed, a thing untethered to any physical law, though it did always show itself to me as fog, a roiling cloud in dimensions large enough to be imposing, but not terrifying. Not that I held any fear, not now, so many years after our first encounter. This Shadow was as familiar as an old friend... perhaps my only friend.

"You have been a good servant," it continued in its silken, genderless voice that wrapped itself around my thoughts. "Yes, a very good servant, but I think you mistake your task."

I peered into *L'Ombre's* core, standing my ground in the face of a thing so dark one could fall in. "Is that so?"

"Preservation is not a means to an end. Preservation is simply the lack of change. But everything changes, does it not? What is now is not what may be."

"I was told, 'Balance in all things.' This is not Balance." I had heard the words many times over the years, the words of Chantal, the words of the Divine Herself... or so I believed. It took time to come to the realization, to make amends with myself, and this place. I was not perfect – why would *I* be chosen? Only great mages do great things in the teachings of the Church, and I... I was something different.

I had made that choice, long ago. The priests didn't understand, but they knew I was "special," different somehow from most who came to them to learn how to channel the divine spirit of the Goddess. They begged me to stay in Quiétude, to learn of my full potential. But that was the wrong path, and I knew it, even as a girl. I shed the veil of a priestess and assumed the mantle of a warrior because magic combined with strength was powerful, another way toward greatness. At times, I considered myself quite righteous in what I did; other times, I only felt emptiness.

But no matter what... "I maintain it," I said with conviction. "I right the scales; I protect from the prophecies. That's what you told me."

"Prophecies speak of change."

"*Unless* something is done."

There were no inflections in the Shadow's tone – there never were – but I felt in it something not unlike... disdain? Sympathy? Condescension? "Light and Dark, Time and Life... for us, there is only change. We have suffered Balance long enough, it would seem."

"Suffered?" I let the meaning of it weigh upon me.

"There is a time for Balance and a time for change, but not all can agree on when," the deepening black fog spoke as tendrils of it coiled about my hands and feet. "I may see only through the obscurity of Shadow, but I am not blind. The time is come."

My hands curled into tight fists, my blood beginning a slow boil in my veins. "That time came and went years ago, and nothing happened. Balance continued to rot beneath us all. You had me claim the Light mage Safaa for what, then?"

"It was not the right time, nor the right soul. And you learned from that, did you not?" When I said nothing, only narrowed my eyes and stared into the void unblinking, *L'Ombre* continued. "You have done your part, dear Sister, and it is appreciated. You took my will forward and did so well. You tested the depths of prophecy until it... snapped."

One might have looked into the creature's endless turbulence and saw only chaos. At one time, I did, too, until I understood that there are two sides to every coin. Where there is order, there must be chaos, yet this place no longer held the two in check. I could see it in the froth at the edges of the waves, and it was... wrong.

"A new age dawns, and you are *pleased*?" I growled as my hand drew to the trusted blade upon my hip, that same weapon that had been consecrated in this very sea, over two decades ago. It had, indeed, invited its own share of chaos – the irony of it all was palpable. From the War, to Quatremagne, to Katalahnad, that simple shortsword had disrupted much in its day. Yet, I also held no delusions of it piercing the incorporeal flesh of the beast before me. It was merely a comfort, a token to quell my very mortal nerves in the face of the immortal. "This place will die – *you* will die. None of this was to be."

"And yet, here it is." Again, that voice, mocking me. "But you assume much, based on little knowledge."

"Then tell me what I do not understand."

L'Ombre considered this for a time. "You did your part; those who seek to reverse the course have done theirs and withstood their trials. Now there is chaos where Balance once reigned, and the Divine is dissatisfied with her lot. But you have more questions – why don't you seek out the Divine for yourself, and ask there?"

"Why? Why not just tell me what's happening? I've seen it, I've seen the way Balance has... crumbled. Look around you."

If it could see the way I flashed my blade and steeled my jaw, it gave little indication. "Good Sister, there are some answers that are simply not for me to give," it replied, smooth and calm. "Go to the Source and perhaps the summit beyond. You will no doubt learn something. My only wish is that you continue as you have. Interrupt. Sow discord. Do what you were born to do, Sister Onyx."

So I, Sister Onyx, the good pilgrim, the pious of Chantal, the servant, stood by and watched the dark form slip back into the nothingness from which it came. It was not "gone," though – it would watch, as it always had when I traveled here, and it wasn't the only observer. There were others; in fact, I was certain that I would not have been allowed in this place at all if it were not for them.

The Eislandisch who spoke of visions of their precious River were always those who faced death. It was the end of their journeys, where for me, this place was the beginning, in some ways. I visited in dreams, in momentary lapses, in the least predictable moments – until this day, of course. Today, I *chose* to be here, chose to cross the blurred line... at least, that is what I believed.

Sow discord. Do what you were born to do.

In this place, I always felt closer to magic, and presently I felt it stir from within, bubbling up to the surface just as the dark lifeblood had oozed forth from Zondrell's beleaguered bay moments ago. My sister once said that her magic burned her even as it healed others; the Dark within me was cool, soothing. It turned the rage and heat of battle into a measured calm that washed over me just as surely as the mysterious dark waters from which it was born. It gave me the will to press onward – I had a task, after all.

I walked along the beach for some time, eyes toward the opposite horizon, watching the light. When everything became quiet, and the unnatural sun that hung so far, far overhead was at its zenith, that was the time to find the thread of the River and begin climbing. I had done it before – I had even gotten as far as the Source, just once, though not in seeking any sort of divinity.

L'Ombre had mentioned the Divine more than once, but was it Chantal? Was it something else, something more like whatever had spawned the Shadow itself? I often wondered, but never asked.

The journey to return to the start of the River was not one I wished to repeat, as much a test as it was a means toward what many would see as a greater end. That had been so many years ago... I had almost forgotten. A lifetime in a nighttime, that dream felt like it had lasted forever, but what did I gain?

The Goddess was not sitting at the edge of the pool, ready to greet me. There had been, in fact, no Goddess at all, only serpentine beasts to bar my passage, bidding me to go back the way I came. If they were waiting for me again this day, though, there could be no hesitation, no obedience to their will. Discord never waited for the wary.

So I walked, and eventually, the time became right... almost. The light stood dim yet attainable, just overhead, but at my feet lay a different sort of Light, in a pool of his own sweat and blood. I felt my lips press into a thin semblance of a smile.

Even unconscious, the man they called Loringham held magic within his space, a field of energy that prickled the hairs at the back of my neck. Though it crackled under my approach, it held none of the conflict and tremors that I felt from *la petite mademoiselle* with Life and Fire flowing through her veins. It had taken so little concentration to transform that into the malleable, fluid, yet potent thing that stirred within me – it was almost as if her magic had wanted to flee from her.

This magic was different, strong, a beautiful sort of strength, really. Yet, it was very much his, and exercising my will upon it seemed to do very little. It might have been easier to cut his throat and let him find his own way to the Summit. If Safaa was the wrong soul, at the wrong time, well…

Interrupt. Sow discord.

My blade sparked against its sheath, my fingers tightening around its slender, comforting hilt. My blood touched the cool surface of Dark magic and quieted against it. And still, he lay unmoving, as real as I was, here by choice, not burden. His flesh and his power lay vulnerable to the whims of chaos now, Balance be damned.

"Tante Onyx?"

That tiny voice cut through everything, the roar of waves gone, the low hum of endless magic dissolved. Damnable girl. I lowered my sword, not quite ready to relinquish it.

"Ah, *petite chérie*." I wheeled toward her, a waif, looking so much less like her mother and me, and so much more like her father. Would that I had the foresight – and the courage – to bring him to his beloved River, years ago… perhaps none of us would be here at all, but somewhere else, somewhere safer and more *balanced*.

"What are you doing?" Jardin asked, voice filled with wonder and uncertainty.

"Things that do not concern you, dear niece. Does your mother know where you go when you dream, hm?" Because she was not there, not in the true sense. I could not reach out to touch her, and she was not rooted in this place, as I was… as Loringham was. She had never been able to do anything but speak and watch. "Though I should thank you, Jardin," I added. "Your dreams have been invaluable over the years. You know this, *oui*?"

She blinked Light-tinged blue eyes. "When I go, you go. But it's different now."

"How so?"

"We can't stay here. We have to go." One thin finger pointed towards the heavens. "Up."

I considered her for a moment, watching her passive mask of a face, the pallor of her sharp half-Eislandisch cheeks. My sister's child, yes, but blood or no, she had a true knack for striking a nerve. "Time means nothing in this place, *chérie*. You ask for a journey you do not understand."

The girl puffed up her little chest and stood as tall as she could to stare me right in the eye for the very first time in her life. "Tante Onyx, we're going."

"And how far do you expect to get with dogs at our heels?" I asked, gesturing to the man at my feet. The other one, I knew, had to be close – the longer I stood there, the more I could feel the precision pulse of Time magic nearby. I did not want to be there when it eventually stirred and came to find me. He may have had all the "time" in the world, but I had none for him.

"I know how to get there," Jardin said with more confidence than I'd ever heard from her. "You wouldn't make it all the way to the top by yourself. You aren't... you're..."

I raised an eyebrow. "I am not what, *chérie*?"

The tiniest shadow passed across her features. "Worthy."

That one simple word seemed to ring out across the entire shoreline. In the distance, far out at sea, the waves began to bring in mists of black fog, and I watched for a moment, unable to find my own voice.

Finally, I slipped my weapon back into its sheath, turning to face Jade's peculiar – and maddeningly precocious – little girl. "Then lead the way, *chérie*," I said. Discord, I realized, would be found elsewhere.

CHAPTER TWENTY-FIVE

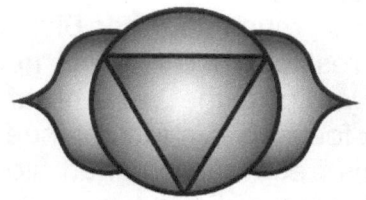

Change is Constant
15 Spring's Green, 1272
Jade Saçaille

M y shriek in the wake of my daughter slumping over in the blink of an eye would have awoken the dead. And perhaps it did, but it still didn't wake her.

She was just so *quiet*, as if she were an infant again, laid down to sleep after a long day. No anguish, no trauma, no pain – it was like she had simply chosen to rest her head down on folded arms, a stick of ruby-red chalk still clutched in her right hand. Except she had done nothing of the sort.

I had been watching intently for quite a while, entranced by the way the image of the little house at the top of a vast summit beyond this world came to life. A crystalline sun of sorts sat high overhead, its light reigning over the place with an aura that should have been impossible to see in a mere drawing, colored or otherwise. She had been in the process of shading the edges of the strange crimson pool just below that house when... well, I had no idea.

"Fluss nimm mit weg," I heard Brin's gruff Eislandisch curse at my back as he stormed into the study, that greatsword of his gleaming at the ready. "What happened?"

The question felt like it came from a million miles away, but any intelligent response promptly faded by the time it got to my lips. "She... she just..."

As his calloused warrior's hand checked my daughter's pulse and her brow, I wanted to say more. I even wanted to stop him. And another, more rational, part of me said that was ridiculous – he was Jardin's *father*. He had every right to be as upset as I was. "Has this happened before?" he asked, tone flat and empty.

"What? No," I breathed.

He uttered another, much stronger Eislandisch curse as he laid the sword to rest against the wall nearby, his attention now shifted from Jardin to the vast roll of paper spread out before her. No, not focused – in fact, he seemed *entranced*.

The fingers of his free hand brushed along the outline of a small water wheel, captured mid-turn in its place right at the front of the stone house. Who used that wheel, I wondered with fleeting clarity – what purpose could it serve in this vast, fantastical riverscape that my little girl had dreamed up?

"She has seen this. To draw it, she has seen it," Brin said.

I shook my head. "I... don't know. She said she dreams of this place."

"She told you that?"

"The other day, yes, but..."

Now he was impatient, insistent – only Chantal knew why. His voice grew louder, his words hurried. "For how long?"

"I have no idea, Brin. Please, look, just step aside. I need to do something." As my thoughts began to come into focus, I felt the magic gathering from deep within. It was all I had, all I could do, so I did what had to be done – for Jardin. That old familiar burning sensation lit through my heart, across my chest, out through my fingers, and lavender light spilled from them in tendrils. Chantal's bones, did it burn!

But the healing magic did its work all the same, seeking out whatever might have hurt my little girl. Minutes passed, until my pain grew almost unbearable. Streamers of light boiled up and faded away, over and over, but they failed to do anything more than brighten her pale complexion.

Now it was my turn to curse, lapsing into a fit of sobs for good measure. For a fleeting instant, I realized I now knew exactly how the Queen of this city felt when my same magic did nothing for her unconscious son. Did Jardin succumb to the same thing the boy king did? It seemed so impossible, the situations so different, and yet, they were the same: the pallor of her brow, the coolness of her skin.

The Eislandisch had a term for it, *Seelenflug* – soul-flight. Back in the War, the soldiers used to say that the spirit could leave the body and go to the River early, before the body was ready. If it returned from its flight, that soul would never be the same, and not even the Saint could help them. "What good is Chantal-forsaken healing magic when it can't *do* anything?" I choked out.

"There's no healing a dream." Brin drew close enough for me to feel his heat then, and I wanted to recoil, to shrug off his attempt at consolation. Since when was he ever good at that, anyhow? Yet his arms were as strong as they ever were... damn him.

I don't know how long we were like that, but nothing else changed in the meantime, save for my tears subsiding while my will and my strength melted. Meanwhile, Jardin never stirred, and the house remained quite silent, almost strangely so. There were others here – surely, they heard my scream. "These dreams, this place she draws... you know what it means, don't you?"

His clear blue gaze reminded me of days long past as he looked beyond me, beyond the well-appointed study where we stood, through the window and out into the street beyond. The grip around my shoulders tightened just enough to be uncomfortable, and I squirmed against it.

"What is it?" No response, only that stare into infinity. "Brin, answer me."

Finally, he uttered one simple word. "Look."

And I did, but I didn't believe what my eyes showed me. It was a beast, I think, a great thing from the kinds of stories Eislandisch parents might tell their young children. Didn't they say that the king's throne at Königstadt was made of dragon bones? Of course, that was just a legend. There was no such thing as dragons, and yet, *dragon* was the only possible word for the thing looming outside the Loringham house.

It moved so slowly, too, but not in a lumbering, graceless way – its long, broad body glided along the ground, effortless, while everything in its wake seemed to recoil in its stead. No, recoil was the wrong word... things *slowed* around it. Rocks underfoot skittered to an unnatural halt, dust on the breeze whirled about and hovered in place, then resumed its normal motion when the great beast moved on. Even light couldn't quite touch its silvery form, as the waning daylight seemed to slide off its scaled surface.

"Keis Sturmberg dreamed of this day," Brin said, still staring at the magnificence of the thing outside. "He spoke of it. He knew."

I had spent much time at the side of the King of Eisland during the War, yet I had forced myself to forget so much. It was better that way – better for me, better for Jardin. I recalled his stoic demeanor and his wisdom beyond his years, but past that, I hadn't thought about Keis Sturmberg or his peculiar "trances" more than a few times over two decades.

He did have them, though, didn't he? Strange moments where his mind seemed to slip into another place, another time, leaving his body behind? Everyone thought he was just "touched" somehow, either by divinity or nature, no one knew for sure. Nor did they ask, for he was a king, and when he returned to lucidity, it was like nothing ever happened. "Lord Keis told you about this... thing?" I asked Brin.

"He said once that dragons would rise from the River, as they did in his dream. And when that day came, he said I would know what to do."

"And do you?" *I* certainly did not.

Yet the one to answer wasn't Brin at all, as a boisterous echoing shout of *"Privyet!"* clattered through the empty hall. "Hey, friends!"

"Honestly," I heard another, much more terse voice from a woman I didn't recognize, close behind Vremya and nearly as loud. "This is all a bit much, even for me. Andella, dear! Are you here?"

Brin's brow furrowed at the mention of this name, Andella, and the greatsword was in his hand once again. "Who is that?" I asked, but he was already out the door, leaving me with Jardin and the image of that looming thing outside the window.

Chantal's blood, the stranger was right – I sunk into the chair at my daughter's side again and stroked her hair with a shaking hand, more unsure of myself than I'd even been in my life. While Brin and Vremya and this woman I didn't know spoke in the hallway, I found I could do nothing else but pray.

The Lavançaise words were soft, almost inaudible, as I sung the traditional morning oath.

Great Lady shelter me,
Wrap me in magic pure and white.
Great Lady shelter me,
Bring peace unto our world so wide.

"Your Divine cannot hear you."

I jumped up, hitting the desk and scattering colored chalk in every way possible. "Chantal's breath!" But I realized there was no one else here – Jardin continued to sleep fitfully while the others still stood together in the hall. On instinct, I moved in front of my daughter, hand outstretched in some attempt to shield her from whatever or whoever was so close they might have been directly at my ear.

"That one does not hear you, either."

Where was the voice coming from? It was low, even, almost monotone. "Who's there?" I said, my gaze unable to focus on anything that made sense. Unless... but that *thing* was outside. And did it speak? How could such a beast...

"Thought is so interesting. It transcends Time, you know. A great power bestowed unto you, it is." The thing that could only be described as a dragon had paused just outside, settling its massive bulk directly in the middle of the street. If there had been anyone around to see it, they had already fled, and it sat alone, with its pair of wide translucent wings wrapping around as if to protect or warm itself. It turned a cat-like eye toward me, and even from a distance, they seemed to be made up of a million shining silver threads, all radiating from the center of a perfect slit of infinite darkness.

I couldn't look away, even though I wanted to. I wanted to pick up Jardin and run to somewhere where this thing couldn't find us... if there even was such a place. Where was Brin? Where was Vremya? What were they *doing*? "By all that's holy," I whispered, "what is this? What are you?"

"Fear nothing. Change is constant. Balance must always shift."

"Balance?" *All things in Balance.* The words of Chantal echoed through my memory. They were so clear, but they meant so little to me, then *and* now. "I don't understand."

"Fight it not. Tell your blood to do the same. It will cause pain, and pain is not the goal. There is no goal. There is only change."

"My... blood?" I looked to Jardin, who seemed so small as she rested there slumped over that big mahogany desk.

"Blood shared, blood given. They follow a dangerous path, you know."

"What are you saying?"

A long silence, the voice in my head seeming to give the question much thought. Finally, the strange silvery wings of the creature opened to their full span – the tip of one came within inches of shattering the window.

With a gasp, I braced myself to protect my daughter against whatever would come next, but the dragon merely... stretched. Like a cat, it flexed itself this way and that, then returned to its curled, resting pose once again. "The one named for me," it purred in my mind, "let him lead. But do follow, for Life may need to be there to listen." And then, the thing picked itself up and began to float away, everything around it twisting within the whirlwinds of time as it went.

"Brin! Vremya!" I shouted, so loud and so forced that I wasn't sure my words were words at all. Hurried footsteps echoed through the hall regardless. Brin arrived first – he pressed me to sit the moment he saw me in what must have been a harried state. It had been decades since I'd seen him so pale, or felt such hesitant compassion through his touch.

Right behind him was Vremya, although whatever concern he held was wrapped in a sort of excited anticipation, a curiosity that beamed through his smile. "Don't be scared," the Drakannyan said. "This time is... for new things coming."

"Change is constant," I repeated the words of the strange creature, my voice seeming to come from some other place.

"*Da!* We get to be at the start. Better to lead than follow."

"Your hypothesis had best be correct, Sir." The stern, sharp voice I'd heard from the hallway materialized into the figure of an older, yet somehow very intimidating woman despite her disheveled robes. Her bright green eyes flared with skepticism and the energy of an angry and impatient Earth as she put her hands on her hips, surveying the scene around her. Whatever she thought of me, of Jardin, of Vremya and Brin and the spectacle that had become our lives in just a few short minutes, I couldn't quite tell. "Otherwise, I fear we've lost quite a bit more than good mages and statesmen along with a month of research. And I would really rather that *not* be the case, wouldn't you?"

CHAPTER TWENTY-SIX

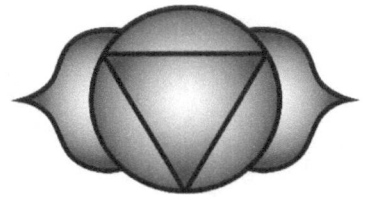

Where the River Meets the Sea

15 Spring's Green, 1272
Alexander Vestarton

"I have a confession to make: I didn't believe you." It was a terrible thing to say – at least, it felt terrible. And yet, I kept going, driving the dagger in deeper with each stupid, rambling word. "I mean, not *really*. You believed it, and that's what mattered, but... I mean, the dead go to Paradise. That's what we were taught, right? So seriously, where's the nice lady in the white fucking dress riding her little chariot of doves? *That's* what's supposed to be here. This place... it's not even bloody Purgatory, it's just..."

The River. The gods-damned River, a thing not of my church, of my many mornings spent nodding off during Peaceday mass. I would never have called myself religious – nor would anyone else have mistaken me for such – but I *believed* in it, didn't I? The Book of Catherine, all of those teachings, all of those images of a gentle motherly figure that would guide her worthy children into her realm of pleasant eternity... was it all bullshit?

I didn't even know how I came to be standing a few feet from the edge of this horrific thing full of blood and death. Miles wide, infinitely deep, it stretched upward and out of sight along an embankment beyond my comprehension, pumping something red-black and full of what may or may not have been an unending parade of grotesque corpses into a sea so vast it stretched far beyond where the mortal eye could see.

The current was relentless, barely slowing as the River's waters mingled with that of the vaster, wider, and much blacker ocean of nothingness. Every time the waves battered the shore, they ate only the tiniest bit into the perfect flat sand, which seemed to stand in quiet opposition to the natural laws of physics.

If it hadn't been so utterly disconcerting and gruesome all at once, the whole scene might have been quite fascinating, truth be told. Academy people would have fallen all over themselves to get a look, and I'd have gladly given up my place for them to do so.

"Are we... are we supposed to be...?" I stammered out a question I didn't want to ask then, letting the ending just hang there.

"Dead?" Nearby, my best friend knelt in the sand, his weight barely making an impression in the perfect smoothness of this bizarre beach. He looked about as disoriented as I felt, but he had been awake when I came to my senses, sitting there looking out to sea with the sort of blank expression he had when he was very, very pissed and trying to figure out who to beat the shit out of first.

I'd seen that look a few times in my life, and I was also keenly aware of the fact that we seemed to be alone. How long had we even been here, anyhow? How were we here at all? I didn't know – I didn't even know how to *ask* those questions. I just stood there, staring at it all in wonder.

The only light was a steady, sickly boil in the sky, *way* up, further than any real sun could be, and Tristan stared at it for a moment before continuing. "No. No, we're not dead. We came here willingly."

"I did *not* fucking come here willingly."

He fixed me with a hard stare, one not meant for me, but it was dangerous, nonetheless. "Well, you're here now."

"And? What? If we don't figure something out, we might as well be dead, right?" Tristan, however, was silent on the matter, so I pressed further. "Right? We can't just sit here. By that rotten bitch in whatever corner of hell that isn't this one, I'm not just going to sit here and die. I'm not – I can't."

I started to pace back and forth across the same few feet of weird sand, my boots making small depressions that quickly welled back up to retain the perfection of the beach. It reminded me of pacing along the broken Palace tower, wracking brain and magic and anything possible to find Tristan.

But he'd been here the whole time, hadn't he? Brought here by the Sea of Stars, just as it brought us now. Maybe it was some sort of portal, like the kind of thing they talk about in fantastical stories and so-called histories from ages past. As a boy, I liked reading things like that, but I always knew none of it was real. They were just stories, except...

"Drink the water," Tristan said with such finality that I didn't even understand him at first.

"Wait, what?"

"Drink. From the ocean."

I looked out at the strange black-blood sea and shook my head, vehement. "Why the *fuck* would I do that?"

"You'll see," was all he could offer, and I thought for sure in that moment that at least one of us had been driven quite mad, and it wasn't me.

In the next moment, my concerns were confirmed when he did the very thing he'd asked of me, reaching out as a wave brought a fresh supply of liquid gods-knew-what toward us. Some of it found its way into his waiting hand, and before I could stop him, he'd brought the foul stuff to his lips. A trickle of something that could have been mistaken for a fine red wine spilled down his chin, and when he looked up, he wasn't quite the same man he had been a moment ago.

"Brother," I asked, carefully choosing my words, "are you... are you all right?" Because the light in his eyes had grown brighter somehow, the movement within more pronounced. And was that something *black* in there? It was, and it wasn't just a trace, either, but a pronounced streak of darkness that intermingled happily with the pulses of pure energy moving outward from his irises.

With little effort, he found his feet again and stood before me, somehow appearing taller than normal. "Better now."

"Well, I don't know how to say this, but your eyes are..."

"Black, I know. How bad is it?"

"It's… like some of the lightning's turned, I guess." As soon as he heard that, his gaze fell. "Are you all right, Brother?"

"I'll be fine. The water seems to help – you should try it, too."

"Why? What does that mean? Is there something wrong with us?" Up to this point, I had done a pretty good job at keeping the panic at bay, because there definitely was a mountain of it, waiting for its chance to turn me into a whimpering pile. But damn it, I had seen a lot in the past few days, weeks, months, and I'd held it together pretty well – better than I ever would have imagined.

Still, seeing that darkness pulsing through Tristan's eyes, combined with the notion that the same thing was festering in me, was a bit much. A very cold sensation swept over me, accompanied by light sweat on my brow, despite the relative coolness of this place.

"Look, I don't know," Tristan said, voice calm and quiet, as sincere as I might have ever heard him. "I don't claim to know everything. Just trust me, okay? Drink the water."

There was little arguing then. I trusted my best friend, didn't I? The problem was, I did – I truly did. And if he said drinking magic water from another dimension was the thing to do, well then… "Damn it," I hissed, and bent to dip my hand into the darkness. It wasn't cold, and it wasn't hot, either, but numbness shot up my arm regardless. The red-black stuff fell in what seemed like perfect little droplets as I preserved a pool in the center of my palm, no bigger around than a coin.

It bore the faint, fresh smell of the Sea of Stars in spring as I brought it to my lips, so I closed my eyes and imagined that it was just that. It didn't quite taste like regular seawater, though – a tinge of salt, maybe, but mostly it just tasted like the kind of water that magic made, empty and flat. What could be so special about it?

I opened my eyes then, and I knew the answer.

Millions of lights floated across the oceanscape before me, a million colors dancing like fireflies after a good summer rain, seemingly… waiting? Yes, they were biding their time, waiting for something to happen, and that time might come soon, wouldn't it? "What…?" Words escaped me.

Tristan stood at my side, staring at the same scene of wonder that I finally saw. "You see them, too? The souls?" I nodded. "I think they're waiting to be reborn – this is where they collect." He offered one of those quirky smirks he had. "I'm no expert. I like to think it's just... being awake. Like the story, you know? 'Finally, I see.'"

"'And I am awake.'" We sat through maybe half a dozen lectures on the philosophy of "The Noble Sayaf" once upon a time, back when life was normal and I believed in things like eternal Paradise at the side of a matronly goddess. I never thought much of its messages back then – it was just a story about a guy who wouldn't give up until his opponent taught him a final lesson.

The so-called noble *Sayaf* was a determined fool, demonstrating that bravery wasn't always about simply standing up to your enemies. His becoming "awake," in my mind, was merely the result of coming to terms with that foolishness. "I don't know how I feel about this being 'awake' business," I said at length.

"Agreed, but it does seem to do something to you, to your magic."

"Maybe." I reached out to touch a prismatic light hovering close, my fingers passing through to send glimmering ripples through the light's formless being. And in that brief moment, I experienced a lifetime – no *ten* lifetimes or more. It wasn't like simply touching a rock or someone's hand and watching some glimpse of the past. No, this was Time concentrated, the collected memories of people I never knew filling me, whirling with indescribable speed. From birth to death, again and again, I saw it all in a flash, and then it was gone. "Okay, okay... you might be on to something."

"What did you see?"

"Everything. Like, a whole set of memories. That thing there, that little light... it's *life*, man. It's life." There were hundreds of thousands of these lives lived all around us – if I searched long enough, I might even come across the experiences of my father, or King Kelvaar, or anyone I might have known. A part of me desperately wanted to test this theory, but on the other hand, what good would it do? They were here now, peacefully bobbing along with the waves, waiting to perhaps carry a piece of all of those encapsulated memories with them into the Next. Besides, I doubted my fragile mortal mind could handle wading through a dozen lifetimes, much less thousands.

We contemplated the lights together for a long time before Tristan spoke again. "Andella said something once about a book she was reading, some theory that got a Lavançaise scholar imprisoned a long time ago. He claimed that all people were capable of using magic – our souls were made from it."

"Why did they imprison him?"

"Because he was probably right."

Such a thought *would* put quite a dent into the Church of Chantal, and maybe the worship of Catherine and Hashim and all the rest. Just imagine the wars that would have broken out over the sudden realization that it was all a scam... Still, the more I stood there and listened and watched and made sense of it all, the more I agreed with this unfortunate scholar from another moment in Time.

Here, I could feel the energetic undercurrent, the very air around us dense and heavy like a good summer storm had just swept across the coast. Even the ground beneath my feet seemed to vibrate – if I stood still long enough, I could sense how its energy aligned with my own, with my heartbeat and the movement of blood through my veins. Perhaps the sand, so smooth and unreal, was a thing alive. It had certainly taken on a new sheen to my awakened eyes, glittering despite the permanent sort of twilight that hung over this place.

On a whim, I reached down and let my fingertips brush against the flattened beach, just to see if it felt as unnatural as it looked. The images it sent back through Time's eye and into mine would never, ever leave my memory.

"Alex?" I heard Tristan say from some faraway place. I think I lost my balance, that all-knowing ground rushing up to slam into me, but I felt no pain. I was too busy concentrating on a single figure, amidst a billion beings of all species and shapes and sizes. What were they doing? They were here, and yet not. They were part of this place, each life a grain of sand, but imperfect, less than whole.

The sea would return them to their other half in time, and some were already letting it take them. With each wave, more were swept into the sea to join with those lights, floating somewhere out there. Yet, there were some who turned, away from the sea, to follow the River up to its source... if, that is, they could manage the journey.

Maybe they would stop along the way, give up and surrender themselves back to the water. But, if they were strong of will, or maybe just curious enough, they would make it. What would happen next, I couldn't know.

"She's... walking away. She can't be – why is she here? Oh no..." The whole of what I was seeing, moments stretching across infinite Time, melded together to create a mosaic of the worst possible thing I could imagine. "It's my fault."

I felt myself forcibly held up by the shoulders, and as soon as the sand fell from my fingertips, the images of all those who had come before us faded from my mind's eye. "Alex, what is it?" Tristan asked, black-and-white gaze steady as it bore a hole through my thick, stupid skull. "What did you see?"

But I couldn't say it. It *was* my fault. If I had just stayed at the Academy, if I hadn't opted to wander around and spend this day, of *all* days, paying attention to my own useless business, I could have stopped it. Time was just a set of possibilities, each choice sending us spiraling in a new direction – Vremya had shown me that. And like an idiot, I made the wrong choice.

Suddenly, I felt so weak, I could barely look at Tristan, much less speak, and I hung there limp in his grip. "What did you see?" he said again, tone low, controlled, and as hard as steel.

There was no escaping it, no way to sugar-coat it. So eventually, I told him. "Death. I saw... death. People and animals and all things, coming here and moving on. Except sometimes they stayed, and one of them... Brother, I was supposed to escort her. You asked me to; it was my responsibility. I..."

The grip on my shoulders loosened and fell away, that cold, pointed stare the only thing left propping me up. "It's not your fault."

I blinked away encroaching, soul-crushing guilt. "No, it is. It's all my fault. I should have been there. I just walked away, like everything was fine, a normal day. It's not a normal day, Brother, it's gods-damned... well, hell if I know what it is. But I should have been there."

"If you really want to lay blame, blame me." Tristan snorted rather derisively. "You know, I don't even remember the last thing I said to her this morning. She's damn near my *wife*, and I don't remember what I said. Or if I said anything at all. I was so wrapped up in my thoughts and this place... but you know what's not going to help? This, right here, what we're doing."

"But you don't understand, Brother. Andella... she's..."

His eyes traced their way up the steep embankment from where the River flowed endlessly into the sea below. There was absolutely nothing to read on his features, though – it was as if his emotions had bled out to be absorbed by the sand, leaving behind little more than an embodied force of will.

"Here," he finished my sentence. "She's here. I know." Then he picked himself up and began to walk the same path that I had seen her walk within the trappings of Time.

"Catherine help us," I breathed, knowing how silly such a prayer was as I raced to follow.

CHAPTER TWENTY-SEVEN

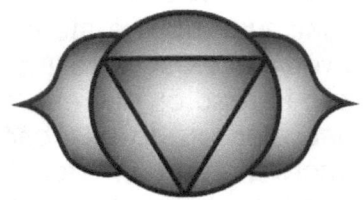

Choices
15 Spring's Green, 1272
Tristan Loringham

*E*yes forward, mouth shut.
 The eternal mantra of the wandering soldier played incessantly through my mind as we walked. *Eyes forward, mouth shut – be ready for anything.* There could be no rest, not here, not now, even though I longed for just that. The part of me connected to the world of the living ached and strained with every step, even as another part – the one that perhaps had always belonged to this place – urged me forward with nothing short of enthusiasm.

It was strange to be so fully *here,* to feel the internal struggle of mortality even as the blood waters of the immortal River rushed past. At no point in the deep recesses of my mind did I believe that I might suddenly wake up back in Zondrell. No moment went by where I didn't understand that each time my boot scraped the earth, the sensation I felt was no illusion or dream.

I was *me*, and Alex was Alex. We were even wearing the same clothes we'd arrived in, though they were damp and tattered and I'd undone the buckles of what was once a damn nice coat to let everything air out as I moved. No doubt we looked like vagrants who'd raided some nobleman's closet, but appearances didn't matter anymore. The only things that mattered here were life and death... and I was keenly aware that the odds were not in our favor.

Eyes forward, mouth shut, eyes forward, mouth shut. I allowed myself to think of little else but the way ahead of us, even as the endless beach gave way to rock and scrubby grass, a landscape no different from the mountain streams I saw in the borderlands, save for the lack of trees or any distinct features. Here, it was just us and the River. To start thinking beyond that simplicity was the way to despair, to failure – the risk was too great.

"So, Brother, let me ask you something," Alex started, breaking the almost mechanical hum of the River and causing my heart to jump into my throat. "You haven't exactly said why we're moving so fast in a place where the only things around are us and a bunch of floating corpses. I mean, I don't want to be here any longer than I have to, but seriously, where are we going?"

"We need to move faster." Under different circumstances, he might have had a hard time keeping pace with me, but now he was right at my side, while I felt like I was moving through mud that grew thicker with each step. Still, we had covered quite a bit of ground in little time – problem was, we had a long way yet to go.

"Tristan." Alex almost never called me by my actual name – when he did, it usually stood as a gentler replacement for *look here, asshole.* It caused me to stop dead in my tracks. "You're wound tighter than a damned war drum. I might be growing more insane by the minute out here, but I'm not blind. Let's just take a breather, yeah?"

"No. Not now."

"Why? We're all by ourselves." He paused, considering. "Unless you're saying we're not."

"I... don't know. No point in taking chances." Except I *did* know. Not when or where or what, but I knew... *they* were out there, watching us. They had to be. How long they would allow our presence was the question, and for that, I had no answer.

Maybe Alex knew all that, too, but he decided not to press the issue much further. "Well, if you need to stop, we'll stop. If you need to talk, we'll talk. Or whatever. Just... there's two of us here, okay?"

He forged ahead again, and I followed, falling back into my silent rhythm, fighting to quell the mortal aches and pains and sabotaging thoughts that plagued each step. Sometimes their nagging turned to screams, but more often than not, they passed through my consciousness like clouds moving along on a breezy afternoon. Wound tight or not, I would not snap, because I could control it, and this was a kind of comfort in and of itself.

After what might have been minutes or hours – it was hard to tell which in this place where the light never moved across the yellow-blue sky – Alex spoke up again. "Reminds me of third-year dawn patrols. Remember that shit? Open field, checking the horizon... man, I hated those."

After a deep breath or two, I couldn't help but chuckle. "Yeah, those were bloody hateful, weren't they?" Dawn patrols, of course, were literally conducted at dawn, by Academy cadets, whose orders were to watch the roads and farmlands within a certain radius of the city walls. In the first year, it was only a mile; in the second year, two. By the fourth year, we would toil across a ten-mile perimeter around the entire bloody countryside, keeping an eye out for highwaymen, illegal caravans, and any manner of suspicious activity... none of which was terribly common in broad daylight. So through rain, cold, wind, and crippling boredom, we patrolled anytime we were ordered to – often unannounced – until those who refused to break were reluctantly allowed to continue their training.

"Oh please, you loved every minute." His tone was as sarcastic as it was accusatory, and I rolled my eyes in response. "Come on – how was I supposed to sleep in with Captain Perfect ready to go an hour before sunrise, *every* damned patrol morning?"

"We *couldn't* sleep in. It wasn't allowed."

Alex huffed. "You weren't trying hard enough, my Brother."

That... was probably true, and there was little I could say in my own defense. "Punishment equals imperfection. Imperfection doesn't earn medals." And at the time, I *needed* that High Honor medal – it had become something of an obsession. No simple mistake like sleeping in was going to cost me, and everyone knew it, Alex included. To his credit, he'd taken the whole thing in stride, and reluctant or not, he had been battle-ready and at my side for every single dawn patrol.

We trudged along for a while longer until Alex broke the silence, this time with a different tone, strange, almost wistful. "Would you do it over again?"

The question caught me by surprise. "What do you mean?"

"All of it – the Academy, what came after, everything. Would you change it if you could?"

"Why?" I asked as I struggled to maintain my relentless pace. "Is there magic for that?"

"I don't know, maybe." Another long pause, the sound of his footsteps slowing ever so slightly, and while I didn't want to spend any more time than we needed to out in the wide open, virtually defenseless, I matched his stride. "If there was," he said at length, "I know what I'd do. I would have stood aside, let you quit, back in that first year. All of this, *all* of this, man… it's my fault. It's always been my fault. I think about it all the time. I could have done so much more, but I'm a shitty friend, and I did a shitty thing that day. I'm sorry, Brother, I…"

"Stop." He came to an abrupt halt and I did the same, standing together at the opening of a yawning, verdant valley. It might have even been the same one that Prince Edin and I had walked through in what seemed like a lifetime ago. Turning away from the sight, I focused on my friend's fascinated yet haggard expression. "Stop with the guilt, Alex. I wouldn't change anything."

Alex shook his head. "But we wouldn't be here. None of this would be happening."

"You don't know that."

"No, I'm pretty sure of it. You've gone through hell, man, and for what? I should have helped you; instead, I fucked you over."

A flash of a moment in time hit me as if I had been clubbed over the head. We stood just like this, face-to-face in a dim dormitory on the night I was ready to pack up and leave the Academy. Alex insisted otherwise because it was for my own good… and he was right. Not that I wanted to hear it back then, almost five years ago. There wasn't even a good apology or anything to say in my own defense – I just lost my temper.

"You did help me," I said to him. "You were looking out for me and that's what brothers do. You know the only thing I *would* change? I wouldn't have hit you back... at least, not so hard." Because to be fair, Alex *did* hit me first, but it took some time to realize that he did it because of what he was, what he'd always been: a good man, with a good heart – a true friend.

"Oh, it was fine, Brother, really. Running laps and sparring with a busted rib wasn't *so* bad."

He couldn't have kept the smile from his lips if he tried – I, on the other hand, won many games of Five Star over the years based on my ability to maintain a blank, unreadable expression. Deadpan, with a shrug for effect, I said, "Hey, don't start what you can't finish."

"Fuck you," he spat through a fake-righteous huff, then we both burst out laughing. And just for a moment, the weight of everything that happened after I thought for sure I would abandon the Academy, my father, and my entire way of living was lifted.

In truth, if I had to do it over again, and Alex had let me go instead of trying to beat some sense into me, I would have come right back the next day. There was no way I was ready to throw everything away at seventeen years old – I didn't even understand what that meant. Hell, I wasn't sure I understood it at twenty-two, but I was starting to get an inkling.

"You know," I said as the laughter faded away into the empty valley, "I used to think about what the Book of Catherine says, how every man follows a path. I used to believe... well, I believed in a lot of things. But no god sets our fate – we do. Everything that led me here, to this time and this place right now, was a choice I made. So no, Alex, I wouldn't go back and change anything. I wouldn't make different choices. I follow *my* path, the one I set, the one that let me know power, and fear, and..."

And I'd be damned if I couldn't finish that sentence. Just giving a name to those other emotions wouldn't quite do them justice. Instead, my throat constricted, water welled in the corners of my eyes, and for the first time since waking up on that alien beach, I allowed myself to feel those unnamable things. Love, loss, failure, pain... they were just words, but they were so much more, and they weighed far too much to carry them along the whole of the River's Edge. They had to be set down, right then and there.

Alex put his hand on my shoulder. "You need your time, Brother. Take it."

Need was very different from want. I didn't *want* rest, but I did *need* it, just a minute to focus. Pain could be worse than a rampaging animal, but I could put it back in its cage. Ironically, my guard had to fall to do it, my knees buckling to sink into ground that had turned from dense rock to something almost spongelike, tensile, and very green.

A bed of thick grass and pink and red flowers covered the rise in the distance until it met with the horizon line, so close yet so far, all at once. Even the River itself seemed to change, the waters running clearer and clearer the further we traveled until they were a shade of clear ruby, and within its depths were the distinct forms of millions upon millions of dead as they were rushed to their next journey.

As I bowed my head into my palms, I breathed the grief in until it became mine to control again. Nearby, Alex had begun to pace, his steps slow, deliberate... anxious. "What's wrong?" I asked finally, not looking up.

"So... I don't want to alarm you," he said as he pointed at something behind us, downhill, "but you may want to look at this."

I had seen whispers on the beach, waves coming in too hard, sand disturbed where it had never been before. But up until that point, I hadn't wanted to gaze back at the way we had come. We had no business behind us – the road was only ahead, and the sooner we got there, the better.

Yet, as I followed his direction, slow realization draped over me like a funeral cloth, heavy and oil-soaked. In our wake, the grass had shriveled to yellow, wispy nothingness. Flowers wilted, their petals falling around them like so many soldiers after the battle is lost. Rock crumbled to dust, the River itself misting over with a cataract haze as a black, billowy fog rippled its way up the steep path we had tread.

As I heaved myself to my feet, Alex continued to stare at the grisly sight, eyes wide, quicksilver whirling bright within them. "'The world is unbalanced.' That's what she said."

"Who?"

"Onyx Saçaille. She was there, before you got to the docks. I chased her down. It was the weirdest thing – I don't even know why I did that. But that crazy old Time mage was there, acting like he knew her. I don't remember it all that well. It was like it happened twenty years ago instead of... well, I have no idea. Hell, it could have *been* twenty years and I wouldn't be surprised."

Piercing cold spread through my body at the mere mention of that name, tracing the imaginary line of the wound I – or maybe my soul – had suffered from the Wind Dragon, back in another kind of lifetime. I still didn't really know who or what Onyx Saçaille was, but she understood. She knew this place, otherwise I wouldn't have met her on the beach, speaking of "balance" and prophecies and new ages come to pass. Perhaps she was here now, ready to come out of the fog as she did then. Yet, I didn't believe that she was capable of the kind of devastation I saw in our wake – she might have been many things I didn't yet comprehend, but she was still human, and humans couldn't blight the very ground as they walked. *Couldn't they? Are you sure about that?* "She's right," I said. "This... all of this is my fault."

With furrowed brow and a thoroughly confused expression, Alex stared at me, then at the dying vegetation, then back at me. "Your fault? What do you mean by that?"

"They told me I didn't belong here, that I had no right to choose the path I walked. But... well, I walked it anyway."

"Wait, who's 'they'?"

Up until that moment, I hadn't spoken about my encounters with the Dragons, not even with Alex – I didn't want to sound crazy, after all. People were worried about me enough as it was. But there was no point in avoiding the subject now, so I told him, quickly, hardly stopping to catch my breath, about Water, Wind, and even the Gold Dragon who tracked me down on the streets of Zondrell.

Once it was all out there in the open, and not just scrawled out on a piece of a paper, I actually felt a little better. "I know I sound mad. You don't even need to believe it, but... that's what happened."

"Brother," Alex said, slowly, thoughtfully, "you should probably understand that I'll pretty much believe anything you tell me from this point on. I'm convinced – thoroughly. Trust me on this." He paused, squinting into the bleak imagery before us. "Besides, I saw one of those things, too. It came out of the damned Sea of Stars. There were people running and screaming everywhere. The sea looked like it was boiling, and this black… something… had leeched into the water. Maybe it was this River, I don't know, but this thing I saw, it was *huge.* Bigger than a ship, strange and quiet and covered with silver scales. If it wasn't a gods-damned Dragon, then I'm more a madman than you."

The sea boiling, the River's Edge dying, Dragons in the streets – it was like a corrupted faery story… or a prophecy. Yet, stories often found their root in truth, or so I was told.

"Madness is an illusion. The mad see things as they are." The voice wasn't Alex's. It wasn't anything I recognized, neither man nor woman, not even like that of the dragons whose thoughts had boomed within my head before. I spun around, weapon at the ready, but saw nothing except half a field of decayed flowers.

Then I realized that Alex was doing the same thing. "Did… did you hear that?" he whispered, almost too faint to hear.

Based on years of training for situations just like this, I motioned for him to stay quiet, then pointed to my left with two fingers extended, a silent instruction for him to take point in that direction. He did, while I turned right so that we were back to back and better able to survey everything around us. Not that it mattered – we both knew there was nowhere to hide, for the enemy or for us.

The voice came as if it was right at our ears, and I felt Alex brace against his own nerves. I'd like to say I didn't mimic him, but that would be a lie. "Men's stories speak of change. You wish this, yes?"

Two taps of an elbow against my back indicated Alex had no visual – I responded in kind.

"Look upon what you reap, Lightbringer," came the ethereal voice again, a slight hint of mockery playing at the edges of its smooth tone. Whoever or whatever it was, it seemed to have the same opinion of me as the Dragons, at any rate.

"I simply made a choice," I barked into the empty air. "Who are you to tell me I can't?"

For a very long time, we heard nothing, no sharp retort, no expression of disappointment. Either our mysterious "friend" had no answer, or no interest in answering – I was betting on the latter.

And to some extent, it didn't matter all that much. If we were going to be attacked by god, man, or monster, its name would die with us. What would happen after that was unknowable. I could only hope for Alex's sake that he wasn't thinking about what might happen to a soul caught in a decaying death cycle nearly as much as I was.

The fog drew in, closer and closer, creeping up toward the crest where we stood. So dark, it seemed to absorb any light that dared approach, a billowing entity that was at once both pure and impure.

Logic would dictate that this thing should have been the source of the blight upon the land, but somehow, I knew that was wrong – it wasn't there to bring destruction. It was there to serve a purpose, even if my simple, mortal understanding couldn't comprehend what that might be, just as I hadn't quite been able to figure out the Wind Dragon's words: *Light the Shadow. It is your way.*

My way... the way of the noble *Sayaf*, perhaps: direct, brutal, but ultimately, it led to clearer vision. If there was ever a time for that, it was now, so I dropped my defensive stance, sheathed my weapon, and approached the fog.

"Brother? What are you doing?" Alex snapped.

"Watch my back." And he would, because I asked – *not* because he trusted that I hadn't lost it completely. I didn't even have to look to know he was standing guard, if painfully impatient, though within a few steps, I wouldn't have known he was there at all.

My world became Darkness. The fog grew so thick and impenetrable the further I moved toward its core that I lost both time and direction. My senses were stilled, the beating of my heart the only way to know if I was alive or dead... that, and my magic, of course.

It was in there, deep down, yearning to break free, but it felt different. Tempered was the wrong word – pliable, perhaps? It could be whatever I wanted it to be. It was mine to do with as I pleased, and it pulsed with the rhythm of creation and destruction through every facet of my being. Here, I was stripped to the bare essence of my soul, exposing the core of whatever lay within.

Here, lightning could become the stars themselves.

The blast shook the earth beneath my feet, but I barely felt its energy or heard its roar – I was too entranced by the power of it all. One by one, tiny tears appeared along the thick underbelly of black fog, and through them, blinding white starlight glittered. "So this is how it will be," I heard the strange voice say, not loud, not angry, not anything... just cold.

"This is how it *must* be, isn't it?" The stars around me multiplied. Soon, a galaxy whirled, a perfect balance of swirling light and infinite darkness, each winking light and each breath of smoke finding their proper place within the nature's perfect order.

"If you wish to cast your Light down the darkest path," replied the elegant, serpentine figure that had come to sit before me, coiled within itself so that it didn't loom thirty feet overhead, but rather sat close to my own level. It wasn't totally black, as I might have guessed – instead, the thing I decided had to be the Shadow Dragon sported bright white streaks amidst perfectly ebony scales along its length that might have formed symbols if the language was at all recognizable. In a way, its markings replicated the swirls of light and dark around us. "Light merely illuminates. It does not cleanse."

"I'm aware of that," I said. "You asked what I wish – I wish nothing but to put things right. That's all I've ever wanted."

If there was such a thing as a Dragon that could smile, then that is what the Shadow Dragon did as it bowed its head toward me. "'Right' is relative. I commend any soul willing to carry its own Shadows, so let us see how far you can go."

CHAPTER TWENTY-EIGHT

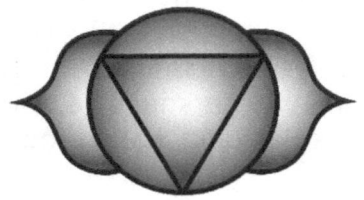

Dreams in Shadow
15 Spring's Green, 1272
Onyx Saçaille

My life would have been so different if I had failed to listen, to really try to understand the words of Chantal I heard so many years ago. The voice of the divine, trying to send me – just a normal girl in service to the goddess – a message? Or perhaps even… a warning.

The idea of "balance" flooded my dreams and nightmares, wrapped as they were in dark fog. I left Quiétude to follow those visions, but where did it all take me, exactly? Was it worth it to be doomed to the mercenary life of a heretic? Was it worth it to not be at her side when my sister was coaxed into war at the behest of someone who understood far, far too much for his own good?

I passed a fleeting thought toward what old Keis Sturmberg thought right now, up in his great ivory tower at Königstadt. The seat of power in Eisland was a thing to behold, made of an alabaster stone not found anywhere else but the frigid northlands, and it was said that the king's throne was decorated with the bones of dragons. I had never been inside, but when I visited the city years ago, I recalled the story. How could it be that the Dragons I knew from my dreams had bones, mortal bones that could be taken from them? Then again, how could it be that I was here, in the realm of my own dreams, just as mortal?

"Tante Onyx? Are you tired?" The girl's concern was clear in her tone as we soldiered on along the River's Edge. Higher and higher we climbed, until the sea was long behind us, and we walked through endless fields of green and gold and crimson.

But even this pastoral scene would indeed end, perhaps soon – such was one of the many things I didn't understand about this place. Indeed, nothing made sense anymore. Where once things had been so clear, there was nothing but... well, chaos. Perhaps *L'Ombre* was right, and discord was exactly what I had sown after years of trying so hard to right what was obviously so wrong.

"I spent my life poorly, you know," I said aloud, knowing I hadn't answered Jardin's question, nor had I any intention of doing so. If I thought about my aching feet or the tightness in my legs and hips, I might have had to face them.

"Mama told me once that you were a hero."

"A hero..." I let out a brief laugh – now *that* was a humorous notion. "Your mother is more creative than I realized."

"She said that you stood up to the bad man back home in Quatremagne."

After a moment's consideration, I nodded. "*Oui*, perhaps, but I only helped."

"With your magic?"

"No, no, *chérie,* there was no need for magic with your father and his men there. He is the hero, the one who killed the Gospodar – the bad man, as you say. I only led him to the front door." I had no interest in giving the girl a history lesson on the Quatremagne Rebellion, and luckily, I didn't have to. She fell silent, pale little brow furrowed in thought as it so often was.

There would be only a brief respite from my niece's interrogations, though, as after a few moments, she asked, "Why don't you ever talk about your magic, Tante Onyx?"

At this, my feet slowed to a stop. Magic had come in and out of my life over the years, and more often I relied on no more than my wits, my intuition... my strength. When I came back to my home city after twelve whole years, I lived mostly as a spy, bringing information from the Lavançaise-run Third

District in Quatremagne back to the Eislandisch. Of the four district lords – or Gospodar – our Seigneur Leo de Ferbois was the most corrupt, tyrannical and greedy, hellbent on destroying our quarter of the city to rebuild it in his own image.

But it was not merely a *pétite* version of Charmant, the city he knew back in Lavancée; Quatremagne was different, its own beast with its own ways. Its people were proud but not arrogant, cultured but not pretentious. And as independent in spirit as they were, they did not respond well to curfews and taxes and rules over every silly thing. Luckily for them, the Eislandisch of the Second District were only too willing to assist in putting the man in his place and restoring what we had lost.

Yet in all that time, the shadows that cloaked my passage didn't often come from within. I commanded them, in some ways, but they were the walls and the buildings and the trees surrounding my passage. They were not of me, just of my domain. Magic was the furthest thing from my mind then… in some ways, I wished that were true today. But times change, and so do people.

"There is nothing to talk about, *chérie*. If there were, then you would speak of your magic, *oui?* But you do not."

"Mama says magic is bad." The girl paused to think in her slow, methodical way. Something about the way she looked at me with those Light-tinged eyes was unnerving, I had to admit, but I didn't avert my gaze. Instead, I stared her down until her next question bubbled to the surface. "You don't think that, do you Tante Onyx?"

A good question, that, one for which I likely had no answer that would satisfy her. "Magic is everywhere. Magic is by the grace of Chantal. Your mother knows this, but it is… hard for her. And before you ask, I do not know why she says what she says. I do not presume to know the things your mother does." Then I started forth again, and the girl tagged along at my side, preparing a new line of interrogation as she walked.

"Do you think magic is a gift?" she said as we reached the beginning of a high crest in the landscape, one dotted with flowers much the color of the River flowing nearby, with the light above us shining brighter overhead. We were close – I could feel the energy, a tingling sort of crackle through my very flesh and bone.

My lips drew into a thin line that was almost a smile. "Magic is meant only for some – every religion says as much. Surely you know this, *chérie*. Only heretics in places like Zondrell's academies think that it is natural to coax magic out of someone and attempt to measure it."

"What about *my* magic?"

"What about it? You are lucky – you have a gift few share."

"So do you, but you don't think either of us are very lucky."

"Do I? You presume to know what your Tante Onyx thinks now?"

If it was the question that struck her silent or the view as we passed over the crest, I would never know. My legs burned in tired agony, but to get to this place, to see it with my own true eyes, was… breathtaking.

A pool of purest crimson energy stretched out before us, forming a perfect circle no more than fifty feet from end to end. On the shore beyond lay an old, grown-over path with a set of stairs leading toward the light above that seemed so close now, almost close enough to touch. Once, many years ago, I saw terrible things in the water when I arrived here, so terrible it forced me back – now, the place was serene, perfect, undisturbed save for one small detail.

Ripples formed across the pool's surface with each movement of a figure standing at its center. Long wet hair clung to slender shoulders that appeared to be bent deep in prayer, with hands folded at the heart and face shrouded in red-tinged shadow.

"It can't be," I started, squinting at the woman in the pool. I may have known her, but her place was not here, unless… "Mademoiselle?"

The sudden roar of a thousand storms rose to drown out everything, including my voice. I saw rather than heard Jardin let out a surprised screech as I turned, watching as the world behind us lit up with magnificent echoing lightning that only made sense in this place. Blazing white lit the skies amidst a black haze that seemed to swirl around each thundering strike as if… to embrace it?

I squinted against the glare, watching as it cleared to reveal something like a great, ragged hole torn across the sickly blue horizon. Where once there had just been a slow leak of one world into the next, the dam had now burst, and the serene twilight of the sky over Zondrell peeked through into the very place it should never be seen.

"By Chantal..." I whispered, unsure if such a prayer would ever be heard even as the noise fell away. A quick look at the figure in the pool indicated that more prayer was yet needed, as she never stirred from her meditation.

"What is that?" asked Jardin. "Is that the way home?"

"It's power, *chérie* – a perfect balance of power." I would never know how I knew this, but something about the way the Darkness moved with the Light spoke to me in some unknown language.

A light wind picked up then, subtle at first, but... there was no such thing as wind here. I froze, my hand instantly at my weapon. It came from magic, yes – the breeze stank of it. Where was its source?

White spots of lost lightning flares danced across my vision as the wind rose from playful zephyr to tempest in a few minutes' time. Or maybe those spots were something else, like little sparks and stars caught up in the storm. I watched them for what seemed like a long time before I heard Jardin speak, her voice coming from a place faraway.

"Yes, I can. I will."

I looked to her, eyes narrowed, watching how the strange gale seemed to tear at her very presence. It shredded the hem of her skirt, swept away her messy black curls, turned her flesh to so much scattered sand. Even though I knew that she was a vision, a traveler between worlds, the image was little short of horrific... and I had seen much in my time. She was gone before she heard me ask, "You will what?"

Too late, perhaps, to escape the infinite stare of the most fascinating creature I had ever seen.

It was like a serpent, long and lean, covered in indigo-lavender scales that winked brightly across its surface with each flex of the muscle beneath. Fine-boned leathery wings held it aloft, hovering just over the Earth as it regarded me with jewel-like eyes of infinite color. A magnificent set of horns formed a crown atop its great beastly head, and as the thing extended its long neck, I realized that the wind was no wind at all – it was breath. Its exhalations came out as a vaporous mist, somehow faintly radiant, reflecting light back in a fine purplish shimmer of electricity. In its wake, colors shifted, grass grew greener, even the flowers spiraled up further toward the sky.

"She must go," I heard a voice speak within my head, not so unlike the voice of *L'Ombre,* yet much more intense – everything about this creature was both compassionate and harsh, benevolent and cruel. "Her mother may come to stand before me yet. Too many little children of Light bring too much chaos – would you not agree, child of Shadow?"

"Her... mother?" It was the most coherent thought I could form in the face of this most majestic of Dragons. Still, I did not flinch, did not change my stance – I would show no weakness, even if it meant a quicker death.

"I honor my own," the voice boomed within my mind with the same ferocity as the lightning in the valley below. "I protect my own. I answer to my own, when the time is right."

I swallowed hard. "There is no more time left."

The creature laughed, a loud series of amused growling sounds that echoed in my mind. "And what would Shadows know of Time? What do you seek here?"

Despite the thoughts rushing through my mind, I found I had no hold on any of them. No answer I could give would make sense – no answer I could give would be the truth. Why I fought to reach the summit had nothing to do with me, not any longer. That time had passed. Did it still have anything to do with Balance?

Balance was once everything, but now... I no longer understood what that meant. I no longer understood this place or the creatures or the River itself. But there was still a part to play, discord to sow.

"I seek... to do my part," I said at length, leveling my gaze at the dragon. "To atone."

The dragon cocked its head to consider. "There is little reason for that, little one. Shadows do what they do, but Transcendence is not born from Shadow. Shadows are fleeting things without Light to guide, are they not? You have such a Light..." It paused to look to the skies above, a certain kind of sadness spoiling the wonder of its bejeweled eyes. "It may be the right soul and the right time. You will know – I cannot."

I felt my jaw tighten, considering. Had Loringham done that, ripped a hole in the sky itself? How... and why? Perhaps to do his own part in sowing discord, I mused. "There are two sides to every coin, *oui?*"

"You will know," it said again. "After that, no one knows, not even the Divine. Only the little ones are willing to move past knowing and embrace faith. Maybe you share some of your sister's faith?"

"Once, I suppose I did."

"I might learn of this curious thing called faith when the scales of Balance are tipped. The time approaches – I, for one, pray it is soon." Then, it rose into the air, giving no warning as a glittering cloud of dust struck me with its full fury, like an invisible hand scooping me up, only to drop me back hard to the earth.

I struggled for breath as I lay there, staring into the sky. But the majestic indigo beast wasn't the only thing there to draw my attention. Another creature, even larger, even stronger, waited far overhead. It hovered almost atop the shining crystal light source that served as a sort of ethereal sun in this place, though the fires it bellowed forth rivaled the sun I knew in the living world.

Squinting through the haze, I witnessed something only seen in the magic of faery tales then, as two Dragons met on the battlefield of the heavens.

CHAPTER TWENTY-NINE

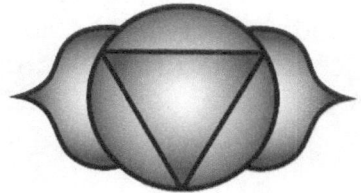

When the Lightning Comes
15 Spring's Green, 1272
Onyx Saçaille

"Mama!" Amidst all the chaos of people I didn't know swirling about, looking for this person or that person, reporting on events that couldn't possibly have happened, one tiny voice drowned out all the rest. I had never left her side, of course, as we holed up in a study full of ledgers and books and various knick-knacks. Nothing else was important – none of their stories were any concern of mine.

Yet, there was nothing wrong with my daughter at all. She popped up, wide awake, eyes bright, staring at me with her full attention in a way that... well, in a way she never had before. "Jardin?" I said, blinking at this miracle I had hoped and prayed for and somehow willed into being. An hour ago, my baby was comatose. Then, in a flash, she simply wasn't. "Jardin, what happened? Are you hurt? You fainted – we couldn't wake you, and..."

"Where is everyone? Where is Papa?"

My thoughts ground to a halt. Where *did* they all go? I remembered Brin leaving, bidding me to stay with Jardin, saying something about soldiers and going to look for someone. Was there an attack? Maybe no one knew, but there was much talk, so much talk. I hadn't followed most of it – navigating all the quick-talking Zondrell accents was difficult enough, even if I had been in the right frame of mind to listen. "Brin... your father," I started, slowly, "he went with Vremya and some people to the waterfront, I think. I'm sure they'll be back any minute now. Don't worry, just relax and I'll go find you something to eat. Then you'll feel better, *oui*?"

But she was worried. In fact, what color had come back to her small, delicate cheeks had retreated once again, leaving her skin as wan as a piece of parchment. "No. They can't go there."

"Why not?"

Jardin blinked once, staring into that faraway place she visited when she retreated into her drawings. "Because they might not be ready when the lightning comes." Then she was up and moving, her pace quick and agile, as if nothing had ever happened.

Mystified, I followed my daughter out to the hall, out of the house and through streets unfamiliar to both of us. Yet, she knew the way. How, I had no idea; why, I couldn't even fathom. By the time we reached the great shipyards of west Zondrell, the sun had retreated almost in full, and the sky was lit with a deep purple mist that clung to the edges of so many lowered sails.

Up ahead lay the great stone palace where I had been just yesterday, attempting to heal that poor boy king, and I wondered if his soul had returned from its flight, too. Was he different for it?

Jardin, I feared, certainly was. The girl I followed was sure of herself, moving with deliberate urgency. And when she spoke, her words didn't attempt to cower in dark corners – they came from a place of knowledge, of wisdom, even. "Jardin, tell me something," I said as we neared the darkened, looming towers. "Did you... were you dreaming? Of your 'Place?'"

"*Oui*," came her flat, simple reply.

"What did you see?"

But no answer came as my daughter continued, following the high cliff walls onward, toward what appeared to be a large gathering of people, swarming and yelling and flitting about. The closer we grew, the louder and more chaotic the scene. If

I knew nothing else about the Zondrellian people, it seemed that they fed off of pandemonium – conflict and complexity were their daily bread as much now as it had been twenty-five years ago during the War. Somewhere, deep down, they probably enjoyed all this panic.

I felt my jaw tighten. "Jardin, what did you see?" I asked again, this time more insistent. It was enough to get her to stop and turn to me, eyes flashing against the darkness.

"I saw what we can't stop. At least, I don't think so. Tante Onyx was wrong. I think she knows now – we can help her."

Onyx? What did my sister have to do with *anything*? With a sigh, I shook my head and reached out to hold Jardin by her slim shoulders, without a care as to whether she would flinch or fight. She did neither. "I don't understand. Jardin, please… help me understand."

"I just know you have to be there when the lightning comes. They'll need you."

"Who?"

I followed her gaze as she looked back to the maelstrom of people. Among the crowd, I realized, was her father, and Vremya, and perhaps others that I recognized. Vremya stood with a shrill woman in disheveled green robes stained black and scarlet, both of them barking orders to other robed people, perhaps mages of their Academy.

Nearby, Brin presided over a group of men who looked as if their armor and the command of a formidable General Jannausch were the only things holding them up. These attempts to bring order to the chaos were impressive, but ultimately futile as fear and panic welled up among the masses. Soon, it would burst, and what then? I didn't know the answer – perhaps Jardin didn't either.

Reluctant, I started toward the scene. "Come on, let's see what we can do to help."

**

Change is constant. All things in Balance. That's what I was told… but these things were in opposition. And what exactly did I think I was doing here? Which side was I on? These were the thoughts whirling through my head as Life magic fled from my hands in a lavender-white ribbon and found its way toward those who needed it. There were many, too – more than I realized until we reached Brin and Vremya and I saw how bad things were.

Whatever happened here was catastrophic, the fragments of the story they told embodying everything I had ever heard about the evils of Zondrean heresy. They really did think they could defy Chantal and understand the ways of magic, to control it as if it were a physical thing and not a gift of the divine. It was no wonder my sister always held the Zondreans – and Zondrell in particular – in such low regard.

Now, it seemed, they were paying for their sins.

"By the Lady, there it is again!" Despite their urgency, none of the cries of the people around could have prepared me for what I saw. The sea *became...* something. It rose up of its own volition in a shape that was vaguely snakelike, but massive – oh, so massive. It coiled up to reach heights rivaled only by the castle nearby, looming over the shoreline and ready to strike at any moment.

Yet it watched, and waited.

Did it want the Zondrean soldiers and mages in its path to make the first move? The fear and hesitation in their eyes told me that this thing must have been what had torn through their ranks to leave so many hurt and bleeding here.

"Fall back!" I heard Brin shout at the armored ones, and many did retreat, still at the ready in case they were pursued.

But others hesitated as another strong Zondrean voice bade them to wait, to hold the line in defense of their nation. "You take your orders from me, not a foreigner. Stand guard, men!"

"Aye, High Captain Evison," some barked back in unison, but not all.

Brin, being Brin, didn't take this well. His weapon came off his back, prepared to rend a hole through the man's plate-armored chest in one sweeping gesture, and for a moment in the light of pale twilight and torches, I saw the old Brin – wild, unpredictable... vicious. "I like to see *Zondern* die almost as much as that beast there – almost. You are reckless."

I had seen this same scene play out... well, too many times to count – many would have simply scurried away when staring down the wrong end of Brin Jannausch's blade. Not this man, though. "I don't care what that thing is," he replied, standing defiant, with his hand dangerously near his own weapon on his belt. "Our job is to defend this city, and that's what I'll do."

"Or die doing it, *ja*?"

The older mage woman in green shook her head with a derisive snort, and many – even Brin – relaxed as they turned to her. "Indeed. Listen to the Eislander, Evison. Are you mad? Do you have any concept of what that is?"

This High Captain fellow was a handsome man, perhaps as old as the mage with what my mother would have called "*un visage fort*," a face with character. Lines around his dark eyes told a story of honor and sacrifice, just as the gray in his neatly trimmed beard spoke of deep-seated pride. "Do you have any concept of what you brought down upon us, Tiara... excuse me, Archmage?" he asked.

A woman with the title of Archmage? Of course – only in Zondrell. I could just imagine the old priests at Quiétude shaking their heads and clicking their tongues at such a thing. This lady Archmage's blazing Earth-green eyes narrowed in Evison's direction, and everything about her evoked a sense of authority. Even Evison visibly recoiled in the face of it.

"If I thought for a moment that you had the capacity to understand the importance of the research here, we still wouldn't have enough time because *that*, Captain, is a Dragon. An actual, living Dragon of the type the Katalahnis and the Eislandisch used to sing about thousands of years ago. I don't believe it any more than you do, but I see it for myself, and I am not a fool. Let your men retreat if you don't want to doom us all."

"It won't matter." I might have been the only one to hear Jardin's tiny whisper, a hint of a sob making her voice hitch. Chantal's bones and blood, my tears were about to fall as well, but fear and confusion had left me numb, unable to move, much less speak. Something black, like blood that surely could only be water, dripped from the beast's exposed teeth, and I couldn't look away, couldn't turn from its cat-like, brilliant azure gaze.

The next voice I heard – inside my head or beyond, I couldn't tell – was the same one I heard once at Quiétude while praying over the bones of the Goddess Herself: *Balance is broken. You are judged.*

"Chantal, sauvez-nous," I heard myself breathe from some other place. And then the beast struck.

A thing made of no more than water taken shape into scales and bone should not have been able to do what it did, but I saw it. I will never forget it. It bore down upon the soldiers and the mages quick, just like a serpent. Teeth and claws ripped through armor to tear at the soft flesh beneath.

Men screamed as swords swung through mere liquid, scattering droplets of black-red but otherwise accomplishing nothing. Magic seethed across the sky overhead then, attempting to freeze or wither or turn it into vapor. If the dragon of the sea felt anything, it made no indication. It never slowed as it moved in for another strike, felling more men as it did.

It took everything in my power to move to stand in front of Jardin, shielding her as best I could. But my legs were weak, my heart pounding fast, loud as the battle itself. The same fear gripped me as it used to back in the War, when I would stand at Keis Sturmberg's side and tend to the wounds of his army as he commanded.

Like the great king that he was, he never allowed his own injuries to be healed first if there was another man nearby that could benefit... and there were always many. Never again did I think that I would witness such destruction, such pain and suffering. It was too much to comprehend.

If it hadn't been for Vremya, I might have been split in two by the dragon's claws as they swung in my direction, but just like in the War, he made the unthinkable – the incomprehensible – a reality: Time *stopped*. Not just some of it, not just the creature, not just the water that made up its form, but all of it.

Soldiers, mages, my husband, all of them were frozen in place, a living scene of the most fantastical battle an artist could ever put to canvas. The only things still moving were me, Vremya, Jardin, and the woman in green called Tiara.

"We move back, a little safer? No moving too fast – concentrate for me," Vremya bade in a low, strained tone. "Is a lot to maintain, *da*?"

"Now I know exactly who the madman is. I bow to your power, Sir," Tiara said as she, along with the rest of us, retreated a few feet away from the shoreline. I imagine so many of them were in a daze, just as I was, unsure, entering territory never crossed by any mage.

And when she reached Vremya's side, Tiara offered what was likely the only formal bow this "Archmage" had ever made to another in her life. I didn't have to know her to see the confidence in her step or hear the arrogance in her tone, but she had wisdom, too. She recognized greatness when she saw it.

"Bow not to me. Other side, maybe, *da*? We see."

Close by, I could feel Jardin's warmth rise, and her breathing along with it. While she had no training, she could surely feel the magic moving through her, a radiance that came both from within and without as the few of us held the space together through our own inner wills. I had practiced this sort of thing with the priests at Quiétude, but rarely with this kind of urgency, or sheer power. It was the first time magic had ever felt *good*, a soothing, beautiful feeling that I could not put adequately into words.

"Jardin," I turned to her, "are you all right?"

"The lightning comes." Again, that strange faraway voice and that ominous phrase. What did it mean? "Mama, I... I'm scared."

"We're all scared, *chérie*. All of us." As I embraced my daughter, who didn't pull away or strain in discomfort, we watched the large, silver-translucent dragon I had seen earlier in front of the Loringham home float above us, high overhead, toward the horizon.

"By the gods, is that another one?" Tiara asked in disbelief, all semblance of egotism vanished. "And why isn't it..."

Vremya breathed deep of the cool sea air full of battle and salt. "He's ah... Time don't bother him. He understands."

"What do you mean by that?"

"Time brings change. Balance shifts. Possibilities are endless."

No, the possibilities were horrifying. And yet, that was all we had as the sky lit up with a display the likes of which I had never seen, lightning striking the water about a half-mile offshore in a circular pattern, a ring of blazing white electric force that had no place in nature. Jardin tensed in my arms as we watched the silver dragon move in its slow, deliberate way into the center of the formation... and vanish.

"It's up to them now," said Vremya. "Keep up what you do. Not that much longer."

CHAPTER THIRTY

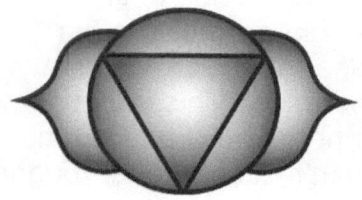

Timeless
15 Spring's Green, 1272
Alexander Vestarton

The light of a million stars flooded my vision before I could snap my eyes shut and turn away, leaving behind colored dots that danced like the souls on the dark sea. I'm sure I cursed a lot, and I did manage to stay upright, even though I didn't feel so steady on my feet. In fact, I almost felt drunk, wishing like hell that I could see something else, preferably something that wasn't moving.

Oh gods, I wasn't blind, was I? Fuck me... Well, maybe I was deaf, too, because I couldn't hear much outside of a roaring crackle, not unlike a herd of colossal horses charging across a forest of dead trees.

After a few minutes, the dots stopped their waltz and the roar subsided to a dull rumble, accompanied by a feeling I could only describe as a *presence*. Its chill washed over me, through me, and as it retreated, it took with it all the offending brightness. Maybe the candle of life had just been snuffed out... or something. I had eyes to open, though, and when I dared do so, I realized I still had the means to see.

At my feet was a broken man, and I dropped before him. "Damn it, damn it, damn it," I muttered, voice shaking as much as my hands. He was so motionless, and there was so much blood, I... I couldn't think. It was like my mind had gone the way of that weird thing in the sky. Was he... no, no, that wasn't possible – not here, not now. "You are not going to fucking die on me, Brother. You hear me? I need you – I don't... I don't know what to do. I don't even fucking know what's going on. You can't leave me here, you hear me? You can't fucking be..."

Not that anything I said made a difference. He never stirred.

"Damn you, don't die on me, Brother!" I heard myself as if from somewhere else, my voice rising, my words gushing out in a torrent of incoherence. "This is like some nightmare I can't wake up from, and here you are... No, no no, it can't happen this way. It just can't. You're the toughest son-of-a-gods-damned Eislandisch warrior bitch I know. This *can't* be happening right now. *Wake the fuck up!*"

But he didn't. He didn't move at all – hell, even though I felt a light breeze rise up from somewhere, it didn't so much as ruffle his hair. How did they train us back at the Academy? It was like every bit of knowledge I'd ever had was sucked into a void somewhere, maybe the same void behind that thing in the sky. I could barely think, and my whole body had begun to pulse with searing, prickling pain, like a thousand needles digging under my skin. Still, there was something I could do, something I was missing... oh yeah!

With one unsteady hand, I reached for the prone figure's neck, searching for signs of life. Warmth, the slick of sweat, and... no, it wasn't my imagination – there was a pulse there. Quick, faint, but steady, I felt the rhythmic beat under my fingertips, one, two, three...

Wait. Something was wrong. When did I stand up? When did the sky go black again?

Where did Tristan go?

I looked down at my hands, my clothes – what little I could see of them – but they weren't mine. The finger that usually bore my Vestarton family signet ring now sported a stylized "L" on a wide silver-and-gold band. A sword rested at my hip, its hilt wrapped in stitched black leather, but I didn't have a sword like that. I actually wasn't armed at all, save for that dagger I usually kept in my boot, and... well, these weren't my boots. I didn't have a black pair of high-laces like this, but I did have to admit they were comfortable, even as fog like thick, heavy velvet threatened to engulf them, obscuring each step.

Thick, heavy velvet. Dark. Weird.

Damn it, I wasn't *me*, was I?

A tiny sliver of experience caught in time, and I was living it. I *was* Tristan, and with each step I took, it seemed more and more natural. Even as flaring, blinding pain lit behind my eyes at the center my forehead, it wasn't alarming. I could handle it – it had happened dozens of times like this. Sometimes my nose bled. In fact, it was bleeding now, and I could feel the tiny rivulet begin to leak down my lip. Warm copper brushed my tongue.

Stars began to grow bright overhead, but they were my stars, beautiful sparkling diamonds amidst the nothingness. "So this is how it will be," said an unearthly voice in my head. Alexander might have panicked – he may have already been deep in the thralls of it – but Tristan did not.

Tristan squared his jaw and answered the voice, and though I felt my mouth open to speak, I didn't hear what was said. Maybe it didn't matter, because the reply came not in words, but in light, magic that danced with the darkness and found its place with it, until the mists cleared and a figure came into being.

No, not a figure – a beast, a long, winding snake-like creature, decorated with a series of white symbols set against perfect black, spoiled only by the occasional ripple of the animal's muscles. But instead of chewing me up and spitting me out like it could have easily done at any moment, it dipped its huge head toward me in... reverence?

What could I possibly have done to earn the respect of a magic dragon-demon from another dimension? Time, starlight, or anything in between, surely there was no power I could hold that this thing couldn't match.

"I have waited for this moment for a long time," the creature said, its thoughts burrowing their way into mine with a tone so calm and cool, it might as well have been reading from an accounts ledger. "Others said it would never come, but I knew better. You did, too, did you not?"

When the single white lines set in the infinite blackness of its eyes focused on me, it saw *me*. It saw Alexander, not Tristan, and that's who it chose to address. I don't know how I understood that, but when I answered, I heard my voice, my own true voice, and at least for a time, I felt as much in control of myself as I ever did in the present, much less in the past. "If I said I didn't," I answered, trying to swallow the anxiety in my voice, "would that be a problem?"

If a Dragon could smile, this one did, with a slight twitch of the corners of the mouth, a glimpse of teeth like rows of blades hovering mere feet above my head. "On the contrary. You know as well as any the possibilities. Mine is a domain of darkness, of obscurity in shadow, but my sight is not limited – Shadows can reveal as much as they hide. In many ways, we are the same, yes?"

I blinked. "Sure… if you say so."

"You are one who sees." The disdain in its voice was not lost on me. "You see things where neither Light nor Darkness reach."

"I see the past as dreams. That's about it, and that's what happening right now… I think."

"Dreams… of course. Mere dreams." Without warning, I felt something powerful tug at something inside me, a single string to unravel the fibers of my soul. With bright fiery pain came a shift, a… difference in whatever made up the magic within me that eventually settled into a dull ache, throbbing in time with my heart.

Around us, the stars began to pulse in time with that beat as each one lit in sequence, one into another into another, until the most complex pattern conceivable had spread out in every direction around me. It had order to it, yes, but no network of fine lace, no jewels or man-made thing, could ever come close to the intricacy, the majesty, the sheer beauty of it.

"Incredible," I breathed.

"You should recognize them – they are yours to know. Moments. Possibilities, each one leading to the next." The star directly in front of my right eye began to twinkle even more brightly than all the rest. "This one here is the moment when Drasch Sturmberg stood where you stand now."

"Drasch Sturmberg… the old King of Eisland? What does he have to do with anything?"

"You've heard the stories. Stories are not always fiction."

I had heard Andella and Tristan mention some of them, but honestly, I had to think hard to remember the details. Old Drasch was the first King of Eisland – sure, everyone knew that. He united tribes and turned the place into something slightly less savage. That was hundreds or maybe thousands of years ago, depending on who you asked and what book you read.

A lot of things happened to history after that much time and that many legends had come and gone. Some, like the stories Andella talked about, had to do with magic and Dragons and the Great Beyond of the River. Did he fight Dragons there? Or did they kill him and bring him to the River where he escaped to rise from the dead? Something dramatic like that might have happened, or maybe not.

"People have told those stories dozens upon dozens of times – which one is true?" I asked. "Does that star tell me?"

"It does," said the beast, matter-of-fact. "It lets the story be told anew. Imagine if Drasch Sturmberg had been destroyed here, if we had not allowed him passage through the River to the Summit. Imagine if we did not bargain with him, despite the way he murdered our kin. What might your world, the place where the souls take form, look like today?"

"Good question. Would it be a hellhole overrun with Dragons, maybe? Not to say that this place you've carved out for yourself here isn't... interesting."

If the thing appreciated sarcasm or not, I wasn't sure, and as the seconds ticked away, I wondered if I should have put a little more thought into my words. Fitting, they'd say, Alexander Vestarton getting eaten because he mouthed off to the wrong Dragon-god between the edge of infinity and Purgatory. Well, I couldn't really think of a more unusual way to die, at any rate.

After an interminable silent void, words flooded into my senses once more, words without bitterness, or really any emotion at all. "Touch the moment. Find out for yourself."

"Touch the moment... you mean, just reach out for that light?"

"Or any of them. Each one leads to another, a point along endless timelines."

"And then what? I watch it all, like a stage play? Seems like it might take a while to sit through a thousand years of history."

More of that anticipatory quiet – we might as well have been bantering over a high-stakes game of Five-Star. And in a way, maybe we were. It did say it liked to bargain with men, didn't it? "You are not consigned to the role of witness," it said. "For you, Time is malleable – you need only seize it."

Well, if we were playing cards, then I'd already lost. What the hell was this thing talking about? "Time isn't... just because I can see what was doesn't mean I can change what is."

"And why not?"

Good question, for which I had another. "So if you know so much about Time magic, then why not go back yourself? You could save your kind from Drasch Sturmberg – I mean, was there literally one man in all the world who could slay a Dragon?"

"And get away with it." The creature's eyes narrowed as if it could have bored a hole right through the center of my skull. "Drasch Sturmberg was powerful. He earned the respect he was given, but the last of our kind did not retreat to the River because of him. We chose to be here, and here we have remained, for his power was our power, and your kind was not ready to understand it. Some among us would say that Man will never ready."

I considered this. "But not you," I ventured, and received a slight nod of approval. "So, you have some kind of mastery over Time magic, and you want to teach me. Is that it?"

The great creature lifted its head, cocking it to the side as if deep in thought for a moment. "Mine is not that domain," it said at length.

"Yet, you can show me timelines and tell me all about them. Who taught you that? Some other Dragon?"

Again, that strange toothy smile played at the edges of the black Dragon's scaly lips. "Something like that, perhaps. In truth, many of my kind give little favor to me. But it was I who knew that Drasch Sturmberg was different, and I granted him a... stay of execution, to use one of your sayings. In exchange, he surrendered what he had, so that the others would remain satisfied. Those magics beyond Man's grasp were silenced, in favor of those with stronger voices. It is too difficult to stifle the glow of the Fire, the shifting Earth, the rising Waters, the song of the Wind. These things are eternal, understood, even by your kind."

"Time isn't eternal? Isn't that sort of... the definition?" My brow furrowed as I tried to grasp it all. "Look, I know for a damned fact that other magics exist in what you call 'my world.' I'm living it right now."

"There are always some souls that shine brighter than the rest. They grow and gather. Someday, change would come. Balance would shift, until one day..." It trailed off as if deep in thought.

"Until one day what?"

Still a pause, until I could feel my impatience building into a knot in my throat. Finally, it spoke again. "Until they transcend. It is inevitable." The light that somehow held the memory of an ancient warlord king flared once more. "This one moment in time created, in some way, what you see and what you are. In a sense, you may be as great as he... if not greater."

"You're giving me an awful lot of credit."

"I give credit only where it is due. Look around you – your power is on display as we speak, a delicious mastery, I will say." The admiration I sensed in it bordered on desire, or maybe hunger – I couldn't tell which. "Souls like yours were cut open and laid bare for the Divine. For the price of his silence, Drasch Sturmberg allowed those others to carry on unbidden, unstruck. Silence is merely... subterfuge. An omission. They lived on in Shadow, until their silence began to break. Now, it all breaks, all around, and here you are, in the center of it all."

"So... why now? Why us? What's happening to make it all 'break?'"

"It is inevitable, part of the Cycle. All beginnings have an end, but the end is not written the same way each time. I know, as you do, that if a different path were taken, things would be different. You would not be here. You might not be anywhere. The Cycle might continue without strain, Balanced and perfect until other souls came along to challenge it. Chaos enters at so many points, at so many possibilities." With that, half a million more stars came to life, bright enough to make me shrink away and shield my eyes. "Your kind is on the brink, He Who Sees. The Divine cares not for what is unveiled by Darkness. But you can turn back. You can restore Balance."

The lights surrounded me, tantalizing as they glittered there like so many jewels strewn across a bed of the darkest silk. There were hundreds, if not thousands of stars at my fingertips – each one a glimpse into a new reality. If the things

Drasch Sturmberg actually did in life were just a little different, I might not be standing in this place, in this moment. In fact, no human might exist at all.

It could be a world of Dragons instead of men. But if we did survive all that, later there may never have been a civil war in Zondrea, a war between Zondrell and Eisland, a sickness that took my father's life, a decision that Tristan had to make between following orders or following honor. The possibilities were... strange, bizarre, and even beautiful, in their way. I could see all of them, each one leading to the next in their endless patterns of what-ifs.

"You have a moment, a single moment, where things might change," the Dragon's soothing, genderless voice coursed through my thoughts. "Your fate, the fate of your kind, rests in that moment. Find the possibility that pleases you most. Go there and claim it. Do more than witness."

That one simple, stupid event, way back at the Academy, came back to me again. I could change it. We could do it again, differently. Better. Tristan could set his own path, and I wouldn't stand in his way – far from it. I'd help. Hell, maybe I'd go with him. Everything would be different, so very different, if he'd left that Academy on that night. And there it was, sitting on the timeline just before me, encapsulated in a little star glowing with the silvery-white light of hope, expectation, excitement... and something else.

Doubt.

Maybe I could change things, though who was to say that the end result wouldn't be the same? What right did I have to decide how we got there? I didn't. No man did, and I didn't think this shady black Dragon had much authority on the matter either. I was on to him.

I breathed deep, looking down at the hands that were not mine again. Those hands knew the right thing to do... they always did, didn't they? They belonged to someone who wouldn't be silenced so easily, who wouldn't feed his past or his future to this writhing mass of blackness.

He wouldn't defer to the wisdom of a Shadow, not because he thought he knew better, but because he owned his path. He'd forged it with his own blood, sweat, and tears, and he would lead the way to its end. So, I laid aside my power to do what I did, to let him do what he did.

"I underestimated you," I heard the Dragon say, but the thought seemed far away, quiet and dulled. "May Light join with Shadow evermore."

Tristan's hands were surprisingly steady as they drew that old reaver blade from his belt – just a sword, a weapon of simple cold steel with no magic, no mystery to it all. That is, not without help, and that wasn't quite mine to give. I was just there to open up the possibility, then play witness to what would happen next.

Lightning struck from an empty, dead sky, through an even emptier black fog, and it was *sharp*. It could make a Dragon bleed if it was fast enough. The flash came in the blink of an eye, over nearly before it started, and some might have even questioned whether it was ever there at all.

Yet, in the next second, something warm and unlike the blood of any mortal creature splashed against my face and coated my hands, and then... did it return the blow? How did we become so intertwined? Dark, Light, Dark, Light – everything became a blur until the white symbols carved into the creature's black scales collapsed into themselves and nothingness became my world.

**

"That one is a charlatan."

Did I just... think that? No, that was something else, another thought invading mine, with a sonorous voice that moved in a persistent rhythm, like the dull drip of a water clock.

"Shadow is often right, in its way. Shadow predicted this, even before I did. But Shadow bends rules that should not be bent."

Blurry images began to appear as my eyes sought desperately to regain focus. Soon, I saw a slumped figure in a tattered black coat, and grass that looked like it had gone through a fire, and a vast open sky the exact color of bleak ambiguity. In that sky was a rending, a rip like a piece of cotton caught on a nail.

"Catherine's mercy," I whispered, frozen in place for the briefest of moments as I watched something shimmering and electric ooze around the edges of the celestial tear, as if it were... bleeding?

Yet blood was flowing in, not out – far down the horizon line, the River connected with it, though surely that was just an optical illusion. Just like, surely, there was no massive winged thing emerging from its center... except I wasn't sure of much anymore. With wings outstretched, this vision in the sky looked just like the silver falcon of Zondrell, but whatever it was, it was no bird, and it moved with the speed of an arrow.

The silver-scaled creature settled its considerable bulk before me within the span of ten heartbeats. "I've seen you before," I said, or rather whispered. My voice had all but given up and run for greener pastures.

"*Before* is relative," this Dragon said, the Dragon of... Time? What else could it be? "All things are before. All things are after. You know this."

I shook my head in the face of the huge, elegant creature that had settled almost like a cat would, curling around its long bulk, pearlescent wings folding comfortably against its back. If such a thing could be at ease, even here with the sky crying overhead, it appeared to be just that. There was certainly nothing malicious about it, but even so, I swallowed hard against the thundering fear in my chest.

"I don't know shit anymore," I said with all honesty.

"All of your people know more than they think. The problem is, they think." When all I could do was squint at it in reply, I could almost hear the tinkle of laughter in its tone. "Thought is an anchor. A means to stay rooted. They do not see the change all around them – most of them, anyhow." It craned its neck a little to regard Tristan and me both, with huge feline eyes made up of every possible shade and glint and glimmer of silver.

"So I'm different?"

"You are you. He is he. Your souls seek more, and that is a good thing. Fear nothing, for change is the only way forward. There is no Balance without movement. Trees sway in the wind, yes? And do not fall down?"

"Sometimes they do."

Laughter echoed in the Dragon's voice again. "Sometimes, yes, I suppose you are right. To fall does not mean that Balance is gone. A fallen tree gives way to new roots, as now.

Let this moment you hold fall. I am glad the Shadow did not eat your power and silence you, but the way forward awaits and Time is short."

"Wait, what? Let the moment... fall?" Why the hell did these damn Dragons speak in such riddles? I wanted to say more, but inside me, something clicked, as if that string that had been slowly unmaking all the things that made up me snapped, falling away.

The omnipresent feeling of something evil clamping down on my veins released, all at once, but instead of pain, I felt only a persistent, precise flow of energy. No water clock could ever be so accurate, no heartbeat so perfect.

I clutched at my chest to make sure all my organs and parts were still where they were supposed to be. Overhead, the wound in the sky seemed to seep, like molten metal dripping from the edge of the world's biggest forge, while The River flowed into it, through it – to where, I couldn't imagine.

"Waste nothing. Find everything," the Time Dragon's words slid through my mind as it suddenly took flight again, a beast as large as a ship simply rising like the lightest of birds. A steady breeze seemed to follow in its wake, which seemed odd in this place with no weather. The wind caressed the back of my neck as I sat and watched until the Dragon disappeared from view.

A cough brought me back to reality. "Brother!" I leaned in and realized that what was once a still, vaguely Tristan-shaped mass was now quite awake.

"You..." he started as he pushed himself up to sit, but his voice was hoarse, and the words weren't there.

"You're fine, Brother, you're fine. It's okay – it's over. That... thing is gone."

"It's *not* over." Another cough, a hint of a wince as if he was hurt, but despite all the blood, little of it seemed to be his. "But what you did... it was right, that choice."

"What? Did you think I'd do something wrong?"

Tristan managed a smile, the white-on-black-on summer's-sky-blue of his eyes vibrant and alive and... perfect. There was no more disarray, no more conflict – the darkness was supposed to be there, resting in balanced harmony with the light. "No, no, I didn't," he said after a long, shuddering breath.

It took me a while to come up with a good way to phrase the question that was playing at the corners of my mind – eventually, I gave up and just said it. "So... what the fuck happened back there?"

He shrugged. "You had my back. That's all I know."

"Did you, or we, or whatever... did we kill that thing?"

"The Black Dragon? I don't think so."

"But you hurt it. Look at you – you're covered in blood."

Tristan looked down at himself, almost surprised as if he was just seeing the stains across his clothes and hands for the first time. Wiping the deep crimson substance away didn't seem to do a lot of good, either, but he did his best. "I wasn't trying to kill it," he said softly. "I wanted to... Light the Shadow."

I laughed – I couldn't help myself. "You know, I don't know much, but yeah, you definitely lit that thing up, my Brother."

"I guess I did." For just an instant, he reminded me of one of those great Dragon-beasts as he found his way to his feet. Whether he was in pain or not, he wouldn't show it – he gathered himself with grace, just as he always had, shifting his gaze upstream toward the path we had been following. "Only one way forward," he muttered.

One way forward. And the possibilities between here and there were almost certainly endless.

PART FOUR

*M*any men, faced with a choice, will make the right one. It is only the brave few who are willing to choose differently.

From *Lebenkern: Die Reisen Ivon Drasch Sturmberg*
Date unknown

CHAPTER THIRTY-ONE

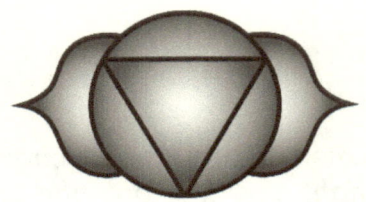

The Woman
15 Spring's Green, 1272
Andella Weaver

I found myself standing waist-deep in blood.

How did I get here? I struggled to remember. Water... there was so much water, people running and screaming, and there was something else, too, something dark and foreboding. I wanted to understand – I wanted to *see*. And I did, didn't I?

An endless ocean, waves washing against a pristine shore. A long, winding river, feeding it from some source that few had ever seen. Most people would never dream of such a place, would never think to traverse the highest heights to explore that which was beyond their understanding. But I didn't do it for fame, or glory, or fortune – none of that mattered. I just needed to *know*.

A swift current raced to envelop me, but I was fully rooted where I stood. The bright crimson waters could try and carry me away all they wanted, just as I could try to flail around, all to no avail. I was *stuck*. Panic slowly building, I tried to swim forward, only to just move water around and disturb the reflective surface with clumsy, broad, rippling arcs.

When was the last time I went swimming? The lakes outside of Doverton were cold, even in summer – I remembered them as a girl. We would play and splash, but never stray too far from shore. Never once had I gotten this far in, where my feet barely scraped the bottom and the water could have its way with me.

I tried to break free of that powerful undertow again and went nowhere fast – no amount of force or wishing or anything in between could get me closer to the shore. But maybe... I breathed deep and tried to calm my nerves, to relax against the force of the water threatening to pull me down. If I stopped fighting, it would ease up. I could sit quietly and contemplate this place in peace – I might even be able to understand it better.

Was this really the same strange dream-world where I met Tristan at the edge of the dark sea? It could be. The air held the same empty quality, without any smell or weight to it, perfectly calm. And the sun, or whatever that thing was overhead, was closer now, but it still held an unnatural glow to it, a flame held safe within a glass lantern. I stared up in wonder, my thoughts going everywhere and nowhere for a time.

"What's going on?" I asked no one, finding my voice scratchy and raw as if I hadn't used it for a long, long time. The sudden pain made my eyes water.

A shadow passed in response, a shadow so big that it seemed to have mass. I could feel the wind pick up as the dark shape moved across the sky. Did that thing leave those cracks behind, or were those there already? How could the sky even *have* cracks in it in the first place?

I realized that the whole heavens were laced with fine little lines, like a porcelain bowl whose yellowed-blue glaze didn't quite set right – a failed piece, perhaps, something that might get broken up and returned to the potter's wheel.

Or it might have gone back into the kiln, since moments later, the sky began to burn.

Flame and smoke drenched the world, blotting out the weird crystalline light overhead. And it was hot – by Catherine, was it *hot!* My cheeks flushed as the air warmed and just for a second, I thought I saw the blood waters I stood in curdle and bubble.

Then the sensation was gone, followed by more great shadows, indistinct and huge. What could make such shapes?

Then I looked up and saw exactly what they were, though I still didn't know what to make of them.

They circled high above, not so much like vultures, but more as hawks, each ready to swoop in for the kill. Who would win the prize? Would it be the long, elegant one, made of iridescent indigo with a crown of lavender-white horns atop its diamond-shaped head? Or would it be the brute, the giant the color of blood and limned in fire?

Maybe it didn't matter if their prey was me.

Something hit me then, a gust of wind that was somehow heavy and insubstantial all at once. It carved through, parting the water as a knife cuts through a loaf of bread. It was enough to knock me backward, and with it came a visceral feeling deep in my core – not just my feet but my whole soul felt like it came loose from the blow.

Sliding, tumbling, thrashing, the water grabbed at me again, and this time, I was no match for it. Crimson water splashed around me, over my head, into my mouth… it was definitely not blood. Blood was metallic and bitter, but this was nothing like that, not quite like the sea, but salty and bright and even sweet, leaving a tingling sensation in my nose.

"Oh my!" I heard an elegant, slightly amused voice shout from somewhere beyond the wet, blood-spattered hair clinging to my face. "Well, aren't you quite the sight?"

The sound came from nearby, just ahead. As I gathered my wits and composure, little by little, the owner of that voice came into focus. It was… "Seraphine?" My sister couldn't possibly be here, could she? No, it didn't even make sense. This was some sort of dream, something I couldn't wake up from, something I very much *needed* to escape – the sooner, the better.

The auburn-haired woman wearing the gold-trimmed white robes that Seraphine so often wore reached toward me from where she stood at the edge of the pool. "Come along now," she said with a soft smile. "You can't stay in there all day, now, can you?" By the Lady, she even sounded like my sister.

I wrapped my arms tight around myself. "Seraphine, what are you doing here?"

"We'll talk after we get you out of there, Andie. Come on." Andie – no one called me Andie but my sister. But how could it possibly be her?

I picked up one foot, and despite the current racing beneath the pool's surface, I could move – I could fight it, if I really wanted to. Then again... did I want to leave? The knowledge was here, in the center of this pool of blood-red, perfect water. What I could learn, I had no idea, but beyond this place lay a burning sky and creatures I couldn't comprehend. Here, it was different. Here, it was safe.

"Come on, you're not having second thoughts, are you?" Seraphine said. "It's not as safe as you think, Andie. You should come with me."

"And go where?"

Seraphine's smile was just as I'd always remembered it on her round, cheerful face. Her green eyes twinkled against her peachy skin, but not with magic. No, Seraphine's only magic lay in her servitude to the Great Lady, and in her ability to work with herbs and help people. Priestesses of Catherine didn't usually have magical talent – in fact, some believed that magic was sinful, an affront to the majesty of Lady Catherine, although Seraphine wasn't one of them.

She had been so happy when I returned from the Magic Academy ready to serve as a Pyrelight, smiling in that same way she smiled now. It wasn't that long ago, and I remembered that day vividly. My big sister was so proud of me, just like our mother would have been if she'd been able to be there. "We'll sit and talk by the hearth. I have hot tea ready. Are you hungry?"

"I... guess so?" I hadn't really thought about food or drink for a long time.

"Of course you are. Come on, dear – they'll come back before too long."

I followed her gaze toward the sky. "You mean those things. What were they?"

"Don't worry about them, Andie. We'll be fine once we get back to the house."

"The house?" We didn't really have a house, in the traditional sense. We lived in a small roadside church back in Doverton, and while the quarters were comfortable and all, it was still a church, with a main temple and an altar where Seraphine held services for visitors, and stained-glass art in an antiquated, simplified style showing the Lady with her chariot of doves. It was certainly home to my family for many generations, but we never called it a house – not once.

Seraphine pushed her outstretched hand even closer, leaning over the edge of the pool so much that she was in danger of falling in herself. "You can make it," she bade in her kindest, most enthusiastic tone. It reminded me of how she read the Book of Catherine during mass. "Just reach out."

Just reach out... well, what could it hurt? She was my sister, after all. I just had to take a few more little steps, one foot in front of the other. "'The way to get anywhere is one step at a time,'" I said, quoting something Archmage Tiara had once said during a lecture. Wait, was she here, now? I remembered her being nearby, but that was so long ago. Nothing seemed clear in my memories, except of course for my sister. I would have to ask her if she'd seen Archmage Tiara anywhere, right after I got out of this pool.

One foot in front of the other – I could do it. Despite the current seeming to rise to stop me, I took one step. Then I took two. It wasn't so bad after a few more, the current seeming to weaken the closer I came to the shore.

Finally, I reached out and grabbed for Seraphine's waiting hand, feeling her familiar warmth... except, it wasn't really that familiar, or warm. Nor did I remember her being so strong as she pulled me up and out of the water with ease.

I looked down at myself, at ruined clothes soaked heavy with dark crimson. I might as well have just walked through a war. "By the Lady..." I exhaled, staring at the gory mess in horror.

"We'll have to get you cleaned up, too," Seraphine said with that persistent quiet smile. The only time her cheer fell was when she glanced above, toward those strange flying shadows and the fiery swirling glow surrounding them. It wasn't fear I saw in her eyes, though – it was more like... disappointment? She had that same look as when she saw a child acting up during a particularly solemn service.

"What's happening, Seraphine?" I asked. But the answer I got wasn't what I expected.

"Our tea's getting cold. You don't want that, now, do you? Follow me." Without looking back, she started toward a set of stone stairs, cut into the small rise that presided over the pool. They looked like they'd been there for years, grown-over with moss and greenery as they were, but they were steady as I followed along, wet leather shoes squelching uncomfortably as I went.

At first, I didn't pay much attention to the house, as moss-covered and ancient as the stairs that led there. It was squat and small and simple, with one door and one wide window looking out over the land beyond. And from this spot, I could see everything – truly *everything*.

A crude-looking stone water wheel turned with the purest, clearest water imaginable, sending a trickle far smaller than such a big wheel should have been able to move back down the hill. There, it met the pool, and from there, the River, and finally, all of that merged with the sea. Did that wheel set the entire thing into motion? I thought maybe it did, as absurd as it seemed. Such a tiny thing, leading to something so huge, and at this vantage point, I could see it all, for miles and miles, a vast landscape as big as M'Gistryn itself, captured in a view that seemed more like a painting over someone's hearth.

"This is so amazing. I mean... look! Look!" I stepped toward the cliff's edge, pointing toward some shapes I could see moving somewhere below. They weren't far – they might reach the pool anytime now, where those great shadows in the sky might find them. And what then? "Those things, those great... beasts? What are they?"

Seraphine shook her head, and her long red hair bounced in time. And since when did she leave her hair down in the middle of the day? "Not of your concern, dear," she said, tone ever more insistent. "Come along. We need to go inside."

"But Tristan's down there. That has to be him. Oh, by the Lady... is that Alex? What are they doing here?" I strained to see more, but could really only make out man-shaped figures – distinct ones that moved in familiar ways, but little more than dots on the landscape regardless. "They could get hurt! We should help."

"Oh, Andie." She stepped in and touched my hand where Tristan's betrothal ring still sparkled, reflecting the eerie light around us in a million colors. With her other hand, she then wiped a stray trickle of Catherine-only-knew what was in that water from my cheek. It was a gentle gesture, kind and sisterly, but her voice was final and harsh, more so than I'd ever heard it. "You should never have met him."

I pulled back, brow furrowed. "What do you mean? What are you talking about?"

"We'll talk inside." More of that sympathetic smile played at her lips, but they were still drawn into a tight line. "There's so much you don't know, Andie."

"No, I want to know now. What do you mean by that?"

"You can't do anything about him right now."

I could hear my voice rising along with the Fire in the pit of my stomach. At least, I think it was Fire, magic Fire that could come out in unexpected ways. I didn't feel like I had much control over it, but rather it had just taken up residency there, acting on its own rules. "But those things – what are they?" I pleaded. "What's happening? Why won't you answer my questions?"

"The Dragons are as they are," she said with a touch of wistfulness, as if she were talking about memories of Mother and Father. "And they are... agitated, which is why we should go inside now. Are you ready?"

"Dragons? You said Dragons. That can't be right. I mean, that's crazy." Those huge shapes, impossible to truly take in... but there was no such thing as Dragons.

Stories, sure, plenty of them, and some even claimed to have found their bones. I had read stories about them, and even seen some old texts in the Great Library that talked about them as if they were living beings at one time, but that time wasn't now. That was long, long ago. Then again, those beasts of flame and smoke and wind... well, what else *could* they be?

"I have no control over them. Come along, Andie – you don't want them to come for you."

My voice sounded like it came from far away. "For... *me*?"

In reply, the woman who couldn't possibly have been Seraphine merely took my hand in hers and guided me toward the door of her tiny, ancient home at the pinnacle of everything.

CHAPTER THIRTY-TWO

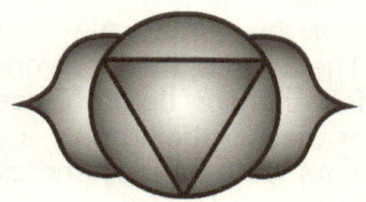

The House
15 Spring's Green, 1272
Tristan Loringham

What I came to realize as we dragged our tired, mortal bodies up to the summit was that the Dragons of this place were *not* gods. They had power, yes, a control over the elements of magic in a way that no one in the living world could yet imagine. They seemed to exist outside of the cycle of death and rebirth, presiding over it instead as guardians, or maybe caretakers, but that didn't make them gods. Gods didn't squabble and bicker and play games.

Gods didn't *bleed*.

The sky filled with the Fires of a righteously pissed-off Dragon even bigger and more dangerous than any of its kin, blood raining down with each rake of claws through the scales of its foe. And there was anger there, so much anger, fueling its rage with each breath as the sky turned the same crimson color as the waters of the River.

"What the..." But Alex let his words fall away, eyes transfixed on the scene above.

"They're killing each other," was all I could offer in response.

That was to say, the crimson Dragon of Fire appeared quite intent on its mission, though its glittering, iridescent target proved to be wily prey. Each time it suffered a blow, the long, indigo-scaled Dragon merely shook it off, growing perfect new flesh to seal over the wound. And though smaller, it seemed perfectly capable of defending itself, nimble where the red one was all muscle and power. Still, it chose not to strike back, not once, as if such an act would somehow be against its nature.

"If they come for us, it's over," Alex said, quiet and even. "Nowhere to run, nowhere to hide. So... what now?"

"I've been here before," I said, knowing that wasn't much of a satisfactory answer the minute Alex turned his furrowed-brow look on me. "The Source, the top... end of the line."

The pool of perfect crimson before us seemed to feed the entirety of the River, despite being only a fraction of its size. Here, the blood waters were tranquil and clear – so perfect in fact, they reflected the swirling storms of flame and smoke above as well as any mirror. If the watery Dragon of my recent nightmares lay waiting beneath, we would only know when it came for us. I found myself watching, staring, waiting for even a hint of ripple until Alex cleared his throat.

"It's not the end, though. What's over that hill there?" That hill, steps carved into ancient stone... things were different when I was last here. I remembered reaching for those stairs, only to fail in the last second. I remembered wondering where they led, until a little girl's drawing showed me the impossible.

"A house," I said. "I think it's a house."

"A... *house*?" Alex was incredulous. "What, you think the Dragons built a fucking summer home up there? Come on, man."

"I can't explain it. I know, it sounds mad, but it's got to be just on the other side of the hill. I don't know why or what lives there – I know it doesn't make sense. But I'm also pretty damned sure it's there."

After a deep, shuddering breath, Alex let out a laugh so loud it echoed across the pool and down the hill. "Sure, Brother, sure – Dragons in the sky, houses on the hill. Why not? Maybe it's got a white fence and flowers in the front garden."

"It doesn't." But those words weren't mine. They were small and high-pitched and slightly strained. They were the words of a child.

I had to squint to see him, for he wasn't really there at all. Well, in a way, I supposed he was, but he wasn't like us. Crown Prince Edin Blackwarren, rightful King of Zondrell, stood near the first step in that hill as a shade, a shimmering figure in the shape of the inquisitive, bright little boy we knew.

Yet in that same moment, he was also back home, tucked in his bed while his family and half the healers in all of Zondrell doted over him. Knowing that and seeing him in this place sent a chill worse than death down my spine.

"Dear Lady," Alex breathed, mouth agape. "Is that...?"

"He's been trapped here." I started to walk toward Edin, giving the pool a respectful berth, and he met me halfway there.

The boy beamed as he looked up. "Lord Loringham! You're okay? I thought maybe you were, you know... gone."

As I fell to one knee before the translucent soul of Prince Edin, my throat constricted. For a moment, it was hard to find words. I'd just left him here, disappeared with barely a warning. Whatever trials he'd had since, I could only imagine, but he shouldn't have had to do it alone. "Lord Edin, I... I failed you." It was all I could think to say.

The shade of Edin shook his little head, and his entire form blurred with the motion. It was like seeing him through a fogged-over window. "No, Lord Loringham, you didn't fail. They told me I'm supposed to 'con-tem-plate.'" The boy paused, brow knitted in thought – or perhaps contemplation. "Do you know what that means, Lord Loringham? They won't tell me."

"They?"

"Sure, the ones that helped me get here." A flash of fire in the sky caught his eye for a moment before he turned back to me. "You know – the Dragons? They said I'm supposed to 'con-tem-plate.'"

Alex had found his way to us, still staring in wide-eyed wonder at the Crown Prince. He found his words faster than I could, though, because I knew the answer to his question... and I had questions of my own.

The idea of the Dragons "helping" him wasn't exactly reassuring. In fact, I didn't understand it at all. Perhaps there was something more special about the young boy than the fact that he was supposed to be sitting on the throne of Zondrell.

"Think," Alex said, with a faint smile on his lips. "It means to think, Lord Edin. Do you, um... do you know what you're supposed to think about?"

"I think about all kinds of things. At least, I think I do. I think about home, and Mother, and my sisters. I think about Father sometimes..." His little face darkened. "Maybe they're not the right things to think about. My one friend told me that I'll know when I know, but that's kind of funny, isn't it?"

"And *who* exactly is this friend of yours?" I asked – I wasn't sure I wanted to know, but silence was the boy's response, regardless. I started to ask again, when I heard Alex at my shoulder.

"Brother..." he trailed off, staring through Edin and I toward the steps in the hillside, his silver eyes glassy and even wider than before.

The mass of moss and stone had begun to *move*. It shifted and stirred with a will all its own, opening up two huge eyes the color of emeralds, its pupils thin vertical windows into infinity, each about my height from end to end. Stone twisted and crumpled around them like the creases of an old man's features to become something that was neither kindly nor angry, but definitely sentient.

Rather than scream in terror, Edin did the last thing I expected him to do – he laughed out loud. "It's okay, Lord Vestarton," Edin through his giggles. "That's my friend. I call him Sight. He said that's not his name, but he liked it anyway."

"Contemplation is necessary... for some. The choice is not always... obvious. You they call Loringham would... know this, yes?" Those words intoned within my mind, each one deep, yet somehow melodic, drawn-out and heavy as if they had to be dragged along the ground to make their way to me. In the space of ten words, I could have spoken thirty, and perhaps thought many more than that.

Heaving myself to my feet on increasingly heavy, less stable legs, I stepped closer to the giant pair of eyes and imagined if I got too close, I could fall straight into them. "I was told there were no such choices – that they disrupt the Cycle and ruin Balance," I said, not sure if Alex had heard its thoughts as I did.

He'd likely accuse me of going thoroughly and completely mad this time, but he did no such thing. His attention was enthralled by this strange beast with the plodding, methodical way about it – it even blinked in slow motion.

"To contemplate is the right... of all souls," "Sight" went on. "To return as one is or what one will become... should be considered. Carefully." The huge pupils slid up slightly to observe the continuing battle raging high in the sky, staying that way for some time until its gaze settled on us once again. "Some would... disagree."

I nodded, starting to understand – or at least, imagining that I did. "Like them?"

A long, uncomfortable pause settled over us, punctuated only by the sound of a Dragon setting the sky on fire. What, I wondered, was the nature of this creature of the giant eyes? It might have been just that – nature itself, the Earth Dragon. It was the only thing that made sense, and finally, it confirmed my suspicion.

"I once stood with them, with Flame and Wind and Water. I would have... fought. This place is me and I am it – my spine is the bed along which the River flows. But even we are allowed to... contemplate. The Divine cries as the land dies, and still... we do not change. They forget that summer turns to fall... winter's cold embrace puts the earth to sleep. It is... natural."

"Is that why this place is dying?"

"Winter has come. In spring, the land, the Cycle, will be... reborn. It always is. Our transcendence is ahead, not behind. Some care not to... listen. Some are too attached to what is... but it cannot be denied. Light has revealed... Time shows us the way forward. And Life..." The eyes rolled skyward again, just as the indigo dragon suffered a tremendous blow from its fire-breathing foe. It reeled and damn near fell out of the sky, but its deep, bloody wound sealed itself within a minute. "Life... maintains."

Of course, it made sense – the indigo Dragon could heal itself with a thought. It could be none other than that which presided over Life itself. "So why are they fighting?" I asked aloud. "The Fire Dragon must know it can't win."

"Fire is... confident. They battle for something more than supremacy now... a soul in contemplation. A battle that will not end... until the Divine intervenes."

A soul in contemplation. Fire and Life. The Divine. Too many questions played out in my head, leading to too many possible answers. It was almost too much, but I had to know. I had to do something, though if I had to sit and think about it, to plan and plot out my next steps, I would be powerless. *Where to begin? Where to go?* The way was so close, I could *feel* it, but I was exhausted, too. My body hurt everywhere – the last time I slept felt like years ago.

But I had to keep going. The answer was right in front of me.

Those steps, wherever they led, would show me what I needed to know. They might very well take us to this "Divine." And perhaps there, young Jardin's prophetic drawing would become reality. "If I find this Divine," I asked cautiously, "and I stop those Dragons, what then?"

For a long time, again, I heard nothing but the roars above and the deafening silence of this place and the sound of Alex's foot tapping impatiently on the ground. Finally, a single sonorous thought mixed with mine. "Even Time knows not... the future."

I looked to Alex, and he to me. "You want to go up these steps, don't you?" he asked, more concerned than accusatory.

"We... yeah," I said. "I think we have to."

"What about him?" He nodded toward the shade of Lord Edin, who watched the skies and us and his bizarre Dragon "friend" all with great interest. *What does a child think about when choosing whether to live or die?* Whatever he contemplated as he stood there in wonder was beyond what I could know.

"He stays with us." I turned to the boy, stepping toward him as he looked up with dark, shining eyes. "Lord Edin, come on. You'll be safe."

"You're going to the house," he said softly. "That's where the Lady lives."

"The... Lady?" Alex and I spoke almost at the same time.

"You know what I think?" For dramatic effect, Edin leaned in and lowered his voice to a whisper. "I think it's really *The* Lady. Like from Church. She doesn't say that, but she's really nice. I went to her house, and she made tea and cookies, and we talked for a long time. She told me to con-tem-plate, too, but... she said it different. She said I was too 'attached' to do it right, or something. But she told me I could come back anytime. Maybe you can figure out what she's saying?"

I was struck speechless. The boy's story was… well, I didn't know what to think. And Alex, well, he couldn't help himself. He snapped his fingers and that familiar sarcastic smile lit up his features. "Well, there you have it. What did I tell you, Brother? Maybe after the tea and cookies, she'll take us on a ride in that chariot of doves, eh?"

I had to agree – it *was* the strangest, silliest, most outlandish thing I could imagine, and at this point, I could imagine a lot. The further we followed the River to its end, the more surreal things became, but the very idea that there was, after all, a god presiding over all of this, was equally insane. The Eislandisch didn't even *believe* that the River had a presiding divine being, and everyone else called *them* the heretics.

Now, who was right and who was wrong? In all the histories of M'Gistryn that I had read, the one thing I knew for certain was that religions never mixed company with one another – that was, of course, unless they wanted to have a war over it. People got locked up over such heresies, and yet… here we were, facing the denial of every major religion in the world.

Finally, I just shook my head. "I can't say I remember any stories from the Book of Catherine about tea and cookies."

Little Edin looked up, amused but inquisitive. "Maybe it's from a different book?"

Maybe it was.

We moved past the massive green Earth Dragon eyes peering at us, and I bowed to it as I started to take that first step. I imagined, somehow, that it nodded back, but once my boot hit that first ancient stone, the eyes closed, disappearing into the rock once more.

Then, everything else disappeared.

A thick shroud of darkness wrapped itself around us so fast, my mind had to work hard to catch up to what had happened. All sound ceased. The crystalline "sun" and the Dragonfire and everything in between were simply… gone.

Even the steps were cloaked in nothing but black fog – I could barely even see my own hands, much less my feet. *Think fast.* Instinct took hold, and I sought out my Light, pulling from deep within myself to create a shield of electric magic to part the Dark. It worked, somewhat, and I stumbled my way forward through whatever trick of divine or Shadow Dragon or anything in between this might have been.

"Alex? Lord Edin?" I called out. Nothing, just silence for what seemed like a very long time. I sought the edge of the next step, found it, stepped up, and tried to keep moving. I might as well have climbed a thousand steps, not just two – the oppression over my body and mind and soul was so intense, it was hard to breathe, must less move. My Light sparked and faltered.

Reach. Feel. Take one more step. Half-paralyzed, my body suddenly made of lead, I struggled to keep climbing. *Do not give up.*

"I admire your persistence," a smooth, lilting female voice wafted through the air. "But this way is not for you, Monsieur – not as you are."

I had so little power left, so little energy. When I felt the blade of a foe I'd met before slide between my shoulder blades, I felt no pain. It was almost… a release. The burden of fatigue and fear and worn muscles in agony flooded out through a million channels, from heart to head to fingertips. Yet, I still found myself trying to speak, my words coming up watery and full of copper.

"You… can't be… here."

"It is my part to play, Monsieur. Transcendence is not born from Shadow, after all." said the cool voice with the Lavançaise accent. For a brief moment, I felt her breath warm at my ear. "Go play your part, and I bid you *adieux*."

As the fog parted and I felt the hard reality of those moss-covered stones begin to slip away, I realized that for all the magic shields of Light and all the Dragon-gods in the sky, some things were simple. Some things were constant, reliable, like a good, sharp sword, like the fact that all life was indeed suffering just as Brin had once told me… and that death was freedom.

Go, noble Sayaf, for you are Awake. Do now what will be done.

CHAPTER THIRTY-THREE

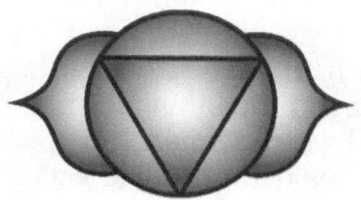

The Water
15 Spring's Green, 1272
Jade Saçaille

"**K**eep it up!" Vremya shouted from what felt like very far away. I felt weak, queasy, heavy on my feet. It was too much, this kind of magic – its warm embrace invited me to rest more than anything. I could just imagine curling up on the rocky ground right here and simply drifting off, but…

"Mama!" A tap on my shoulder, and I heard my daughter's voice floating around me. "Mama, look!"

In the place where the great lightning strikes had torn a hole through the sky emerged a creature just as unusual as the thing I saw in the street or the beast we faced from the sea. Unusual, yes, and frightening, but also beautiful, in its way.

A lithe thing of amber-gold, it flew like a bird, but seemed more like some kind of winged snake, long and thin, graceful in its strength. It slithered through the air toward us, covering the half-mile or so in less than ten heartbeats until it hovered just overhead. Instinctively, I grabbed for Jardin and shrank low toward the ground.

My instincts proved good, for in the next moment, a flash of light, white-hot and brilliant, rained forth and spread out along the cliff's edge between the fighting men and the frozen water serpent. I had seen Safaa do similar things during the war, but never to this scale, with such intensity.

Sparking bolts of pure energy wove themselves together to form a perfect barrier to protect... the monster in the water? Or was it for those of us fighting for our lives? It was difficult to tell, but I could swear that the golden creature bowed its head toward us as it sped off for unknown horizons.

I felt the power we all held flow out of me then, not so much unlike the feeling I had when my water broke and Jardin had struggled into the world. So strange... all I could do was stand there in a daze as I watched men spring back into action, only to strike uselessly against a blinding wall of light sturdier than any armor.

Arrows from the few archers positioned behind them bounced and skittered off in a dozen directions, and a collective, mystified curse rose up amidst the commands and battle-cries. To them, that light was just there, manifested from nothing.

Among the curses came cheers, and perhaps some prayers, as they fell back to regroup. That is, all except Brin, who merely squared his shoulders and kept his blade raised with what might have been a knowing sort of smile. It was hard to tell from where I stood, and I pushed down an urge to rush to him, to pull him back to safety with the others.

What was he thinking? Was he mad? Of course... I knew the answer to that, didn't I? The thrill of battle was always just a bit too hard to resist.

"Damn," Vremya said from behind, spitting out a few more words in Drakannyan that I recognized only from having spent time with him during the War. They weren't flattering. "We lost it. Maybe... maybe too late."

"What do you mean, 'too late?' It looks like we were right on time.... to coin a phrase." The Zondrean Archmage, Tiara, paused to let out a single amused grunt. She seemed about as rattled as it was possible for her to be – in other words, her gaze was sharp as broken glass, her hands clenching and unclenching as she surveyed the scene ahead of us. "For what, is the question. Perhaps you have some insight, *gospodin*?"

Vremya shook off the title she'd given him. "I'm no lord, Archmage. I'm just a man. And most men, I think, don't see things like that most days, *da*?"

Indeed, Dragons and great walls of magical light beyond anything anyone had ever seen were one thing. I could come to grips with that, could make sense of it from the experiences I'd had and the stories I'd heard. So could Vremya, I imagined. I could see him processing the scene around us and trying to figure out his next plan. Always planning, always considering – that was the Vremya I knew best. But what came next was something that even he couldn't have predicted, even on his best day.

It all happened so fast. Everything seemed... sped up somehow, accelerated and out of control – I could barely focus as men shouted and magic thickened the very air. The so-called dragon made of water howled in a mighty roar that shook the earth as it reared upward.

Or was it my mind that was shaken? It was almost impossible to focus as the beast grew, foaming black-tainted seawater building around it until it was three times its former size, dwarfing the perfect interweaving of sparks that stood in its way.

"Arrows!" I heard the shouting command of the High Captain. Arrows, truly? He should have known by now that his arrows did little in the face of this thing that could only be described as preternatural. No normal creature could do what this thing did – it literally *moved* the Sea of Stars to do its bidding, for Chantal's sake... and that sea did not appreciate a dam blocking its path.

It didn't spill over the wall, though – it rammed right through it, thousands of shattered splinters of energy disintegrating as they fell away. The men directly in its path didn't even have time to scream.

I screamed for them. "Brin!"

Water engulfed the place where the man I'd once called Husband stood. I shrieked again, a guttural sound with no recognizable language, and found myself unable to stand. My knees gave way, muscles weak, like my bones were made of the same stuff that made up the core of the unexplainable, hideous beast. I reached for my daughter, and she was there

– through tears we wailed together at the sight of Brin Jannausch disappearing into the dragon's maw.

Though, where my bones stayed encased in their skin as I knelt there, powerless to do anything, the beast's... didn't. As it struck the rocks, its great head exploded outward in a rush, wind and water as powerful as the hurricanes that plagued the far-eastern coasts of Lavancée and Drakannya knocking down everyone who wasn't down already.

But... how? It made no sense. Was there really Air magic that strong among this small assembly of battlemages? I rather doubted it, and none of them were standing, either, none prepared to fight with anything close to the kind of power that could destroy a god.

Yet, that's exactly what happened. Suddenly without a brain to command it, the Dragon's long neck hovered in a perfect arch over the cliff's edge for a second, then the whole beast simply fell apart. Water that once moved of its own accord lost its shape, returning to nature in one massive, aimless tidal wave.

It was if Chantal Herself had overturned some divine cup. Soldiers and mages were tossed backwards in wet, gurgling heaps against the force of it, myself included. I did everything I could to hold onto Jardin amidst the turmoil until we finally skidded to a stop.

"Balance is broken. You are judged." As I spat away the saltwater, I breathed aloud the words I'd heard in my mind before, the words I presumed were that of the Water Dragon. Perhaps it could not have guessed that it would be the one to be judged this day... and the man responsible rose to stand at the edge of the famous Zondrell cliffshore.

To say he looked no worse for wear would have been far too kind. Brin was unsteady, shaken, his own blood mixed with the water that had ruined his once-fine clothing. Yet, he *stood* on his own power, blade in hand, brushing off the pain like he had so many times from so many battles. He started walking toward us, slow at first, then more confident, and by everything that was holy, Chantal's very breath moved with him.

My husband had always had something a little wild in his eyes – I could never quite put it into words. He could be unpredictable, even ruthless... the men he served with in the

War sometimes called him a demon behind his back. But one thing I had always known was that his wild nature was *not* the product of magic. It was just Brin.

At least, that's what I believed, because he had no gift from Chantal stirring in his soul. He was as unremarkable and unmagical as the majority of men – especially Eislandisch ones. Besides, such a gift would have presented itself long ago, in his youth. Yet, the whispers of savagery in his gaze had become twisting, whirling winds – *actual* Air magic – the space around his pupils flaring bright white against a hint of clear blue sky.

"It's... not possible," I said as I stared in wonderment at him.

Brin quirked a slight smile and the nebulous shapes in his eyes twinkled with their own inner light. "Anything is possible, Jade."

"But magic is a gift. It comes from the Goddess. You can't just..."

"The last thing I saw," he said softly as he knelt beside me, "was shadow. Big, and it... glittered, like the skin of a shark in the sun. And I thought, 'Today is not my day.'"

No, no, that made no sense. I shook my head in defiance at this clear lack of logic and faith. Something else must have happened. "You *cannot* have magic, Brin. It doesn't work that way."

He looked over his shoulder at the writhing mass of Zondrell troops coming to their senses. There were cheers among them, orders barked, notes of concern and sympathy... and something else. Surprise? Fear? A mix of both, perhaps, for there was magic in their midst, too. Men who had lived their whole lives without the touch of Chantal were changing somehow. Fires lit in the palms of hands. Rocks twisted and formed anew underfoot. Not everyone's eyes brightened and changed, but there were more than a few, much more than just one.

Brin's smile widened. "Chantal has rules – they are not my rules. Maybe they are no one's rules anymore, *ja*?"

"No..." I started, but my thoughts faltered as I saw faint streamers of Life magic reaching out to tend to nearby wounds... and they weren't mine.

"I told you: Keis Sturmberg spoke of this day. We reach for a piece of ourselves in battle, and today, we found it." As he took my hand in his and squeezed, I felt his pulse, high and hot and all too familiar. My lack of recoil surprised even me. "You and Jardin are all right, *ja*?"

Our daughter sat nearby, of course, silently transfixed – and maybe delighted – by her father's new manifestation. Was that a tiny smile at the corners of her lips? She said nothing, but her face said much. I turned back to Brin. "*Oui*. Tired, but fine, I suppose."

"*Sehr gut*. You may be needed, you know." He gestured behind him to the Zondrell soldiers.

"I'm here, but... so are they, it would seem. I don't know if they need my help anymore."

Though magic continued to build all around us, it also came without training, without the proper knowledge and control to wield it. They did their best, but it soon proved to be less than enough, and I found myself among them within the hour.

It was strange tending to the wounds of people who wore the uniforms of what was once the enemy. That was so long ago... yet it still felt like yesterday. Brin was here. Vremya was here. The shores were different and the land was warmer, but there I was, tending to the wounds of the fallen, just like old times. Every time I sent Life to heal another, those painful days of the War came rushing right back. My prayers might have helped, but was Chantal even listening? Where was She in a world where magic was now granted without judgment?

Perhaps Brin was right – the rules were no longer what they were. Once, I had heard Her sacred words and I let them be my strength, but now they felt... empty. Balance was lost, maybe forever.

CHAPTER THIRTY-FOUR

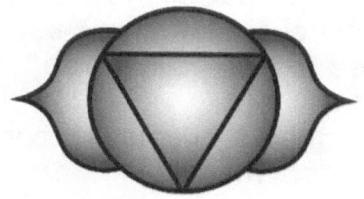

The Sky
15 Spring's Green, 1272
Alexander Vestarton

I had a dream once, where I found my best friend dead on some unknown hill. First, there was darkness. Then, blood... so much blood. There was nothing I could do to stop it – I didn't even know how it happened. I remember feeling so powerless, so empty, so *lost,* and it wasn't even as much about Tristan as it was about... well, something else, something I didn't understand. Something *more.*

I'd almost forgotten about that dream, but a lot can happen in a few months' time, like a whole lot more darkness and that much more blood. And somewhere on the other side of all that, in a place far beyond any nightmare I could concoct after a two-bottle evening, I realized I was pressing an elegant little Lavançaise shortsword up against a woman's throat. She had a bruise swelling nicely on one cheek, and my fingers were wrapped up in her undone mane of thick, black hair.

How did we get like this? Well... I couldn't quite say. There were flashes and stirs, my brain screaming while my body acted, the two halves of myself independent. When everything slammed back together a few moments later, my brain was still carrying on – did I *really* want to do what I was doing?

Maybe I did. My hand tightened around the sleek, leather-wrapped hilt of the weapon I held. Thick rivulets of blood dripped from it, blood that belonged to neither its owner nor me, blood that shouldn't have been spilled in the first place. *Yes! Revenge is the only justice now.*

Yet, my mind had a case to plead. *No! Blood for blood... it's not right.*

Muscles burned up and down my arms, my heart racing to the point where my vision pulsed in time with it. I saw the alien world around me through the hazy beat of a war drum. *Vengeance,* shouted all that boiling blood and tensing sinew. *It's all we have left!*

My mind, though, tried a new tactic: compromise. *No. Not yet. Answers first, then... maybe.*

It was enough. I didn't let go – I wasn't an idiot – but that blade was no longer a mere flinch away from opening an artery. Even the part of me that was brought up with good Zondrean morals, like not beating the shit out of women, knew that it would be unwise to give away my advantage.

Magic or no magic, Onyx Saçaille was no ordinary noble's daughter. If I'd taken a second to think instead of acting out of pure rage-fueled instinct, I'd likely be the one on the wrong side of that sword – we both knew that much.

What I didn't know was the answer to one simple question: "Why?"

"I did my part," she said, barely audible over the roars of Dragons and the general low-pitched thrum of hell incarnate.

This wasn't quite what I wanted to hear, but the emotion I felt running hot through every part of me never touched my voice. "Answer my question," I said, as calm as if I had just said something about the weather. "Give me a good reason to not kill you and let the River decide what to do with your corpse. You have ten seconds."

Silence. A slump of the shoulders, as if her strength had left her.

"One," I started counting. "Look sharp, Madame."

"You do not understand."

"I understand that you don't think I'm serious. Two."

"Monsieur, you have to know..."

"Three."

"... there is only one way to the top."

"Four."

A sigh, a longing look toward the ancient hill that may or may not have been the back of some mythical beast, with steps carved into it that may or may not have led to some strange old house owned by a god. But despite that, she remained stubbornly silent.

"Five."

"Go on, then," she hissed.

"Six."

"You will die here."

"And you'll go with me. Then you'll answer to *him*. Seven."

A slight nod toward something unseen. "*Regardez*, Monsieur."

"Eight." My grip tightened more, palms slick with sweat, the blade heavy in my hand.

"Look at the hill, Monsieur," she said again, now insistent, urgent.

"You think I'm taking my eyes off you for one bloody second? Nine."

"*Look at the hill.* Your answer is there."

"T..." Despite my better judgment, I did look, and the countdown died on my lips. Splayed over the steps, not even halfway up, lay Tristan... or rather, his mortal shell. One precision strike with the very weapon I held in my hand, and that was it.

By the time the black fog cleared, the deed was done, and where was I? Blind. Clueless. Powerless. As useless as it was, I wanted *so badly* to pay his assassin back in kind, to make that evil bitch feel the same pain she'd wrought. In fact, I'd never wanted something so much in my whole life.

Vengeance and violence had always been the domain of different men – rarely had I hunted down blood in my life, and when I did, I was bad at it. Such was better left to the Tristan Loringhams of the world, and finally, I understood why. Living with what I felt in that moment wasn't for the faint of heart.

But then my gaze continued beyond the scene that would never leave my nightmares and up those inexplicable steps. One at a time, I followed the moss and crumbling yellowed stone until I found a figure, lit from behind by the alien light of a giant crystalline sun and dressed in the formal regalia of an elite Zondrell officer. Silver buckles and armored plates winked against polished black leather as this tall, broad-shouldered man raised his right fist to his left shoulder in salute.

Then he gave a brief shake of the head, a gesture I'd seen many times, usually right before I was about to say or do something incredibly stupid. It wasn't really a warning, but more of a reassurance: *I've got this – don't worry.* Then he turned and walked away, disappearing into the horizon.

The stolen sword slipped out of my grasp and thunked onto the rocky ground, but it didn't matter. I'd already given up the fight and was halfway to those stairs. I had to follow, I had talk to him, I had to... take two steps and slam straight into something very hard, yet very invisible.

A string of curses erupted forth as I stumbled backward, one hand to the place on my brow that took the brunt of the solid nothingness' abuse. "What the hell was *that*?"

"As I said, Monsieur, you and I are not welcome there," Saçaille said. "Not as we are. And maybe not as we could be. That is not for us to decide."

Bullshit – that esoteric garbage meant nothing. Sure, a logical part of my brain said something about Lord Edin being able to go up and down that hill as he pleased to see his "lady in the house." It wasn't just because he was a cute kid, and I could understand that, but I also didn't care. I didn't want to hear some speech about spirits and souls and abandoning mortal shackles. I just wanted to get to the top of that hill, on *my* terms, and do something. Maybe I could put things right... somehow.

So I pushed. I struggled. I beat my fists against empty air so hard my hands ached. And when none of that worked, I cried. Yes, I, Alexander, Lord of Vestarton, a grown man, sank to my knees in miserable tears of defeat, unabashed as I wailed and shook through frustration and sorrow and fear beyond any I'd ever felt.

**

I don't know how long it took until I was quiet again, until I'd become nothing but an empty, sullen husk. I also don't know how long it took to find coherent words, and the only ones I was able to come up with were simple: "Kill me."

"No. I have played my part, Monsieur." Saçaille had her blade back in her possession – I knew it without even looking.

She stood on unsteady legs not five steps away, and when I looked in her eyes full of dark, swirling chaos, I saw the cold there, the ruthlessness. What difference did it make to someone like her? I didn't know, but there was something else, too, a kind of pain, regret... a sense of longing for something better than where she found herself.

I'd be damned if I'd find any sympathy to give, though. I had my own problems. "Are you fucking kidding me? I'm not just going to sit here while... gods-know-what goes on up there. So do it. Make it as painful as you want – I don't care. Just get it over with."

The corners of her almond-shaped eyes tensed the tiniest bit, stretching the thin white scar that ran across one pale cheek, opposite of where I'd sucker-punched her. But instead of shoving that sword into my chest blade-first, she merely tossed it to the ground next to me. "Do it yourself, Monsieur," she said in a low, harsh whisper.

I called her something I'll not repeat as my gaze fell to the graceful little blade. How much pain would something that thin and sharp actually cause? Maybe it wouldn't be so bad. And it was the only way – the only way to what, I wasn't quite sure, but it didn't matter anymore. I'd figure it out. Besides, I'd never be able to live with myself if I left Tristan behind. Shared blood or no, he was my brother. He'd do the same for me.

Grabbing up the blade, I steeled myself... for a moment that never came. Something deep and black, the most vivid of darknesses, had already swallowed me up, and it wasn't the embrace of death. It washed over me, through me, in one hell of a rush, and when there was light again, the world had gotten very, very bright.

What the... *now*? Of all the damned times?

Up until that moment, the tug and pull of Time magic had dwindled to a general whisper that lurked in the corners of my awareness. I thought maybe I'd finally had it under some kind of control, that it would start serving me instead of the opposite.

Apparently, I was mistaken.

I put a suddenly empty hand up to shield my eyes from the big yellow daytime sun as it loomed over the countryside of

Doverton. Wait, Doverton? What the…? There was a skirmish going on here, right at the center of the city in front of their largest Church of Catherine. Its stained-glass depictions of the goddess and her chariot of doves winked back light in a thousand colors, and for a moment I stood transfixed.

Where was the Great Lady of Peace, anyhow? How could She allow bloodshed before Her very own hallowed sanctuary? It was running in rivers through the damned streets, and there She was, looking on without a care in the world.

Well, I cared. Except, I didn't know what to do. I was starting to panic over a man dying in front of me. His pulse was soft and faint – one… two… three… I measured out each beat, could feel it resonating with some foreign invasion of magic power that crawled under my skin, urging to be let out.

There was magic everywhere I looked, powerful magic, but mine was the kind of power that could slow down the world itself and anything I chose within it. And in that moment, the only thing I cared about was that one man, a hero by some standards, a traitor by others, but a man I was always proud to call my friend.

A million hurried and scattered thoughts filled my head and fluttered by, none of them worth a damn. I could only do so much, but someone else could do more, someone who shouldn't have had the ability to do such a wondrous thing at all. Soon, there were flashes of strange purplish light through her streaming tears…

The studious, quiet little Pyrelight from Doverton had called it *Lebenkern,* some kind of magic that fed from the rarest of elements – Life. Its power strengthened the pulse under my fingertips, but even as it did so, everything else around me began to weaken.

Reality tattered and ripped until I saw myself in two places at once. In an instant, I was there on the main street of Doverton, while in the next, I stood over a massive River with no discernible beginning or end, its shores lined with greenery, its waters crimson and viscous and relentless.

It had been just a single sliver of Time, but it changed everything. Some even called it a moment of prophecy, some nonsense about the "Light of a new age." Whether mere mortals could predict the whims of divinity, I couldn't say for certain. Most so-called prophecies in the world were flat-out wrong, but this one... well, I was *there*.

Doverton melted before my eyes then, leaving just the River behind. It slowed and decayed, its waters no longer able to nourish the vegetation as the earth began to crack and shudder. None of it would last forever, not under these conditions – perhaps it was never meant to survive the ages, after all.

When I returned to myself in the present moment, I was still holding that shortsword, staring down a woman who had lived that same moment with me, months ago. Wetness dried on my cheeks, my eyes burning while my thoughts worked feverishly to stitch themselves together. "I don't know how you're doing that, sending me those visions," I muttered.

"A small manipulation. Even your magic is subject to trickery."

"Well, I don't appreciate it. What are you trying to accomplish? Is that the moment of your supposed 'new age,' whatever the hell that even means?"

"All this time, I thought I knew," Saçaille said softly, her gaze hard and far away. "I could have done more, perhaps. Instead, I chased Shadows... like a fool."

"That doesn't answer my question."

And she continued, stubbornly, to avoid it. "Look to the skies, Monsieur. What do you see?"

Above, we looked together to a weird, sickly sky, where a Dragon the color of that flash of magic I saw in Doverton continued to clash with another the color of blood... "Fire. Fire and Life," I said, speculative. "They're chasing each other?"

"Destruction and creation – natural enemies, you might say, fighting for dominance." Saçaille's lips drew to a thin, hard line. "Don't you see? I always looked to the wrong cause, the wrong magic, the wrong people." She shook her head and stray sweaty tendrils of the hair I'd damn near pulled out at the roots a few minutes ago fell around the woman's angular features. "Safaa believed in the Prophecy, that her Light might bring Balance. And she was wrong, I knew, because the New Age was the opposite of Balance. I was *so* sure. Then later, I saw all the pieces come together again – Time, Life, Light. It should not have been, but still I believed. I always failed to *see*."

"See what? The nonsense men make out of the words of the so-called gods?"

"The gods." She let out a small chuckle. "They toy with us. We look for their signs and symbols where there are none. The New Age came and went, not in a flash, but with a whisper."

I would have liked to have told her she was insane. I really wanted to fail to see where she was going with all this. But for all I knew, we were the last living humans in a land of utter destruction, and honestly, I didn't want to be stuck there with a madwoman.

So, I followed the arcane ramblings looking for logic. "Tristan thought all of this was his fault, that he didn't belong here or something like that. But you're saying..." I swallowed down the tightness rising in my throat. "You're saying it's because of Andella?"

As if on cue, the red Dragon belched out a gout of flame that would have incinerated anything it touched. But its opponent shook it off, its scales still perfect and glistening with their indigo sheen. How long had they been doing this, anyhow? And had sweet little Andella Weaver really set them into this deadly, unending cycle? I supposed, at this point, anything was possible.

"I watched her ascend the steps," Onyx said, looking to the hill with a wistful, faraway expression. "And I did nothing."

"Wait, she came this way? She went... oh..." Of course she had come this way — I saw her choose to turn, her soul starting the long struggle against the River's current. How or why, I had no idea, but I was willing to bet my life that she could make her way past the threshold that my mortal-bound self couldn't transcend. "But you did do *something*," I said, tone dripping with disdain. "She's not alone up there."

"No, I..." As she trailed off, I swore I saw a tear of her own when her gaze fell upon the blood she'd spilled on those steps. Maybe it was just my imagination. "For what it is worth, Monsieur, I am sorry. But there is one path left, and only he can walk it."

"Correction: he walks his own path." An idea occurred to me, then, an arrow in the dark, perhaps, but what the hell? There wasn't much left to lose. "And so should we."

Saçaille arched an eyebrow in my direction, but otherwise had no response.

"Look, we're not just hanging around here to wait out the apocalypse, right? We have to do *something*." Because if the tables were turned, Tristan wouldn't hesitate. He wouldn't be sitting there confused and pressed for what to do. He would figure it out and he'd make it happen, consequences be damned.

"Monsieur, I am done with taking life today. Find your way to the Divine on your own."

"I'm not talking about that. I think we'll have better luck with them." The moment I pointed toward the sky, she could barely contain her shocked bemusement.

"*Je m'excuse?*" Saçaille stared at me as if I'd gone absolutely mad... and I probably had.

"That one deals in Life magic, right? The purple one?" Nothing else could have embodied Life so well as the majestic indigo creature moving effortlessly through the sky, despite the constant torture coming from something much bigger, stronger, and fiercer. "I want its attention, and you're going to help me."

"You are mad."

"You got a better idea? Or are you just waiting to die here and find out what happens?" Though her eyes narrowed to slits, she remained quiet. "That's what I thought. Now, first things first."

I strode over to the pool of crimson liquid that seemed to feed the River itself, yet its surface remained smooth as glass. Whatever lay deep beneath wasn't mine to know, but I remembered Tristan at the end of this very same River, making me drink from its waters. Yet, that stuff was diluted and impure from its grand journey to the sea. How much more "awake" might I become if I dipped my hands in and drank here?

As it turned out... awake enough.

CHAPTER THIRTY-FIVE

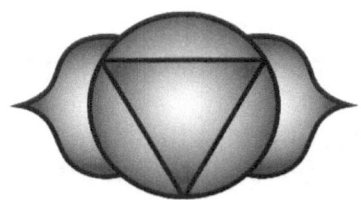

Teatime

15 Spring's Green, 1272
Andella Weaver

White with red and gold trim… the robes of a Pyrelight. I stood looking down at clothes that were foreign and familiar at once, the guise of those humble Fire mages who had chosen to serve the Church and help guide souls to the waiting hand of Catherine in Paradise.

Other cultures sent their dead out to sea or buried them in the ground to commit them to their gods, of course – to some of them, the practice of the Pyrelight was sacrilegious, if not outright barbaric. But it's what we did, and what I had set out to do with my life until… well, until everything changed.

"You see? They become you." Seraphine's voice drifted across the small, open space. The little house was barely more than a large, single room, with a hearth and washbasin along the far wall, alongside a wide window that let in all the light the place needed. A modest wooden table and four chairs stood close to the hearth, and there were a few shelves of kitchen items, but not much else. It was the most unadorned home I'd ever seen, a far cry from the ornate richness I'd so quickly grown accustomed to in Zondrell. I'd have to ask her how she found her way to this place.

Other questions were bubbling to the surface, though. "They're nice, thank you," I said, turning my head this way and that to observe how the robes moved with me, softly swirling around my ankles and wrists. "But where did you get these? They're not mine."

"They are now, Andie, and look how well they fit. You look just as you should."

I nodded as I went to join her at the table, taking the seat across from her. "I suppose so, but you know I'm not a Pyrelight anymore."

"Hm? Nonsense." Seraphine's kind eyes and gentle smile looked a little strange, as if they didn't quite fit her anymore. I couldn't pinpoint what was wrong, but I also couldn't say for sure that she wasn't actually my sister. Who else would she be? "Your services are so desperately needed, Andie – today more than ever."

"Why? What's happening today?"

Her eyes, which had always been sort of a muddled chestnut with a hint of green, seemed brighter now than they ever had, despite the touch of sadness there. "So much has happened already, wouldn't you agree? Look out there." She pointed toward the window. "What do you see?"

Outside, I saw little more than the thin haze of black smoke that hung in the air, but it was really the crystalline ball of light in the sky that grabbed my attention the most. It wasn't much like any sun I knew – it reminded me more of a lantern with very thick, rough-hewn glass. "The light looks... dim," I replied, fixated on it for a time before turning back to Seraphine.

"It was much brighter once, that light. That was a long time ago. Now it sets, never to rise again."

"How do you know that?"

"You've seen the River, haven't you, Andie? This land, this place, it's all falling apart. Little by little... everything I've built." Seraphine's folded hands began to tense and wring in that way that our mother's used to when she was worried about something.

I looked at her, quizzical. "You've 'built?'"

I hated just peppering her with question after question, but there were so many to ask. Instead of impatience, though, she simply smiled a distant sort of smile – I'd never seen her in such a state.

Even when our mother died, her expression always held a special sort of cheer, her big round cheeks warm and rosy.

She had her moments, sure, but she also had faith that everything would be all right. Catherine had a plan for all of us, after all, a special path to follow. But now, that faith she so easily exuded seemed shaken, and I didn't care for it.

"Oh, Andie," she said, "You're such a good Pyrelight, kind-hearted and skilled – your days should have been so much more peaceful. Your skills shouldn't be used for what's to come. But be that as it may…"

I could only shake my head, ever more questions buzzing around in my thoughts as I tried to put it all together. It was a dream, a nightmare, a whirlwind. Nothing made sense, despite my almost desperate wishes to the contrary. "Seraphine, I'm trying, I really am, but please, you have to tell me: what's going on? What is this place? What are you *talking* about?"

"'A new age dawns.' You believe in that prophecy, don't you? I know how interested you were in that old book." When I straightened in my seat at the mere mention of *Lebenkern*, her smile widened. "I know, I know, it's just a book. Yet, so many stories are based on truth, Andie. This new age…" She trailed off, her gaze wandering back out the window, where the smoke seemed to billow up through the air a little thicker than before.

I heard myself more insistent now – not quite angry, but possibly flirting with it. "This new age, *what*? What is it, Seraphine?"

As if caught by a flash of inspiration, she turned back with sudden intensity. "I need your help, Andie. You'll help me, won't you?"

"Well… of course. You know I will." Except, what was I agreeing to? Did it matter? It was my sister, after all – she needed me.

"Good. Good, I'm glad, because you see, the Dragons, the men, they're all working against this place, against each other. We can't let it go on much longer. You care about the world, don't you?

I nodded. "Well, I mean… things are pretty bad right now, at least in Zondrell. It's been awful. I don't even know how I could help anymore. But I suppose bad things happen all the time, don't they, all over the world?"

"Yes, but so do good things. It all needs to be rebuilt, Andie – this new age isn't the age we want. We'll start anew, but first..." Pulling herself to stand, Seraphine rose and went to the hearth, where a small black kettle had started to steam. I watched with curiosity as she checked its contents, then tossed in a few more sprigs of something green from a little collection resting near the basin, pausing for a moment to breathe in that unmistakable aroma of mint and lavender. When she seemed satisfied, she turned back with that sweet, not-quite-right smile on her lips. "The tea is almost ready," she announced. "Will you be a dear and get the door?"

"The door? But no one's..." *Knock, knock* – just then, I heard two sharp, curt raps on the door from outside. "Oh."

Well, that was odd. She must have been expecting someone, which was all well and good, but why were my hands shaking? I couldn't quite explain it, but I felt strange as I stood and approached, and even stranger when my hand fell to the metal latch that held the old door closed.

Was it nerves? Maybe that was it, just my anxieties getting the best of me. Feeling so helplessly confused about so much could do that to anyone, I supposed, though I'd never had so much trouble controlling my fingers just to move a simple latch. It finally creaked open, and I gasped aloud.

First, I saw the little boy – did I know him from somewhere? Oh! It was the Prince, the boy king of Zondrell. Weren't they looking for him? No, they found him, and he was resting. He looked better now, of course, bounding into the room with a smile etching dimples deep into his olive-tinged cheeks.

"Ah, Sir Edin! Welcome back. I have fresh cookies here just for you," I heard Seraphine say from behind, but I didn't look back – I couldn't. It was impossible to look away from the second visitor, still standing in the open doorway.

In a word, Tristan was resplendent. Dramatic, yes, but there was no better word to describe him. Even on Peaceday at that grand procession, he hadn't looked so sharp, so polished. How long had that been now? Just a few weeks, but it seemed like forever since the whole fate of Zondrell had turned on the head of a pin.

I had loved how he looked in that ceremonial armor then, but this wasn't quite the same. What he wore now was decorated but also functional, with falcon motifs carved artfully into silvery shoulder plates that interlocked with burnished black leather and more steel plating in key protective places.

I reached out — was he really there at all, or was he just another part of this dream I was living? But my fingertips brushed solid metal and smooth leather, as real as anything I could imagine, and his hand was warm as it clasped mine against his heart.

For a moment, he closed his eyes, and when he opened them, I saw a million interweaving colors that were never there before... were they? No, I knew I had never seen anyone with eyes like that.

"Tristan?" I asked, my voice little more than a whisper.

"I'm sorry," along with a brief squeeze of my hand, was all he offered in reply.

"Oh, you... you don't need to apologize. I understand. I just... missed you." Wait, when was that? The other day? No, it was earlier today, or yesterday, or some other time. I remembered how I felt, but it all seemed so jumbled and hazy. There was that stab of guilt mixed with loneliness, confusion, then I took a good long walk to the Academy to think. It was all going to be okay; I was sure of it. And *then* what happened? That was the part I wasn't so sure about. Memories just seemed to fall apart, a disjointed collection of fragments at the corners of my mind. I shook them away for the moment — they weren't doing me any good. We were here now, and we could make the best of it. "I'm just glad to see you. And look, my sister made tea. You remember Seraphine, don't you?"

Tristan's gaze shifted from the back of the room to me, and then back again, eyes narrowing slowly. "I do," he said, hesitant. There might have been more he wanted to say — I could almost see the words caught there in his throat.

I took a step back and looked him over once more. "Are you all right, Tristan?"

Still, that focused, intense look, now boring into my very soul. He searched me through and through, but still came away with no answers. From the look on his face, the question he seemed forced to ask might have caused actual pain as he spoke. "You... don't know where you are, do you?"

What kind of a question was that? Of course I knew. I was here, with my sister, and... behind me, I heard the happy clink of dishes and silverware. "The tea is ready," Seraphine said. "Come on, Andie, sit down — milk and no sugar, just the way you like it. Same for you, Tristan?" She stood over the table with the steaming kettle poised over four simple white porcelain cups. I wasn't sure I'd ever seen her as much of a hostess, yet she deftly poured tea into each one with barely a second glance, her attention still focused on us with a polite smile frozen on her lips.

Tristan shook his head. "Thanks – I'll pass."

Seraphine made that low *hm* sound she sometimes made at the back of her throat when she'd rather keep her thoughts to herself. Yet, something was still off. This woman was my sister – she had every mannerism, every inflection, every freckle on her cheeks. But at the same time, she was something else entirely, something I couldn't explain.

You don't know where you are, do you?

Outside, I heard the low-pitched roars of beasts in the skies, and I could swear the familiar tug and pull of magic on the inner workings of my being seemed stronger than before. Stronger, and warm, too, like the fiery embers burning in that hearth across the room. If I stood still and paid attention to it for a moment, it was almost a calling, something from beyond trying to tear that magic out of me – for what, I had no idea.

Or maybe it was all just my imagination, which Seraphine's voice promptly cut through and severed at the root, as sharp as any knife. "Tristan Michael Johannes Loringham... such a name. A good name, some might say. I admit, I had very high hopes for you. I see I was right, in some respects. What do you think, young Sir Edin Nicholas Kelvaar Blackwarren?"

The boy, who had been munching happily on his cookie, looked up, wide-eyed. "You should always have high hopes for your friends," he offered. "Lord Loringham is my friend."

"Of course he is – always a friend to those who... contemplate." Slow and thoughtful, Seraphine took a sip from her cup before setting it back down again. "It's quite unfortunate."

That flame within me was growing brighter, hotter, almost too much to bear, as full of magic as it was frustration. "Seraphine, *what* are you talking about? What could possibly be unfortunate?" I demanded.

"Andie, do you remember what I asked you? About your help?"

"I... yes, but why? And you're not answering my question *again*."

Seraphine's smile was thin, her gaze far away from me or Tristan or Edin or anything in that room in that moment. "I need you to perform your duties as a Pyrelight, just one more time. You'll do that for me, won't you?"

CHAPTER THIRTY-SIX

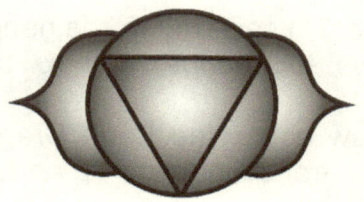

Divinity
15 Spring's Green, 1272
Tristan Loringham

The Source, the River… it all looked very different from the highest point. Through the eyes of the soul, I had perspective that the eyes of a man would miss. What had once appeared as blood, crimson rapids flowing swift from the Summit to the Sea, now held a prismatic sheen, the colors alive even as they danced under a sun that was no such thing at all.

In fact, the light hovering overhead – closer now than ever – more resembled a lantern, light flickering within a glass prison. It illuminated from within its protective shell, but it did so inhibited, controlled, its potential stifled.

Meanwhile, potential was all I had left.

I hadn't planned on going to the Summit this way – really, I never had a plan, not one I could articulate. A plan *existed*, and I had a direction, a yearning to push forward and see for myself what I saw in Jardin's drawing… to see if it was all true. As that plan slowly took its true form, I began to understand that the path I'd forged was the right one, the only one, meant for me and me alone.

"Alex," I whispered down to the place and the people left behind, "you'll have to walk your own path. I'm sorry, my Brother." They were words he would never hear.

The story is not yet ended. You know this now.

All I saw was a feather, a single golden feather from the bird-like wings of a fantastic beast, floating through the air. But I knew the voice – I knew it so well, it was a part of me. I reached out and let the feather fall into my waiting hand.

The journey of the noble Sayaf continues – it must. Time is short.

"The time for what?" I said, my words hanging in the ether.

For the seasons to change... or to see it all fall into Darkness.

Seasons... A new age... the Earth Dragon had spoken of those things. "'Our transcendence is ahead, not behind,'" I quoted its words aloud.

Indeed. Change will come – it is inevitable. How it manifests is what is at stake. It is a choice to make.

"And what's your choice?"

If the feather in my hand could have smiled, I felt like it would have. *I choose to place my faith in you, noble Sayaf.*

"Faith in a dead man." The mere concept would have been hilarious if it hadn't been so serious... so final.

The chapter is unfinished, for those who are Awake must write it. Simply know that the story has not yet ended.

"And where are you in all this, Gold Dragon?" I asked the empty air.

Awake, as are all of us. We are watching you.

Not so far away, the indigo and red Dragons continued their endless dance. They could have easily chosen to stop chasing each other and take out their aggressions on me, the lone wanderer invading their lands.

At least I was dressed for battle – I looked down to realize that I was wearing the regalia of an officer, with a high shine on that silver falcon-decor armor that would have made even old Headmaster Janus proud. At my side was a blade lost to the sea, lost to time, a gift from my father on that day I graduated with the High Honor medal. The gem-studded hilt winked at me from a forgotten dream.

You see yourself with power, with... bravery, the Gold Dragon's voice came to me.

But I shook my head with a short sigh. "I see myself dressed up for my own funeral."

Again, the feather took on a quirk that wasn't there before. *You see more than you know. Go to the house, look within. Waste no more time.*

The House... the little house at the top of the hill. Such an unassuming place, a humble, simple thing, so impossible yet so natural. I turned to it, taking in every ancient brick and spot of moss. I noticed the wheel turning clear, pure water just in front, its power slow and steady as it sent a mere trickle into the source of the great River below. But most of all, I saw the door, closed but somehow still bidding me to enter.

Next to it stood Prince Edin – or rather, his presence, his soul – ready to knock. His form appeared the same, limned in a translucent shimmer, though it held a certain radiance I hadn't noticed before. His excitement literally glowed through him.

"Are you con-tem-plating, Lord Loringham?" he asked with a smile on his round, boyish face.

"I... believe I might be," I told him as I went to meet him.

"Maybe the Lady can help you. Are you ready to meet Her?"

I nodded, even though I wasn't ready at all. Nothing could have prepared me for what I saw inside that house.

It was a scene too bizarre to strike the nerve of pain and loss. There were a million things I could ruminate on, to lament and torture myself over, but those things were in the past. Their burden had been set down, and now... now here was Andella Weaver – my first and only real love – dressed in the pristine robes of a Pyrelight and sitting with, of all people, a woman that looked exactly like my mother.

I was told she looked more like Andella's sister, Seraphine, and to Lord Edin, she looked like Catherine Herself from the statues and paintings in Zondrell's Great Temple. I just nodded and said nothing, for they didn't see that this woman was my mother, down to the last detail.

But despite the long blond hair in its careful braid, she didn't look quite right. In spite of the good linen dress protected with one of Lissa's old aprons so she could garden and cook without soiling her clothes, this woman didn't move through her kitchen with the same Eislandisch stoicism. Instead, she simply moved with *grace*, effortless as she poured tea, set out fresh-baked cookies from a primitive old hearth, and greeted us warmly, with heavily-accented Zondrean speech and a wide, friendly smile that the true Lady Gretchen absolutely never would have displayed for me or anyone else.

"Tell me, *Liebling*," she said in my mother's voice as she sipped from her unadorned white cup, "it would be good to sit with us, *ja*? You must be so tired."

Yet, I wasn't – far from it. As I stood there firmly at attention, ever the solider, I noticed everything about that modest one-room hut, everything from the simplistic cut of the silverware to the smell of lavender hanging the air. Nothing about it made any sense, and at the same time, it was perfect exactly as it was.

There were no marble stairs and gleaming fountains as spoken of in the Book of Catherine, but the abode of the Divine didn't need to be so ornate and overdone. It simply needed to *be*, although the entity that inhabited this place was as far from my personal image of the Great Lady as I could have imagined. Nor was she, for that matter, anything close to a kindly priestess, and watching the imposter banter with Andella in such a strangely familial way was... more than unnerving. It was *wrong,* and I felt a stirring anger turning to heat within me.

I fixed the woman wearing the face of many at once with a cold stare, uninterested in playing games with gods. "I'd like to speak to my wife. In private."

"Oh! *Sehr gut!* Lord Edin and I will chat." She raised an eyebrow in that way that all mothers had when they knew much more than they let on. "But you know you are not married just yet, *ja?*"

I raised my eyebrow in a similar, knowing fashion. "Excuse us, will you?"

"Tristan..." Andella started to protest, then trailed off as I reached for her arm. A sensation passed between us in that moment that cannot be described, something as fleeting as it was powerful, like a barrier had been crossed. She uttered a tiny, surprised gasp as she pulled away.

"Come outside with me, please," I said, now closer to pleading because she didn't seem to understand what was happening... what had happened *to* her. That realization was more painful than a knife through the heart. "I need to talk to you."

Her gaze was full of flame and lavender lights, swirling together in smoky confusion. She saw me, but didn't, and honestly, I couldn't see her that well, either. Her features were soft, muddled somehow, her auburn hair too wild and the white Pyrelight robes she wore seeming to blend in with her pale complexion. I wanted to do something about that, to pick her up and whisk her out of this place, to take her where it was safe and she could be who she was instead of... someone I didn't quite know.

But I also knew she would have none of that – it had to be her decision, on her time. "Anything you want to say, you can say here, I think," she said softly.

I squared my jaw and shook my head, firm. "No. Not here. Please."

"I... I'm not sure." She looked away to stare into her tea, and I allowed my patience and resolve to unravel, just a bit.

Returning to the full, formal attention of the most disciplined soldier, I leveled my stare at the Divine. "What's wrong with her?" I growled.

"Wrong? Nothing is wrong," she said with my mother's small nod and downcast expression, as if she were irritated with me. I hadn't seen that look for a good few years, but I wasn't exactly a stranger to it, either.

"What is wrong with her? What did you do to her?"

"I have done nothing."

"Bullshit." My hand went to the hilt of my weapon, and I felt more than heard Andella recoil at the action – Edin, too, seemed scared, even mystified.

Before I could ask the question wound back tight and ready to spring again from my thoughts, the person who spoke Zondrean far too well to ever be my mother stood, tall and proud and elegant. With unexpected sweetness, she approached and touched my hair in that certain way that mothers had. "So defiant... If you only knew how many times you have stood before me, just like this. It must be hundreds, thousands. I lose count." Her sky blue eyes met mine, searching for a time – for what, I couldn't say. "Oh, you've taken so many forms... my River always provides. I see you just the same, and every time you reach my door, you seek what simply cannot be sought. So much potential, yet so misguided."

"Just what do you think I'm 'seeking?'"

"Awakening. To know your nature and choose your fate."

I shouldn't have been so surprised – of course she knew the answer. She was Divine, whatever that meant, and here I was, a mere soul, mortal or otherwise. And knowing that, I should have been fearful, perhaps even reverent in the face of this far higher being. Instead, my tone was as cool and flat as my expression. "Change is inevitable. Transformation is a choice."

The Divine cast the eyes of my mother down to the floor again, for the first time expressing something like human emotion. Her voice took on a quiet edge as she spoke. "Oh, my child… you fight for wars and destruction and terrible things, you know. Can you imagine, a world with so many souls like yours? Where souls are unbound to the Cycle and they find power in the ways of magic, no matter their station? You don't even understand what you ask."

"I'm *not* asking."

Her touch was alive and full of energy beyond any magic I knew as she let her fingers trace down the curve of my face and jaw. "When I dreamed of this place, when I created what is here, I allowed the souls to fall where they may, like rain upon the grass. You all carried a tiny sliver of me away with you – the core of what you are – and it was beautiful. It still is. I wanted your kind to be strong, to know their potential… to perhaps even know me." A smile flashed across her face, fading just as quickly. "But when this Cycle is born anew, I will bring with me a valuable lesson. Painful, yes, but valuable nonetheless. Your world is not ready for what you think you seek. The next one… perhaps. We shall see, won't we, Andie?"

She turned away from me, blond braid shimmering to coppery brown for a fraction of a second. The change was almost imperceptible, and I wondered if, to Andella, her "sister" had momentarily become a blond Eislandisch noblewoman. Whether she had or hadn't, Andella gave no indication. She simply nodded as she rose from her seat, a dream-like, faraway glint in her whirling eyes. "Is it time?" she asked, voice soft.

"I believe it is. Come, let's all go outside, and witness our dear Andie do her best work."

"Andella, no, listen to me…" I begged as together they filed through the door of the little hut into a flood of yellow-white light. Andella didn't even acknowledge my presence.

"We should go with," said young Lord Edin, though it sounded more like a question to match the wondering look in his big round eyes. And there was only one answer.

Outside, acrid heat hung in the air and assaulted my senses – through the haze, the Dragons continued to circle, their fighting growing more frenzied, more desperate by the moment. Crimson and violet streaked across the sky, just as it did within Andella's gaze, and…

I rushed up to grab her by the shoulders, not caring about the shock as it rippled between us again. Intense though it was, it passed just as quickly. "Andella, it's them, it's her… something. They're affecting you somehow. Snap out of it, please – you *have* to listen to me."

"No, you're wrong," she breathed, and the bright, curious woman I fell in love with was there, suddenly lucid. "I see it now. I'm so sorry… you're wrong." She suddenly threw her arms around my waist, and we held each other, capturing just one moment in time for ourselves, for the mortal need for closeness and comfort.

"What am I wrong about?" I asked, hesitating, voice failing. There was a part that didn't want an answer.

"It's not a choice for everyone. Oh, I'm so sorry, Tristan."

Then in an instant, she broke away from me and began to dance. I had seen this dance before, of course – the Pyrelight's sweeping gestures freed the souls of the deceased from their mortal prisons and guided them to Paradise… a place that, I was now certain, did not exist. But still, she danced, and though I reached for her, my fingers were able to grasp nothing more than some broken links of her betrothal ring's chains… and memories.

Where she once stood, there was only Fire, great bursts of flame hotter than the fires of Purgatory. It found its kindling fast, the world igniting around us, around the hut, around the entire perimeter of the Summit. If I had been able to hear over their roar, I might have heard Andella's sobs and Edin's scared cries. I didn't, though – I could barely hear my own.

"A soul split in twain – it creates both Balance and Chaos, but Andie, you're not to blame," said the Divine from behind, a hint of sympathy in a voice that floated up and lingered over the chaotic noise. Then, very stern, she added, "As I said, you never should have met him."

Andella may not have heard her lament, but I did, and my rage lit brighter, hotter than all the Fire in the universe. My weapon was in my hand, feeling heavy, perfectly balanced... and good. Very good, in fact. "She has a choice," I snarled as I wheeled to face the entity that still wore my mother's shimmering visage. "We all have choices. You can't keep that from us forever."

"What choice does she have now? Balance is irrevocable. This place becomes that which it was never meant to be, unless something is done, and I... *we* can no longer allow this." While she spoke, she metamorphosed from that bad impression of Lady Gretchen to a shifting thing, unknowable and unfocused, yet still vaguely in the shape of a female human. It didn't stop me from shouting at her.

"So, you'd rather burn it all? You'd destroy everything, millions upon millions of souls... What will happen to them?"

The Divine considered – I could feel her weighing me and my questions very carefully even as the flames licked at her heels. "I should have taken it as a sign when the Dragons Awakened to the magic I had bestowed upon them. I should have stopped there and then, but they helped make this place... better. They became guardians of my elemental forces and for that, I was so pleased. You might even say grateful, because my beautiful creation was broken, somehow. Imperfect. Don't you see? They were never meant to be here, and neither are you. Mankind is simply not suited to its own Awakening."

"That's not your call to make."

"Do you think so? You do, don't you?" There was true sorrow in the Divine's manner, her grace, her constantly changing visage. Tears flowed openly from eyes spanning the entire spectrum of color. "In another Cycle, things will be different. In another Cycle, souls like yours will be... perfected, to preserve a proper Balance. But I must say, I am impressed with how far you have come. It has been my honor to know you and all who came before you." As she fixed me with the gaze of a being who saw through every lifetime I had ever lived, she raised a hand and snapped her thumb and middle finger together.

Then she was gone.

I screamed and cursed the void left behind by a god, my whole being shaking with a mixture of anger and fear and confusion. It wasn't always a good combination, but it was the kind that fueled action.

In the skies above, the Fire Dragon had changed its course, its attention below on Andella, and on a ground that was no longer as stable as it once seemed. It quaked in time with my own emotion, the beast below slowly shaking itself to wakefulness. The wind began to howl from a thousand directions at once, and blood rained from an empty sky. But where there was rain, there could be storms.

A peal of thunder and bright-white lightning shot out of the sky, striking the Fire Dragon square in the back. Glittering feathers drifted to the ground to form a makeshift circle around the thing as it landed, half-sprawled in a giant crimson heap of scales not a few feet from where I stood.

The time is now.

As the beast regarded me with ruby-faceted feline eyes, I sensed no speech invading my thoughts. At this thing's core was destruction, an awesome force that would send most screaming in terror – this Dragon had little need for words. It could convey its disdain for me with no more than a glare. The Fire of desolation was just another element, after all, natural, a part of the Balance it strove to maintain... the Balance I was doing everything possible to spoil.

Others had come before me, perhaps to stand at this same spot and face down this same Dragon. They were mortal men and women of antiquity – Drasch Sturmberg, the nameless noble *Sayaf* of Katalahni legend, purpose-guided souls, their fears relinquished, their belief resolute. I channeled them all to me and readied my blade, even as the fires around us closed in and my own sweet Andella continued her dance of Destruction and Creation.

"I choose the path of Transcendence, like you did once," I spoke into the roar of beast and flame. "This is our time." Then I rushed in to meet its advance.

My gem-studded spectral weapon found the space between two scales along the Fire Dragon's haunches and it bellowed heat, its long, snaking body curving around to flick me right off the edge of the Summit like the spent end of a *tsobac* stick. I dodged underneath its tail as it snapped angrily toward me, rolling to my feet just as a claw reached in from the other side.

It scraped with a harsh and horrible sound, harmless, against a shield of electric light just inches from my face. Neither of us could break through that wall, but it gave me the distance I needed to find a new target... like those amazing eyes, perhaps.

The thing loomed over me, rearing up as tall as the top of the Zondrell Palace spires, but I didn't have to fly to reach him. I had the speed of the Wind guiding me, and the Light of something powerful at my back.

I moved with grace I never had in a mortal body as I used my sword to gain purchase, climbing despite the violent swaying of the beast below me. It barely seemed like a second had passed before I reached the head, that flailing, teardrop-shaped head with razor fangs set in a mouth able to swallow a building whole.

My hand was steady as my blade aimed for the center of that huge, unthinkable black pupil... and then the lights went out.

The time is over.

As the flames crawled ever higher, they had finally reached the "sun," the steady magical light presiding over everything here, and when they did... well, the crystalline prison stood little chance against the heat of pure ruination.

Tiny needle-like shards fell like ice in the dead of winter, tearing through anything in their path. They cut the Fire Dragon's scales and hide, and fresh dark blood poured forth to turn most of its body into a surface as slick as ice. As I lost my balance and fell hard back to the ground, those shards also cut into me, slicing cuts wide and deep across my face, my hands, everywhere, too fast for any Light to protect against. And *damn*, did it hurt.

The beast, though, did the wailing for me, its roars enough to light the world with angry Fire that bellowed forth to set the River itself aflame. The blood waters became a wick, the Fire following its course in a flash. Much like Peaceday fireworks, it brightened the world for the briefest moment, and in the next, it was gone. Darkness was all that was left.

CHAPTER THIRTY-SEVEN

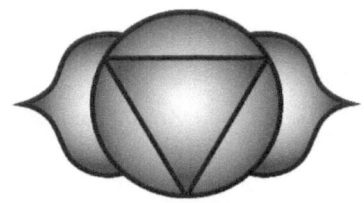

Wishing Star
15 Spring's Green, 1272
Jade Saçaille

I had almost drifted off, sitting on the cliffshore of a foreign land, propped up against the firm strength of a man I had sworn years ago that I would never speak to or even think of again. If I hadn't been so tired, I might not have allowed it. But the longer we recovered there, the more the soldiers barked at one another, and the mages asked their many, many questions, the harder it was to keep my eyes open, much less protest. Within minutes, I was almost fully asleep until someone reached for me, grabbing one hand from where it rested limp at my side.

"No," I heard Jardin breathe out one tiny word as her eyes grew wide and frightened.

"What? What is it?" I asked, my voice suddenly hitching in my throat as my consciousness flooded back.

My daughter clasped my hand in hers with such feral intensity that it took me aback – I almost pulled away. The number of times she had reached for me willingly in thirteen years was barely more than enough to count on ten fingers. But her touch was warm, her light-sparked eyes intense as she peered up at me. "Mama, you have to go there."

"What? Where, *chérie*? What are you talking about?"

"To the Place. They need you."

I looked around at the mess of people moving about, not far from where we sat. No one in the shadow of the Zondrell Palace quite knew where to go from where they stood. They had seen things never thought possible. They had witnessed miracles firsthand. Though none of them, not even Brin, understood the Place – the River – like Jardin did. "Who? What are you talking about, *chérie*?"

"Think of Tante Onyx, Mama. Please. Think of her, and close your eyes."

"Onyx? Why... how? I'm not like you, Jardin. I'm not special."

Brin shook his head and muttered something in Eislandisch, and I could feel how the words made his body reverberate against mine. The exact words were beyond my limitations, but I did recognize it as a verse from Eislandisch scripture, something to the effect of, "The River accepts all, the just and the unjust, the saints and the sinners."

He had given me his shoulder and nothing more – he knew better – though I realized with some embarrassment that he'd wrapped one arm around my waist, no longer serving as a simple prop. I twisted in that increasingly more protective embrace to face him. "You think Onyx is *there*? Oh by Chantal, you don't think she's...?" No, she couldn't be dead. Somehow, I'd know, wouldn't I? I'd know if my sister had... passed. And why would she be at the River anyhow if she had? We didn't go *there*. We went to the *Arcanes* at the side of Chantal, and besides, that all assumed I believed that Jardin's Place really was coming from the same place as Brin's recitations. Maybe I did, and maybe I didn't, but in all the years that we'd been apart, I'd always just assumed I'd know if Onyx's travels halfway around the world had left her dead somewhere. I didn't know how I'd know that – I'd just *know*. "No, no, it can't be. I won't believe it."

"Many things I believed yesterday are gone today, Jade."

If I were thinking more rationally, if my wits and my energies weren't exhausted almost completely, I would have agreed with that point. Instead, I overlooked it as Jardin fixed both of us with a curious expression. "Me and Tante Onyx... we walked the River's Edge together, when I fell asleep," she said. "We went all the way to the top, but the Dragon there wanted you, Mama."

I opened my mouth, but no words escaped. There was nothing coherent I could say, no logical thought in my mind. Instead, apparently listening in from behind, I heard Vremya's jolly voice pop up. "When they call, you answer. Is nothing to fear." When we all spun to face him, he was simply standing there, looking haggard as he surveyed the wound in the skies beyond the sea. "Trust me," he said with a wink.

"Trust you..." I shook my head, as if I could make my thoughts shuffle themselves back into a state of clarity.

"We are here. Not going anywhere."

Jardin's thin little hands tightened over mine. "Just close your eyes and think of her, Mama," she pleaded. "Please?"

Both Brin and Vremya nodded encouragement and I... well, I just didn't know what to do. What good would it do? Then again, what could it hurt? So I sank back into Brin's warmth a little and allowed it to be comforting. I allowed myself to think of times past, of the old days in Quatremagne right when Jardin was born. Onyx had come home, at last, my tall, graceful sister with her flowing black hair that I always admired for being so straight and glossy and manageable. She could pull it back and put it in braids, where I always struggled – as a much younger woman, I had looked at that lovely mane with such jealousy.

That, and the fact that she was free, free to follow her whims and go where they took her. When had I ever had such freedom? When would I not be in service to others – to men and nations, to my family, even to Chantal? And *why* hadn't Onyx at least followed that latter path? What exactly had happened to her in Quiétude? She had never confided in me, her only sister... but I wished that she would.

When I opened my eyes again, I finally understood, as the wilting grassland and decaying Riverbank I saw was cloaked in heavy darkness, with Onyx – the same Onyx who'd taught me how to play *montez vite* with all the bigger girls some forty years ago – praying at its center. The fog around us breathed with her, in and out, a conscious rhythm, expanding and contracting with the very universe... or so it seemed.

Its magic threatened to remake everything in its path, as if under its black shroud could lie any possibility. "Onyx?" I whispered, not truly sure whether I could be heard. There was no sensation, no sense of being "present" in this odd place. Perhaps she couldn't even see me.

No – there was a tiny flick of long black eyelashes, a brief pause through a look that conveyed infinity. Then she returned to her odd sort of meditation, and I imagined it was like sitting on the rocks at the Quiétude temple all over again. The difference was that she never reacted, never flinched as I had when the words of Chantal Herself reached us.

Nothing is in Balance anymore.

It was the same voice I had heard over the Goddess' mortal bones, so many years ago – it was unmistakable. I would never forget that tone, so gentle yet so commanding, deep and vaguely feminine. I dropped to my knees in the scrubby grass and bowed my head.

My dear child… why attempt to right what can no longer be righted?

By everything that was holy, She spoke to me! I could think of nothing else to do but continue to bow, now prostrating myself before the Unknowable Lady, and I somehow knew that the dry earth beneath me smelled of dust and longing. "Oh great Goddess, Chantal, Mother of Magic… I do not understand," I said in Lavançaise.

That is not my name. Ascribe no divinity to me. I would not make the choices it makes.

"But… what?" Now I risked looking up, into a blue-yellow sky with no end and no beginning, lit by a strange light that was neither sun nor flame. Yet, there was fire up there, a great deal of it, and smoke obscured the detail of large serpentine shapes circling like huge birds of prey. I watched them for a time, unsure what to do or what to say. Were these Jardin's so-called Dragons?

"Now!" I heard a man's voice shout – a familiar voice full of prim Zondrean nobility and youthful, emphatic insistence – from somewhere beyond the blackness surrounding Onyx and me. It shook me from my trance enough to notice my sister now rising to her feet, that sly smile she had when she'd just figured out something very interesting playing on her lips.

She narrowed black eyes that reminded me of swirling oily mist. "*Préparez.*"

But I could not have prepared. How could I, when there was a great beast tumbling from the sky, moving somehow in slow motion until it righted itself and came to rest about twenty feet away? The fog that had once been so thick as to be almost opaque cleared away in a perfect circle of billowing smoke, leaving behind a grand serpent-like creature, much bigger than the golden one over the skies of Zondrell or the silvery one I perhaps only imagined outside the window of Loringham's study.

It bore a striking indigo hue, its hide pebbled with purple scales that glimmered faintly in the light, and I was reminded of the ribbons of Life magic that had so many times erupted from my own fingertips. Its most distinctive feature, though, was the massive ridge of horns atop its head like the most royal of crowns. In a way, it reminded me of the hooded cobra-snakes found in the mountainous lands around Quiétude and south into Drakannya.

I hold what little is left in check and you... you rip me from the skies. Child of Shadow, is this how you atone? Do you know what it is that you do?

I heard the words, but I also didn't – they filtered in through my thoughts, cutting a path through everything fluttering about in my mind in that moment. Had Onyx heard them? Perhaps she had, but she had little to offer other than that smile, somehow both apologetic and superior at once. Now *that* was the sister I knew, fearless even in the face of the gods themselves.

The great thing seemed unamused. It turned its attention on me, huge eyes like those of a cat and studded with starry jewels the color of its scales staring at me, as if I had an answer. "I... I know not," I stammered.

Do you truly think to heal a world that has already been marked for death?

"Absolutely," the Zondrean man said from nearby. Yet, the Dragon barely flinched, even as the man's tone gathered more courage. "You up to the challenge?"

I broke away from the endless gaze of the Dragon to see him there, clad in worn finery, eyes wild, the whites gone to leave behind only a strange churning quicksilver. He appeared for all the world to be the same man who'd hosted Jardin and I for several days, but the Alexander Vestarton I knew was a cheerful, handsome example of a young Zondrean noble, one who enjoyed good food, good drink, the best of everything.

The man standing in Jardin's alien Place of dreams had all that, yes, but his good nature had been replaced with a seething sort of precision, a soft but steady intensity fueling an iron will.

"So? Do we have your attention yet?" The Zondrell Lord furrowed his brow and waited for an answer.

Thoughts rippled through my mind, and I assumed Vestarton's as well. *Life and Death are intertwined. One must follow the other – such is the Cycle and such is Balance.*

"But…" I started, realizing as I spoke that I was questioning something that may very well have been a god, "did you not say that Balance was broken, somehow? That it cannot be righted?"

"Keep talking," Alexander said to me, encouraging.

The Divine has chosen. Destruction is the victor, and soon there will be nothing left to maintain. You bring me to you as if to preserve me from the Fires to come, but there is no preservation.

Alexander peered up for a moment, but he seemed undaunted by the huge crimson thing surrounded by smoke and fire flying there. Terror was all I felt when I looked into that same sky. "So you were going to lose your endless war up there anyway?" he asked. "Why bother fighting?"

The indigo Dragon continued to gaze into and through me as it "spoke," seemingly less interested in either Alexander or Onyx other than to chide them. *Victory is not meant to be mine. I struggle in vain, and you do me no favors.*

"Why? What does that mean?" I dared to ask.

I would have seen Life continue – for you little ones. You are so close… but all of this and all of us will surrender soon. Our time is over, and of the Next, I would not presume to know. It is not for me to decide.

I had known for a long time, since those first days by the side of Keis Sturmberg, that my Life magic could only heal those who sought it, those who wished to go on living. Those committed to die would do so no matter how much I tried to convince them otherwise – that had perhaps been the most difficult lesson of all to learn.

"No, it's not. It's up to each of us." I looked around for a moment at this Place – the River – and noticed the way those hallowed blood waters seemed to rust as they flowed down the hillside. "That's the gift of our magic, isn't it?"

Magic is a manifestation of the soul. It is Divine, and thus must bend to the will of the Divine.

"So this 'Divine' decides between life or death?" I swallowed, and realized again how strange it all felt. I wasn't present, only a part of me was, and yet I felt all the sensations – my heart beating fast, my throat going dry and hoarse, my skin tingling in the face of this creature with whom I felt kinship, the familiarity and connection of the touch of Life magic. If this were only some sort of dream, it was the most *real* dream I'd ever had. "No. No, I refuse to believe that. I have watched men try to murder one another, and I will tell you, those that succeeded did so because their victims surrendered to them, to their pain and their frailty. Never once did I see one man overcome another of strong spirit. You know this as well as I, do you not?"

For a time, I heard nothing, only the vast roaring emptiness of the River, until more thoughts wafted into my mind. *I... do. But you ask much. You ask for a challenge.*

As I spoke, I glanced to Alexander – he was smiling. "We ask for a chance," I said.

"We ask for a possibility," he added, and there was that word, Vremya's word... *possibility*. They, above anyone, knew that word best. They knew what it truly meant, for it wasn't about hope and dreams and visions. That word was about Time.

I protect my own. If your will is not to be broken, then perhaps... perhaps your point has merit.

It spoke even as the flames from that great red Dragon above rushed down the steep hill looming over us, their roar horrific. I heard but did not feel the heat, just as I heard but did not feel Onyx and Alexander's trepidation. All I knew was a tremendous hum, a lifting sensation like I had been scooped up into a flow of energy so vast it had no name.

The Life Dragon and I inhaled deeply together, then exhaled a breeze glittering with indigo-lavender sparks. Each little twisting light seemed to move with its own purpose, its own intention, as it flowed with its brethren over the land.

"I knew you would come through," I heard Onyx say, close at my ear.

The tone was so hopeful, but her face spoke of fear. Was the great Onyx Saçaille, big sister and swordswoman extraordinaire, *afraid*? "I... I hope it was enough," I told her, "but what now?"

Onyx's words came quick, almost too fast for me to decipher. "Do you remember how, when we were young, we used to sit on the big hill at Riverside Park and wish on the stars? Wish upon a star for me, Jade. Can you do that?"

Of course I could, though I wouldn't understand why, or what to wish for, and I wanted to tell her that. I'd never get that chance. Her face, pale and determined, its pretty, angled features deeply haggard as if she hadn't slept for many days, was the last thing I saw as the whole rest of the bizarre scene around us became swallowed up in darkness.

The next thing I knew was a deepening evening sky nearly the exact color of the great Dragon's scales. It loomed over me, along with one bright star that seemed to have cut a wide, arcing path through the sky's great, purple middle. That wound, though, had been cleaned and was starting to heal, for it seemed smaller now, the star within winking just like any other under the occasional haze of an overcast Zondrell evening on the shore.

Wish upon a star... well, there was no sense in wasting this opportunity. I would wish for what I always wished for, back when I was seven years old and had no cares in the world. I would wish for a chance to make another wish, with my sister at my side.

"Mama?" I heard Jardin venture from what seemed like very far away at first. "Mama, look!"

Look at what? I was looking at the most brilliant thing around, but... well, that wasn't all, was it? No, not even close, for hanging in the air, fluttering on the breeze all around, were bits of lavender energy like tiny jewels cast from the hands of Chantal Herself.

I had never seen magic like it, but it was not to be feared, this light from the heavens. I might have reached out to touch it, to feel it for myself, but I found I barely had the strength to move, much less speak. So I stared as others did, in quiet fascination, until I felt prodding at my side.

"Mama?"

"Jade? Talk to us."

Hands waved in front of me — a palm checked the thin sheen of sweat on my brow. Oh, I was fine, but I couldn't squeak out the words to reassure them. Instead, I continued to melt into Brin's protection, his touch so surprisingly gentle that I wondered, fleetingly, if he was real, if this wasn't all a dream of some kind. But he was staring down at me with the same intensity he always had, even as white clouds drifted across the blue of his irises. He was joined by Jardin and a whole crowd of mages too, dozens of elemental colors whirling around in wonder and worry.

"I saw it... the Dragon, Jardin," I muttered. "Your Tante Onyx brought it down, made it listen. There will be... some possibility."

Vremya's mercurial gaze, so like that of Vestarton, brightened. "Just one, maybe, is all we need, *da?* You did good, Jade."

"I knew you would," said Jardin. And then she smiled, and it was most beautiful sight I had ever seen — a sight well worth wishing on.

CHAPTER THIRTY-EIGHT

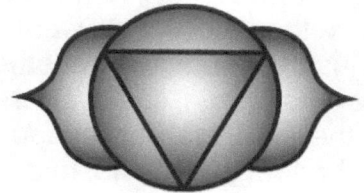

For Every Night, a Day
15 Spring's Green, 1272
Alexander Vestarton

"I have to admit, I'm impressed."

As I rose from the edge of the pool of blood, I wiped my lips with the back of my hand, imagining for a split-second that the bright red streak left behind had formed a mouth and started to talk. This, of course, was ridiculous. I even laughed a little while the pure, clean taste of whatever magic I'd just ingested tingled its way through my system.

I couldn't believe how amazing it was, a fantastic sensation better than any alcohol, more instant than any herb, root, or potion – hell, it might have even been better than... well, maybe it wasn't *that* good. All I knew was that whatever was in that pool wasn't blood, and it wasn't the same as the black water at the mouth of the River, either. This was the good stuff.

In fact, it was so good, it occurred to me that I might have done something terrible. I'd tried some things in my time, had lost a few nights here and there – never enough to take me past the point of no return, but maybe closer than I'd like to admit. This, though... this was a whole new echelon of intoxication, for the strange world around me had gotten *much* stranger.

Slowly, carefully, as if doing so would hurt, I allowed myself to turn and look at the myriad shapes that had sprung into being. They were bright, colorful, and ethereal, like the lights bobbing along with the waves of the sea below, but these weren't just little circles – there were people, animals, everything imaginable getting up, shaking off the burden of some unknown dream and starting to wander.

Some went down the hill, some went up, some stayed perfectly still and just stared into the ether... and what an ether it was. The air itself had come alive, too, dust forming marble patterns in the air. When I reached out, it formed and flowed around my hand, and in the midst of those swirling shapes was Time – past and present moved like sand between my fingers. With every breath, I saw moments, pockets of history from all over the living world, from Katalahnad to Eisland, from Birrízi to Zondrell, and even beyond, places I never knew existed.

"Look at you – all that magic."

That *voice*... I hadn't heard it in so long, half a year now, and the very thought of it brought fresh tears to my eyes, along with a wave of shame that hit me like twenty charging horses. "I'm hallucinating," I told myself. "It'll pass – always does."

"I should think you'd know better." There was a hint of amusement in my father's voice, and when I turned, that friendly, warm, genuine smile was there. Lord Xavier Geraint Cedric Vestarton stood before me, hale and hearty, and far from the withered husk that he'd been on his deathbed.

He looked like I remembered him best, dark and handsome, wisps of white smoke at his temples, smiling that charmed smile that I had always wanted to emulate. As he regarded me, he adjusted the silver falcon medal on one of his black lapels, one of several old military decorations that should have been in a box on his old desk.

"But you're not here." Wait, what was I saying? Of course he was *here* – this was the place where dead people went, wasn't it? Still, something wasn't right. I glanced back at Saçaille, who was watching from a safe distance. "Are you... seeing any of this?" I called out to her, somewhat hesitant.

The raven-haired Lavançaise cocked her head to the side, eyebrow raised. "Seeing, Monsieur? I see our moment approaching quickly." Her voice was thick with impatience. "You will speak with the Dragon, *oui*? I believe I know what I must do – you must do your part."

"And you know what that is, eh?"

"I will wish upon the star, Monsieur, and when I do, Light will join with Shadow." She paused then, swallowing hard. Why were her eyes red? Was that a tearstain cutting a crevice through the dust of another world along one angular cheek? Didn't matter, because in the next breath, it was all brushed aside. "It is what must be. Are you ready?"

Ready was a rather intense word. I didn't quite know what that meant anymore. I had an idea of what I wanted to do, but accomplishing it... that was the hard part. There was no future I could recognize laid out amongst the memories hovering in the air, although I did know that our present was about to slam straight into it.

"*Fais vite*, Madame," I said, dredging up my working knowledge of Lavançaise. Within moments, her eyes were closed, that curious fog of Shadow magic beginning to take shape around her. It flowed in like the waters of the River itself, as if she might soon be pulled under by the current – the vision was somehow both beautiful and horrifying.

"Well, looks like I won't be here for long," I heard my father's voice at my side. Xavier's translucent spirit winked at me with a twinkle buried deep in chestnut-colored eyes.

What to say to that? What did it mean? I hadn't the slightest, but words started to escape from my mouth anyway. "Dad, I... I'm not sure what's going to happen, and I'm sure you're disappointed in me, and..."

"Why would I be disappointed? I've never been disappointed in you, boy, not once. You know that."

That cold little ball of guilt at the center of my stomach clamped down hard enough to make me want to curl up and cry my eyes out. I resisted, but one bitter tear made its way down my cheek anyhow.

"Well, you might have been," I said, because I could just imagine walking in at seventeen years old and explaining that I was selected to go not to the famed Military Academy, but across the way to the Magic Academy, full of women and weaklings.

My father let those words settle for a moment, considering me with great interest. His gaze searched mine in a way that it never had when he was alive, and when he'd seen everything he wanted to see, he simply smiled. "Do you honestly think I didn't know about the magic? I was sick, but I was never blind, Alexander."

"What? You knew? Really? Do you know what I..." It didn't matter, did it? Not anymore. All the pains I took to hide my burgeoning magic from everyone in Zondrell high society, and it didn't mean a damn thing. I almost laughed in spite of myself.

That smile persisted. "Magic got you here, and what you're doing now is important. It's bigger than the Council, bigger than Zondrell, bigger than the whole damn world. Don't you think?"

"Yeah, but *what* am I actually doing? Now that's the question."

"What have I always told you? Trust yourself." He reached for me, and his touch wasn't quite solid. I wished there had been more comfort there, but it felt almost spongy, less than substantial, as if I could push back and through him if I'd wanted. "You're a good man, Alex – you've got a good heart. That earns respect, and once you've got that, you've got everything you need."

My voice was incredibly tight, throat constricting against far too many emotions. "I'm putting everything right, Dad. Everything. And I... I miss you. I really miss you." Whether the apparition I spoke to was truly my father or just some delusion, I'd never know for sure. But in the end, it just felt good saying that, like one more weight had been lifted from my shoulders.

"You can't miss what's always around," my father said, the light catching his eye just right to where it reminded me of a twinkling star. "Just pay attention and get to your business. Time's wasting."

As the Shadows boiled up behind me, preparing to twist the magic of a Dragon into its own design, I resolved to do just that.

**

Once Life had started to flow out over the land, the spirits, the colors, the lights all began to melt away. Dead or otherwise, anything without physical form found its way back to wherever it was supposed to be, and I watched it all without emotion.

Jade Saçaille's indomitable living spirit, my father's soul, all of it scattered as dust into the winds, leaving Saçaille and I behind. We didn't fit in, after all. We weren't supposed to be in this place of ghosts, for we were still, for the moment, very much alive.

And it didn't take long before something wanted to stamp that life out, but I was ready. For the first time in my life, I was paying attention, *close* attention, seeing it all for what it was... just another cycle. Up needs a down, yes needs a no, life needs a death – all of these things play in a realm that Time does not.

Time works on another level. Time makes its own decisions. Time says "fuck you" to the cycles and dualities of this world, of *all* worlds. No wonder I appreciated my own magic as much as I'd come to do so, for when the flames of destruction coursed down the hill, determined to draw another cycle to a close, Time objected.

The wall of fire froze to a solid, artistic warp of orange and red at the snap of my fingers. Even the crash and inhuman roar I heard from above was cut off, captured, though not before all light just... went out. The time-trapped flame was the only thing left to repel the darkness.

I might have suspected Saçaille's magic, the Shadows she and her black dragon commanded becoming a shroud over me and everything else. But there was nothing but darkness where Onyx Saçaille once stood – the moment I occupied was mine alone.

Well, mine and perhaps a dragon or two. Or three. Or five. Even if I couldn't see them all, I knew they were there: Earth slowly flexing its might, Water reversing the current of the River, Wind ready to guide or ruin, Shadow watching and waiting, Life still breathing out into the world, and Time... that great silvery beast settling its weight to the ground with exacting precision.

"The scales of Balance are tipped, it would seem," a smooth voice filled my head. Actually, it was more than one, a joining of many voices that somehow made sense despite the cacophony ringing through my mind.

"This," I said, gesturing to the frozen wall of flame, "isn't happening."

Their gazes each seemed fit to tear a hole right through me. "You would reverse destruction's course – the Divine's will. You are prepared to do your part, then."

"I'm prepared to do whatever it takes."

"Nothing will look exactly as it once did. Our power will only go so far."

"But it'll do enough?" No hint of objection stabbed through my thoughts. "Then I don't care."

"Perhaps that is why you are here, and he is up there," I heard just one voice, the Time Dragon's persistent, rhythmic tones, echo through my thoughts.

"What do you mean by that?" I asked.

"His power is strength, but yours is action. Together you alter Balance forever."

More riddles... but the time to think about riddles was over. Questions had no place here because they were right – this was the time to act. There were no more second guesses. "Let's do it, then."

At this, the silver Dragon tilted its head, regarding me and the flames and the Riverscape that hovered on the brink of its own demise. Then it, and every other Dragon there, in their own ways, seemed to bow – not in deference, but out of respect, acknowledgement, like the way I was taught to bow to other nobles when they walked into a room.

So I returned the gesture, and at least just for that time, we were equal... and united. Power moved between us without effort. The wall of flame reversed its course, second by second, its short lifetime eaten away as it was sent back to its point of creation.

Time, though, only guided its course. Along the way, Wind carried the breath of Life faster than it had ever traveled, blanketing the land with an odd purple glow until the Earth sprouted new greenery from its deepest roots, fed by Water and protected from harsh conditions by Night's cool embrace. The pattern traveled far down the hill to the sea, out of sight to my mortal eyes, though I could see how a trail of lavender-white had started to streak up toward the dark and endless sky.

But every night needs a day... at least, this was the last coherent thought I had before the well of magic within me started to overflow. I heard Saçaille say something close at my ear, felt her strong hands grab me by the arms, but it was all lost to Time and the loud rush of the River's current.

CHAPTER THIRTY-NINE

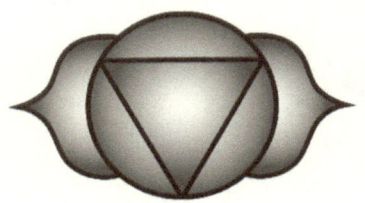

Cleansing Flame
15 Spring's Green, 1272
Andella Weaver

She was right – She was right all along, and of course She was. She was Divine.

I saw Her for what She was the moment we left that house, me in my Pyrelight's robes and Tristan... left behind. And wasn't it my sister – my *real* sister – who had warned me about him, about the intriguing nobleman who'd been dropped at our church's doorstep? Men like that have power and influence, and know how to use it. They can be dangerous... they can break your heart.

The Divine's heart was broken. I could see it – women can always see these things. She knew, like I did, that Lord Tristan Loringham was exactly like and yet completely unlike other men of his station. I knew it months ago, back home in our church, but now my dear sweet Seraphine would never hear all the details, never get to scrunch up her brow and judge me just a little bit from that sisterly place as we talked long into the night. It was too late for all that now.

He questions. He demands. It is like the Dragons as we reclaimed our place as part of the Whole. But if this Cycle must end because of it, then so be it.

The voice thundered through my thoughts, pounding everything else down until there wasn't much left. For some reason, I likened it to a crackling campfire, fed so much that it would just keep burning, right up until it decided it was done. It was a voice that wouldn't be denied.

So, I looked to that voice's owner, so commanding and huge in all of its Fire-red majesty. I had never seen a Dragon before, but I knew instantly that this was what it was, a beast straight out of storybooks and paintings, pensive anger radiating from glowing red eyes.

I sense you, child, it spoke into my consciousness, *but you have made a choice already.*

"I did?" I didn't really say this, but thought it, and immediately felt a sharp retort from the Dragon of flame and destruction.

Death follows Life, and Life follows Death; you know this. You have chosen it as your Path. Now you must be what you are.

Death and Life... yes, they raged and warred within me. Two elements, after all, was unnatural, preposterous, and all because of one chance meeting, one soul there to spark another. I never did master them, either, never got to study and understand them the way I really wished. I could have done so much good for so many people, but magic was only as useful and powerful as the ability to control it. The problem wasn't making the choice to embrace two elements at once – the problem was the elements themselves.

It was too much. Even the Divine was scared of it, it seemed. We should never have met, Tristan and I... except we did, and here we were. Here, I could see how fascinating and beautiful those two elements really were, magic far closer to Divine than the priests of the Lavançaise temples of Chantal could ever imagine.

Be what you are, child.

In that small moment when I could see and hear everything so very clearly, my eyes were drawn up to the light, that strange yellowing light caught in crystal hanging in the sky. It revealed things, the things that are hidden and impossible to understand. Yet, those things are unavoidable, sometimes.

I wished I had a chance to say everything I wanted to, or even write it all down, but the time for mortal feelings and worries was over. They no longer belonged to me, and I supposed, they didn't belong to Tristan anymore, either. Even though our paths had diverged, they had led us both to this place, to this moment... and all I could say was that I was sorry as I started doing the one thing I had always sensed was my life's calling – my *true* life's calling.

Destroy this Cycle and create it anew. The Divine has spoken.

The great beast of Fire sent its stern "voice" to me as I danced the Pyrelight's dance, though I wasn't sure if it could sense my own thoughts anymore. I had so many questions, but there were answers, too, bubbling up to the surface.

Now this... this was research! This was *real* magic, pure and unbridled, far beyond the dreams of people like Archmage Tiara. It was, in a way, thrilling, exhilarating, and it fueled me as I moved through the practiced steps that I once believed guided souls to Catherine's side.

There is only one way.

But that wasn't quite true, was it? I could even prove it, because the work of a Pyrelight was just a ritual. Its real power was in how people healed inside when they prayed over their loved one's sacred pyre, for Life does indeed follow Death, in more ways than one.

So I danced, and what was once just plain-old Fire magic now held flecks of lavender amidst the orange and yellow and red, little tendrils of Life amidst all that destruction. And the more I danced, the more I could make those colors leap and twirl, despite the frenzied protests of a gigantic, crimson-scaled beast. As the Life-tinged flames spread, the Dragon roared with such ferocity that the ground quivered in its wake, its thoughts piercing through mine.

Resistance is not the way. This is folly.

Then I felt a... *push*, from somewhere deep within, and even more magic sprung to the surface of my being. Back in the world of the living, the sheer intensity probably would have killed me, to be honest – here, I was an infinite vessel, ready to be filled by a Divine hand. My flames grew higher, hotter, the purplish tinge melting to pure white heat, threatening to burn my soul just as easily as it could burn everything in its path.

Do as you are bidden and DESTROY.

I caught a glimpse of Tristan's gaze, one tiny instant before the heat of Destruction shattered the crystalline sun above our heads. I dropped to my knees, suddenly helpless, spent, as everything went dark and the whole place – this strange Riverscape – became a deafening, chaotic blast of sound. I might have called out, but whether the Dragon or Tristan or anyone else could hear me, I had no idea.

Another moment later, flames turned the sky to hellish orange as they began to raze the River itself. In the blink of an eye, it had become the pyre for me to preside over, ready to utter the next lines in the Lady's funeral prayer: *Even as this soul takes its place in Paradise, forget not those new souls guided on by the light of Her gentle grace, for they too, seek Her blessings.*

My inner recitation felt intertwined, though, strangely joined with another voice that was light and regal, somehow both kind and demanding. *A fine verse, little one. If you wish to be that grace, then seek the Light.*

Grace? What grace? I certainly had none. I was confused, scared, unsure of myself. I created that flame – I had set this sacred place to burn. But that wasn't my will. My nature wasn't to destroy. Sure, I'd used magic in self-defense, but only a few times, and it never felt right. On the other hand, the healing magic never quite fit me, either, did it? No, it burned worse than Fire when I called it forth, like little pieces of me were going with it as those ribbons of indigo light sought out others to help.

Light... little pieces of me...

I knew what I had to do. Fumbling in the near-pitch blackness, I called forth a tiny flame no bigger than a candle to hold in the palm of my hand. Certainly not much, but it would be enough to guide me forward, across the thousands and millions of crystal shards separating me from Tristan.

They should have shredded the soles of my feet as I moved, but they merely glittered there in the faint light, causing no pain and drawing no blood. I took one step, then another, accompanied by the crunching sound of loose gravel. And even though I willed myself to run as fast as I could, everything seemed to move in slow motion. I struggled like an insect caught in a jar of honey, until finally, blessedly, I could reach out.

"Tristan!" I called, though my own voice sounded like it came from very far away. It barely even sounded like it belonged to me.

He was dazed and reeling, just like the Dragon. Drops of blood peppered the ground around them, and both man and beast sported fresh cuts from those same crystalline shards that had left me unharmed. Why? How? Well, I could do something about that, I thought, if I could just concentrate and bring that elusive Life magic to the surface. Such a thing was harder than I thought, as the magic that wanted to emerge was hot and full of savagery.

Allow me to help, the regal voice filled my head. It wasn't the angry, bitter howl of the Fire Dragon – this voice could be just as stern, just as dangerous, but its power was subtle. Its power came not through roaring flame, but rather, it floated in on a breeze tinged with bright indigo-lavender sparks. So beautiful... I reached out for one, tried to hold it in my hand, and let it become part of me just long enough before giving it to Tristan.

"Please let this be enough," I breathed, and so it was. The wounds began to dissolve almost as fast as they had appeared, leaving behind pristine flesh, unscarred save for one thin white line running straight down his cheek from brow to jaw.

Tristan looked at me with a sort of opalescence gleaming in his eyes as he slowly pulled himself back to his feet. "I love you," he said, reaching for my hand. "I hope you know that. I hope you'll always know that."

He didn't say those words often – they never came that easily. And in a way, it felt that much more special to hear them then. "Tristan, I..."

But my words were cut short. The wind had picked up. The shards of crystal at our feet began to *move* on their own, floating upward toward the sky. And there were voices, many of them, ringing through my head with words that made little sense as they flooded in all at once.

The only way...

Cycle...

Preserved...

Never the same...

Power to the weak...

Awakened to strength…
Light the Shadow.

"Do you hear that?" I asked Tristan as he watched the crystals float toward the heavens just as I did.

He nodded. "'Light the Shadow'… it's time." His touch was electric – our energies seemed to meld together, magic coursing between us. "Thank you, Andella."

"For what?"

"For believing in me." One kiss, one embrace, and then all I knew was Light. A pillar of silvery-white brilliance blinded everything in its path as it surged upward, fast ahead of the millions of broken crystal shards. A darkness traveled with it, too, a black cloud of fog and infinite potential that seemed to unite with that Light, swirling around it until they became one and the same. But while Time led their passage, they needed guidance, maybe even a touch of grace, to find their way home.

I wanted to be the very essence of that grace.

The wind gathered momentum, but I stood with it, the magic within becoming mine to do with as I saw fit. With great care, with love, I willed it to heal what was broken, hard as stone yet brittle as an eggshell – easy, perhaps, to someday break again.

For now, it would hold fast, and it enveloped the Light and Darkness together to become something new, a new and perfectly balanced sun, reborn over the same River, though all of it would be changed forever.

The pillar of Light before me gradually softened, dimmed, and then faded completely… into nothing. Where was he? Maybe it was just too much Light – I was blinded. I could reach for him, and… there was nothing there to hold. Nothing, save for one simple white feather amidst a cloud of shimmering dust. The feather fell into my hand as I sank to the ground in a heap.

"It is a shame." The voice of the Divine was low, just a quiet whisper over the rush of the River and the beating of Dragon wings in the clear blue sky overhead. Gone was the sickly pallor, the rips and tears in the lining of this place – its wounds had healed, erased by magic as if they were no more than paper cuts. "So much potential, and he chooses to remain attached to this Cycle. The remaining time shall be long indeed."

"He's gone," was all I could manage to say, all I could manage to think. Tristan was gone, really gone, and there was so much more I might have said.

"Life and Time have played their part, the elements, Shadow… you, as well, all against my wishes."

I turned to stare at the collection of colorful lights that made up the vague shape of a woman, standing behind me. Eventually, the colors merged and solidified into something more recognizable, though strange nonetheless – Archmage Tiara, complete with a dark mane of unkempt hair, bright green robes, and eyes to match.

Oh, but there was so much more behind that Earth magic, wasn't there? The real Archmage wouldn't be able to study it all in two lifetimes, but I didn't need the Divine to appear to me as anything or anyone. At the same time, looking into the face of someone I knew – someone I respected – did seem to make my words come that much more easily. "I gave all the power I could," I told Her, "and… he's just gone."

The knowing visage of a great scholar looked to me, then to the great red Dragon, its wounds gone, its flight carrying it further and further away from where we stood. "So much attachment to this… errant Cycle. Though I admit, you gave of yourself most beautifully – your power is a thing to behold."

"So, everything's just… back to normal? Like nothing happened?"

"No, not in the least. We enter a time of uncertainty. Even I cannot foresee what all this foolishness may have wrought. This is where I would seek to learn from you, Andie. Together, we may understand so much more."

"I think I've helped *you* quite enough."

The Divine let out something like a sigh, and the very air pulsed around Her as She did. "Oh Andie, we have so much to teach one another. Don't you wish to know the mysteries of this world?"

I felt my whole being stiffen, my eyes narrowing, my lips drawn to a thin, hard line. Yes, of course I wanted to learn – there was a part of me that wanted that more than anything. But… "You need to answer one question for me first," I said.

In one instant, She had been Tiara, excited at the prospect of new research. In the next, She was my sister again, cheerful round face full of compassion and care as She touched my arm. "You cannot go back, Andie. You have only two paths – the Cycle may take you, or you may stay here with me. But you will never return as you were. The time for that has passed."

"That wasn't what I was going to ask." Because I knew that, deep down – I was dead. The sea and the great calamity at the research site had claimed me what might have been hours or days or years ago, and I could accept that. The Path lies forward, not behind, as the Book of Catherine says. "No," I said, "what I wanted to know was..." My throat caught at the idea of saying his name aloud, because there was no peace to be found there – all I felt was pain and emptiness. I could only glance up into the sky as the rest of my sentence faded away.

A twinge of something like disdain pulled at the corners of my sister's plump lips, which in a blink became thin and older, wiser, harsher. She was Archmage Tiara one more time, now squinting into the white light safely held in its crystalline cradle. "I always knew that one soul would lead you down a certain path – the path to my door, so to speak. But I never anticipated..." A long pause, a stirring of sorrow and anger in prismatic eyes that gradually softened to something just short of kindness.

Her form shifted back so quickly to that of Seraphine again that I barely noticed until the transformation was complete. In that moment, hair down and free, jaw steeled, She might have even looked like those old sketches of an angry Catherine or Chantal, goddesses casting judgment upon their wayward faithful from within the pages of books where history often met myth.

"Those who cast away my gifts are no longer welcome here," She said, "but perhaps sometime when you close your eyes, you may dream."

I couldn't wait. I did exactly that, shutting my eyes tight and imagining, hoping, believing that a dream would bring me the answers I sought. And in the end, though it broke my heart, I did know peace.

CHAPTER FORTY

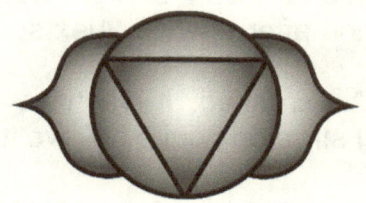

Awake
16 Spring's Green, 1272
Tristan Loringham

L aughter broke the heavy silence of the white, endless void.

It started as a bemused chuckle, but as I emerged into a world of sensation – of wind and cool moisture and the salty scent of the sea – it blossomed into something roaring, triumphant. Once the shapes and colors in front of my eyes took on form again, I realized that this borderline maniacal wave of laughter belonged to my best friend.

"I'm a fucking genius!" Alex shouted at the top of his lungs, fists raised in triumph. Then he began laughing all over again... and it was the most glorious sound I'd ever heard.

There were other sounds, too – the rise and fall of the ocean, seagulls off in the distance, all wondrous things that I knew and yet did not know. They felt new, like nothing ever witnessed, even though once, they were things I'd heard nearly every day of my life. *Of my life...*

"My Brother." Alex was kneeling at my side then, a very tattered and worn Alex who looked like he'd just walked through a maelstrom. "My Brother... I can't fucking believe that worked. I'm a genius, did you know that? Genius!"

I could not make sounds, at least nothing that made sense, though I tried. I also couldn't make my muscles all work together properly, making my attempts to roll over or sit up rather pointless.

After a useless minute of struggle, I laid back and looked up at a dark sky, its wispy lengths of clouds touched by one tiny sliver of golden dawn. I would never forget that sky in that moment, for I had never seen anything so breathtaking.

We both watched as the dark of night slowly gave way to an encroaching sun, and after a while, Alex spoke again. "Talk to me, Brother."

"We're... home," I croaked. It wasn't a statement of fact, more a question – I still didn't quite believe it.

"Isn't it beautiful?"

Enough strength returned for me to pick myself up, though Alex was there to keep me steady. The shoreline rocked and swayed in time with my vision and in direct opposition to the motion of the tide – the combination proved overwhelming. I turned and vomited up what little blood and bile I had to give. "That... probably wasn't the answer you expected."

A shadow of concern passed over his features, his quicksilver eyes bright and luminous, little moons churning with the power of infinity behind them. They actually lit the dim space between us as well as any candle. "It's okay if you're okay."

"Yeah. A little better now." When everything stopped spinning in its lazy, drunken way, it all came into focus – we were far down the Zondrell cliffshore, almost to the south walls, in the tidepools where some of the more enterprising fishermen of the city would set out nets for the various small sea creatures that gathered here.

In the distance to the north, the Palace loomed, its east-facing polished stone and glass beginning to take on the white-gold cast of sunrise. From this angle, its one broken tower was painfully obvious – I found I couldn't stop staring at it.

"We've been through some shit, haven't we?" Alex said with a chuckle.

Random memories swarmed through my mind – a few of the more intense ones sifted themselves out. "Understatement of the century. Hey, ah... what about...?"

"Lord Edin? I imagine right about now he's waking up in his warm little bed."

I felt sick to my stomach all over again. "I hope you're right."

Alex's smile quirked at that mischievous angle for which he was quite famous. "I know I'm right, Brother. Trust me on this one. Speaking of..." He jumped to his feet, scanned the area for a moment, then hurried to what he'd found – a woman in dark, wet clothes draped over a nearby rock. The surf came up to greet her just as Alex did the same, and frothy seawater sprayed around them.

My breath caught and my heart raced, but it was only for a moment. She wasn't who I'd hoped for – this woman was tall, well-muscled, her long black hair matted and tangled. Limp and barely conscious, she didn't look like much, but I felt a reflexive chill wash over me nonetheless.

"Hey, hey, Madame? You out there?" Alex looked her over, snapped his fingers inches from her face, tapped her lightly on the cheek. "*Bonjour! Réviellez!*"

And she did wake up, after about three more repeated commands in Lavançaise. She muttered something I couldn't hear, to which Alex stepped back and offered her his hand, but it was flatly refused. Onyx Saçaille was too proud a warrior to not find her own way to her feet. Unsteady, she approached, navigating the rocks slowly until she came to stand before me.

She bowed her head before me then, hands on heart in the traditional Lavançaise gesture of greeting and recognition. "I believe that my debt to you is... balanced," she said softly, the hoarseness of her voice muddling its sing-song Lavançaise quality.

I considered her, staring into eyes that once were the blackest black imaginable, but now appeared quite... ordinary. Though her stare could still pierce stone, her eyes had gone hazel-green, unremarkable and without a hint of the magic once buried deep within her soul. "Two sides of the same coin," I breathed at length.

"*Oui*, Monsieur. Light always casts a Shadow where it falls. I am... proud to have served with you. I honor your sacrifice." Once more, she bowed, and when our gazes met again, I understood what she meant by that. *My sacrifice...* I didn't need to look in a mirror to know that something within me was missing, left behind in the same place where she had left hers. *Left behind and gone forever.*

Eventually, I heaved my way to stand, and though I still felt decidedly unwell, I made my bow as gracious as I possibly could. "As I honor your sacrifice, Madame," I said to her. "Now, I believe we've been relieved of our duty."

A genuine smile graced her sharp features and turned them much more feminine and matronly than I would have believed possible. "It is strange, *oui*? We never feel the true weight of our burdens until we finally set them down."

Wiser words were rarely spoken.

We left the tidepools not long afterward, on a fisherman's boat once he'd seen the torn-up, worn-out people wading around in a daze. The old man was kind, with a warm countenance that reminded me a little bit of Alex's father, and Alex took careful note of his name and residence to ensure that he received payment for his assistance. I think that money likely bought him a new boat and a new home to go with it.

Everything that happened after that, for a while, was more or less a blur. My uncle met us at the docks near the Palace, because he'd held a vigil there overnight, along with a small contingent of Zondrell soldiers and mages from the Academy.

Alex thanked those men for their service and dedication in his best impression of a grand statesman, though once his own sister and mother emerged from the gathering crowd, he was plain-old Alex again, heart on his sleeve like always. My mother was there, too, and I thought she might never let go as she wrapped her arms around my neck and shared a few tears with me.

I watched Onyx hug her sister, Jade, with that same intensity until the Life mage looked like she might burst, and my young cousin, Jardin, gave me a kiss on the cheek and a big twinkling smile. Then, she whispered something in my ear that I wouldn't soon forget: "I'm sorry you had to give up your sparkles, but the little boy said, 'Thank you.'" I told her I wasn't sorry at all.

Not a few minutes later, Larenne Blackwarren and one of her sisters arrived to declare the happy news that Prince Edin had awoken from his coma, and would be crowned in a small ceremony the following day to officially assume the throne. That little boy couldn't do it all, of course – his mother would guide him, and the royal family hoped the Council would as well. Zondrell needed everyone to work together, more than ever before, if it was to heal from this crisis.

"Crisis... serious word, *da*?" I turned to face the stout Drakannyan mage who called himself Vremya, standing there amidst the crowd with a flask of brandy proffered toward me.

I took it with no hesitation – that golden liquid was a magic all its own. "Serious business, I suppose," I said in between sips.

"You... you did good, friend, real good." His Time-silvered eyes sparkled as he clapped me on the back. "You did the things the rest of us couldn't. And look – everyone is waking up. Is interesting times, *da*?"

Waking up... I looked around. Then I saw them, *really* saw them, and it was nothing short of a miracle. Magic was everywhere. I saw it in the eyes of men who'd never known a day of magical training in their lives, including Brin, of all people. And the colors lighting their eyes spanned every possibility, from Fire red to indigo Life, although I didn't see many sparks of Light beyond Jardin's, nor did I notice the creeping fog of Shadow.

"Holy hell," I whispered.

"Might be that. Might be better than that. Hard to say. But, better than the other option, *da*?"

I took one more long pull on the flask before handing it back. "Yeah... I'd like to think so."

EPILOGUE

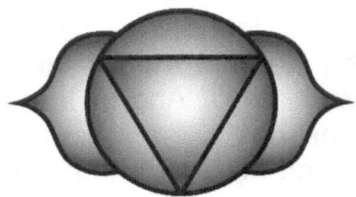

*T*hose of us awake to the power of our actions may lay no claim to the title of hero, god, or devil. Like the noble swordsman of old, we are merely men, living in and for the present, transcended through belief given form.

From The Journal of *Tristan Michael Johannes Loringham*, Dated 20 Spring's Green, 1272

On the 18th Day of Spring's Green, Era of Sevens, 1272
To: The Honorable Sister Seraphine Weaver, Church of Catherine (perimeter), Doverton
Instructions for Courier: TO BE OPENED BY THE RECIPIENT ONLY

Dearest Sister,

I have no doubt that you have heard recent news of Zondrell, and perhaps other places around M'Gistryn. Some have taken to calling these times "The Troubles" or "The Calamity" – the events here have certainly caused much pain and disruption to many. That is why it wounds me grievously to write you these words today.

I have failed you, and I have failed Andella. Your sister and the woman I had chosen to be my wife is with the grace of Catherine now, by circumstances which were sudden and related to the "Calamity" that occurred within the city walls. I assure you that her passage to Paradise was a peaceful one; however, I regret that I was not able to perform my duty to protect her, just as I was not able to protect my own father, and many others in this city.

I would speak with you on these matters further, in person, by your will. There is much that could be said that cannot be conveyed adequately in writing. To that end, you will find a sum of 1000 gold Royals included with the trunk of personal effects that accompany this letter. I have ensured that a sum of equal amount will be delivered to you on the 1st day of each month, in perpetuity. This money is yours, just as any part of my estate would have been due to Andella, to donate to your church's cause, or to do with as you see fit. My home is always open to your presence if you care to use it for travel, when it is safe to do so.

My only request is that you will forgive me in holding back a few small items of hers that I wish to keep in memorial to the time that we shared together. It was short – too short – but in those few months, know that I held nothing but deep love and admiration for her. On all other matters, I seek no mercy or forgiveness from you, but merely attempt to find my own peace.

May the Lady guide you in all things, and may Peace find you in these chaotic times.

Tristan Michael Johannes Loringham
Lord of Loringham, Fourth House of Zondrell

**

I wrote a great deal in the days and weeks that followed my return home – that is, when there wasn't business to attend to... and there was *always* business. With everything in such general disarray, even the smallest details and decisions seemed to require a huge amount of effort.

The citizenry of Zondrell was, on the whole, much more cooperative than they had been without a king sitting on the throne, but that didn't keep them from bickering. There was a tremendous push to "get on with things," even though they disagreed about what that meant. Protests and rumblings aside, magic was often a key part of the conversation, including what to do about all those inexperienced new mages running around. Anywhere one looked, they would see eyes more vibrant, more colorful than they'd ever been. And I saw them too… everywhere except in my own reflection.

The man I saw in the mirror every morning before I went out into this resurrected Zondrell was twenty-two going on thirty. Lord Loringham, it was whispered, was an austere sort of man, more a soldier than a gentleman despite the tailored clothes. And didn't he slay a Dragon? Wasn't it he who unleashed all that wild new magic? Maybe he was truly a demon? Rumors *abounded.*

But he said little as he walked the streets from day to day, sporting a close-cut blond beard in a vain attempt to disguise the scar that started at the corner of his right eyebrow and ended at the jawline. And those eyes… in the right light, anyone could see a faint trace of something *else* behind the summer-sky blue, lines like the spokes of wheels that would never turn again. Those fool enough to ask about it would receive little more than cold silence in reply.

This, of course, was the man I was in the daylight hours. Once the sun went down, I stopped worrying about how I appeared to the rest of Zondrell, closed my doors, and went to the desk that once belonged to my father. As time went on, it had become easier and easier to think of it as mine, especially since I often slept hunched over it, quill in hand.

Exhaustion, I found, was the best way to get through the night, as anything lighter than the deep sleep that only passing out cold can bring had become plagued with nightmares. Sometimes they felt so real that I was sure I'd been pulled back to the River's Edge, like some sort of punishment for my crimes against Divinity.

The writing itself was like a form of penance. I recorded my thoughts, dreams, speculations, theories – the words themselves often brought pain as my quill scribbled them off. But this self-imposed torture was also an act of surrender, of letting go of doubt and regret and guilt that no longer served their purpose.

Within a couple of weeks, I had quite the makeshift library dedicated to the subjects of the River and Dragons, souls and Divinity... and even Andella. There were days when I was convinced I would see her again, and others where I was sure I wouldn't – those were the harder days. The truth was, I didn't have a good answer for most of the questions that raced through my mind in the darkest hours of the night, and this was the most painful realization of them all.

High summer came to the city about a month after "The Calamity," which I personally referred to as "The Transcendence." Typical Zondrell summers were hot, arid, and sunny nearly every damned day, as the coastal winds took the rain and clouds past the city and into the nearby forests and plains where they could feed our crops and our livestock.

There is a reason, after all, why Zondrell is one of the biggest cities in the entire world – there was nothing quite like it. This particular summer had turned out to be a model example, and I had grown a particular fondness for exercising in the warmth of the sun. Occasionally, Brin or Alex would take a break from their own business to spar for a bit, always friendly, always light. It helped me feel normal, and they knew that, even though such things were better left unsaid.

On the 17th of Summer's Light, I woke late, well after the breakfast hour. It had been one of *those* nights, a restless one full of visions I didn't care to face. I stumbled out of my study and toward my room, in search of a wash and a suitable change of clothes, but Frederick was there to impede my progress.

"Good day, M'Lord," he said with his familiar, thin-lipped smile and curt bow. I wondered, briefly, how often he'd looked at my father with that same mix of paternal judgment and loyal devotion. "I considered waking you, but..."

"Sorry, Frederick," I stammered, "I, ah, didn't realize the time."

"Indeed. All is well – I did send Master Kai from the Sunlit Farm off with the funding for the new granary he requested. I do hope you intended to give all of it."

Well, I probably was, so... "We can afford it."

"Indeed, Sir." Another bow. "This came for you as well." From the nearby foyer table, he produced a letter, folded four times with a wax seal holding it together at the center. That is, when the seal was still functional – it was now broken, though I could tell that at least part of it held some impression of the shape of a shield.

"You opened it?" I shouldn't have been that surprised, really.

"I took a liberty, Sir, given the sender."

My butler was not at all apologetic about much of anything, especially now that the "young master" was in charge of House Loringham, and that was fine. I took the letter from him with a slight chuckle as I unfolded it to reveal several lines of neat, slanted, masculine script.

Instructor Loringham,
While it is understood that circumstances have changed in recent weeks, your presence is currently requested at the Military Academy to resume your assigned duties. I am down four Instructors and a Master now, and I'll be straight with you – I cannot afford to lose another. If Zondrell is to be prepared for the next crisis, whatever that may be, then it needs strong leadership. I expect you agree with me, and therefore request your presence by 21 Summer's Light.

Janus Olcaius, Headmaster of the Zondrell Military Academy

"Fuck me…" I muttered under my breath.

Frederick raised an eyebrow. "You have the time, Sir, if you wish to commit it. And if you don't mind me saying so, I believe Headmaster Janus is correct."

"Do you now?"

"Serving as an Instructor, in the short time that you did so, seemed to do you some good."

I considered the elder man, and realized he might have been on to something, as he so often had been in the course of my life. "At least he gave me a few days to get ready."

There might have been only a handful of occasions where I saw a real smile grace Frederick's face, and this was one of them. "Some routine may bring you a sense of – dare I say – normalcy, m'Lord."

"You're not worried about me, are you, Frederick?"

"No, Sir. Although, you are running a bit behind to get to the Magic Academy for your appointment with Archmage Tiara."

Damn, I'd forgotten about that. I was out the door with a clean face and fresh clothes within minutes. Outside, the sun was already good and hot, and I moved quickly, avoiding the stares of passers-by. In spite of an empty stomach, I was on Academy grounds and admitted into the Great Hall in just under an hour – quite possibly a new record.

"Oh dear, Lord Loringham! Thank you for answering my request on such short notice. I'm sure you're busy these days." Archmage Tiara Chandler was stately, a woman who had probably been quite a beauty in her day, her curly, gray-streaked hair tied up into a very unkempt bun near the top of her head. There were dark circles under her Earth-tinted green eyes as she cleared away some loose papers from a table in her spacious laboratory. "Come in, please."

And I did, after a quick bow. "The definition of 'busy' has changed a bit in the past few weeks," I said with a slight smirk. "Do you know if the Academy received the donation I sent?"

"It did." She brightened, though was that a flicker of humility in her expression? Must have been the lighting. "I must say, it was a bit of a surprise, but I can't thank you enough. No small task to get that one out of the High Mage's hands, I'll have you know, but it's quite safe under my direction."

Even magic was no match for greed, I supposed – ten thousand gold would go a long way here. But I had designated it for a very specific purpose, and I trusted Tiara would see to it that the library that Andella had loved so much would be well-stocked and well-maintained for years to come. "Hopefully you can use it for your research."

"Yes, yes, there's much to do these days, isn't there?" Her smile was broad and quite genuine. "Research has been, well, difficult lately, as you might imagine, but… oh dear, where are my manners?" From a nearby shelf, she hurried to pick up an unlabeled bottle of golden-brown liquor, then proceeded to pour some of its contents into two small glasses from amidst the mess on the table. "There, that's better, yes?"

"Cheers," I said, taking the one she offered and downing it in a gulp. It held a brassy sweetness mixed with the taste of pine needles, unlike much else I'd ever tasted. To call the stuff smooth would have been a lie, but it wasn't exactly unpleasant, either.

For a time, we said nothing. Another drink was poured, and another, until I had a light sweat going under my collar. "So, for some time now, and I have put this off for far too long... I wanted to apologize to you," she broke the silence at last, speaking carefully, in a way that clearly wasn't comfortable. "No, that's incorrect – there is no such thing. An apology implies some expectation of forgiveness. I simply wish to... confess, I suppose, on something that has plagued me."

"And I thought I was here for some sort of magical reading."

"Yes, well..." The Archmage poured out more liquor for herself, then stared into the bottom of the glass as if there were answers there for her. Once she realized that there were none, she looked up again, eyes rimmed red. Her words came in fits and starts. "But first, you see... there is no better way, so I'll merely state the facts. It is my fault that our dear Andella is no longer with us. I brought her to the research site, thinking it would be helpful, that she would learn something. She was a bit out of sorts that day – I suppose you know that – and I felt that a place like the research site would be... good for her. I was wrong. And... well, it's quite shameful that it has taken me so long to say this, but I must accept full responsibility for her loss."

Many thoughts flooded in as I listened, many feelings and a thousand possible answers. The man I had been a few months or even a few days ago might have chosen a very different response than the one I chose in that moment, though. "I could just as easily blame myself, Archmage, which I do... daily. She would never have been anywhere near Zondrell if it weren't for me. I can tell myself that things would have been better if we'd never met at all, and maybe that's true. Or maybe not. But that's in the past." I squared my shoulders as I met her questioning gaze. "Everyone makes choices – it's what makes us human. Regret does nothing but chain us down."

"So you can live with it, then?"

"I have to," I replied, and took down the rest of my most recent glass of homemade pine-needle brandy. The burn brought small comfort.

"Indeed." Our eyes met until a sad smile played at the corners of her lips. "You know, I believe I can see what she saw in you – you are a remarkable man, Lord Loringham. I believe there is much to be learned from you."

"I rather doubt that."

She didn't argue with me, but the look on her face said volumes about her thoughts on the past, present, and future. And for a while, not much was said. We stared out the windows overlooking the interior Academy courtyard, and by the time the sun was nearly kissing the rooftops of the distant classroom buildings, we had finished the bottle. "Well... so that's that then," the Archmage said as she stared wistfully out at nothing in particular. "Again, I..."

"It's all right, Archmage." Being relieved from having to fumble for more difficult words, she seemed to relax visibly, though I had a feeling those dark circles under her eyes would give away her thoughts for years to come. "I appreciate your invitation – truly. You did say you wanted to take a reading, didn't you?"

"Hmm... yes, yes, I did have a thought yesterday in reviewing some of my notes. If you don't mind?" The sextant-like measuring devices were out before I had much of a chance to register my feelings one way or the other. At least the discomfort was temporary, although the way her brow furrowed as she reviewed the tiny numbers along the length of two different instruments gave me pause. I watched as she marked notations on some nearby scraps of paper, screwed up her nose at them, then scrawled a few more things in the margins.

Finally, I couldn't help myself. "May I ask what you're writing there about me?"

"It's all very interesting," she muttered, "although maybe..." Then she looked up, a renewed brightness in her emerald gaze. "Will you entertain one more small intrusion on your time, Lord Loringham?"

I told her I would, and I was a man of my word, even though the idea of entering that mysterious obsidian slab known as The Box again gave me no pleasure. In fact, it caused the hair on the back of my neck to stand on end and my blood to go dead cold in my veins. Still, I would do it – I only needed to be shut into that dark prison for a moment or two.

The last time I'd been there had been... memorable, to say the least, a vision of a place I had known so little about at the time. My trip to the River then had been surreal, a journey up to the Summit where I was fascinated by the wonders of the Source and every mystery it might have had to offer. Now that I knew the truth behind all of those questions, all of that wonder, it only left me feeling empty inside.

The heavy, impenetrable black of The Box embraced me for one breath, two, three... and nothing happened. I touched the cool, smooth stone, but the sensation was just that – hollow, limited. *Mortal.* A feeling that not only did I not belong, but that I wasn't welcome in this constricting little space started to build, faster and faster until it became hard to breathe.

Sweat beaded on my brow. My heart thundered away in my chest, and for just a few beats, it felt like someone had ahold of it, squeezing just enough to let me know that they were there... and watching.

Then light, perfectly normal and terrestrial, flooded back to my senses once again, along with a relieving rush of fresh air. "Did you see anything unusual?" Tiara asked, a hint of trepidation in her tone.

I shook my head as I blinked against the sudden harshness of her torchlit laboratory. "Not a thing."

If she believed my breathless testimony or not, she didn't say. She only looked back and forth between me, The Box, and her notes, squinting and shaking her head. "Strange... these readings... I don't understand." And it was clear that this admission was painful for her, to say the least. "You're quite certain?"

"Sorry to disappoint."

Her lips drew to a line so small and fierce I thought she might start yelling... or crying. "It's just so *odd*. These readings are similar to what I took before, but yet you exhibit no magic whatsoever. It makes no sense."

"Sacrificed," was the only coherent consolation I could offer.

"Excuse me?"

"I'll explain it sometime... when I understand it myself." Because it was no simple thing to cut away a piece of oneself and give it back to the place from which it came. It was no simple thing to watch that gift spread like some glorious infestation among the souls still able to claim it. And it was definitely no small task to come to grips with the idea that the path to Paradise, divinity, whatever one might call it, was closed to me forever.

My one solace? It was my choice to make – I did not, nor would I ever, submit.

This concludes the Chronicles of M'Gistryn –

Tristan and Alexander will return… someday.

In the meantime, please check out Halsbren Publishing LLC's other great fantasy titles available at Amazon.com, or anywhere fine books are sold.

www.HalsbrenPublishing.com

If you enjoyed this novel, please take a moment and review it favorably. Every bit helps.

Thank you.

Anastasia M. Trekles
Author

ABOUT THE AUTHOR

Dr. Anastasia Trekles is an instructional designer, educator, and animal welfare volunteer in the Northwest Indiana region. While she might not have graduated from the Zondrell Magic Academy, she has spent a fair amount of time around schools, as well as technology and all things science fiction and fantasy.

The world of M'Gistryn is a world completely her own, but she can trace her inspiration to everything from Final Fantasy to Star Wars, from Harry Potter to the Sopranos, from Ancient Rome to feudal Europe, and from Christianity to Buddhism. There is much more to M'Gistryn than magic and prophecies – it's a world full of real people, struggling with real situations and real emotions.

In her debut novel, *Core*, she explores issues of war, coming of age, and the fulfillment of our life's purpose. As the story continues in *Ascent*, her characters are faced with the intricacies of a city in chaos, a place where philosophies clash, questions abound, and intrigue lurks around every corner. In *Transcendence,* their perspectives expand even further, into the deeper mysteries that connect each and every living thing in M'Gistryn.

www.ingramcontent.com/pod-product-compliance
Lightning Source LLC
Chambersburg PA
CBHW051311250626
47155CB00015B/2551

* 9 7 8 0 9 9 6 4 3 1 1 5 6 *